WHAT BOOKS PRESS

AN IMPRINT OF

THE GLASS TABLE

COLLECTIVE

LOS ANGELES

MASTER SIGER'S DREAM

A NOVEL

A. W. DEANNUNTIS

LOS ANGELES

Publisher's Cataloging-In-Publication Data

DeAnnuntis, A. W.
   Master Siger's dream : a novel / A. W. DeAnnuntis.

   p. ; cm.

   ISBN-13: 978-0-9823542-7-8
   ISBN-10: 0-9823542-7-4

   1. Siger, of Brabant, ca. 1230-ca. 1283--Fiction. 2. Siger, of Brabant, ca. 1230-ca. 1283--Humor.
3. Philosophers--Fiction. 4. Philosophers--Humor. 5. Christian heretics--Fiction. 6. Christian
heretics--Humor 7. Catholic Church--Fiction. 8. Catholic Church--Humor. 9. Fantasy fiction.
10. Humorous fiction. I. Title.

PS3604.E16 M37 2010
813/.6   2010928215

What Books Press
23371 Mulholland Drive, no. 118
Los Angeles, CA 91364

WHATBOOKSPRESS.COM

Cover art: Gronk, *two faces*, mixed media on paper, 2010
Book design by Ashlee Goodwin, Fleuron Press.

MASTER SIGER'S DREAM

A NOVEL

for Patsy

and in memory of Charlie Funnell

PROLOGUE

IT IS NECESSARY, THEREFORE, that in present things there exist
the necessary causes of all future things; and the argument would be the same
should someone appeal to what happened in times past.

> "On the Necessity and Contingency of Causes" (c. 1265)
> Master Siger of Brabant

Now I call 'philosopher' any man who, living according to the right order of
nature, has attained the best and ultimate end of human life.

> "On the Sovereign Good or On Philosophical Life" (c. 1268)
> Boetius of Dacia

We pronounce the sentence of excommunication against those who shall have
taught the said scrolls, books, and leaflets, or listened to them, unless they
reveal themselves to us or to the chancery of Paris within seven days in the
manner described earlier in this letter; in addition to which we shall proceed to
inflict such other penalties as the gravity of the offense demands.

> [Condemned Proposition 40]

> [It is an error to hold] that there is no more excellent state than to study
> philosophy.

> [Condemned Proposition 21]

[It is an error to hold] that nothing happens by chance, but everything comes about by necessity, and that all things that will exist in the future will exist by necessity, and those that will not exist are impossible, and that nothing occurs contingently if all causes are considered. This is erroneous because the concurrence of causes is included in the definition of chance, as Boethius of Rome says in his book *On the Consolation of Philosophy*.

"The Condemnation of 219 Propositions" (March 1277)
Etienne Tempier, Bishop of Paris

[Spoken by Thomas of Aquinas] ... "This figure, which your eyes encounter as they return toward me, is the light of the spirit who, wrapped in grave thought, found death slow in coming. This is the eternal light of Siger, who, when he taught in the Rue Fourarre, proposed in faultless form truths that earned him the hatred of envious rivals."

Dante Alighieri , "Paradiso," Canto 10, lines 132-138 from
The Divine Comedy (1321)

The dawn is here; arise my lovely one,
Pour the wine, but slowly, and touch the lute,
For those who are here will not stay long,
While those departed will never return.
The Rubai'yat of Omar Khayyám (1121)

CHAPTER THE FIRST

LET HISTORY REMEMBER With Perfect Fidelity and Affirm Without Equivocation or Confusion or Debate, that on the Night of December 22, 1277, a Cold and Glittering Rain Fell Hard, and Siger Recognized He Needed to Flee Paris.

Shrouded in billowing blue-black darkness, the towers of Notre Dame sparkled with an icy skin. The same hard rain fell on the Sorbonne, and on a small stone house in the tiny Rue du Fouarre. At the doorstep of this house laid a silver puddle trimmed with pale shards of frost. Its door opened, and a black-cloaked and hooded figure stepped out.

Master of Natural Philosophy Siger of Brabant muttered a prayer to Saint Granache of Bourbon, Preserver of Important Personal Possessions, pulled the heavy door closed behind him, and then using a thick black key locked it. With a sigh he smiled. After days of preparation he was finally relieved of his domestic responsibility, and he enjoyed the blissful conviction that what could have been done, had been. His next-door neighbor, Theodore of Blaumange, had finally agreed to watch his house and care for his hamsters in exchange for a bottle of Scotch. And his temporary roommate, Boetius of Dacia, was now finished packing. He would be gone by morning, and he had all the right connections to escape the city. But after one-too-many mysterious phone calls, Master Siger was forced to admit he needed to see Mistress Jacqueline. Because of him, they were on her trail, too. So she would need to leave Paris, too. All Siger needed to know was how she planned to get out. It was the only excuse he needed to visit her, if just for this one last time.

Siger stepped around the puddle and watched his shadow pass over it. In that silver reflection, tendrils of black vapor seemed to crawl and curl before him, obscuring his path and disguising his intentions. His smile of relief disappeared. He stepped out of the shadows and into the lane, already sweating despite the weather, and more than a little desperate.

Master Siger of Brabant was among the most brilliant philosophers in Paris, and so ranked among the most gifted of his time. He could plan and worry and conspire simultaneously, and still be terrified, his gift was that deep.

Wrapped in his heavy, wool cloak and trembling against the needles of frozen rain flung against his face, Master Siger hurried along Fouarre until he reached Boulevard St. Michel, and instantly regretted it.

Boul' Mich was bright, noisy and packed with holiday-delirious Parisians. Despite the cold rain, the sidewalks were jammed with clusters of Christmas shoppers and revelers. The crush of his fellow citizens pressing against his body as they moved past him in their quiet hysteria made Master Siger nervous, as if, under their collective influence, he might lose his ability to resist the snare of such enchanting rapture. But he would resist because he possessed the power to resist. He was a philosopher, after all, and he had acquired knowledge. The philosopher who possesses knowledge has power. And Master Siger possessed knowledge this hedonistic horde bumping and jostling him could not even imagine. Above all, his knowledge included the fact that the black Continental cruising ten paces behind him with unknown but surmisable intent was stuffed to its roof with the Bishop's thugs. Pushed and turned though Siger was by the crowd, he felt those eyes behind tinted glass watching him as a tangible caress. He had to admit there was something reassuring about such profound attention. Recalling the suggestion from the video movie he had watched with Boetius earlier that evening, Master Siger looked up into a black and impenetrable sky. Its frigid darkness gave up no secrets. All he got was a wet face.

The stream of cars and buses and horse-drawn wagons jamming the boulevard crawled between intersections, demanding enough exposure to force Master Siger to slink and slither within the shadows of that vacuous revelry. But the holiday's sorcery was difficult to resist, even for Master Siger. Slivers of the dazzling street-lights and blazing headlights danced on every rain-glazed surface, celebrating a desperate hilarity, an urgent delirium that could be easily mistaken for joy. Master Siger could acknowledge all of this fraudulent good-cheer and yet refuse to succumb.

He avoided eye-contact as he walked, but gradually he realized this was unnecessary. Despite the many newspaper stories that had featured his photo beside descriptions of his involvement in the student riots, no one seemed to recognize him. Each of the Parisian dailies had run a banner headline denouncing the riots. But they had also chastised the Sorbonne scholars, who they assured their readers were ultimately responsible, and every editorial had denounced Master Siger as their leader. Now bumping shoulders with arrogant viscounts and aloof prostitutes, he could not decide whether his anonymity was a relief or a disappointment. Because of course there still was that black Continental hounding his heels. For a moment he considered simply waving down the Bishop's car and getting in. Perhaps if he asked politely and contritely, the Bishop's men would give him a lift. At least then, he would be formally introduced to his assassins.

Master Siger turned off Boul' Mich' at a slow trot to see if he could lose the Continental in that maze of tiny, dark alleys clustered on the other bank of the Seine and stretching to Les Halles. The cold rain beat against his face, and his cloak had become heavy with icy water. Before he reached Jacqueline's apartment he needed to lose that car. Perhaps the idiotic futility of that aspiration made it a point of honor, but he glumly accepted it anyway.

Siger began to sprint along more black alleys, skidding and almost losing his balance as he turned on the slick wet paving stones. He chose the narrowest alleys and turned frequently, running until finally his breath gave out and his heart pounded in his chest. He stopped then beneath the shelter of a blacksmith shop's awning to rest. To his relief the Continental remained out of sight. He wiped rain from his face with a wet sleeve and reminded himself that his evening had begun very differently.

Master Siger's evening had begun warm and dry and sheltered in his thick-walled house. That sturdy little house in Rue de Fouarre protected his pet hamsters, Abelard and Heloise, his collection of exquisite first-edition books alphabetized and neatly shelved to the ceiling, his sophisticated Japanese stereo system and five thousand phono albums, his Japanese videotape equipment, his case of single-malt scotch, and his four carton-boxes of pornographic video tapes hidden in the basement against the possibility of a disastrous raid by hysterical Capuchins. While the riots had become more violent over the past weeks, the walls of that little island-fortress of cultivated taste had also come to shelter Boetius of Dacia, like Master Siger, another notorious Sorbonne Master of Natural Philosophy. Though their adversaries in the philosophy department, so much like the sharp winter wind, had rattled their shutters and beaten on their heavy wooden door, Fouarre's stout walls and solid doors had kept them safe.

Yet tonight, Boetius and Siger had found themselves confronted by the truth of what, as philosophers, they had always known; every fantasy of safety is an illusion. As brilliant philosophy instructors at the most prestigious and powerful department in the world, they each had recognized the feebleness of their protection, the shabbiness of their defense, and the depth of their danger. So that finally they had to concede that this would be their last night sheltered and safe behind those walls. The rising sun would find each of them on the road and in-flight from the Bishop and his minions, and lucky if either of them got ten miles from the city-walls without being caught.

Warmed by Fouarre's blazing wood fire, these illustrious Masters of the Sorbonne had spent their last night of comparative safety watching a video tape of Boetius's favorite movie. Boetius slouched on a green couch whose tired cushions barely covered its rips and exposed springs, wrapped in a worn bathrobe that he had stolen from Walter of Pannonia. A six-pack of beer squatted by his side on the couch, and the yellow remains of a fat, round joint smoldered between his pinched fingertips. The movie they had watched concerned a group of men at the North Pole fighting against an invader from outer space.

Master Siger guessed that this might be the tenth time Boetius had made him sit through the movie. He liked it well-enough, but he could not fathom what about it might compel Boetius to watch it time after time. As Siger slid down further into his corner of the couch, he decided that it could only be another indication of his colleague's overpowering intellect.

The film had nearly reached its end where the reporter in the film was about to speak into a microphone, and Boetius leaned forward. In echo to the lips of the video image, Boetius said, "Look to the skies; keep watching the skies." Then he smiled. He seemed to find this line of dialogue both profound and amusing. Master Siger had tremendous admiration for the noble mind of Boetius of Dacia, even when he recognized he was unable to follow its perambulations.

Master Siger resumed his journey through the rain, choosing streets and alleys that appeared empty, though several times he hurried past holiday shoppers who carefully balanced armloads of brightly wrapped packages. Since this world could not be what it seemed, he assumed they were not the people they appeared to be. Suddenly, emerging from deep shadows, the grinning, glazed face of a drunken celebrant accosted Siger, insisting that he share a drink to the Lord's birth. Certain he was confronting an agent of the Bishop, Master Siger's dark features and the glare of his eyes sent the message he wished conveyed. As Siger left the stunned drunk reeling in the center of the dark alley, he flattered himself to think he was getting rather good at this trick.

The maelstrom of the riots, the viciousness of the invective spewing from semi-official sources, along with Siger's and Boetius's peculiar choice of powerful and vocal opponents, and worst of all, their proximity to the precipice of heresy, had drawn an ecclesiastical scrutiny to these Masters of Philosophy that they could not survive, and now finally they understood this. Their positions on controversial issues were well-known, and they had both engaged in activities certain to enrage the Bishop's office in public. So they were not surprised that, when the Condemnations were posted, their enemies recognized this chance finally to be rid of them both.

Master Siger had promised Mistress Jacqueline they would spend this Christmas season together in Paris. Once again, he found himself forced to apologize for another promise he should never have made because it could never have been kept.

When the closing credits to the movie appeared, Boetius used the remote control to stop the tape, and then quietly belched. He passed the smoldering joint to Master Siger. "If they aren't after us already," he said, "they will be soon."

Master Siger took the joint carefully from Boetius' pinched fingers. Ruefully he said, "Teaching part-time and being screwed around for five years, but finally I've gotten tenure and regular classes." He eyed the joint with suspicion, and then smoked it. "The rent's been paid six months in a row, and there's real food sitting in the refrigerator beside the beer." He passed the joint back to Boetius. "I even got you three courses to teach this semester." Boetius winced at these words as he took the pinched, brown roach. Master Siger smiled. "But I'll confess that in a way all this commotion is a relief. Because there was a real danger I might start living normal and that I might even get paid that money you owe me."

Boetius of Dacia shifted on the sofa and squinted. "Don't exaggerate when you whine." With the joint in one hand, he used the other to rake his fingers through his blonde hair. "Otherwise people will think less of you." When he grinned, his face collapsed until it was mostly curled lips.

While Boetius smoked, Master Siger looked around at his tiny house and shuddered, still finding it hard to grasp how far they had fallen. "We better assume they're after us." He took a can of beer from the six-pack beside Boetius, popped its top and drank. Half to himself he muttered, "For a while I thought no matter how bad it got, at least we'd keep our jobs." But regret was something Siger was becoming comfortable with. So it was inevitable he would search out Mistress Jacqueline with fear in his heart and apology on his lips.

The rain fell suddenly heavier as Master Siger, hidden within the shadow of a passing wagon loaded with hay, crossed over to the Ile de la Cité. Above him, the bells in Notre Dame slowly tolled midnight. At the end of the bridge Master Siger turned to look back. It seemed unlikely he had lost the Bishop's men, but he saw no one behind him. He continued moving between pools of darkness protected by paths masked in deeper shadow.

This side of the river was deserted, and Master Siger walked its streets alone. The wind blew colder. His robes were soaked through, and he hunched his shoulders against the rain as he walked. He peered hard at doorways and into the bottomless shadows in the alleys. Master Siger reminded himself that his adversaries were thoroughly efficient, and he was being watched even when that appeared impossible. Then he looked up, startled to discover wide, pale flakes of snow drifting among the raindrops. For a moment he considered the question of why the awful pain predicted of Hell was imagined as the pain of fire.

Leaders of the Church had dutifully condemned the senseless violence perpetrated by the police, they had sympathetically deplored official bloodshed, and they had even denounced the vigilante mobs braying at the Sorbonne's gates. But far more insistent, they had bitterly condemned what they labeled as the spreading of heretical ideas, certain that the demonic fanaticism of those revolting Masters had made the mounting carnage of the riots inevitable. The King had expressed his royal dismay, but then claimed that matters of Church dogma were beyond his Church-sanctioned powers to resolve. So now, cowering at the center of this whole controversy, Master Siger and Boetius of Dacia spent their last evening in Paris, and perhaps their last evening alive, sitting together on a beat-up couch in their warm dry house, stoned and watching a movie.

Mixing with enormous flakes of wet snow, the rain fell still heavier. Master Siger's cloak had become soaked entirely through. Wet to the skin and freezing, he trembled as he walked. He no longer bothered to look back for his surveillance, nor even bothered to step around icy puddles of rain. His only thought was to be warm and dry again. He wondered if his situation could get any worse than it was, until a sudden flash of headlights ahead reminded him that it most likely would. Behind those headlights trailed a big dark car. For an instant its headlights turned on him. Master Siger sprinted into the next alley and then he resumed running. The Bishop's fury was another matter that Master Siger no longer wished to consider.

When Master Siger found the time to think about it, he would acknowledge his own collection of various and embarrassing regrets. He would admit he had been reading too much and drinking too much coffee. And he had certainly wasted too many hours talking to too many people on the telephone determined to explain what he thought and why he thought it. He had only made matters worse by calling up his old girlfriends late at night to deliver rambling diatribes that would become more twisted and incoherent as the hour grew late, and always end with vicious and bloody threats against his many dim-witted enemies. To his dismay, several of those conversations eventually appeared as transcripts in *Newsweek* magazine. Master Siger came to wonder if he was in some obscure way afflicted. Burdened subtly by a pseudo-organic malignancy, or a previously unrecognized form of stupidity perhaps? Had the fabric of his mental life, he finally wondered, developed a sort of leprosy? Or might he have contracted a debility of the spirit?

Uncertain of the nature of his mental malady, Master Siger had been satisfied to employ every curative herb, however exotic or expensive, in its defeat. But the recent turn of events finally left him without hope. He had come to doubt even the purposefulness of his own mind. With his shoes filled with icy water and with a small army of large-headed enemies lurking around every corner, Master Siger could only conclude that celebrations are depressing and that Christmas doesn't come for everyone. He approached Mistress Jacqueline's apartment building burdened with the hope she might still be willing to help him celebrate one last time. She would cheer him up if anyone could. Or so Master Siger hoped.

When Boetius of Dacia had reached over to eject the video tape at the end of the movie, he belched again but this time defiantly. "Tempier has gone ahead with the new Condemnations without even waiting for Papal approval. Which can only mean he's desperate."

"The man's just a coward," Master Siger said. His own conflicts with Etienne Tempier, the Bishop of Paris, had been frequent, resulting in an unfortunately voluminous trail of incriminating documents. Long argumentations before members of the faculty and students had been transcribed and offered up to anyone's misinterpretation or distortion. "The appearance of decisiveness means Tempier thinks he's got us. He is a coward but one who thinks strategically. So he must have counted up his friends. And we should assume he has the Papal Legate, Simone de Brion, in his corner. And that means he's got powerful Franciscans in his pocket."

"No surprise there." Boetius tipped his head back and closed his eyes. "The Dominicans and the Franciscans are dividing everything between them. They're choosing Popes. Favors like this don't get forgotten. Tempier has powerful backing for what he's doing, and that's almost as good as having a spine, so he thinks he's going to see this through to the end." He laughed quietly. "Admit that my analysis is clever and to the point. Of course, all it tells us is that when the shit-hammer falls, we know which end Tempier will be holding."

Master Siger nodded glowering at the floor. "These new Condemnations cast the net of heresy as wide as possible." His irritation was a reaction as much to slovenly logic as to canonical arrogance. "Atheism and pure food laws are lumped together with astrology and Satanism and drug abuse. Someone should tell His Holiness it's time he stepped in."

Boetius reminded Siger this Pope was new to his job, having only held the office a few months, and that he had already committed the Church to a crusade for the kingdoms of Castile and Aragon against the Moors. "And let's not forget those grey and pissy Germans," Boetius added. "Pope Nicholas has big stuff going on. Guelph and Ghibelline stuff. You and me are just petty local crap. Tempier will make the decision and the Pope will back him, because he's got way bigger fish on his line." He yawned. "Get used to it. The big guys are cutting us out the hard way."

Master Siger picked the roach out of the ashtray and looked at it wistfully before he began to light it. "Theology and philosophy are about to go their separate ways. Philosophers will be relegated to discovering stuff, but theologians will get last-call on what it all means."

Boetius of Dacia stretched squinting. "Just when we finally get the job, they close the factory." A gust of wind sent a splatter of rain suddenly against the shutters. He grinned. "Still, you have to admit there is nothing more excellent than the pursuit of philosophy. Philosophers alone are the wise of the world."

"Thinking like that is what's gotten us here."

"We thought ourselves into this." Boetius shrugged with a smile. "We'll just have to think our way out."

Master Siger took another hit from the roach and leaned back. "I can't think of anyone we can count on in the Curia. Even old friends of Albertus or Brother Thomas. And those guys have as big a stake in this as we do."

"And that's where you're wrong, my friend," Boetius of Dacia said. "Nobody's got as big a stake as we do." He blinked once and gasped. His eyes widened and he seemed to stare at nothing. Then gradually his expression softened to something resembling relief. He looked at Master Siger with an odd smile. "I know you're going to think maybe I'm crazy, but I've got to tell you something, so listen." Boetius speech was quiet but rapid, as if he worried he might not get out all of the words. Master Siger leaned forward.

"For weeks I've been having a feeling so strange I can hardly describe it. I suffer waves of conviction that, somehow, none of this is real. Nothing, you understand? I flush with the certainty that everything I see is a distortion in some other wave of reality. As if the world itself was a battering series of conflicting waves flowing from every direction, and each moment is simply an instance of impact, but repeated with such frequency it appears to us as constant. This sense of the unreal is almost tangible. So I've become certain that events around us aren't unfolding in their proper order. Something of this world has gone out of harmony with its immediate past. Somehow we are living some different future. And worst, it seems like only I'm aware of it." He looked away as if debating with a furious self, then turned back to stare directly into Siger's eyes. "Has anything like that happened to you?"

Siger studied Boetius awe-struck. He was now certain that Boetius was either the finest mind of his generation, or thoroughly insane. "Unfortunately," Siger said, "I can't recall anything the Divine Aristotle said about whatever it is you're describing." Master Siger was not sure which startled him more; Boetius's confusion, or his own stab of fear over that confusion. He reached for a fresh beer while he watched Boetius carefully.

Boetius's eyes seemed to focus on some threatening but invisible presence. "There have been times when I have literally not felt myself. Truly, although you're smiling, I've lived with the sensation that this body and the world it appears to inhabit are not continuous. As if my mind lived within one reality, but my body existed in another similar, but still separate, reality. I'm powerless to demonstrate any of this, but I'm sure that this moment we are now sharing has become unhinged. Something, somewhere, has gone seriously out of joint."

At the word, Master Siger smiled reaching for the brown paper bag and then began to roll. Boetius turned and looked over into Siger's eyes as if waiting for an answer. Master Siger could think of nothing to say.

"All right," Boetius of Dacia said. "Never mind, forget I said anything." Relieved because that was what he intended to do, Master Siger finished rolling the joint, lit it and then passed it to Boetius.

"Whatever else," Boetius gasped between hits, "we're here and they're there. And there's one simple reason we have no hope for assistance. Nobody else has the following that we do. Not even Brother Albertus. That's why he's left Germany, running back to Paris just to genuflect and kiss Tempier's ring. As long as he was undecided, we had some protection. But with him gone to the other side and nobody else to step in, we're out at the furthest end of the limb. We've run out of places to hide, so the Inquisition can take us any time. And believe it; once du Val has you and me, he'll forget the others. He knows that arresting us will scare the rest of them so straight he won't ever have to bother with them again. It's all part of the same equation. The trap is about to spring, and everybody else knows it." Boetius took another hit and then passed the joint back to Siger.

Master Siger leaned back as he smoked prepared to hear an old argument. "Those guys!" Boetius barked in disgust and shaking his head. "They just hung around Brother Thomas for one reason; just to be in the spotlight, just to get their faces in the papers. We knew it and they knew it. And Brother Thomas must have known it, too. But we know that none of them ever really figured Brother Thomas out. None of them really understood what he was talking about."

Smiling behind a grey-white cloud of smoke, Master Siger said, "The irony shouldn't be lost on us. When those august men acknowledged their ignorance of Thomas's true philosophy, we should have applauded them. When they admitted total incomprehension of his words, we should have congratulated them. Because by doing this they were covering themselves in the most sacred of all mantles, the mantle of Truth." Pleased by his own eloquence, Siger's smile grew.

"And that's why they can't be touched," Boetius grumbled in half-earnest anger. "And that's why we're alone, buddy, left out to dry. You and me, Bacon in England, and maybe a hundred underclassmen; all of us cast into the ecclesiastical sea and expected quietly to drown."

Master Siger hesitated as pulsating waves of terror suddenly crawled over his scalp and his panic rose to just below his throat. But he struggled and managed to fight it all back. "And all of that's your story. In my story, we're completely wrong about all of this. It's Christmas, after all. Everybody knows that nothing really bad happens at Christmastime. Don't you ever go to the movies? And after the New Year celebration, this all blows over. Just like you said, the new Pope's got a lot to think about. Like for one thing, his College of Cardinals is at its own throat so the Pope can't get a blessed thing done. And for another, the noble citizens of Rome are so furious with His Holiness they're threatening not to let him return from Avignon. Just how many fights can the Pope afford? I mean, just think about that, is all I'm saying."

"You keep thinking all that," Boetius of Dacia said. "Me? I'm packing for a long trip. And I'll advise you do the same if you know what's good for you."

Master Siger of Brabant looked around his little house in Rue du Fouarre and at all of his stuff, a lifetime of stuff. Deciding not to decide, he yawned and stood. "Tempier won't do anything drastic so close to Christmas. He'd look bad in the press if he did. Besides, everybody who's anybody has already left town for the holidays. He'll wait at least until mid-January before he makes a move. He wouldn't want to do something decisive with nobody around to applaud."

Master Siger reached for the last can of beer. Boetius of Dacia growled and lunged at his hand, but Siger snapped the top and put the can to his lips. And then the telephone rang. Master Siger stood to answer. As he stepped past him, Boetius feigned a lunge for the can of beer, but then glanced up. There was sympathy in his eyes. "There's nothing more dangerous than a dumb philosopher."

Siger of Brabant had hardly lifted the receiver when he heard the words, "Come now or don't come at all. This is end-game." With a loud click the line went dead. Seconds flew by before he recognized the voice. It was Mistress Jacqueline, and she was very serious. His smile flickered and then faded. He replaced the phone.

Boetius looked up. "Jacqueline?"

Master Siger nodded. "And she didn't sound good." He felt the net tightening.

A subtle sensation, like the draft from a passing thought.

Boetius asked, "You going to see her?" Master Siger nodded. Boetius of Dacia stood. "Well, by daybreak I'm out of here." Then he smiled his squinting grin. "Tell her I send my love. She's always been too good to you. And tell her what I told you." Master Siger slipped into his cloak, then pushed out his right hand, and Boetius shook it.

Master Siger asked, "You still headed to Amsterdam?"

Boetius nodded. "It's still the only place to publish good pornography. And you have that address to write to me, right?"

Master Siger grinned. "Don't worry. When you become famous, I'll be right there to collect."

Suddenly Boetius embraced Siger and hugged him hard. The gesture startled Siger, but he found himself returning it warmly. "Take care of yourself," Boetius said, "and we'll call that a date."

When Siger of Brabant locked the front door to his house, he knew Boetius would already be climbing the stairs to bed. Siger would remember his promise, and hoped Boetius did as well.

The rain fell still harder as Master Siger turned at the entrance to an alley between alleys behind Les Halles. Through a narrow space between two taller buildings he thought he saw a long, black car. It took a moment to convince himself it wasn't the Bishop's Continental. He stepped into the shadow of a house across the alley. Clinging to that shadow he walked to a nearly invisible door. Master Siger stepped out into the middle of the alley and called softly, "Jacqueline." A window above him opened, a bucket released a cascade of brown excrement that flew past him. Master Siger ducked as another window opened, and a soft, feminine voice cried, "Come!"

As on so many past evenings, Master Siger shouldered aside the flimsy, half-hinged wooden door, and climbed the damp, dark circular stairs. On the second landing he passed the old and withered soldier who had lost an arm in the last Crusade but had gained a wretched cough, and who spent his nights sitting on a stool in the doorway to his darkened room. At the sight of Master Siger, the old man nodded and resumed coughing.

Two or three nights each week for the past several months, Master Siger had asked, and Mistress Jacqueline had told him, more about dialectic and the *Analytica Posteriora* than anyone else in Paris, until she would become tired and insist on sex and then sleep. When Siger reached the top of the stairs he did not knock, but quietly lifted the latch.

He saw them as soon as he stepped into her room. Against one wall stood a stack of brown cardboard boxes, and in front of the stack crouched a row of green plastic trash bags. Siger stopped just inside the door and closed it behind him.

Quietly Mistress Jacqueline said, "Two men were here today." She lay in the center of her wide bed with its blanket drawn to her throat. Her thick, black hair was long and seemed to billow around her narrow face. In the center of a large white pillow, her face seemed the bright heart of a black flower. Her green eyes studied Master Siger with dark curiosity. "I wasn't here. Annie told me when I got back."

"You think I shouldn't have come?"

Jacqueline hesitated. "Probably you shouldn't have come. Probably I shouldn't have called you. Probably they have somebody in the neighborhood watching the house. Probably they're on their way up the stairs right now." Finally she smiled. "But who knows, perhaps not."

Master Siger took her smile as an invitation. He walked to the bed and sat down on its edge. "Boetius thinks they're on the move, and he's getting out of town." The rain from his hair dripped past his collar and down his neck. He shivered. The bed and Mistress Jacqueline looked more appealing than he ever remembered.

"That's a good thought," she said. "And so am I, tomorrow. You should think it, too. You've heard about the riot today near the Gare de Lyon. Couple of dozen skulls cracked. The police arrested more students, a group of them went to hospital with injuries and tear-gas. Seems like it's past time you made up your mind."

Master Siger nodded. "Will you come with me?"

"They're after you, not me. I'd like to keep it that way." Although she smiled, her eyes were flat and seemed to see through Master Siger's head. "I hear there's a remarkable convent near Cannes. Very forward-looking, very modern. Top-of-the-line gym facilities with a tennis court and golf course. I hear the food's excellent and it's a five-minute walk from the beach. Very private, very exclusive. I've been thinking that I'm finally tired of being cold." She shivered, pulled the blanket tight around her throat. "I understand there are visitation privileges for certain university masters." Her smile became coy.

Siger thought he detected something ominous in what she said, but he could not make it out. He disguised his confusion saying, "Boetius sends his love. Despite everything else going on, all he's worried about is his probing masterpiece novel of porno-philosophy."

"He's told me about it." Mistress Jacqueline stifled a yawn. "He wants to reveal matter as merely waves of compressed nothing so that what we think to be physical love is materially impossible, and that Pythagoras has described it all perfectly in his mathematics of frequency and harmony."

Siger did his best to disguise his surprise at how much she knew of Boetius' private project. He said, "All he does is whine and complain about all the research he still has to do, and how packing it all up has ruined his concentration."

"He talks a better game than he plays." Mistress Jacqueline grinned. "But he's a sweet guy. And someday he'll prove himself your most valuable friend." She paused. "You know, he was always after me to go to bed with him."

Master Siger could not decipher her expression. "And did you?"

"Wouldn't you rather not know?" Then she said, "Look over at the table." Master Siger saw a small octavo book in a beaten and dark tan vellum binding with a scuffed and ripped spine and battered, blackened corners. Mistress Jacqueline added, "You'll need that where you're going."

Siger picked it up and flipped the cover open. On a browned and foxed flyleaf he read the inscription; "To King Leer, from Queen Sophia." He recognized Mistress Jacqueline's handwriting. The book's title and text were printed in a calligraphic dialect of Syrian Hebrew that Siger recognized from certain remarkable volumes which had passed through his hands while he worked for Balthazar the Bookdealer on the island of Majorca. Transcribed by one Haiam of Aphrodisius, the volume announced itself as "On Comedy: Lecture Notes from the Words of Aristotle." Master Siger recalled certain obscure references in *De Poetica*, and remembered the controversy over whether there might be a second book to his survey of theater and poetry. Carefully he turned page after page of elegant script. He trembled. "And why will I need this where I'm going?"

"If you're about to face the Inquisition, you'll need a sharpened sense of humor more than sharpened dialectical skills."

"This is a wonderful gift." Siger of Brabant was genuinely startled.

"A wonderful gift is one that is not wasted." Mistress Jacqueline asked, "What do you plan to do?"

Master Siger hesitated. "Shop for a coffin?" Mistress Jacqueline did not smile. He said, "I have some phone numbers to try and one or two places to go. Like

Boetius, I still have a few favors to call in. It's only a matter of making the right connection." And then, smiling as if finished with uninteresting business, he said, "But tell me more about your convent. It sounds very accommodating."

Mistress Jacqueline smirked. "Ask no more questions. Tonight, instead of dialectic, we will explore the exercise of humor."

Master Siger hesitated.

"One of the few points," Mistress Jacqueline said, "where Aristotle and Plato agree, is that humor is dangerous because it is invincible against every logic." Siger studied her blankly, as if philosophy no longer held his interest. She might have understood this because, after a moment and with quiet sympathy she said, "It must be very cold where you are." Master Siger recognized Jacqueline's smile of invitation. "And it must be getting colder. Darken the candle and come to bed."

Master Siger smiled with relief. He stood and stepped to the candle on the table. As he leaned forward, he glanced out the window. Within a shadow on the street below, Siger of Brabant thought he could make out a deeper shadow. This shadow appeared to have black legs and black shoes. He flipped the curtain closed and blew out the candle.

When finally Master Siger embraced her naked skin she winced and then laughed. "The thing about spending so much time out in the cold," she said, "is that eventually we become colder ourselves. We resign ourselves to never being warm again. And then entropy claims its own."

Master Siger felt her flesh suddenly grow hot to his touch. He held her tightly, and she sighed. He breathed the warm smell of her skin, felt the caress of her hair, tasted the salt from her neck.

"Come with me," he said. He buried his face in her thick black hair and sighed. There was more pleading in his voice than he had wanted, but he could not disguise his fear.

To his surprise, Jacqueline softly laughed. "Inquiries must end, so I will tell you now instead of tomorrow. I must not go with you. What you must do I cannot help, and where you must go I cannot follow. Tomorrow you must leave too." She turned to face him, looked carefully into his eyes. "But we still have tonight. And we will always have Paris."

Let the Supple Fingers of History Release Master Siger to His Exhausting Pleasure and to His Tormented Sleep.

CHAPTER THE SECOND

LET THE QUIVERING QUILL of History Inscribe for All Eyes to See and All Hearts to Know, that at the Breaking of the Cold, Bleak Dawn of December 23rd in the Year 1277, Master Siger's Eyes Opened Suddenly.

Still muddled in terror from a dream he could not recall, he looked over at Mistress Jacqueline. Her breathing was deep and regular, one arm stretched above her head revealing a pale pink breast. In the grey light and framed by the whiteness of her pillow, her face seemed to glow. Her black hair lay tangled and pulled back from her brow to pour beside her head. Her lips slightly parted in sleep were full and red as if she had been eating cherries, and prayed to be kissed. Siger studied her lips, her throat, her breast. His knees went soft and a space opened in his chest at the certainty that this was the last time he would see her. But he would remember.

Master Siger stood carefully from the wide warm bed, gathered his clothes still damp and cold, and quickly dressed. He draped his wet cape over his arm. His precious Aristotle he tucked into the fold of his clothes closest to his skin. He took what he intended to be his final look toward the bed, and hesitated. Stepping to the sleeping Jacqueline he leaned forward, smelled the skin of her throat, and lightly kissed her cheek. He was about to whisper his farewell, but her eyes fluttered and she softly moaned. Master Siger left the room dreading she might wake before he had gone. Later, he would wonder at his cowardice.

At the bottom of the stairs Siger of Brabant slung his cape over his shoulders, pulled his collar tight and stepped out into the alley. The cold air was thin and still, the sky was granite grey. He paused and looked along both sides of the alley. When he saw no one, he headed toward the river and back toward the Sorbonne, and one last attempt to save himself.

With a pocket full of coins he had gotten from Jacqueline he crossed the square of the Pantheon to the public telephone behind Maurice's bookshop. It was still too early in the day for old friends to walk past him and not turn to offer a greeting, or for students and colleagues to cross the street and not meet his eyes. That part of his life he would not miss. Whatever happened now could only be an improvement.

Among the few former colleagues and associates who would even come to the phone, the verdict on Master Siger was unanimous. He was worse than poison, he was radioactive. Exile, they all said. Get out of this town before you get somebody killed. This consensus was depressing. As Siger made his phone calls, he studied a battered yellow Volkswagen of indeterminate vintage parked at the other end of the square. After some reflection he concluded that Tempier would never use a car that looked that bad for a stakeout. The Bishop of Paris, after all, had a reputation to protect. Eventually, Master Siger ran out of phone numbers to call. With the last few coins rattling in his pocket he walked to Boulevard St. Germain, and Simone's Café.

He drank his cup of coffee slowly, first because he could not afford another, but also in order to think. This seemed to Master Siger the appropriate time for thought. The moment had come for him to consider and weigh and compare. His circumstance demanded to be pondered, and he was a guy for pondering. So, between sips of coffee, he briefly outlined his situation.

This strategy exhausted itself quickly. He concluded that he had run out of options. By default, the only course of action still available to him was flight from the city. He must leave Paris and savor no hope of return.

With Aristotle secure within his cloak and his passport and credit cards snugly bound deep inside his pocket, on the night before Christmas Eve, Master Siger of Brabant scuttled along Boulevard St. Germain. Up one side of Embassy Row and down the other, Master Siger made certain he knocked on every door. He was, he knew, in pursuit of the rarest of God's creatures; a prince prepared to confront the Bishop of Paris, the Pope, and the Inquisition, in support of a penniless and powerless scholar. Siger understood that, even had he been a duke with a stock portfolio thick as a phone book, his was an impossible case. So he chose this strategy unburdened by optimism.

Eventually he reached the last door on the block, the sub-consular ministry of the Duchy of Belgium. He climbed the stairs and knocked. As if he had been observed the entire time, the peephole-slit in the door instantly opened, a small piece of paper fell through, and a voice whispered, "Ask for Guido." The opening then closed.

On the piece of paper Master Siger read, "Only an asshole like you would read a piece of paper like this expecting help. Eat me." Master Siger did as he was told. As he swallowed he felt a tap on his shoulder. He turned to discover standing behind him a man with greasy black hair, badly pock-marked skin and a milk-white left eye. Master Siger smirked. Tempier's associates were infamous for their good looks.

"Guido?" Master Siger asked.

The man nodded. "The boss needs to talk to you."

At the bottom of the stairs Master Siger watched a black '67 Continental pull quietly up to the curb. He recognized it immediately. Guido shoved him into the back seat, got in beside him, and then slammed the door. Master Siger sat behind the driver, a large, thick-necked man with a round, shiny pink head the size of a melon. The car lurched silently from the curb into the afternoon rush of traffic. Master Siger decided that good help must still be as hard to find as ever.

Leaning back into his leather seat, Master Siger experienced an oddly consoling sense of relief. He had done his best to follow his light and embrace his destiny. But that phase of his struggle had ended, and he was finally resigned to placing his fate in the hands of others. It was time for him to admit that, in the end, this must be his fate. So he sat in the back as a pupil once more, attentive to instruction by others.

Beyond Master Siger's window, Paris raced by hurrying to spend a few precious moments beside its mistress. The Continental sped beneath garlands of glittering lights and decorations strung for the holidays. The early violet twilight creeping above the horizon was already bringing these carnival lights to life. For a moment pleased by what he saw, Master Siger almost smiled. A second good-bye to someone he loved with its uncanny resemblance to his last look at Mistress Jacqueline, but so much worse.

The realization he no longer had friends in the city left Master Siger oddly calm. No acquaintances to gather with in celebration of the holiday, even his old friendships had become too worn and frayed to renew. Neither he nor Boetius of Dacia had been invited to a single Christmas party. This, he recognized, would have been a lousy Christmas no matter what had happened. Even in the company of Mistress Jacqueline. For a moment his thoughts returned to her in bed. Master Siger's sense of calm resignation turned to despair.

The Continental came to a stop in front of the Hotel de Ville. As they got out of the car Master Siger asked Guido, "Do you remember an old Christmas carol that goes, 'Deck Us All With Boston Charlie'?" Guido turned his blind eye to Master Siger and his expression did not change.

Master Siger followed him to an obscure side-entrance. With a key from his pocket Guido opened the door, ushered Siger inside and then locked the door behind them. From there Master Siger obediently followed Guido. At the end of a long corridor, narrow and grey and doorless, they reached an elevator. Though Master Siger had never passed along this entrance, he was confident he knew where they were going.

The elevator reached the fifth floor and the doors opened. This corridor Master Siger recognized instantly. Wide and covered by a thick and darkly-figured carpet, along either wall of this hallway stood pieces of elegant furniture and other priceless expressions of the wealth and majesty of Holy Mother Church. The air was foggy with sweet incense and the profound, low-pitched hum of money being counted and power exercised. Though Master Siger knew this route, he allowed Guido to lead him past identical tall, polished wood doors. So he recognized the door where Guido finally stopped. Master Siger had been here often before, too. Guido leaned his ear toward the door and then quietly knocked. Master Siger heard a murmur from the other side, and Guido opened the door. He nodded to Master Siger and then turned back toward the elevators.

Inside, Master Siger found himself as unsettled as always by the august presence pacing behind a desk the size of a small boat.

"So nice of you to drop by," Etienne Tempier, Bishop of Paris, said into his chest as he continued to pace. He did not look up nor glance at Siger. "Grateful you could find the time in this joyous and busy season to join us." Large, handsome, silver-haired and dressed in full ecclesiastical garb of Advent green for the liturgical season, Tempier's voice was deep and round, perfectly tuned to communicate the divine presence, to address the heavenly host, and to bring the fallen back to the Church. "Finished our Christmas shopping, have we?" He snorted a quiet laugh. "With the few friends you have left and the little money you make, I expect that's hardly an issue."

Master Siger struggled to find the appropriate retort, but Bishop Tempier continued. "Only a few days ago it suddenly occurred to me how refreshing a quiet chat with you might be." The Bishop looked up finally and stared hard into Master Siger's eyes. Siger could not hold his look and he turned away. In a darkened corner of the room he saw a slim, dark-haired man sitting with his knees crossed, who also seemed to be studying Master Siger. Though Siger knew him well, disguised by the shadows it took a moment for him to recognize the Papal Legate, Dr. Simon de Brion.

In a sudden gesture of ecclesiastical enthusiasm Bishop Tempier stopped pacing behind his desk turned to Master Siger and opened his arms wide. The man seemed to tower, his body all but filling the room. "This is, after all, the season of forgiveness and reconciliation. We all should take advantage of its precious opportunity to renew our old friendships." Carefully, as if distracted by thought, the Bishop slowly sat down while his eyes held Master Siger's. A smile seemed almost to come to his lips.

More to the ceiling than to either of the men in the room, and in a tone far from satisfaction, Tempier said, "All of Paris celebrates your stimulating intelligence. And with great justice, after all. For that intelligence seems to generate thoroughly provocative views on every issue." The Bishop's smile flickered, and then the tone of his voice became wistful. "How unfortunate, then, your addiction to these embarrassingly sophomoric pranks." The Bishop sustained his smile and this demanded discipline, a struggle obvious to Master Siger. He studied Master Siger with a distant, speculative interest, as if perhaps considering the grave this body before him would occupy. Finally he nodded Master Siger toward a chair that faced his desk.

As Master Siger sat down he glanced again into the darkened corner of the room. But nothing was being given away tonight.

The Bishop said, "I have taken the liberty of inviting our old comrade-in-arms to join us. I hope you don't mind." Bishop Tempier's smile for a moment became avuncular. "This might surprise you, but only moments before you came in I was saying to the good Doctor that the Sorbonne is nothing like it was in our day. The young ones, I tried to remind him, are always keen to understand, but they never do. That is why they come to us. When the young are born with the acute understanding they each presume to possess, all of us will be out of jobs." The Bishop quietly chuckled as he leaned back. Dr. Simon de Brion sat straight and quite still, unimpressed by the speculation.

"An invitation from the Bishop of Paris," Master Siger said struggling against panic, "is impossible to resist. But of late it appears I have caused Your Holiness more consternation than consolation. My struggle with the thought of an obscure heathen philosopher seems to have tested the patience of even those who are well-informed."

Bishop Tempier sighed a sigh of patient tolerance stretched to its limit. "As good Brother Thomas so often said, reconciliation is the true virtue of every season. And despite my lack of intellectual gifts, I have always benefitted from your insights. In turn, however, I have flattered myself to think that our meeting this evening might stimulate your own thought as well. Perhaps for once I might even add to your astonishing knowledge."

Tempier glanced down at the several newspapers spread over his desk. With a quick look, Master Siger realized that all of them either mentioned his name in a headline, or featured his photograph. He returned his look to the Bishop.

Bishop Tempier waited, as if he was choosing his words, or awaiting more from Siger. In a tone of mild exasperation he continued, "Perhaps we should begin by clearing something up. Forgive my bluntness, but it seems to me that people like you think people like me sit in big offices like this doing nothing except hump the secretary and take long lunches. Do I have that about right?" The Bishop's smile faded, replaced with an expression that hovered between boredom and hostility. "You and those pimple-faced jerks who follow you around always think people like me have nothing better to do than decide questions of Being and Essence. As if that was anything I might get paid to do. As if that was all there was to being the Bishop of the largest Catholic diocese outside Rome." Tempier's voice rose, his forehead creased with consternation. "Because if that was all this job took, even you could be the bishop."

The Bishop's eyes slid to the dark corner, he gritted his teeth and breathed deeply. He said, "People like you just stir up the perverts with all this talk. Who really cares about that stuff? Just you and that bunch of assholes just like you. And what good could come from all this crap? Half of Paris running around yelling at the other half, nobody doing what they're supposed to be doing, nobodies listening to nobodies going nowhere and accomplishing nothing. Talk like yours just gets the weirdos worked up."

Master Siger wanted to defend himself. The words rose to his throat and clotted behind his tongue. But he clamped his jaws tight, reminding himself that what he did not say could not be used to attack him.

"Well, I've got a message and here it is. This is all going to stop, and right now!" Bishop Tempier leaned back again, looked over at Dr. Brion, and then glanced up at the ceiling. Master Siger waited and clutched his Aristotle tighter.

When Tempier turned to Master Siger, his generous smile had been refreshed and re-lighted. "So you think you know my job? And you think you know how I should be doing my job? All right, then. Since you know so much, take a guess what kind of day I've had?" His smile broadened as if something truly delightful had just occurred to him. "Well, before we all die of suspense, let me tell you. A delegation of Corporalists stopped by this afternoon."

The mention of the name startled Master Siger. He shuddered and could not disguise it. He knew all about this sect, had been hearing about them for several years. Hardly more than muttering to himself, Master Siger said, "God made you, He said you are sacred, He made your body, therefore it is sacred, therefore all your body's parts are sacred, therefore you can't throw any of them out."

"Exactly!" Eyes bright with surprise, Tempier turned. Addressing the shadow within the shadows he said, "Sounds to me like our friend here has been reading some books." As if reverting to Master Siger's days as the Bishop's philosophy student, Tempier asked, "So what happens if, for example, you have a tooth pulled? Or if your appendix gets yanked? Or if maybe a leg gets cut off in a war?"

"Our bodies are a short-term loan from God," Master Siger said, disguising his disgust with a hint of boredom, as if he had already taken this exam, "and the Lord expects them returned when our time on earth is done, and just as they were given to us."

"And too bad," Bishop Tempier added with undisguised sarcasm, "if that piece of His Perfect Work weighs twelve pounds and smells funny. Whatever it is, He gave it to you and expects you to carry it with you, even if it has to be strung around your neck in a sack. A theology like that puts a whole different meaning to the Great Accounting."

Master Siger shuddered but bravely grinned. "Just the sort of people Holy Mother Church accepts easily. I hope your Reverence was not his usual rude self. This is, after all, the season of Reconciliation."

Bishop Tempier ignored the sarcasm. He continued to smile like a man holding lots of really good cards. "Don't get me wrong, I'm not prejudiced.

Liberal Corporalists I can almost deal with, they're cosmopolitan by comparison. But that wasn't these guys. And it wasn't the Corporalist Separatists, so much the worse for me. Ever heard of that bunch?"

Caught between boredom and horror, Master Siger trembled. His personal contacts with members of this sect had always ended badly. "Another idiocy that's seized the words of Revelation and stripped them of any responsibility to logic or to the Church on dogma."

Tempier's eyes went suddenly round with an angry astonishment. "See what I mean?" He slapped his hand loudly on the desk, then glanced toward Dr. de Brion for support. "The problem with guys like you is you spend too much time in the classroom. No offense, but you don't ever get to see the loonies up close."

Master Siger snarled, "You haven't been in my classroom recently."

"That's funny coming from you. I'll bet you get a laugh at every faculty party over that one. Do me a favor and just remember where you are right now. There's a fine line," Tempier said with grim authority, "between impertinence and ignorance, Master Siger. And you're sitting right on top of it." Tempier shook his carefully trimmed silver mane. "People like you never seem to be around these guys when their eyes blaze and their lips foam as they describe the latest abominations they've gleefully perpetrated on themselves or each other."

"Or worse," Master Siger added, "on some perfectly innocent stranger. All of it for self-purification in their obedience to God as described by some syphilitic prelate." Master Siger struggled to disguise his contempt. "Some misguided country priest possessed by delusions of communion with God and demanding blind submission in exchange for eternal salvation. Responsible to no authority, no formal laws or informal rules beyond his self-inspired and delirious reading of Scripture."

Bishop Tempier appeared to try very hard to smile. Master Siger admired the struggle, but did not mistake his grimace. "It's really too bad," Tempier continued, "guys like you can only think about Being and Reality. It's a great limitation. People like you discuss this stuff the way my friends discuss the stock market. With your blackboards and your chalk, your great failure is that you can only think about looniness in the abstract. Meanwhile, real people are living under real bridges bumming spare change from strangers while they mutter, utterly unsurprised when they realize they are God, and relieved they simply have to answer the voice that keeps talking to them."

"Perhaps Your Holiness would prefer that we all just stop thinking."

For a moment Master Siger thought he heard the Bishop's teeth grinding behind his grimace. "People like you think, 'What do I think is really loony, and why?' But all the time they're already out there, camping on doorsteps and flopping around in trash dumpsters." Tempier's anger finally slipped its leash. "For each one of your heretic buddies in the University, there's a thousand wandering the roads of Christendom, invisible except to that handful of Christians doomed to damnation for listening to them."

Master Siger felt his face redden, he clenched his fists as he spoke. "And only Your Holiness and the Inquisition can save us from this horde of marauding sons of Satan. Can their heresies be so persuasive and enticing they must be obliterated?"

Bishop Tempier glanced with exasperation toward Dr. de Brion. But gradually his face relaxed, and then the hint of a smile appeared. "So, how about the Corporalist Fundamentalists? Ever run into any of their persuasion?"

"They go the Corporalists one better," Master Siger said. He smiled even as his throat tightened recalling an unfortunate encounter less than a month before. "They even include what the body excretes."

Amused by Master Siger's discomfort, Bishop Tempier nodded. "So according to them, you have to keep all your hair and finger-nails and your toe-nails and all your blood and all your shit and piss and everything else. And according to them you've got to save it all in bottles or something. They're Fundamentalists mostly because nobody will go near the smelly imbeciles."

"A sort of theological leapfrog," Master Siger added, finally finding his balance. "Sets them apart from those wishy-washy liberals. Of course, they haven't dropped all appeals to reason, just the reasonable ones."

Bishop Tempier again glanced at Dr. de Brion. Then he leaned forward, opened a polished wooden box on his desk, brought out a long black Havana cigar and began carefully to trim it. Master Siger noticed he did not offer one to Dr. de Brion, or to himself. "But I promised," Tempier said, "I'd tell you about my day. Okay, just to make this merry season merrier, the Mucosite Corporalists dropped by. Now, just for the sake of argument I'm going to bet you've never heard of them."

"Given the grand varieties of pollutants," Master Siger said with a sneer, "I expect every perversion will have its flower."

"Well, well!" Tempier said turning in Dr. de Brion's direction. "It seems there's at least one thing our notorious scholar doesn't know about. So perhaps his enlightenment is in order." He turned back to face Siger.

"But let me set the scene for you. The head of this bunch is a doddering abbot from a monastery outside Mainz with two wives, a concubine and twelve kids, and who insists that eating radishes confuses the mind and pollutes the soul. But as a Corporalist, this little old guy goes the Separatists one better. According to him, every time you sneeze or spit or cough, you've got to do it into the same snot rag, a snot rag that it's a sin to wash."

Master Siger felt his body suddenly flush, and his damp clothes become a furnace.

"The Lord made all the parts that excrete," the Bishop continued, "and that includes all the parts that make mucus. So this creepy old man sat the whole time right there, right where you are, spitting and sneezing and coughing into this bath towel of filth he wore across his shoulders. And on the floor beside him he had his sack with the festering odd body-part and leaking jars of putrescence of every description."

Master Siger could not resist glancing around his chair, then nervously across the room, his eyes finally coming to rest on Simon de Brion. For a moment Siger thought he could see Dr. de Brion smile. But when he looked again the smile was gone. The Bishop got the cigar lighted and leaned back to release a long jet of grey smoke. "So today, he and his two very young female acolytes put themselves to the trouble of stopping by to harangue me for more than an hour." Tempier paused and then sighed. "And just guess who they were on about? I'll give you one guess."

Master Siger noticed he had begun to sweat despite the chill dampness of his clothes.

"Its stuff like this," the grinning Tempier said wreathing his face in grey smoke, "that makes Christianity really great. So long as you don't contradict us we'll humor you. But let me just ask you this. How does a person like me, who is normal, tolerate people like them? I hang out with cardinals and fashion models and nuclear physicists and football players. I'm knowledgeable in the fields of art and music and finance and deciphering the NCAA basketball championship. What I'm asking is, does this seem like the kind of job for a person with my sensibilities? This is what I want to know."

"Your sensibilities are not at issue," Master Siger said. "Where the Church finds a heresy too vile to be tolerated, the heretics simply disappear. If these fanatics were a genuine threat to dogma, they would no longer exist. It's because they are intolerable to everyone else that the Church feels safe to embrace them. A heresy going nowhere is like a benign tumor, safer ignored than attacked."

Bishop Tempier rubbed his eyes with the heels of his hands. "Holy Mother Church does a pretty good job of tolerating creeps like you and your goofy friends, too. So now I'll tell you a little secret, just between you and me since you're so interested in knowledge. What you don't know about loonies is going to get the rest of us killed. And being killed is something likely to piss me off. Because, believe it or not, I like my job. The money comes in regular and there's paid vacations and health insurance and nooky when you can get it. What I'm saying here is, I myself can't complain about these working conditions."

Across the room Dr. de Brion cleared his throat and re-crossed his legs. Bishop Tempier rubbed the ash from his cigar. "So, in the spirit of the season and the privacy of this conversation, we'll forget the implications of your suggestion. Day before yesterday I had Henry of Ghent in here screaming at me. Just because I let him put the Condemnations together, he thinks he can just bust in here any time he wants. And you want to take a guess who he was screaming about?"

Master Siger glanced over to Dr. Brion, and found no assurance.

"Do you know what John Peckingham said to me a couple of days ago about you? He said, 'You'd think that little prick was the first turd on the moon.' You know what he's like. But does that make any sense to you? Is that the way you philosophers talk about each other, with mixed metaphors?"

"I am not without resources," Master Siger said.

"Yeah, right, and pull the other one." Bishop Tempier leaned back staring at an invisible place, smoke leaking from the side of his mouth. Finally he leaned forward, half closed eyes finally finding Master Siger. "For a while now you've been telling yourself we had to be kidding up here; that we were always really only talking about somebody else. The Condemnations of 1270 should have been clear enough, even to you. And the Council of Lyon in '74 was another hint you didn't get. So now I'm showing you the whole book. These new Condemnations spell out everything we've got on you and your pecker-pulling associates. Every one of these clauses is clear as my piss-water. No more screwing around with any more words. You are now hearing the last one." Bishop Tempier leaned back and carefully blew a wide grey smoke ring, watched it drift toward the ceiling with undisguised pleasure. Then he sat forward and stared at

Master Siger. "Could you really be so stupid as to think we were just going to keep looking the other way?"

Dr. Simon de Brion coughed quietly. Bishop Tempier hunched his shoulders forward, lowered his voice still further. "Listen, I'm going to tell you exactly what I told that drug-addict pimp creep Boetius of Dacia. If Pope Nicholas thinks so highly of you two, do us all a favor and go be his problem for a while. Get out of Paris and don't come back." Bishop Tempier leaned back again, his look unmistakably grave. "Think of this as your final warning. If I find either of you inside the walls of this town tomorrow, I won't protect you from the loonies you pretend to respect. I will not defend what the Church condemns. Whatever you two are up to will not be sheltered here. What do you say, pal, cut us all a break."

Master Siger of Brabant pressed Aristotle to his breast. "The Church prides itself on its adherence to formal rules of procedure. So I remind you that the University and its Masters all enjoy the direct protection of His Holiness the Pope. No official council has been gathered, no formal presentation or debate of issues has been convened. The 219 Condemned Propositions have not even been reviewed by the Curia. As far as anyone knows, Papal authority has not been extended to this Inquisition."

"You're in France, boy," Bishop Tempier announced. "We do things a little different around here." The Bishop began to laugh. Its sound was broad and deep and infectious, and Master Siger fought the urge to smile along with him. "And I'll confess that I love all that talk about intervention from Rome. That kind of stuff just tickles me up one side and down the other. Because I want to be there when you spout all that to Monsignor du Val as he burns the skin under your arm. He'll be very impressed by your subtle knowledge of Cannon Law, believe me. And he's not an easy guy to impress."

Dr. Simon de Brion coughed again. The sound attracted Tempier's attention. His expression became grim. Quietly he asked, "Remember the Albigensians? We still haven't finished counting those bodies." He paused, smoked his cigar as if thinking words he could not speak. "You're here because you just don't understand when a nice guy is doing you a favor. But ungrateful as you are, here's one more favor. Just a bit of information, a hot tip, if you will. Think of it as a Christmas gift, from me to you. Monsignor Simon du Val of the Paris Inquisition plans a heart-to-heart talk with you the day after Christmas." Tempier grinned. Master Siger barely suppressed a gasp. This was very bad news, and news he had not prepared for.

Bishop Tempier continued, "Now don't get me wrong. Du Val's all right once you get to know him. But on the other hand, I don't like him so much that I'm ready to make him look like a hero when he starts ripping your nipples off."

"In the face of eternal damnation," Master Siger said, "the threats of mere men are nothing. My conscience is at peace. To open men's eyes to the world around them is to open those eyes to the Work of God. Mastery of the world will reveal the face of God."

The Bishop stared at Master Siger for a long moment, as if wanting to be sure he was heard clearly. "These riots will stop, Master Siger. If I have to grind you into sausage meat, and personally feed you to the fish in the Seine, these riots will stop. And I don't need du Val or anyone else to do my cutting for me. Believe me when I tell you I know exactly what needs to be done, and I would genuinely enjoy doing it. You know the old expression? Cut off the head and the body dies."

In the silence that followed, Master Siger could hear his own heart beat.

Suddenly Bishop Tempier smiled. "But I'm such a nice guy, and it is Christmas, after all. So guess what I'm going to do?" De Brion cleared his throat again and shifted in his chair. Tempier glanced in his direction, then reached into his pocket.

Etienne Tempier, Bishop of Paris, handed Master Siger of Brabant the keys to his gold Chrysler Imperial, a generous gesture since it left him with only four limousines for the Holiday season. Then he handed him an envelope. Master Siger glanced inside to find five hundred francs. "For once," the Bishop said almost pleading, "do yourself a favor. Take these keys and this money and drive as fast as you can to Avignon. You're hearing the final word from me. If you value your life even just a little, and I have my doubts about that, be inside the gates of the Papal Palace by sunrise. Or something really Aristotelian will result. Think of it as a formal causality."

"And what about Boetius? Is he gone, too?"

"Left before sunrise. My colleagues followed him until he was well out of town. He's a real smart guy. He knows when somebody is doing him a favor. Not like you. Anyway, he left word he'd meet you in Avignon." The Bishop stood slowly, as if the effort was barely within his power, until his frame once again seemed to fill the room. With his ecclesiastical robes fluttering behind him, Tempier stepped around his desk.

Master Siger stood to meet him. Bishop Tempier put an arm across his shoulders. Master Siger shuddered with disgust, as if the carcass of a dead animal had been thrown across his back.

The Bishop grinned, triumph in his quiet voice. "Meanwhile, forget that woman near Les Halles. She can't even remember your name." He brought his grinning face close to Siger's. Master Siger tried to keep any sign of interest from his expression. Bishop Tempier continued, "And don't bother going back to Fouarre, either. We burned all your stuff and turned your dump into a pizza parlor. You won't recognize the place." Bishop Tempier's grin expanded showing rotted and blackened teeth. "Have yourself a merry little Christmas."

Let the Hand of History Inscribe that Smile into the Hearts of All Men, Lest They Fail to Fear the Wrath of Power.

CHAPTER THE THIRD

LET THE PROFOUND Hand of History Command our Silent and Awe-Struck Attention with the Account of that Long and Complicated and Demanding Night Before the Night Before Christmas in the Year of Our Lord 1277.

The black air had become warmer, and the fat white flakes of snow turned to a rain that fell in sparkling sheets through Master Siger's headlights. Holiday traffic in the center of Paris was a hopeless tangle of recrimination and doubt. Its congestion suggested that every soul in the city had decided to get into a car and drive somewhere other than where they were. Their blare of horns, like a cacophonous chorus of ten thousand howls, conjured a world in upheaval, a terrifying emancipation, a community torn from itself and floating free. He peered through the windshield at the sullen vehicles moving slowly around him, driven by miserably autonomous individuals, anguished by the affliction of their self-sufficiency. And thus he recognized his membership in a profound brotherhood. In some inscrutable but inevitable way, their fate was his fate, their misery his. The delusion of individuation drove all of them, no less than they drove their cars. A collection of self-hoods scrambling deliriously, rushing forward and back, beguiled by the belief that they exist. Their cars, things they believed they possessed, confirmed the lie of personal existence. And their struggle to accumulate possessions was their best, though delusional and useless, effort to increase the likelihood of a personal existence. Staring into the cars around him, Master Siger suddenly recognized himself standing before a mirror and accepted the image that stared back. After all, he still could not help but regret the loss of his collection of phonographs. In some perversion of the logic for which Master Siger held such profound respect, it was all extremely creepy, and so he decided to stop looking.

The Bishop's Chrysler crawled within the mass of glittering metal, giving Master Siger time to count and regret his losses, and to wonder at the Bishop's decision. Clearly the Holy Office had stepped in, and just as clearly an exercise of the Bishop's power had been blocked. He understood that, had the decision remained with Tempier, Siger's shrieks of pain would be entertaining du Val right now. As a prerogative of the Bishop's office and sanctioned by his role as defender of the faith, Tempier's decisions to torture needed no permission from any Pope. So Siger was puzzled.

The majestic office of the Bishop of Paris should have defended this prerogative as if its survival depended on it, because it did. And Tempier had many powerful allies. So Siger's release to the sanctuary of the Pope was a provocative gesture by the Papacy that could only have deep administrative roots and obscure political branches. Master Siger had to recognize himself as merely a pawn in a game far larger than his understanding could encompass. Which was only another way for him to admit that he had no clear idea of what was going on, or why it was happening to him now.

It wasn't just that Master Siger had been reading too much. He had taken far too much of what he read to heart. Now, in the intimate confessional of the Bishop's Chrysler, Master Siger wondered if the thrill of the intellectual chase had worn thin, and if the rabbit had begun to look as tattered from its chase as he felt. Once again he endured the sting of Brother Thomas's absence.

In the three years since Thomas's unsettling death, Master Siger had revisited the man's work, and always with profound regret. Time after time he caught his breath at the care and subtlety of Thomas's arguments. Brother Thomas assuredly was gifted by God, and so particularly capable of leading Christian thought into a new dawn. Master Siger had followed his progress enraptured by the brightening glow of that dawn, finding hope in the elusive but profound distinctions Thomas was able to draw, and even more, by the promise of the treasures of thought just beyond the horizon. Fortunately, Brother Thomas's powerful mind had also brought him powerful allies.

All of this left Siger wondering if his release to Avignon and Papal shelter might be the result of the intercession of some anonymous confederate, more loyal to Thomas's memory than to Siger's well-being. After all, the Condemnations had singled out several of Thomas's own philosophical positions. Perhaps there lurked in the heart of the Curia some scrupulous prelate who found himself suddenly unable to tolerate a victory for Tempier and his colleagues. Particularly a victory over a partisan to Thomas's cause who also labored on behalf of the works of Aristotle.

Or perhaps it all had to do with something else, something unknowable to Master Siger, like that world out there beyond his headlights.

If Brother Thomas had still been around, Siger decided, Tempier would never have dared to go after him. Though always searching for conciliation, Brother Thomas had been determined to defend human knowledge. So perhaps Brother Thomas was, in an odd way, defending him even from beyond the grave. Siger regretted his inability to witness the way the good Brother would have sent those dogs running.

Finally Master Siger's Chrysler broke through the clogged streets at the center of the city, and joined what seemed like a clear highway. But twenty kilometers south of Paris and just past Fontainebleau, a tractor-trailer jack-knifed and Siger became caught in the line of traffic behind it.

Trapped and motionless, once again he studied the faces of the drivers and passengers around him, though his thoughts had moved elsewhere. In only a few hours he would look squarely into the face of His Holiness, Pope Nicholas III, the most powerful man in all Christendom. For the first time since he left the Tempier's office, Master Siger recognized he was genuinely frightened. In just a few hours he would be expected to explain to this man why it was that Aristotle represented no threat to his empire, and no impediment to his schemes. Master Siger would attempt to clarify to the Pope of the Roman Catholic Church the distinction between Being and Essence that had triggered the outrages of the past months. In Siger's imaginary encounter, his explanation would leave the Pope relieved and no longer tempted by thoughts of Siger's execution. The faces in the cars around Master Siger returned blank stares. Once again Master Siger found himself unencumbered by optimism.

Which of his fellow-citizens knew there was a defensible distinction between Being and Essence? Which among them would recognize the difference between the Prime Intellect and the First Intelligence? And who could name the five most influential Islamic thinkers of the previous two centuries? Could any of them even acknowledge that there could be such a creature as an Islamic genius? More importantly for Master Siger, could His Holiness do so? And if Siger could not make this explanation to the most powerful man in the world, what chance did he have of making that defense to someone staring back him from behind the wheel of his car, with kids to raise and a mortgage to pay and a life that very convincingly appeared to be his own?

Master Siger's hands tightened around the steering wheel. Defending heathen Islamic geniuses had gotten him into plenty of trouble. The fact that they were not the ordinary, run-of-the-mill Islamic geniuses only made his indiscretion worse. Avicenna, Algazeli, and the most Aristotelian of them all, Averroes. These men were thinking a century ahead of their Latin brothers, a fact that made Master Siger both shudder and smile.

Months before, under Boetius of Dacia's by-line in *Sports Illustrated*, Siger had ghosted a profile of the new Moslem quarterback at Sienna State. In a passage calculated to seem a discreet and harmless digression, Master Siger had written, "If Western philosophy insists on keeping out the likes of al'Khwarazmi and his *Algoritmi De Numero Indoriu*, Western scholars will be condemned to an eternity huddled in caves, scratching Roman numerals onto pieces of tree bark. Try inventing the computer based on Roman numerals and tree bark." As far as Siger was concerned, Boetius himself could not have made the case more profoundly.

It had taken Master Siger much time and tremendous effort to appreciate Brother Thomas's strategy of forming distinctions within Aristotle's philosophy using Averroes as his non-Christian foil. By acknowledging the Moslem's subtle brilliance, Thomas's refutations gained even greater esteem. So Brother Thomas got to have it both ways. He could create categorical distinctions, and then assert that the Being who does not manifest these distinctions must be God. Brother Thomas had turned tautology into an element of ontological proof. Master Siger recognized this sleight-of-hand, but against his best efforts, had come to admire its audacity as much as its subtlety. Now he wished he had something up his own sleeve more subtle and profound than an arm.

The cars and trucks around him sparkled under livid orange street lights. Siger recognized himself trapped in a slowly rolling wave of metal that, in the rain and under those lights, glistened like a mass of large, mechanical insects. Through the steamed windows in the cars around him, Master Siger saw empty and grim stares. Stranded alone in the middle of that highway and at that late hour, Christmas suddenly seemed to him very far away.

Master Siger suddenly endured a gust of gloom pass over his heart. He wished he had the powers of Brother Thomas, but better still, that Brother Thomas was by his side. Brother Thomas's death had been as profound a political loss as it had been philosophical. And thinking this, Master Siger wondered again if Brother Thomas had been helped into the next world. Then he began to shiver. Despite the car's heater blasting hot, dry air into his face, the chill seemed suddenly to sink straight into his bones. He flipped the heater to high, opened his collar and exposed his throat. For a moment he recalled Mistress Jacqueline, and feared he might never become warm again.

For the political purposes of the Franciscans and Dominicans, the timing of Brother Thomas's death could not have been better. The decision reached by the Curia to suppress heresy while expanding the Inquisition into Italy undoubtedly would have challenged Brother Thomas's notion of Christian virtue. Meanwhile, the call by Pope Gregory X at the Council at Lyon for another Crusade to rescue the Holy Land had forced a split among even the very highest clergy. The previous Pope had insisted on a Crusade against distant heathens, despite substantial opposition from his bishops. They had complained to His Holiness that, despite yearly increases in tithes, their dioceses were starved for the money needed to repair their churches or feed their poor. So the political stakes for this crusade could not have been higher. Master Siger had no doubt Brother Thomas would have been among the dissenters, for whatever good that position might have done.

Two hours later and five kilometers south of Sens, traffic stopped completely. After an immobile ten minutes Master Siger veered onto the shoulder and drove to the next exit. He got into line behind other cars at a one-lane cutoff that had no road sign. There was no turning back. Paris might as well have been a foreign country, or not exist at all. There was only Master Siger and this thin metal shell to protect him, and then the whole hostile and alien world beyond. The darkness could not have been more dark, his solitude in this lightless universe more abject.

Master Siger's involvement in the Paris riots had destroyed any chance for him to negotiate between the conflicting forces. Now, even if he found someone to negotiate with, negotiation itself would appear a compromise with forces of Evil, and merely make his own position suspect. A sudden recollection forced Siger to smirk with embarrassment.

Only days before, in their dining hall decorated for the annual faculty Christmas party, a very drunk Master of Arts Siger of Brabant had delivered his Advent Quodlibet before a crowd of even more drunken Masters of Arts. While elegantly praising and subtly exploring Brother Thomas's remarkable insights, he had defended his own upcoming article that made a powerful case insisting that necessary causality excludes the possibility of Divine Action. He assumed his conclusion would prove provocative, but he was startled and mildly pleased that the reaction of the crowd to his news was a near-riot of fistfights and broken furniture. Siger and Boetius barely escaped before a squad of the Bishop's men arrived, night-sticks flying. What particularly frightened Master Siger was that the squad was led by the notorious Brother Edouard du Carcassonne, Director General of the dreaded Franciscan Highway Patrol. Here he was, head of the Franciscans, leading the forces of the Bishop of Paris. Master Siger suppressed a smirk at this remarkable collaboration of the forces of repression. Meanwhile, in the midst of his drunken and confused flight from the hall, Master Siger spied one of Tempier's lizards perched in the back and scribbling furiously. This alone should have put Master Siger in the clutches of du Val. But here he was, speeding from the scene of the crime ignored and abandoned. Or so he hoped.

A half-kilometer beyond the off-ramp the road split. The street lights continued left, and the rest of the traffic followed those street lights and a wide, high road-sign to Aix-en-Provence. Lightless and signless, Master Siger turned continuing south. Hurtling into the darkness, rain fell through his headlights like a storm of broken glass. He kept the heater going full blast against the damp cold. The wall of darkness at the edge of his headlights could have been the limit of the physical world. Yet he drove on moved by that faith shared by all late-night drivers, that the road always leads somewhere.

Master Siger's speech had grown out of his most recent research. He had arrived at a new theory of causality that provided a logical extension of the work of Aristotle and Averroes. Against the idea of an omnipotent and ever-present Deity, Master Siger had concluded that God is completely detached from the Universe, has no idea what's going on, and is powerless to affect it in any way. And Master Siger based this on the irrefutability of Necessary Cause, a case he had finally committed to paper and titled, "On the Necessity and Contingency of Causes," scheduled to appear in the February, 1278 issue of *Playboy* magazine. Master Siger hoped that the Playmate of that month would be a blond, since blonds always drew the most readers.

The rain picked up and suddenly began to pound against his windshield in a clattering torrent. The darkness became thick and time moved as if through pudding. After several kilometers, in the distance he saw lights. Drawing closer, he discovered that the lights decorated a long, one-story road-house framed in thick logs and looking self-consciously rustic. In the building's windows were hung red and green holiday decorations. The edge of its roof was trimmed with multicolored lights, and near its peak and beside eight glowing reindeer stood a tall, glowing Santa Claus. To one side, three glowing elves clustered together like muttering conspirators. As he turned the Chrysler, Siger realized the parking lot was empty. Suddenly this did not seem like such a good place to stop for a drink and directions. But he ignored that voice of caution and drove in anyway.

Master Siger was sitting at a table by the window when he saw the patrol car pull up. Two tall, broad-shouldered members of the Franciscan Highway Patrol got out and walked through the rain to the door. He watched as they entered and then stepped to the bar. Neither looked toward Master Siger, as if it was possible they did not notice he was there. Their dark brown cassocks bulged at the waist, and each wore an ear-piece that trailed pale wires beside their dark hoods. Neither turned to watch when the innkeeper served Master Siger a double cognac and a Perrier. The innkeeper was short and round and balding, and when he returned behind the bar he gave the men a wide, round smile. He took the dirty grey towel from his belt and began polishing the top of the bar before them.

"Ay," he said, "but it's a heathen terrible night out there. You'd hardly think the anniversary of our Lord's birth was just a day away." He turned and reached to a shelf behind him, brought a bottle and two glasses to the bar. He filled each of the glasses and pushed them toward the patrolmen.

The older, heavier patrolman said, "Please, kind landlord, pour one for yourself and join us." Siger could not see the faces of the Franciscans but he could see the innkeeper clearly. The innkeeper continued to smile as he followed the patrolman's suggestion. When his glass was full, the three men muttered a prayer and then drank. Their glasses returned to the bar with a thud. The older Franciscan hunched his shoulders forward but he spoke in a clear, undisguised voice.

"This weather does seem odd and sort of unholy, don't it?" He addressed his partner without turning. The partner was thin and younger.

"Unholy's the word." The younger Franciscan gestured as he spoke. Even his voice was thin. "Lacking all holiness, an absence of the Blessed Presence, like water upon fire, like a fire made with green wood."

"Just what I was thinking," the older patrolman said. "As if a cloud of malevolence was passing over us. As if a putrid miasma was emanating from Paris and billowing over the countryside like some abysmal fog. A vile, gaseous substance that burns eyes and throats, and forces up bilious fluids."

"I have to admit," the innkeeper said bravely, "I haven't been feeling all that well myself. The wife says it's too much dairy."

In a lowered voice the older patrolman said, "And worse, I hear there's a bunch of these heathens running about. Necromancers and witches, or so I've heard, all of them running from the Bishop of Paris. At least that's what they say. Scattering they are, panicked like rats from the Holy Inquisition. And just like a bunch of rats I hear they're spreading themselves everywhere. Seems you can't hardly turn around without seeing one."

"Never did like rats," the innkeeper muttered as he glanced down at the floor. "You never get just the one." With his towel in hand he returned to rubbing at a spot on the bar. "Do terrible damage and stink to high heaven when they're dead."

The older patrolman rubbed his arm. "Not unlike these heathens. Me and my partner are out on these roads day and night. We see things, and people tell us things. For a while now I've been getting this feeling that something real bad is roaming around out there and just waiting to happen." He turned to his companion. "You remember me telling you that?"

"Sure thing," the younger one said. "Said it a couple of times just today. You say it just about every day."

"What I meant was," the older one said impatiently, "all that stuff we been hearing. The rumors. And all them reports. Riots in Paris. Bulletins from the Bishop's office." He reached his hand under his hood and scratched his head. "It's true what they say, landlord. It just ain't possible to be too careful when one's immortal soul is at stake."

The younger one looked up from his drink. "What my partner's trying to ask is, you wouldn't serve any of them heretics here, would you?"

The innkeeper gave the officers a round, bright smile of utter surprise. "You boys know I give service only to the Lord and the God-fearing."

The older one said, "There've been reports of a free-thinker in this neighborhood. So my partner and I just come by to warn all you proprietors. This is just the type of place he might stop at." Then the two patrolmen finished their drinks together with one motion.

The younger one said, "According to the bulletin back at the station, this guy is a holder in the double-truth heresy."

"And there's a rumor he contradicts Augustine," the older one added. "I'll tell you this guy is just poison. So we're making the rounds, warning everybody of the peril to their immortal souls and what have you."

"What with filthy Arabs everywhere you turn," the younger one said, "a good Christian can't be too careful."

"Well, I'll tell the wife to start locking the doors again," the innkeeper said re-polishing the spot on the bar. "One thing about these heretics, they're always in with the sex. That and the bottle. My wife likes giving me advice. Do this and don't do that, be careful of this and watch out for that. She's a good woman who thinks she knows more than she understands. But you fellows must know all about wives." The innkeeper looked up, his round face reddened.

"We know what we need to know," the older one said, "about the salvation of souls. All else is unimportant."

"Easy for you to say," the innkeeper said and retrieved his smile. "But I tell my wife the same things. I say, 'Those Franciscans know a lot more than you or I do. When one of those powerful fellows tells me something, I take it for truth.' That's how I say it."

"Take it any way you wish," the younger one said. "Just understand what my buddy is trying to tell you. Salvation is the only thing any of us needs to worry about."

The innkeeper's smile broadened as he refilled the officer's glasses. "I'll drink to that, brothers. And I'll be obliged if you join me in that drink. Here's to wives, the Lord's gift of peace." The three drank together.

The innkeeper finished his drink with a sigh of satisfaction. "I'm much obliged to you officers going out of your way like this. How about one more for the road?" Without waiting he refilled their glasses. "Meanwhile, I promise to keep my eyes peeled for any unsavory types. And if one of them comes around here spouting that filth, I'll throw him out on his ear, and sic the dogs on him to boot."

With the innkeeper's assurance he would faithfully inform on his neighbors, the patrolmen thanked him for the drinks and prayed God's blessing for his family at Christmastide. Neither looked toward Master Siger as they left.

When the door closed behind the patrolmen, the innkeeper stepped to Master Siger's table. "Drink up and get going," he said. Master Siger opened his mouth to defend himself, but the innkeeper waved him off. "I can stand all kinds of trouble, but if the Franciscans put a prohibition on my place I'm done-for. I've got a wife and kids and bills to pay. Get up and finish your drink walking."

In the parking lot Master Siger discovered the rain had stopped, but the wind had gotten colder. When he got the Chrysler out onto the road, a pair of headlights appeared in his rearview mirror. His first thought was that he was being setup. He was about to be driven off the road, taken somewhere remote and killed by persons of ungenerous intent. After a moment's reflection, Master Siger resigned himself to God's Will, and the faith that God would allow neither his death, nor his life before it, to transpire without meaning. But just to be safe, Master Siger drove turning randomly, taking each intersection as an opportunity to test his pursuer and assure himself that the headlights remained behind him.

Master Siger consoled himself that it was only reasonable and appropriate he contradict everyone else. After all, this was the lesson he had learned from the other Masters, and what he had trained himself his entire life to do. Perhaps this was the reason his attempt at reconciliation with Brother Thomas months before the man's death had done nothing to mollify his critics. For some, that gesture only confirmed that Brother Thomas, though brilliant beyond compare, had suffered a fiendish confusion in the face of the mesmerizing heresies of Mohammed, and that this confusion must be recognized as a warning to every lesser mind that subtle argument was insufficient defense, and that their immortal souls were in continual danger. Grudges died hard even in those days.

Suddenly the narrow road ended, merging with a four-lane highway. With a flat, straight stretch of open road before him, Master Siger trod on the gas sending the Chrysler forward with a lurch. When the speedometer reached a hundred he let the car drift down to ninety. Glancing into the rearview mirror he saw that the headlights had disappeared. He leaned back but did not relax.

With heretics ripe for picking, Etienne Tempier as not simply Bishop of Paris, but also a former theology master at the Sorbonne, recognized a chance to demonstrate some sophisticated zeal in defense of Revelation while also settling some very old scores. Tempier had tried more than once in the past eight years to undermine Master Siger and strip him of his supporters. A natural ring-leader, Siger could whip up a small army of rampaging Masters of Arts, accompanied by a fair number of adoring students, at any time. Tempier's distrust of Siger was as tactical as it was doctrinal. Master Siger of Brabant had more than just Boetius of Dacia, some Moslem geniuses, and Aristotle on his side. There was politics both personal and professional to think of, and Siger could raise a pretty good stink. But when Brother Thomas died, all the good cards suddenly went to Tempier's hand. The rest of Paris had realized this, and Master Siger finally was learning it as well.

By the time he sped through Lyons the horizon had begun to brighten. The sky was cloudless and the air had become dry. Master Siger knew that, as a result of his flight from the city, a third of the Master of Arts faculty at the Sorbonne were about to be dragged before the Inquisition. Without a leader, they would succumb to arguments as subtle as the Western mind can conceive. Would they be tortured? Was Tempier still so fearful? Or worse, was he that stupid? Master Siger wondered if those Masters would end up suffering the blows intended for him, and hoped they all had already escaped and saved themselves. Because finally, to make their situation impossible and turn an intellectual scuffle into a war, Boetius of Dacia had come to a position that made even Master Siger crazy; the double-truth model.

According to Boetius, given that there are limits to human reason and it is therefore fallible, a position that might appear true philosophically, could still be theologically false. Yet - and here was the tricky part - in good conscience, divine revelation must be acknowledged superior to every philosophy, and so in this way theology would always remain master to philosophy, regardless of philosophy's revelations. This position was heresy bald and unadorned, and just the sort of indiscretion Tempier and the Inquisition kept their knives sharpened for.

As Master Siger approached the outskirts of Avignon he glanced again through his mirror. He saw no cars, yet he acknowledged his ignorance, and that only appearance suggested he was safely alone.

So, at dawn of the day before the Feast of the Birth of Our Lord in the year 1277, as the sun's edge appeared above the horizon, Master Siger drove up the ramp, through the main gate and into the inner courtyard of the Papal Palace of Avignion. Finally sheltered in the shadows of those high stone walls, Master Siger said a prayer that Boetius and Jacqueline and all of the others would also find shelter from the rampage of the Inquisition, and then he put the car into park.

From out of nowhere appeared a shirtless valet wearing red candy-striped trousers. As Master Siger got out of the car, the valet slipped behind the wheel and drove the Chrysler away. A man in the robes of a Cistercian monk, his cowl pulled down to cover all but his mouth, stepped from the morning shadows and walked directly up to him. In a conspiratorial whisper he said, "I like a guy who likes to cut it close." With a nod the Cistercian turned and Master Siger decided he had better follow.

Let the Hand of History Record that, as Master Siger Trailed His Cistercian Companion Into the Maze of Dimly-Lit Halls and Mysterious Stairs That Was the Papal Palace At Avignon, He Realized He Had Abandoned Aristotle on the Front Seat of Bishop Tempier's Chrysler.

CHAPTER THE FOURTH

LET THE ELEGANT AND ARTFUL Fingers of History Part the Purple Mist of Time and the Silver Haze of Exhaustion to Reveal Master Siger and His Mysterious Cistercian Companion Walking Together in Sacred Silence Across the Courtyard of the Palace of the Popes in Avignon.

In the hard and golden first light of morning they entered the palace, climbed narrow stairways, followed twilit corridors, and passed through silent passages. The Cistercian finally stopped before a door, knocked and then entered. Inside, sunlight pouring through large windows momentarily blinded Master Siger, even as he thought he observed a pair of pale pink buttocks disappear through a side door, gender indeterminate. When his eyes became accustomed to the light, Master Siger recognized sitting in a chair across the room Dr. Simon de Brion, the Papal Legate. Combined with his own exhaustion, these two sights unnerved Master Siger. And then he glanced over to the bed.

His Holiness, Pope Nicholas III, Bishop of Rome and Shepherd to the Flock of Christ, lay propped up by several large pillows in a massive bed canopied by a huge, purple velvet counterpane. Master Siger followed the Cistercian to the bedside. While the Cistercian knelt to kiss the Pope's ring, His Holiness looked up with small grey eyes into Master Siger's eyes. With the slightest grin His Holiness said, "To remain vigorous and alert for Mother Church demands great effort." He resisted a yawn. "Relentless effort. We who do Our Lord's work understand relentless effort." The Cistercian stood and stepped aside. As Master Siger knelt and kissed the ring, His Holiness continued, "But I guess it's what they pay us the big money for. And the sacrifice is to the greater glory of the Lord." When Master Siger stood, His Holiness smiled. "Coffee?"

The Cistercian stepped away from the Papal bed and sat down in a chair beside the door. When he slipped back the cowl of his cassock, he revealed the thick face and wiry grey hair of a middle-aged man with the flinty eyes of someone who spent long hours staring hard into the void.

Pope Nicholas III sipped from his cup and sighed with pleasure. "Please take that chair," he said. "This is really excellent coffee, Master Siger. You ought to try some. I get it once a week from a dealer in Marseilles. Comes over in a Moslem ship from Morocco. Those Arabs can really make a cup of coffee. Sure you won't try some?" Now Aristotle-less, Master Siger sat down carefully but said nothing. His Holiness shrugged. "Like the man says, you'll never miss Paris if you've never been there." He glanced in Master Siger's direction, but his eyes took in all three men.

"Speaking of which," he continued addressing Master Siger, "my sources report Paris is a bit warm for this time of year." The Pope spoke as he put the cup and saucer on his bedstead, and then took up a stack of pale file-folders from his side, some very thick. "Is this true?" The Pope slipped on a pair of steel-rim bifocals.

Master Siger said, "Where one is surrounded by loyal friends, the weather is always temperate."

The Pope's laughter rumbled deep in his chest. "Yes, of course, temperate. That's a word any man could like. Temperate. It even sounds temperate." He searched among the folders as he spoke. "Of course, Dr. Tempier, faithful brother and bequest from our late Holiness John XXI, has behaved less than temperately. Yet, we must not forget that his congregation is among the jewels of Christendom, and so his efforts are that much more precious to us. He remains indeed loyal and obedient to the Chair of Peter." From the stack of folders His Holiness drew out one and returned the rest to his side. "His obedience is the reason you are here, and beyond the grasp of certain devout defenders of our Glorious Faith." His Holiness opened the folder while watching Master Siger. "Just so there is no uncertainty on this matter, let us all remember that it is submission to the will of God and His agents that moderates the acts of men."

The Pope leaned back into his pillows and slipped off his glasses, his attention took in all three men. "Still, it is a great blessing for our Holy Mother Church that so many of our most powerful cathedrals are in temperate cities. One is almost tempted to surmise that the simple presence of these cathedrals brings about a favorable moderation in climate. Could that be so, Dr. de Brion?"

Simon de Brion shrugged. "Like all else, weather fair or foul is Our Lord's prerogative."

"Well put," the Pope said. "Very nicely phrased. Divine Providence is active in all things. On the other hand, and still speaking of weather, I'm put in mind of those miserable Mohammedans. Now doesn't that provide an interesting conundrum. It is remarkable, after all, that the holy places of the heathen Semite are in the most hellish climates and in the midst of the most barren wastes. Tell me, Master Siger, doesn't that seem to you nearly Biblical?"

"The thoughts of Your Holiness on such a matter elude this humble mind." Master Siger spoke quietly.

The Pope laughed. "A Parisian Belgian, what a treacherous blend. I really wish you'd try some of this coffee. It's awfully good."

Master Siger shivered. "I'll consent, provided the good Dr. de Brion agrees to join us."

Simon de Brion lifted his hand without smiling. "I am touched by the generosity of Master Siger's gesture. Although I must refrain, I beg Master Siger accept the hospitality of His Holiness."

"Like the man says about Paris," the Pope said with a shrug. He pulled a bell cord that hung beside his bed, then glanced over the sheets of paper within the folder. "Now, it says here you were a member of the golf team at the Sorbonne." The Pope looked up, fixed his eyes carefully on Master Siger. "What average?"

"Your Holiness appreciates I am sure," Master Siger said feeling for his absent Aristotle, "that golf is a frivolous activity only redeemed by the sociability and increase in comity among men opportuned in its pursuit. The tally of anything except good will and fraternity is hollow at best."

"I carry a seventy-five."

Master Siger swallowed hard. "My best efforts have yielded a ninety-six."

Slowly the Pope smiled. Turning to Simon de Brion and pointing to one of the sheets in the folder he said, "That's not what it says here. What do you think, Dr. Brion? It says here his average last year was a sixty-nine."

Simon de Brion glanced at Master Siger and then shrugged. "If I may observe, it is possible Your Holiness fails to appreciate the imperfections of the human mind in the pursuit of truth. Simply a transposition of numerals. Something I expect happens frequently in scientific calculations."

His Holiness chuckled. "And never in your paycheck."

The door opened silently, a young acolyte entered carrying a cup and saucer. In response to a gesture by the Pope, he carried it to Master Siger. To the acolyte the Pope said impatiently, "Would you give our guest a cup of coffee without a table to leave it on?" The acolyte trembled causing the coffee to spill into Master Siger's lap, which caused Master Siger to leap in pain, which caused the spill of the rest of the boiling coffee onto the acolyte, which caused the acolyte to shriek and flee the room, which caused the Pope to laugh.

"It is prudent," the Pope finally said, "to defer to the Inquisition and allow it to do its own work. If we must demonstrate your theories, Master Siger, let us at least wait until the judges are all assembled."

Still standing, Master Siger brushed hot coffee from his robes. "I understood that was the reason I've been called here."

The Pope ignored his response and returned to the sheets of paper in the folder. "We have built a golf course just beyond the pear orchard. I must have you come out with me sometime. The back nine is especially nice. Originally commissioned by Celestine IV, it's a pity the man died before ever stroking a ball. I have added a few modifications of my own. It's quite a challenging course. Besides, there's all that fresh air and sunshine one gradually learns to tolerate. Clears out the cobweb, is my hope. But it also lets a couple of fellows get to know each other a bit better. What do you say?"

Master Siger returned to his seat determined to keep his own counsel. "I am always at Your Holiness's disposal."

"Very good. And I promise you my best game." The Pope returned his attention to the file. After a few moments he looked up, stared at a spot on the far wall and slowly removed his glasses.

"Dr. de Brion, you said something very interesting just a moment ago. Something about scientific calculations. Now I can't recall it precisely."

Simon de Brion said, "Perhaps Your Holiness refers to my comment concerning the imperfection of the human mind."

"There you are, the thing itself exactly. And unwittingly I have provided you with a perfect demonstration." The Pope laughed. "Master Siger, could the demonstration of this fundamental human imperfection have been more succinct?"

"With all respect for the intelligence of Dr. de Brion, it may just as well be that Your Holiness has demonstrated how important it is that the fallible human mind takes advantage of the devices of the modern world created by men to compensate for their weakness. If, for example, Your Holiness had availed himself of a quill and parchment and recorded Dr. Brion's sagacious utterance, there would be no question of what he had said."

"Or for that matter," the Pope said, "if I had been using a tape recorder?"

"Precisely the point," Master Siger continued. "Such a device would not only record the words, but even the inflection of the speaker's voice."

"And what makes you think I haven't?" The Pope glanced around the room. "How do any of you know there aren't microphones in every corner of this palace? Gentlemen," the Pope said grinning, "exactly how indiscrete can we afford to be?"

The silence that followed created a throbbing pain at the back of Master Siger's head. Finally, Simon de Brion said, "But of course we are only speaking hypothetically. A kind of historical phantasm."

The Pope leaned forward, a subtle satisfaction around his eyes. "Of course. Hypothetical. Inferential. The Universe of Additional Universes." He returned his attention to the folder spread across his knees. After a few moments of study, the Pope looked up. "Master Siger, I will ask you a personal question. You must know that your permanent record is remarkably voluminous. From it I learn that not only have you not yet repaid all of your student loans, but that you also did not follow the Trivium and Quadrivium in the conventional fashion. Beyond your rather deplorable transcripts, additional reports from the Inquisition indicate you have taken on the role of hell-raiser among your colleagues and students. The Inquisition has catalogued a number of unsettling reports, including one concerning a gang of Picards and the kidnapping of a student, a man named John d'Ulliaco. According to this, you and your companions broke some heads kidnapping him in order to raise some money by holding him for ransom. Another reports that about a year later, you and your colleagues kidnapped a certain Cannon William for the same purpose. And still another report states that, in retaliation for your earlier arrests, along with one Simon of Brabant you interrupted the Office of the Dead being conducted for our late brother William of Auxerre, by taking the Books of Hours right out of the hands of our French brothers. The result of these hi-jinx is constant friction and mistrust among the Nations. Fortunately for all of us, in his capacity as Papal Legate, Dr. de Brion managed to reconcile the collegium shattered by your very intemperate enthusiasm."

"I can explain all of that," Master Siger said quickly. "Besides, as your Holiness must also know, all of that happened more than ten years ago. I live a very different life now."

Pope Nicholas paused to observe him with an indulgent smile. "I'm certain you can and I'm certain you do, and I'm certain you deserve our congratulations for all of that. But in the meantime, we have these riots to consider. Allow me to frame my question. There are recorded here some three years and nine months when you were neither enrolled in any courses nor were you legally employed. Somehow during this period, you attempted to elude the ever-observant gaze of the Inquisition. Dr. de Brion may want to review my mathematical calculations of the amount of time involved, but I am enormously curious to hear the narration of what lies behind it. So my question is quite simple. How best can we fill in the account of those years?"

Master Siger leaned forward, his heart swelling with the apprehension that events were not proceeding well, and he began to wonder how it is that all he had ever done could so easily come to less than nothing.

"Your Holiness knows," Master Siger began, "perhaps better than any of us, that a fine education, like an abundant harvest, can only be gathered from many trees. And that those trees may be in many orchards. And that those orchards may be in many lands. For part of the period Your Holiness finds curious I collected unemployment checks, and for another part of that time I collected welfare, and for part of that time I worked jobs under the table. But during all of that time I pursued serious study, such that when I returned to the Sorbonne I advanced in my courses very rapidly. Nothing of great mystery occurred during that time. While there may be little in my record to be proud of, there is certainly nothing unorthodox."

The Pope leaned back into his pillows as his small grey eyes glanced up toward the ceiling. He slipped off his glasses and slowly smiled. "So, Dr. de Brion, is that a pretty tale? Does it not stir your respect for this adventurer of the spirit? Conjure in your mind an image of our impoverished young Master Siger hunched over a small electric space-heater, fingers white with cold and pouring over his dog-eared copy of Augustine or the Pseudo-Dionysus. Imagine him, hands clasped around a bowl of weak broth, memorizing another page of Greek declensions, or some choice morsel of Plotinus. Scribbling, no doubt with a worn pencil stub picked up off the street on paper stolen from some dull-witted retailer. Or better, paper and pencils boldly swiped under the eyes of hostile security guards, representatives of our repressive bureaucracy. One can't help but find it a tale both harrowing and uplifting."

Dr. de Brion smiled conspiratorially with the Pope, cleared his throat and re-crossed his legs. He sat very straight.

The smile left the Pope's face, replaced with something disheartened and yet wistful. "With all of your great gifts, Master Siger, you disappoint me. Can you truly believe that you have ever drawn a breath that was not observed? Suppose, my brave Aristotelian, I tell you that for those nearly four years you lived on the island of Majorca. I am told that Majorca is very sensual, very beautiful. And from your reluctant smile I must believe this is so. While resident of that island, you worked for an old Jew rare-book dealer named Balthasar of Antioch. The report continues that you lived in a two-room flat above his bookstore. This bookstore just happened to be on the same street as the Kit-Kat Klub. A clip-joint with a clientele of the hippest dope dealers, on an island infested with clip-joints and dope dealers."

Master Siger leaned forward unable to resist the panic that drove him to defend himself. He opened his mouth to speak, but the Pope looked hard at Master Siger and then held up his hand. "I agree that these reports, thought irreproachable, are merely circumstantial. I acknowledge that in fact they may even be exaggerated. Still, let us continue. Into this web of circumstance let me introduce Miriam, the water-carrier. A towering, raven-haired beauty still in the first flowering of her youth, with whom you became fanatically infatuated, and over whom your lust poured endlessly." The Pope shuffled through pages peering over his glasses until he came upon a particular one. "That's the word the Inquisition's agent used. 'Endlessly'. Seems you have earned a reputation as especially gifted in that regard. But to continue, let me stir all of this a bit more by suggesting that from these jolly acquaintances made at the aforementioned nightclub you might have developed a very serious heroin habit. Because it is only within such a scene and under such circumstances that you would have had contact with certain volumes of dubious scholarship."

Master Siger trembled, glanced to see if his terror was apparent. "With all respect due Your Holiness, the point at issue really concerns my research into the work of a pagan Greek philosopher dead almost fifteen hundred years. Any misadventures among non-believers, you'll agree I am certain, are matters to be taken up with my confessor and the Lord Jesus Christ."

Dr. de Brion half-stood with sudden anger. "Impertinence. You deepen your heresy by daring to explain to the Pope his duties and responsibilities and the limits of his power."

"Humbly I suggest I am misunderstood. I merely wish to confirm my complete submission to Our Lord and His Representative on Earth in all matters pertaining to my eternal salvation."

The Pope laughed quietly. "Eloquently spoken. So now let us speak bluntly, Master Siger, shall we? You know why you are here and now you know that we know a great deal more about you than you may think. You have been a continual scourge to authority in all its forms, and you flaunt your temerity by the insistent claim to complete autonomy in your thinking. So let us begin by remembering that the written word, regardless of its antiquity, can be the source of confusion and outright error for even the most sparkling of fallible human minds."

Master Siger said, "Correct my misinformation, Your Excellency, but recently you personally condemned Roger Bacon to prison for his teaching of Aristotle. This, despite the fact that the ban against the works Bacon taught had been lifted almost forty years ago."

Dr. de Brion stood, snorted with derision and began to pace. "Bacon was a fool! No one cared about his jabbering about Aristotle or Astrology or Spontaneous Generation. But he scorned the Order of Francis. As the Franciscan minister general at that time, His Holiness Pope Nicholas made the appropriate decision. Any other course of action would have betrayed his office and his order. Bacon's criticism of our order stimulated an unhealthy skepticism that would have led to the destruction of the order and a serious wound to the Church."

The Pope held up his hand. "My decision concerning Bacon may have been brilliant or it may have been stupid, only Time and the Lord will know. But Holy Mother Church has sustained many wounds and will sustain many more. We are each of us simply a tool for our Master's plan. In any case, you and I should agree that Master Siger represents no such dire threat." His Holiness turned to Master Siger.

"Meanwhile," the Pope continued, "rest assured Master Siger that the facts are before us, and we shall think about you long and hard, and when we have finished our thinking we will pray for your soul and for guidance from Our Lord in this matter."

Dr. de Brion spoke urgently to Pope Nicholas III. "My sources have received

dire warnings concerning a particularly pernicious reading of the works of
Aristotle. And even more so, the readings of certain heathen Arabs. We now
have an incomparable opportunity to provide the faithful with an example of
both our power and our determination to protect our faith."

"In war as in politics," the Pope said beginning to look bored, "it is worse than
irresponsible to fail to distinguish between the skirmish and the battle. It is of
some value to recognize how small a threat is represented by a drug-addicted
bookstore clerk, even one as brilliantly gifted as our Master Siger. Our decision,
therefore, will be measured and proportional to this threat. I must confess that
I am gravely disturbed and also annoyed by the distressing case of this silly
Grecophile bookworm. Why it has been referred to my attention I still cannot
understand. But my flock has besieged me to take the matter in hand, and this I
will do, with God's help. Now, if all of you will excuse me, I will take some rest
and ponder this further."

Pope Nicholas suddenly turned a warm smile to Master Siger. "Meanwhile, it
is still Christmas Eve and much remains for us all to do. Frère Jacques will see
you to your quarters and then accompany you to the chapel. You'll be staying
with us a while, Master Siger, and I'd really like you to get to know us a bit
better. There's an Advent ceremony this evening after dinner, please be sure to
attend." The Cistercian who the Pope had identified as Frère Jacques stood up.
Master Siger had forgotten the man was even there.

The Pope continued. "Despite the holiday, Master Siger, please don't attempt to
make any phone calls, and promise me you will remain within these walls. You
have complete access to our palace and all its amenities, including our library,
projection room and swimming pool. After the Advent thing there will be a
celebration of the Holy Filling Station and a display of the Sacred Spark Plugs
that allowed the Holy Family to make their flight into Egypt. Then there will be
a dinner to celebrate the arrival of Sheik Mustansir, the Sublime King of Tunisia.
A charming and uniquely intelligent fellow, he comes every Christmastide to
purchase missals. And then at midnight we will celebrate a High Mass. There
will be a great feast immediately following in celebration of the birth of Our
Lord. So heed this warning, Master Siger. As you value your life, eat slowly while
you are with us and eat a lot. Our kitchen staff is the very best in Christendom."
His Holiness's confiding grin seemed sincere.

The others stood and prepared to leave when Master Siger suddenly asked,
"What has become of Boetius of Dacia?"

The Pope looked from Dr. de Brion to Frère Jacques with concern. "Should I know about him?" He took up the pile of file-folders beside him and looked through them. "Do we have a file on him?" From the Pope's expression, Master Siger detected genuine confusion. "Where is our file on this man?"

Dr. de Brion looked at Frère Jacques as he spoke. "I promise Your Holiness I will retrieve that folder from Paris. It will be here by sunset, you have my word."

"So can we answer Master Siger's questions?"

After a silent moment Frère Jacques stepped forward. "My sources tell me there was a change of plans. Seems he remembered a woman he knew in Brugge and decided to see her first. But the word is he's coming down just before New Year's Day." Frère Jacques did not smile. Master Siger looked around. The expression of concern on the Pope's face was genuine.

"So we must suspend our considerations until complete materials are at hand." The glare from the Pope toward Dr. de Brion was unmistakable. Turning to Master Siger he added, "Meanwhile, our luncheon will soon be served. Frère Jacques will see to it you are well-fed."

Frère Jacques stepped forward and kissed the Pastoral ring, Master Siger followed, and together they left, while Dr. de Brion remained behind.

Let the Mist of Memory and the Shroud of Time Fade to Insoluble Darkness as Master Siger Discovers that Between Fear and Ignorance He Has Fallen into a New World for Which He is Entirely Unprepared.

CHAPTER THE FIFTH

LET HISTORY, SPARKLING Clear as Water Flowing Over Diamonds, Revive the Memory that, after a Grand and Delicious Luncheon Following His Intriguing Interview with His Holiness, Master Siger's First Morning of Arrival at the Palace of the Popes Drifted into a Warm and Bright Afternoon.

Side by side, Frère Jacques and Master Siger left the crowded and noisy refectory, to stroll in the silent shadows of the cloister. With Siger's stomach full of food, his night-long drive seemed to have happened days before. Each step deepened his lethargy, as if his feet had become heavy, and even the weight of his head had begun to strain his neck. For moments he thought he was about to fall asleep as they walked. Sunlight cast a glazed translucence over everything it touched. In the dry winter air, the motionless green leaves of the rows of orange trees sparkled. As a background to the songbirds, a stereo system cunningly disguised in the pale stonework softly played Bing Crosby singing "White Christmas" alternating with Burl Ives singing "Rudolph The Red-Nosed Reindeer" continuously and with remarkable fidelity. Master Siger looked for a place to sit down.

To Siger's annoyance, Frère Jacques continued his slow walk, his eyes cast down into his breviary. "You never ate better in Paris," he said as if speaking to his breviary. "The head chef is here from the Hyatt Regency near Musée d'Orsay. Hell of a guy though he's mean when he drinks. But if you think that luncheon was good, wait until the dinner for Mustansir. His Holiness has brought the head chef of his Castel San Angelo for the party. You never had Arab food like you're going to taste tonight."

"And such beautiful weather," Master Siger said. He intended to praise his surroundings and convey a fraudulent pleasure for where he found himself. He tried to gesture, but his heavy arms hung by his sides like over-sized salamis. "His Holiness is fortunate to have this retreat of prayer and contemplation."

Frère Jacques stopped and turned. With a smile he said, "Look, we've both had a belly-full of great food and more than a few glasses of wine. Let's forget the formalities so I can tell you what I really think." He paused and looked around with a bright smile. "You're right, my friend, this is a hell of a place to pass the time. And I'll remind you of something else. Brother Thomas had it right when he said, 'Shit in one hand and wish in the other; put them together and what do you get?' I mean, what's to wish for when you've got everything? Am I right? Tennis court, swimming pool, golf course, private movie theater, servants and clean sheets everywhere, telephones and fax machines, five cars in the garage, you get your pick. Even a depressed guy like you could live good in a place like this."

Master Siger stopped. Light-headed from exhaustion, colors swirled before his eyes and grew bright, sounds of the birds and Bing Crosby became painfully loud. Studying the expression on Siger's face, Frère Jacques said, "Being the guest of the Pope is not the toughest job there is." Across his lips passed the shadow of sneer. "Even has a big library with a lot of books, if you like that sort of thing."

Frère Jacques continued, "I mean, why would anybody want to leave a spot like this is all what I'm driving at. So you won't be roasting beside your buddies over du Val's grill back in Paris. As it is, a guy like you hasn't got enough friends to make a card game."

Master Siger trembled. The world swirled, halos surrounded every object as the light seared Siger's eyes. "My brother hopes to present my prison as if it was some sort of health resort."

Frère Jacques snapped his breviary shut, took Master Siger's arm firmly and pushed him along a narrow, empty gallery. "Call yourself a prisoner?" Frère Jacques hissed as they walked. "Just because you can't leave? Just because you can't go just anywhere you want? Like there's so much waiting for you out there."

"What is waiting for me is my role in the great battle to bring to light the work of the one true Philosopher."

Frère Jacques laughed bitterly as he pushed Siger ahead. "What's waiting for you is a small army of big guys with bigger knives. My friend, you spend too much time indoors is your problem. A couple of pimple-faced kids tell you you're a cool teacher, and suddenly you think you have pull in that town. So let me ask you. What do you think Tempier would do if he got his hands on you?"

Master Siger was quiet for a time. "There'll be sweeps, won't there," he said. "The Inquisition will round them all up, as many as they can get their hands on. Hundreds arrested, the finest minds in France shoved into dank and putrid cells until their one-way trip to the basement. That's how it will happen, isn't it?"

Frère Jacques slowed his pace. Though he kept a firm grip on Siger's arm, he would not hold his glance. "Maybe all that's going on right now. And maybe you should be at least a little grateful you've been spared." He led Master Siger as if he had someplace in mind. "Convenient you forget there's all kinds of pressure going on over you. Everybody wants your balls for a trophy. If the Franciscans turn up the heat, maybe suddenly the Dominicans forget how to protect you." He paused and then turned to face Master Siger. "Ever think of that?" He turned then and led Siger down another corridor.

"I know your type." Frère Jacques continued speaking quietly as he walked and his voice resounded more with resignation than anger. "You're thinking maybe you could make a break to Sicily, get some protection from Simon of Catania or Augustus Robustus. But get as far as Palermo and I promise you either of those guys will kill you just for the reward money. And be happy to do the Pope the favor. So much for the courage and loyalty of intellectuals. You know you can't go back to Majorca. Where else? Constantinople? Give me a break." Frère Jacques stopped suddenly, pulled Siger so close they could have kissed. "In case you haven't heard, your poster is up in every university town from Oxford to Baghdad. There isn't a pool hall in Christendom safe for you to shoot a game of eight-ball. At what point will you get the message?"

Master Siger leaned his shoulder against the cool sandstone wall. For a moment it seemed the weight of his own body might suffocate him. It wasn't just the hamsters and the collection of videos burned by Tempier. Slow walks through the Luxembourg at twilight, traffic and bright lights, music pouring from shops along Boul' Mich'. Restaurants and cafes on Germain under a quality of light nearly frivolous. The smell of coffee and cigarettes, arguments about football, the horses, government and taxes, greetings and partings. And the sight of a slow, burning kiss. Master Siger could hardly explain all this to himself. How could he even hope to explain it to Frère Jacques?

As if conceding something, Frère Jacques took Siger's arm more gently and resumed their stroll. Suddenly he laughed. "Listen, we're starting all wrong. Here I am with one of the smartest guys in the world, and I'm trying to wise him up. Me. And here, all I want to do is be friends. Tell you what. Let me introduce you to some people. Fun types, if you see what I mean. Besides, you'll feel a lot better when we get to Rome. I know a lot more people in that town."

"We?"

"Sure," Frère Jacques said, "you and me. I'm telling you, we're going to have a great time, and we get to be great friends."

Master Siger felt himself stiffen with anger. "Insisting I remain against my wishes breaches the natural laws of God. My brother must acknowledge that mankind's natural state is a state of freedom."

Frère Jacques glanced once into Siger's face and then spat into the dust. "Mankind's natural state is a state of being dead, and don't kid yourself. Count all the years you hope to be alive, and divide by the years you aren't, and tell me how it turns out."

Master Siger shivered. "The Lord's Merciful Love will shield me, in this life and in the next."

"The Lord will deal with each of us as the Lord decides, and in His own time. Far be it from you to decide how the Lord will dispose of us and The True Revelation of Holy Mother Church is our only guide. Only a fool pretends to know everything he needs to know to be able to say what's going on in this world. Past or present."

"The Lord gives each of us freedom so that we can be saved by our faith."

There was an expression of sadness in Frère Jacques's face, as if he was seeing Siger from a great distance and the light was beginning to fade. "We're as free as circumstance allows. We're even free to skip this Advent ceremony. Of course, if we do that we lose our freedom to decide anything at all." Frère Jacques chuckled as he led Master Siger back to the Papal Chapel. Siger followed burdened by an annoyed resentment that could find no focus, so that it seemed merely to swirl within him without direction. Though Master Siger knew that everything Frère Jacques said was true and he should be relieved by his situation, his legs carrying him to the chapel moved as if encased in mud.

When they arrived, the chapel was jammed and the service had already begun. The hundreds of lighted candles cast a thousand dazzling reflections over glittering robes and colorful gowns. Master Siger and Frère Jacques pushed past a surly aristocracy and made their way to the cluster of clergy at the front.

Dressed in nearly oriental splendor, Pope Nicholas led the Procession of the Sacred Spark Plugs down the chapel's center aisle. Master Siger and Frère Jacques just reached their places as, in slow solemn tones, the assembled worshippers began to chant the Fourth Incantation titled, "She's My Little Deuce Coupe."

His Holiness swayed as he held the Sacred Spark Plugs high above his head, and clear for all to see. Congregants particularly moved by sight of these precious relics approached, knelt, and kissed the bright red tassels of the golden pillow that displayed them.

Master Siger had read about these relics responsible for saving the Holy Family in its Flight into Egypt, but he had never seen them until now. The power of his own response, the way seeing these holy objects suddenly swelled his heart, startled him. He prayed fervently, asking that if he be found worthy, Christ remove all confusion and doubt from his soul.

He had struggled for years in theological controversy, yet this material evidence of His Salvation overwhelmed Master Siger with the terrible weight of what he had undertaken. For a moment he recognized himself in the place of Joseph, forced with his family from their home and left to wander among strangers beset on all sides by a host of dangers. How fortunate for Joseph that, at his moment of greatest need, he encountered Blessed Ernie. Master Siger prayed that in this moment of anguish, he too would discover Blessed Ernie poised on Siger's path and prepared to give him comfort. Master Siger prayed for strength, and most earnestly for the Light of God's Grace to enter his soul and illuminate his heart. As the six gleaming objects approached he felt himself tremble, and tears came to his eyes as Pope Nicholas carried them passed his pew.

When the Sacred Spark Plugs had been returned to the altar, Cardinal Egobardt of Vienna stepped to the pulpit and read the passages from St. Phyllis that tells the story of Blessed Ernie, the Gas Station Attendant. And how, when the Holy Family arrived broke, gas tank empty and engine about to give out, Blessed Ernie gave them a fill-up, tuned their engine and replaced their spark-plugs, and then refused their offer of payment, only wishing their safe arrival in Egypt. At the end of the reading, His Holiness led the congregation in the singing of the Ninth Incantation based on "Hallelujah, I'm A Bum." As Master Siger stood and swayed with the congregation, he felt himself renewed as a weight seemed lifted from his heart. For the first time since his arrival, he smiled.

Afterward, the congregation made its way to the Reception Hall, grandly decorated for the Christmas celebration. Wreathes and chains of holly, bright lights and dark green trees were everywhere. On a long broad table set up against one wall, a hundred varieties of food and wine were laid out.

"Our Holy Father isn't your typical, tight-fisted cleric," Frère Jacques quietly said with a grin. His eyes sparkled with the light of a thousand glittering reflections. The glow on his face bespoke a pleasure he struggled to contain, a giddy delight as much from the brilliant company of dignitaries and their trophy companions as the creative adornments to the hall. Templars and Hospitalars, Monastics and Charitables, Franciscans and Dominicans and Benedictines and Cistercians, and even a few Capuchins, circulated with bright smiles and quiet voices. "When he's got the King of Tunis for dinner and a High Mass," Frère Jacques said, "the Pope of Rome knows how to spend money. His Holiness is no piker."

Dazzled by the waves of color and sound, along with the sight of the well-dressed men and gorgeous, elegant women, Siger turned to ask a question, but Frère Jacques whispered into his ear, "Check this out!"

On a cue from an invisible trumpet, two huge black men carrying swords almost as tall as themselves entered the room and stood on either side of the entrance. Behind them appeared a dozen young women whose slim, naked bodies were not concealed by their brightly colored, transparent veils. The women arranged themselves along either side of the entrance. Then, with a soulful flourish from an unseen jazz band, Sheik Mustansir appeared. Applause was immediate and enthusiastic while the smiling Sheik—short, heavy-set and wearing a broad, black belt—waved his hand in acknowledgment. As he passed, each of the veiled women fell in line behind him.

Meanwhile, on a broad dais at the opposite end of the hall, His Holiness Pope Nicholas III appeared and seated himself beside a second throne awaiting his visitor. To sustained applause, the Pope stood while the Sheik climbed the three stairs to the throne by his side. The women, each adopting a different lascivious pose, arranged themselves on the steps leading up to the dais while both men continued to offer smiling acknowledgment to the gathered throng.

At a signal from Cardinal Rigatoni, the band then began to play. Those in the crowd began to speak among themselves or moved toward the food-laden table. A few like Master Siger simply stared at the ravishing women who surrounded these powerful potentates.

To Master Siger, Frère Jacques whispered, "The Sheik makes this visit every Christmas Eve. The Pope makes a deal with him for a load of free missals to be given out to the Christian subjects of Tunis. The Sheik likes this because the hand-out keeps his Christian subjects docile."

"Isn't that risky for the Pope?"

Frère Jacques shrugged, but his grin did not fade. "His Holiness needs oil if he expects to continue the Crusades. But the Pope also believes he can limit how many Christians are killed over the coming year. In either case, His Holiness is an optimist. He is certain that eventually the Sheik will see the Light of Christian Virtue and convert. He's a guy who likes to keep channels of communication open."

Then, as if he had recognized someone across the room, Frère Jacques excused himself. This left Master Siger confused. It occurred to him that, since the moment he stepped from the Bishop's car, Frère Jacques had not left his side.

At liberty now, Siger moved directly to the buffet table. With a plate balanced in one hand and a drink in the other, while most in the crowd scrutinized every look and gesture of two of the most powerful men in the world, Master Siger continued his study of the reclining women. Gradually he discovered himself mesmerized by a certain fair-haired Circasian, sullen and blue-eyed, and who's bold smile and delicious gaze seemed entirely his own.

The two men on the dais leaned toward each other. With some muttered words and friendly smiles, Pope Nicholas III and Mustansir, King of Tunis, stood. Their actions turned every head toward the dais. A small door just behind the pair of thrones opened, and the Pope and the Sheik disappeared through it, followed by their councilors. The last councilor, a large round man with a strangely pink face, stopped and took his position beside the open door. Immediately the women around the dais stood and, one by one, passed through it. When the last one had gone, the large man glanced up and bowed, and then closed the door behind him. Master Siger's heart sank. He had hoped for an interview with the Sheik to ask if he knew the location of more of the writings of Averroes. Or something like that.

Suddenly Frère Jacques appeared by Siger's side. "You still standing here?" He was smiling widely. Siger surmised a considerable amount of drink had been consumed. "We've got a couple of hours to kill before Mass, and this is quite a crowd. Why don't you circulate a bit, practice saying hello? The exercise'll do you good." Frère Jacques winked grotesquely. "You're better known around here than you think."

As if responding to an invisible signal, Master Siger suddenly found himself in conversation with Archbishop Guido of Pavia, the senior baseball writer for *Time* magazine. Tall, bespeckled, and all together foolish-looking, the old prelate launched into a rant about the Dodgers' chances for the World Series next season and how lousy their new pitching rotation looked. Though Siger was determined to remain polite while the drunken sports reporter prattled on about era's and innings-pitched, he confessed to himself regret for his own unfortunate indifference to the game.

Meanwhile, Master Siger overheard a conversation between Brother Alfons of Sevile and Abbess Catherine of Logrono going on behind him. The point of contention seemed to be a certain acolyte the Abbess believed would prove a great addition to her abbey. Food and drink were helping Master Siger relax while giving him something to hold in his hands. He politely excused himself from the Archbishop to return to the table and refill his platter. Just as he turned toward the table he looked up.

In a corner at the far end of the reception hall, Master Siger saw Dr. Simon de Brion standing alone. And Dr. de Brion seemed to stare directly at him. Master Siger continued past the table of food and moved toward a large cluster of people. He was determined to wander among conversations that put him as far from de Brion as possible.

Just before midnight and at a signal from Cardinal Rigatoni, the congregation returned to the Papal Chapel for High Mass. As if from nowhere, Frère Jacques reappeared at Siger's side to accompany him to the Chapel.

Inside, Mustansir, King of Tunis, sat in the choir loft surrounded by his counselors as His Holiness led the Mass. The women apparently had been left behind. The High Mass was being broadcast by satellite into the home of every Christian the world over. Master Siger felt himself part of a great reverential movement toward the righteous path of Christ.

Master Siger sat between Frère Jacques and Bishop Harold of Exeter. The Bishop was asleep before the end of the Introit and snored loudly. Master Siger ignored him and throughout the mass prayed fervently for guidance. The Bishop awoke with a start at the Communion, stood and stumbled to the altar-rail to receive the Host. During the Communion ceremony, Master Siger turned. Simon de Brion sat almost directly behind him and three rows back. Master Siger intensified his prayers.

Immediately after the Mass, the congregation reassembled in the Reception

Hall. The hall was now laid out with three long tables with chairs and place settings. The tables were piled high with food and a flagon of wine sat beside each place. The jazz band had been replaced by a chamber music group. Now Master Siger found himself sitting between Frère Jacques and the Abbess from Logrono. A charming, middle-aged woman with green eyes and thick, red hair, she seemed determined to ask Master Siger something personal, but kept glancing toward Frère Jacques.

Brightly dressed servants of both sexes hurried between tables refilling plates and avoiding amorous embraces. The dinner continued through several courses. For dessert, the gathering was invited to move to an antechamber where sweets and coffee and various bottles of cordials were set out on another long table. A local rock band played for anyone who wanted to dance. Many took advantage. Again unexpectedly, Frère Jacques disappeared from Siger's side. As Master Siger looked around the room to locate him, he suddenly spied another familiar face.

Mistress Jacqueline of Paris stood in conversation with two clerics, one of whom kept his hand on her forearm as he spoke to her. She was dressed in a low-cut forest-green gown that accented her glowing pale shoulders, and Master Siger realized he had never seen her look more beautiful. He moved without hesitation, stepped between the two men and turned to her asking, "May I have this dance?" Without waiting for her answer he led her onto the dance floor.

With a smile she whispered, "Since when have you taken up dancing?"

Master Siger did his best imitation of someone dancing. He whispered, "Whatever happened to your convent-by-the-sea?"

Mistress Jacqueline laughed quietly. "Sidetracked. Life is like that."

Master Siger danced her slowly away from the crowd. "They tell me I'll be here some time."

Jacqueline's gaze traveled beyond him and around the room. "We should all be so lucky."

"Luck has nothing to do with it," Master Siger said. "By the way, I was told Boetius would meet me here. Have you heard from him?"

Mistress Jacqueline suddenly stopped dancing and looked darkly into his eyes. "No one has told you?" She took his arm, a gesture that alarmed him, and held it tightly to her side leading him slowly toward a secluded corner. "He tried to flee to England," she said quietly. "They say he fell over-board. The captain didn't discover he was missing until the morning. Helicopters were sent out. They think he's gone." Again she looked into his eyes. "I'm sorry."

Through the haze of wine and food Master Siger staggered. Mistress Jacqueline leaned into him and he regained his stride. "Really, I'm so sorry. He was your best friend." When Master Siger looked up, she continued to stare into his eyes. He glanced past her face. Across the room he saw Simon de Brion watching them. Siger adopted a grim smile. He bowed. "We're being watched," he muttered through his smile. "Shall we resume?" His choices, he discovered, had suddenly come down to just one.

When her face brushed close to his Siger said, "We've got to get out of here."

Instantly, Mistress Jacqueline's laughter was bright and clear. "Oh dear, don't be tiresome. There is no safer place to be than in the bosom of the Church. And unlike Paris, here you will be regularly fed. Besides, as long as you remain here I'll know where to get in touch with you." Then she looked past Siger's shoulder, and her bright smile suddenly became languorous. Master Siger turned.

Just inside a small door half-hidden by tapestry stood a man. Tall, trim and dark, with thick dark hair and chiseled features, and dressed in the well-tailored clothes of a lawyer, he surveyed the room with intent eyes. "Finally," Mistress Jacqueline said with a sigh. "My escort has arrived, and just in time to save me from having to endure your maudlin pout." She curtsied graciously. "I know you'll excuse me, Master Siger. And I'm sure you will heed the good council of those who think well of you." Master Siger found himself unable to watch her go.

Still abandoned by his personal escort, Master Siger left the reception and made his confused way back to his room. When finally he closed its door behind him, he sat down on the edge of his bed, and for a long time he remembered Boetius. He felt himself forsaken, and yet too heart-sick to weep. He saw himself more alone than he ever believed he could be. His choice appeared suddenly obvious now, a choice that perhaps had always been unavoidable. He waited in his room until four hours after midnight. When Frère Jacques did not reappear, and long after Siger was confident the other guests had retired, he made his escape.

Master Siger's first obstacle was at the end of his corridor. On a bench beside the door a guard fornicated with a very large prostitute. Master Siger did not need the weak light to pass unnoticed. Outside the Palace, Master Siger discovered the gate beside the Papal garages standing unlocked. When he passed beyond the Palace walls, Siger raced along the side-streets of Avignon, lost and stumbling in complete darkness, trying to guess in which direction to turn next. When finally he reached the outer walls of the town, he found a narrow gate that was unattended.

Passing through this gate seemed like crossing an invisible barrier, and on the other side Master Siger began to run through a mowed field that, under the bright starlight, appeared to be dusted with powdered silver. He could just make out in the distance a dark alley of forest that seemed to lead upward and into the hills. With all his strength Siger ran toward that darkness. The last dozen yards to the line of trees left him gasping for breath. Patches of color appeared before his eyes as he strained for air.

But then he was sheltered in their shadows and he collapsed. He rested only a moment before he began to climb toward the crest of the hill. But then he stopped. Something moved noisily in the fallen leaves uphill, and the noise seemed to be moving toward him growing louder. He looked in the direction of the sound. Moving steadily toward him, three black shapes emerged from the darkness. Master Siger scrambled to run, but after a few steps his legs collapsed.

"Hey, man, Merry Christmas." The clear voice came from one of the advancing figures. Master Siger recognized it immediately. "You ran a good race," Frère Jacques said gasping and coughing between each phrase. "But now we should all sit down and take a break. What do you say?" Master Siger sat down heavy with despair and his chest was aflame with pain.

"You kept us going," Frère Jacques continued, "you can take some satisfaction from that." He sat down beside Master Siger, breathing hard as he pushed back his cowl. The other dark figures remained standing in shadows a few steps away. "You know, the more I see of you, Master Siger, the more impressed I become. You wasted as little time as possible making your impressions of us clear. And your escape was worthy of an astute student of Aristotle and associate of drug-dealing murderers. Five minutes one way or the other, and it would have taken us a whole extra day to catch up with you. Unless some jealous husband mistakenly shot you first."

Frère Jacques then reached behind his ear. "It's been a long night, man. What do you say, smoke this joint with us. Let's take a break. We can pick this all up again tomorrow. Let's get high, man. It's Christmas. What do you say?"

Master Siger glanced at the joint, slim and ghostly-white, one end already smoldering, its orange point the only light in the darkness. As he took it, Frère Jacques reached behind his ear, brought out another and lighted it.

The two other dark shapes came forward and sat on the ground across from

them. As Frère Jacques passed one of the lighted joints to the figure nearest
him, they both slide back their cowls. To Master Siger's surprise they were both
young women.

"Siger of Brabant, Master of Arts of the Sorbonne of Paris," Frère Jacques said,
"allow me to introduce to you Celestina of Toulon, Mistress of Computerology
and Guardian of the Back-Up Files. And Marguerite of Montpellier, Mistress of
Biochemical Engineering and Genetics. And Mistress Marguerite has brought
us some wine." Frère Jacques nodded to a young woman with abundant dark
hair and narrow face, and eyes that glittered even in the darkness.

From the folds of her robes she brought out a skin of wine on a cord. She
passed it to Master Siger. The sack of wine was warm in his hand. She watched
his hands and smiled. Master Siger drank a long time.

Mistress Celestina said, "We insisted Frère Jacques arrange for us to meet you.
We've been told so much about you." Mistress Celestina's hair was golden, and
her face was more round than Mistress Marguerite's. "I was fascinated by your
interpretation of Augustine's rebuttal of Pasquale of Padua.

"And the way you interwove," Mistress Marguerite said in a voice that was
soft and deep, "quotations from Marius Agrippa of Alexandria. I wanted to
meet the man whose argumentation is as elegant as chamber music."

To Frère Jacques, Master Siger asked, "Where is Mistress Jacqueline?"

"Funny you should ask that," Frère Jacques said. "Seems Sheik Mustansir has
taken a great interest in your sexy Parisienne genius. Apparently he is cultivating
a keen interest in dialectic. She's joined his entourage headed to Marseille and
then to his palace in Tunis. Lucky girl, if you ask me."

"So who asked you?" Master Siger said.

"It ill becomes a philosopher to play the sore loser. Besides, maybe she got tired
of philosophy and went looking for adventure. You know how young girls are
these days. She asked me to send you her regards, and she promised she would
write to you. I expect that'll be a fascinating correspondence."

Master Siger said nothing, curious to learn how he had come to know her,
but instead of asking smoked at the joint without enthusiasm.

"Hey listen," Frère Jacques said brightly, "it just so happens I brought this
big thick blanket, which is what slowed me down." The blanket appeared from
under the folds of his cassock. "I'll just spread this out here and then we can all
stretch out for a bit."

Later, as Master Siger removed Mistress Marguerite's robes and caressed her pale soft skin in the shadowed moonlight, it occurred to him he was now prepared to doubt everyone, everywhere, about everything, and forever more.

Let the Silver Light of that Round and Splendid Moon Shine Upon this Moment's Peace for a Profoundly Unhappy Soul Benumbed by Carnal Delight, and Let Fall That Merciful Curtain of Memory.

CHAPTER THE SIXTH

LET THE SUPPLE AND ELEGANT Lips of History Quietly Remind Us That on the Sunny and Joyous Christmas Morning of 1277, the Palace of His Holiness Pope Nicholas III Had Been Transformed into a Dungeon of Misery.

Piped throughout the Palace, Christmas songs wafted along hallways and up stairways, drifting even into those chambers still wreathed in slumber. It flowed even over the wide rumpled pile of bed sheets and pillows that concealed the contorted form of Master Siger of Brabant. His firmly shut eyes did nothing to block the gleeful hymns of the season as they pounded against his ears. Siger swept his hand slowly over the space in the bed beside him. With a weak grin of relief he concluded that beneath his mountain of wrinkled white affliction, he was entirely alone. This was his first discovery. His second discovery was pain.

Master Siger discovered that his bed contained only this body and its pain. And his pain was a commingling of many pains. Siger's face and head seemed swollen with a vile, pulsating fluid, and its searing throb seemed all but translucent. Sunlight pouring through his window with its fiercely unnatural brightness blasted his eyes, another pain that amplified the pain of his head. Siger moved his tongue slowly over his lips to discover flecks of some indescribable material. And then there was his stomach. Nausea twisted and roiled its center, creating a pain that could almost have been hunger. His very bones had become possessed by a wretchedness that could only have been a premonition of death itself. Besieged by the anguished joys of this glorious season and the misery of his body, he wondered about death, a thing that he reminded himself frequently was inevitable, but which Siger still aspired to put off as long as possible. But now he found himself muttering a prayer that the pain of his death would not be this pain. Then finally Siger agreed to open his eyes.

For a time and without lifting his head, Siger watched as shadows slowly crossed the ceiling. His memories of the previous night came to him in shreds, brightening for moments and then fading, to darkness. But the profound anguish of his physical state overwhelmed every continuous recollection.

The gradual movement of the light mocked him and his wretchedness and his paralytic immobility, while it smirked and leered at his misery. Siger remained utterly still as he searched for corners of his being not yet compromised, in an attempt to gather what little strength remained. When he concluded finally that his stomach and his head were prepared to obey his wishes, he dressed and stumbled to the refectory. He was, he believed, very hungry.

The large room was nearly empty. To one side, a Benedictine sat alone, and at the other side a Hospitalar and two Templars huddled silently together over whatever victuals could be tolerated. Light-headed and unsteady, Master Siger dizzily prowled the breakfast buffet table in search of acceptable nourishment. While he perused the morning's offerings, he was suddenly startled to recall more of what had passed the evening before, enough to frighten him but not enough to satisfy his distressed curiosity.

Holding a cup of coffee he could hardly wait to drink, and some bread and fruit he hoped he might successfully eat, Master Siger chose a table as far from his few companions as this room's walls would allow. What he began to remember of the previous evening somehow managed to involve Boetius and Jacqueline and Frère Jacques, and then two young women named Marguerite and Celestina. All of it came to him wreathed in a silver green fog. Though he mulled over all of it as he sipped his coffee, he could only conclude that either his memory was defective, or his debauchery had been extraordinarily shameless. He lifted his eyes from his darkly carnal thoughts to find himself suddenly living in a world sheathed by a sticky, vile-smelling mucous of lust. But his head remained filled with concrete, and it was all he could do to prop his face over his cup.

He glanced up to the door of the refectory to see Frère Jacques enter. The man nodded toward Master Siger with a smile, an expression that struck him, at that moment and under those circumstances, as even more perverted than his own memories.

He watched Frère Jacques fill a cup from the urn at the buffet table, and then carry it to Master Siger's table. Still several steps away he called out with an odd glee, "Merry Christmas." Master Siger offered no response. Frère Jacques took a seat across from Siger. "You look like a guy who could use some company." Frère Jacques glanced down into his cup and laughed again, but more quietly. "If you think last night was a great party, stick around for New Year's Eve. You'll see things you never imagined in your philosophy, I can promise you that."

Thoroughly incapable of argument or debate, Master Siger simply sipped his coffee. Frère Jacques watched him. Slowly the smile creasing his face changed. When Master Siger recognized it he cringed, finished his coffee, stumbled to the urn, refilled his cup, and then returned to the table. At his return, he discovered that Frère Jacques's smile had turned into a grinning leer. Frère Jacques reached across the table and slapped Master Siger on the shoulder hard enough to spill a bit of coffee from his cup. "Who would have thought the humble study of philosophy would nurture such amatory brilliance?"

Now annoyed as much as frightened, Master Siger said nothing, sipped what was left of his coffee and looked sullenly out the window. Frère Jacques's laugh was sudden and loud enough to embarrass Master Siger.

Frère Jacques's expression slowly changed to surprise. Master Siger shifted uncomfortably. Frère Jacques leaned toward him. In nearly a whisper he said, "For your sake I hope you have not forgotten a night neither Marguerite nor Celestina will ever forget." The new expression on Frère Jacques's face made Master Siger tremble.

"And you know how girls will talk," Frère Jacques said. "By sundown their imprimature will get you a date with any female in this palace." Stunned and with his thoughts completely muddled, Master Siger swallowed hard, stumbled back to the urn, refilled his cup and then dizzily returned to his table.

When Master Siger sat down again he sighed with a kind of exhaustion. "I don't think I want to know whatever it is you're talking about."

Frère Jacques scratched his unshaved chin thoroughly perplexed. Then he shrugged. "Well, answer me this then. Are all philosophers such humble and self-effacing champions in the saddle? Brother Abelard's exploits are notorious, but I thought that was just the result of prayer and fasting. Maybe you picked up something from that woman you knew in Majorca? Something that drives them wild, perhaps?" This time Frère Jacques's laugh was so good-natured Siger could not suppress a grin.

Siger said, "Mistress Jacqueline told me about Boetius last night." With this recollection he decided his head had begun to clear.

Frère Jacques's smile did not flicker. "So there you are. When can we expect him?"

Master Siger searched Frère Jacques's expression. "She told me he was dead." Frère Jacques's eyes widened, his smile disappeared. "Lost at sea crossing the Channel."

In a voice Siger could hardly make out, Frère Jacques asked, "Where did she say she heard this?"

Master Siger shook his head. "She didn't. And I didn't ask." The veil of his hangover was finally beginning to lift.

After a moment Frère Jacques asked, "Do you believe her?"

"She believes it." Master Siger hesitated. "I don't think she would lie about this."

"Even if she was ordered?"

Master Siger bit his lip against doubt. "You told me she had left in the company of the Sheik. Couldn't we catch up with them at Marseille, and talk to her there?"

"Gets pretty sticky, diplomatically." Frère Jacques suddenly looked depressed as his thoughts drifted far away. "You don't know who he tried to contact in England?" Master Siger said nothing. "Roger Bacon, maybe?" Frère Jacques wondered aloud. "He's the kind of maniac who would hide Boetius." Master Siger held his thoughts beneath his tongue.

Frère Jacques let his arm fall to the table, snorted in disgust. "His Holiness is going to hate this."

At the time Mistress Jacqueline told this to him, Master Siger had not doubted her account. Now, Frère Jacques's questions bothered Master Siger in a way that interfered with his recovery.

Slowly Frère Jacques's expression relaxed. "Let's wait until we've heard this through official channels. What do you say? The Pope's got ways of finding this stuff out." Again he reached across the table, this time gripping Siger's forearm with fraternal affection. "Let's wait until we've heard it from the big guys." Then his look brightened.

"And before I forget to remind you," Frère Jacques continued, "there'll be a Christmas banquet tonight. Afterward, His Holiness sits beside the big Christmas tree in the Diplomatic Lounge and gives everybody a gift. And guess what you're getting? A set of golf clubs. Thought you ought to know. Expensive as hell, of course, and very nice. You'll like them. Just make sure you act surprised. And pleased."

Master Siger shrugged perplexed. "I haven't played in years."

"He really wants you out on his golf-course," Frère Jacques said. "You're probably the only one in this Palace who'll play with the cheating old fart." Then he glanced up at the clock above the door. "We have a couple of hours to kill. What do you say we go for a walk?" Master Siger's only desire was to return to his room and sleep off the rest of his hangover. But Frère Jacques's interest in Boetius forced him out.

To Master Siger's relief, the passageways they followed were breezy and dry and, shielded from the sun, their cool, pale light rested his eyes. He followed Frère Jacques's lead until they came to a wide, enclosed courtyard open to the bright blue sky, but everywhere well-shaded. Surrounded by pale yellow sandstone walls three stories high, the upper stories were interrupted evenly by wide windows.

Frère Jacques tossed his breviary onto one of the stone benches ranged along the walls. Master Siger took a seat at the other end of the bench. He glanced across the courtyard and then up at the wall opposite to its third storey. What he discovered there did not seem real at first. Filling one of those windows, a woman stood facing the courtyard. A pendent fold of drapery hid her face, but her torso was naked, motionless, and young, and it glittered in the sunlight. Startled, Master Siger looked away.

Frère Jacques spoke quietly. "Brother Thomas always said yours was the finest mind in all of Europe. I wouldn't lie to you about this. Flattery never got me very far with a philosopher."

Master Siger grinned, embarrassed and annoyed at his own gullibility. Frère Jacques continued. "But did you ever see that movie where the guy makes the monster, and then the monster gets away? The townspeople get scared and go after it with pitchforks, but they don't stop at just killing the monster. They go after guy who made the monster, too."

Master Siger said, "You believe Aristotle is some sort of blood-thirsty beast."

Frère Jacques looked away. "I don't know anything about any of that. I just know that if the Pope tolerates heathens and Arabs and Jews going around contradicting Holy Catholic dogma, what will happen next? If he tolerates the interpretations from these heathens, what'll he be able to say to the believers who disagree with him? Looniness only gets loonier from there. Tolerance reduces the Pope's control of the Church. Pretty soon everybody is running around believing whatever they want. And there's no worse kind of anarchy, an anarchy no Pope can abide."

Master Siger glanced up to the window. The sight of the woman's brilliant flesh refreshed him. It occurred to him his hangover had finally begun to fade so that now all he felt was tired.

"A smart guy like you," Frère Jacques continued, "might think a little anarchy isn't all that bad. People give up their belief in the hands that are running the show, and for a while they'll think they're free and therefore happy. But sooner or later they come to your house with torches and ropes. The blessing of freedom always becomes a burden, and the liberators are always punished for its crime. Even a guy smart as you would be surprised what upsets people, and what they do when they're upset."

"What upsets people," Siger responded finally feeling caught up in this challenge, "is when they see heads being split open. Pretty soon somebody asks what's going on, and why all the blood? And when that person only gets his head split for an answer, that's when he gets really upset."

"You got to be kidding me." Frère Jacque's expression of stunned disbelief was almost comical. "You really think anybody cares about your right to think? Then you must think people are pretty stupid. What they care about is what you do with all this thinking once you're done thinking it. Curious people die young, but smart people die first."

Master Siger did not smile. "The Lord has given us minds, and minds fill with questions. Those questions, and the curiosity at their source, must be a part of the Lord as much as the mind that possesses them. I have no desire to overthrow the world, even less to overthrow the Papacy and disturb this cozy corner of Christendom. But answers can only be found by pressing against the boundaries. And according to what I have read and observed, I am not alone."

"Don't believe that, my friend." Frère Jacques glumly studied the stones beneath their bench. "A guy like you is always alone. Your mind is troubled, and you want to ease it. Your questions are a burden, so you tell yourself, 'I will solve this little riddle, and that will bring me peace. And after all, what could mere thoughts matter?' So let me tell you. The things that you think don't matter, there's somebody out there who looks forward to getting upset. You say you don't care who gets upset, or what they do when they get upset, am I right? Your only interest is in the truth. Am I right?"

Master Siger glanced up again to the third floor window. The woman's torso was still there, molded in peach-tinted shadow and golden sunlight. Master Siger sighed quietly. "Ever been to Majorca?"

Frère Jacques nodded.

"Then you know Eucalyptus Street. There's a little cafe on the south side of the street just past the docks called Virgilio's. Sunday mornings I would sit at a table in the shade under the trees drinking, and follow the horse-races in Paris on the TV above the bar. Crowds of men carrying pencils and racing forms would fill the place yelling to each other, making bets and cursing the miserable horses who nearly always failed their intuitions. Every Sunday I was privileged to witness men make choices of wager and odds. So much earnest effort expended to replicate logical thought. So many proofs offered why one horse would beat another. So much reflection upon the jockey's skills, or the results of a previous race, the weight carried, the weather, or the other horses. The atmosphere of seemingly-critical thinking was intoxicating. Irrational, as enthusiasm always must be."

"Of course, no matter how often some bettor's hunch turned out to be accurate, it was always just a guess, with no demonstration of how any outcome might be more or less likely. All in such poetic contradiction to the series of proofs offered by Aristotle, and elaborated by Islamic thinkers, of the distinction between necessity and contingency. A science that cannot predict an outcome within a definable context is just another kind of faith."

Master Siger glanced up to find the woman remained in the window, motionless and thrilling. "One Sunday, the cup-race at the Bois de Bologne had come in at a dead-heat. You'll like this story. Men were screaming, hands were flying, faces were red with sweat and excitement. A big and fairly drunk man was sitting with his friend at a table beside mine. At the height of the commotion he stood up from his chair with his back to me, reached into his back pocket and brought out this big, red handkerchief to mop the sweat from his face. Along with the handkerchief, a five-hundred franc note, folded a couple of times, flew out and landed on my table. Suddenly it was sitting beside my glass of wine as if I had just put it there. But worse, just then my waiter came along. He scooped up the banknote as if I'd left it to pay for my drink, made change that he replaced on my table and then passed on. I did not hesitate." Master Siger grinned. "With a swipe of my hand I put all that money in my pocket."

Master Siger studied Frère Jacques's expression. But the expression on Frère Jacques's face did not change. His indifference seemed a faded version of boredom.

"I left the bar immediately, walked back to my place on the square by the Moorish tower with that money bulging nicely against my leg. When finally I climbed the stairs to my room above the bookstore, I felt wonderful. I lay down and slept a dreamless sleep through the rest of the afternoon, and awoke with the orange setting sun almost in my eyes a happy man. And that day I learned a profound truth. The rich do sleep very well." And then Frère Jacques's expression changed. Master Siger watched the faintest of condescending smiles tug at the edges of Frère Jacques's face. Suddenly Siger regretted telling the story.

"But here's the main thing," Master Siger continued. "What bothered me then was not guilt before an Omnipotent Deity, but by what chain of actions and decisions that fateful moment came into being. Was this simply an aberration in a clock-work world having to do only with me, or was this how all wealth was acquired, all success achieved, all victories won? What machinery forged that chain of events into a series of necessary and interlinked causes? Or was that chain merely apparent, some figment of my own mind? This was something even Augustine had dealt with by a sleight of hand. I could trace the series of actions that led to that bill falling on my table. But had all of Universal History been building over the eons of time just so that bill would fall on that table at the precise moment I was sitting there and in the most need?"

Frère Jacques had let his eyes drift over the courtyard while Master Siger told his story. Now his faint smile took on a degree of tolerance, something resembling brotherly sympathy.

"I had gone to the bar that Sunday," Siger said, almost dizzy with the desire to justify his desperation, "intending to bet some of the races. Simply put, I'd gone to test contingency. But race after race, I never found the nerve to put my money down, I never risked a bet. So later as I lay in that bed I recognized that simply my presence had become a sort of wager. I had gone there to see if some event would leave me with more money than when I arrived. Did it really matter whether it came from a fast horse or a drunken neighbor? In a way that I had never considered, contingency had provided, and its chain seemed clear to me. But was I the recipient of some beneficent act of Providence? Had the Lord stepped into History just so I wouldn't starve? Had He smiled down on my need? Around that time I began reading Averroes and Avicenna and, finally, Aristotle."

"Or maybe it was just dumb luck," Frère Jacques suddenly said. "So what?" A note of impatience entered his voice. "So maybe God does play dice. And maybe accidents are real."

Master Siger's eyes became large. With a grin he leaned close to Frère Jacques. "So then, you do understand. You see what the question is."

Frère Jacques waved him away vaguely distracted. "That's all very interesting. Fascinating, in fact. Contingency. Such a big word. Something you philosophers like to think about. Really, I wish you the best of luck figuring it all out. But I'll give you advice about what little I know about. And my advice is, if you want to keep your head attached to your shoulders you'll back off from the Arabs. There's no contingency there, nothing having to do with luck at all. Keep the Arabs out. The Pope'll listen to almost anything as long as you stay away from them. It's one thing for the Pope to invite a powerful Sheik over for dinner. What you're up to is a lot more dangerous. The situation is dynamite and you won't even wear gloves. Worry all you want about that other stuff, but just leave the Arab thinkers out and the Inquisition will fall asleep over the rest."

"And then I'll be allowed to go back to Paris?"

Frère Jacques looked suddenly wistful. "You really know how to hit low. Why do you keep talking about leaving? You're getting me interested in all this philosophy stuff, but deep inside you're still trying to bust out. In four weeks we'll be in Rome. Celestina and Marguerite are both crazy about you." Frère Jacques paused then, as if captured by a new thought. "Say, speaking of which, I could fix it up so they both come along with us to keep you company." His grin became a leer. "Just say the word."

Frère Jacques studied Master Siger's eyes as if waiting for something. Then he glanced down and spoke very quietly. "Here's something else to consider. You know that His Holiness has announced another Crusade to capture the Holy Land. He claims it'll be good for Christian morale. He's only been Pope a couple of months, so maybe he thinks this display of zealotry will give him some leverage with the Curia. But think about what a Crusade would mean. Christian men and women lying dead around Haifa or Beirut or Jerusalem, that's what. And what'll people think of you and your Arab thinkers then? Some people use real bullets, you know. Same in Majorca. Same in Baghdad. So do at least one of us a favor and stop talking about leaving."

The look of disappointment on Frère Jacques's face surprised Master Siger. Frère Jacques continued, "You think a guy like me hasn't got feelings. And the Pope, he's got feelings, too. Here we're ready to hide you and protect you and take you to Rome, take you to all the great bars and restaurants and the best parties, introduce you to interesting people. This isn't all that complicated. All you have to do is stick with us and you'll have a good time."

Master Siger of Brabant looked up to the window and saw movement. Two hands reached around either side of the torso and tipped it to one side. Master Siger realized that he had been studying a headless store-window mannequin. Through his disappointment he said, "Tell me something then. Is Brother Bonaventure behind all this?"

Frère Jacques smirked. He studied Master Siger with mild disbelief. "You think you've got a glimmer." Frère Jacques quietly laughed. "Guys like you always kill me. You've finally figured it all out. This little light has gone on in your head. You're sure there's some conspiracy, and the conspiracy has a leader. Guys like you always think like that."

Surprised now by his own anger Siger said, "Brother Bonaventure's advocacy for Augustine is expressed entirely in Aristotelian terms, yet he refuses to acknowledge that debt. All he really wants to do is push his friends up the ladder. He and his cronies got those Condemnations going in the first place. The Condemnations of 1270 weren't enough. He's turning up the heat again to push Eustachius of Arras, and worse, that reptile Matthew of Aquasparta, into the limelight. Tempier sees his chance to bet on a fast horse, and he doesn't want to be wrong."

Still smiling, Frère Jacques stood and began to pace slowly before Master Siger. With his shoulders hunched and face tipped forward, in profile he reminded Master Siger of a tall stout bird. "You still think this is all about you. You think this is some little game of badminton over your future. Which side has how many points, over the line, fair or foul, safe or out. With all due respect for a Master from the Sorbonne, either start thinking bigger or get a bigger head. You expect there'll be some punishment for Brother Bonaventure or Bishop Tempier, like you and those guys are all just pals. Wake up, I tell you. They haven't been in your league for years. They're thinking about stuff and involved in stuff the likes of us don't even want to know about. You're just kidding yourself, believe me. Big as you think you are, you aren't big enough to break a fart over. You know how much money a good conspiracy costs these days? If, for even one minute, one of those guys had a serious worry about you, they'd already be dragging the Seine for your carcass. These are not the people you think you see on TV."

Master Siger said, "So, if I'm so small-time, why am I here?"

Frère Jacques stopped. For a moment he looked at Master Siger. "You're here because they want you here, and because you want to be here. If you didn't want to be here you'd tell them that it was all just a mistake and apologize for the bother. They already know what they'll do with you, and when it's time, they'll do it. But His Holiness has a plan for you, too. He told me so himself. I don't know what it is, but he thinks you're important. And he's certain you're going to be useful to him."

"I'd be a lot more useful to His Holiness back in Paris."

"There you go again, talking about going back to Paris. Don't you listen even a little? That town is poison for you. There are so many knives sharpened for you, you couldn't even get out of the train station with your balls still in your pants. This is a real nice day, and we're having a real nice time here, you and me. It rains in Paris, didn't you ever notice? That's one of the problems with that town. And the women aren't all that good looking, if you want my honest opinion. Not like in Rome. We got it good here, but Rome'll look even better. You stick with Frère Jacques, is all I'm telling you."

"Stick with you and I'll never get back to Paris."

"You and me are headed for Rome on the biggest gravy-train in history. And Rome makes Paris look like a hamlet. The Pope's got plans for you. Just do him and me both a favor and get Paris out of your head."

Master Siger shrugged and then stood. He felt his hang-over coming back. "I need a drink."

Frère Jacques smiled, threw an arm across Master Siger's shoulders. "That sounds like a real philosopher talking. How about I buy us both a drink?"

Master Siger did not feel more secure, but he was sure at least he'd feel better soon.

Let the Fiery Sunset and Ghostly Hues of Twilight Cast Uncertain Shadows Upon Our Wary Friends as their Figures Side by Side Recede into the Dark Shelter of the Papal Palace in Avignon, and into a Dreaming History.

CHAPTER THE SEVENTH

WITH CLEAR THROAT and Dry Sinus, Let the Voice of History Echo Down Every Hall and From Every Window of the Palace of the Popes in Avignon That Suddenly, and Without Ceremony, Master Siger of Brabant Discovered His Shoulder Being Shaken.

Master Siger opened his eyes to the bright, hot morning sun of the Feast of the Holy Innocents. Then, through that joyous light a shadow moved. His room, he realized, had been invaded. Two large men, heads covered and faces obscured by the hoods of their black cloaks, lurked.

"Hey, shit-head." The tall one poked Master Siger's shoulder hard again with a thick index finger. "Pope wants you at the first tee in twenty minutes. Hey," he leaned closer. "You deaf or what?"

Master Siger sat up slowly and rubbed his eyes.

The taller one stepped back. "We're being nice, right? So get the message, right?"

The other loomed toward Master Siger from the foot of the bed. "Wake up, you creep, or wish you were dead. Twenty minutes. You been told." Then they were gone. Master Siger discovered himself remarkably awake.

The Papal golf-cart perched, sparkling and unembarrassed by the rising sun, at the summit of a long green hill. So glorious and glittering, the cart to Master Siger resembled an enormous ciborium. From the driver's seat His Holiness waved as he watched Master Siger approach. An appropriate goal for such an arduous trek, Siger decided. Eventually he reached the cart.

His Holiness turned with a smile and gestured Master Siger to the seat in the cart beside him.

"So good of you to make the time, Master Siger. Perfect weather for a round of golf, don't you think?" Grinning, he gestured toward the sky. "It's as if the Lord Himself has blessed this special occasion." Master Siger recognized the golf club heads, propped up in the back of the cart in their blood-red leather bag and gleaming in the sun, as those given to him by the Pope the evening before. Siger had hardly taken the seat beside His Holiness when the cart lurched forward suddenly, and he fell back hard.

To Siger's terror, His Holiness drove the golf cart with the self-abandoned excitement of a teenager. Careening to shouts of Pontifical pleasure, they traveled in great, broad arcs around trees, around water-holes, and up and down hills. Over the whine of the motor, the Pope cried out, "You do believe in God, Master Siger, don't you?" Siger could only nod. The Pope threw his head back and laughed. An eternity of terror seemed to pass for Siger until finally at the first tee they came to a stop.

His Holiness stepped from the cart and led Master Siger to the tee. He spoke as he used his putter to point. "This first hole covers nine hundred and twelve yards, and fifty-three is par. Half way along you'll just make out a dog-leg to the right. The fairway passes a lime green '57 Chevy mounted on cinder-blocks. A hundred yards further, there's a sand trap bigger than a football field and shaped like New Jersey. I hope you're getting this picture, because the green is at the edge of a thirty-foot high bank that runs eighty feet in both directions. And the pin is set at the center." His Holiness beamed. "Bet you've never played a course anything like this!" It seemed to Siger that His Holiness took great pleasure in the recitation of statistics.

Pope Nicholas III finished setting his ball and then hesitated. "It must occur to you, Master Siger, that I've invited you out here for a reason. So let me confess something to you. As Shepherd to His Precious Flock, I am deeply concerned. This concern, I believe, is well-placed and urgent, for I have seen evidence for what I fear. With all of the time you've spent in Paris among our enlightened brothers, can you guess what this fear might be?" Master Siger shrugged.

His Holiness sighed. "I have watched the finest minds of your generation hopelessly re-reading an evening's TV schedule searching for something worthy of their attention. I have prayed over thumbs cramped and contorted from abuse operating a remote control. Daily I counsel brilliant intellects whose finely-tuned minds have found themselves utterly adrift, lost in a sea of bright colors and loud sounds, a cacophony, in fact, that signifies nothing more than its content. It is for this reason I've come to suspect some darker magic has leaked into these minds resulting in treacherous and deceptive whirlpools. These vortices of confusion have overwhelmed their efforts to contemplate the supremely divine. These whirlpools churn and spin relentlessly, creating a powerful agitation that defeats all coherence. In their violent motion, these dismal vortices absorb all light, all heat, every spark and fragment of energy. So that, tormented by the ebb and flow of that unruly ocean of bodily sensations, these minds have become disoriented, poised on the verge of drowning. This, to me, is an urgent yet insoluble riddle, a riddle that exists, yet refuses to embrace a solution."

Gripping his putter, the ungainly Pontiff swung with a mighty papal swing, sending his ball high into the bright blue sky. He tipped his head to one side as he followed the ball's soaring white arc forty-five yards dead center on the fairway before rolling to a stop.

Master Siger called out, "Brilliantly played!" In deference to his host, Siger set his ball and then brought out his putter. He took his position over the ball.

Pope Nicholas scrutinized Siger's grip as he continued, "For those spirits so miserably burdened, their search for enlightenment is relentless, as its thirst is unquenchable. Although such mighty spirits are the very foundation stones of this towering castle of Our Faith, the fact that the Church is unprepared to accommodate these same burdened spirits should not surprise us. No more than we should be surprised that a foundation stone is of no value mounted to the roof." Master Siger took a practice swing as the Pope said, "I acknowledge that there are others who are somewhat relieved by their baffled state. For them, it is better that these powerful intellects drift rudderless into that torrent of contentless images, rather than encourage those intellects to bother over issues of substance. How do you see this, Master Siger?"

At the question Siger held his swing. "Your Holiness must excuse my plea of ignorance. For the purposes of my work, the days are always too short and always end too soon." And then he swung.

"Well put," His Holiness said. They watched Siger's white ball arc through the clear morning air. "It is refreshing to see that those who are deeply engaged in the search for enlightenment abjure any superficial satisfactions." Master Siger's ball flew thirty-four yards to the right, bounced weakly twice and then died in high rough. His Holiness nodded with approval. "You make a worthy opponent, Master Siger. Happily, our exertions will be rewarded with refreshment."

Master Siger followed His Holiness down the center of the fairway. For a large man encumbered within a body-tent of gorgeous yet heavy ecclesiastical robes, he moved quickly and with surprising ease. Master Siger made a note as he hurried to keep up.

When they reached the Chevy propped on cinder blocks that His Holiness had described, the Pope nodded toward the passenger door while he opened the door to the driver's side. Pope Nicholas closed his door and then turned on the radio. An orchestra was working over "Joy to the World" with more urgency than pleasure. Master Siger guessed these musicians were being paid by the note.

The Pope opened the glove compartment and brought out something made of gold with a bowl of figured crystal so bright it sparkled even inside the car. A bong, gorgeously wrought with brightly-colored enamel images of naked angels that looked like women. Siger was thoroughly impressed. When His Holiness filled it and got it smoking, he took a Papal hit and then passed it to Master Siger.

"What I don't understand," the Pope said as he held the smoke tightly in his chest, "is this obvious and unashamed delight in all these confusions worked upon the rest of us. In my humble opinion, the mission of Holy Mother Church can be summarized in a single phrase; eternal dedication to the propagation of order. Don't you agree?"

Master Siger nodded as he smoked. His Holiness responded with a plume of blue smoke of his own. "In the end," the Pope continued, "Satan is Chaos personified. As it was before the Creation, so it shall be afterward. The Lord created this World out of the flesh of Chaos. The Devil is Disorder, and Chaos is that Hell inevitable from our Fallen State. The battle of the truly righteous is against the multifarious, the plentitude, the plethora. What all religious belief seeks is homogeneity. Every religion is a political structure in disguise, and all politics strives for an emergent order. You and I and all of our Brothers-in-Christ are mere field-hands in the cultivation and maintenance of Our Lord's orderly fields. Our orchards are planted in rows. Order is the fruit and we are His pickers." His Holiness paused. "So it should come as no surprise that to some, you and your associates appear determined to spread the foul and pernicious weeds of Disorder."

Master Siger spoke slowly through a plume of silver blue smoke as he passed the pipe back to the Pope. "Though it is not my place to remind your Holiness, the objective of philosophy is precisely the same as that of the Church. Aristotle organized his thoughts into books determined to impose order on all knowledge. And your Holiness must admit that his works on logic and reasoning have been of great value to the Church."

His Holiness smirked. "Of course, you have no wish to instruct the Church on what She must acknowledge." Grey ribbons of smoke trailed from Pope Nicholas's nostrils as he passed the pipe back to Master Siger.

With the tip of his finger Master Siger poked at the grey ash in the bowl. "It seems to be my trial to learn only through error."

His Holiness reached forward and flipped on the air-conditioner. "All of us, my son, are mired in a depth of error so profound our only hope is the Church's teaching. The Holy Spirit guides our contemplation of the Revealed Word, and Revelation is the Lord's way of keeping us in the center of the green." His Holiness brought out his score card and a tiny yellow pencil. He gestured toward Master Siger, who surrendered his own score card.

Pope Nicholas III pointed with the stump of pencil out the window. "This golf course extends eight miles. There is something grand about an eight-mile long golf course." His smile seemed to Master Siger both regal and humble. "But this palace and this golf course, and the grounds all around us are not my personal property. All of it belongs to Our Holy Mother Church. But once, all of it was part of an estate called Venaissin. A very interesting story, if you are curious. And perhaps even instructive."

"I am at the disposal of your Holiness, and will follow wherever he leads."

Putting the cards on the dashboard, His Holiness drew thoughtfully on the bong, passed it to Master Siger and settled back into his seat. "All of this, everything you see, once belonged to the family of Raymond, Count of Toulouse. Your generation never reads history so I'll remind you that a Holy Crusade went on around here. Avignon itself was besieged and occupied by King Louis VIII in 1226. A remarkably bloody mess, as you might imagine. But you wouldn't think of any of this to look at it now. And all of it a horrible and bloody battle simply over some words."

Past the Pope's shoulder, Siger watched as, at the edge of the fairway, a man chased a woman. Master Siger said, "Charmingly naive though the ravings of those whimsical lunatics were, your Holiness can't possibly compare their confusion to the depth and precision of Aristotle." The woman Siger watched did not appear to be trying very hard to get away.

"So you have read a book or two." Pope Nicholas smiled with quizzical surprise. "But misguided souls they certainly were. They called themselves the Cathari, although people your age remember them as the Albigensians because so many were slaughtered before the Cathedral at Albi."

As if suddenly delighted to see them there, His Holiness sighed as he glanced up at the score cards lying on the dashboard. "But let us continue this game as we talk." He turned to Master Siger. A wet, almost glistening sparkle appeared in his eyes. "That's what I love about golf. One can play and talk at the same time."

The tiny yellow pencil looked even smaller in the Pope's thick hand. He spoke as he wrote. "Now as I said, this first hole is a par fifty-three. I am certain I will shoot thirteen, leaving me forty under. Unfortunately your rust is showing. You will shoot an embarrassing seventy-seven, leaving you twenty-four over. But never mind," His Holiness said and then patted Master Siger gently on the knee, "twice the number of the Apostles attending Our Lord's Last Supper is undoubtedly a fortunate number and a powerful omen that your game will improve." Pope Nicholas paused as Master Siger passed him the smoking pipe. "But it does seem a justifiable outcome, given our divergent skills and abilities." The Pope drew energetically on the pipe. "But fear not Master Siger, you impress me with every stroke."

Master Siger shrugged. He was already higher than he wanted to be, but he hoped that as long as the Pope was as high as he was, he was safe. Pope Nicholas turned shifting noisily in his pile of ecclesiastical robes until he faced Master Siger. He glanced at the cards and pencil in his hand, and then tossed them forward onto the dashboard.

"Listen closely, Master Siger, and understand the story I'm about to tell you because I believe it says something valuable to us both. And I know you will, because you're a very smart boy." The Pope settled back into his seat and folded his hands in his lap. "Now, Innocent III was the Pope at the time. One day a legate he had sent to investigate these Albigensian heretics was murdered, and his murder took place close enough to Toulouse that it was almost in Count Raymond's living room. Innocent had been mildly furious that the Count permitted these heretics to believe whatever they wanted, but this murder of his emissary was the proverbial last straw. And none of us could have blamed him. So he excommunicated Raymond. As I am sure you understand, by that simple act Innocent literally had offered Raymond's vast and productive lands to any Christian who agreed to act on behalf of the Pope and smite the rebellious Raymond down. Drastic stuff, I admit, but His Holiness was on the spot. If he ignored his own agent's murder, his very powerful enemies would exploit this sign of vulnerability, while even his friends would lose respect for him and his holy mission." Pope Nicholas glanced quizzically into the bowl of the pipe and then re-lighted it.

"Now, Philip Augustus was the king of France at the time but he was already busy, once again attempting to conquer England. Unable to help the Pope himself, he gave blanket permission to any of his vassals with an ambition to do the Lord's work and go after Raymond. Armed with this permission of the King of France, Count Simon de Montfort finally took up the Pope's offer. Simon turned out to be a man who knew what he was doing when it came to war. In his first major battle at Beziers, he overwhelmed Raymond's army, and then his troops butchered, raped and plundered the people of the town and the lands twenty miles around. Beziers is a very lovely town perched in the hills somewhere between Montpellier and Carcassonne. We should take a ride out some time. I find it always instructive to look at places where humans have suffered indescribable misery. Reminds us of our ability to be appalled, if you see my point."

The Pope's words seemed to pop into Master Siger's head as if the thoughts were forming an instant before his lips moved. Looking up, Siger realized how dirty the car's windows were and how hard it was to see clearly out. The world beyond those windows appeared a smeared and obscure blur. His mind awash with visions of bloody death, Master Siger imagined himself safe and motionless at the bottom of a fish bowl.

"Count Raymond," the Pope continued, "had been driven from the battlefield by Simon in a bloody rout, so immediately he made his submission to the Pope. And as was the Pope's Christian duty and obligation, Innocent begrudgingly accepted this submission." The Pope crossed himself and then smiled. He reached for the score-cards and pencil sitting on the dashboard. "Now, this next hole is a bit tricky. There's a very thick rough on an incline to the right, and to the left a water hazard runs almost the length of the fairway. You know," he added smiling, "sometimes, along with a few friends, we put boats in it and have marvelous outings. I should take you out some time. Anyway, this hole is twelve hundred thirty-eight yards par eighty-six.

Tell me, what will you drive with?"

Master Siger could no longer tell whether the fog outside was less confusing than that within. He shook himself awake. "What's the biggest club I can use?"

The Pope snorted. "That's what's wrong with your generation of intellectuals: no finesse. Don't make me cross or I'll forget my story. Anyway, as you might expect, Raymond's agreement with Pope Innocent did not work out for the old Count quite as he had expected. His patrimonial lands had been spared, but de Montfort and his thugs continued to attack the lands of Raymond's fief and those of his vassals. And then later, Albi was plundered and burned, with the massacre of its population. Raymond protested this furiously to his Holiness, insisting that he had made his submission and that his Holiness was now obligated to call back de Montfort and his army. Unfortunately, in the vehemence of his insistence, Raymond's Languedoc arrogance so angered Innocent that he was excommunicated again." Pope Nicholas smiled. "There is no misery that cannot be added to." Then he began to write.

"Now, having watched you this morning," Pope Nicholas said, "I expect you will be unable to avoid all of that water. And your lack of skill with the chip-shot will cost you dearly. You'll shoot ninety-three, putting you seven over, while I birdie for an eighty-four under."

"My feeble efforts embarrass us both," Master Siger said, so high he could no longer remember which hole they had reached. "For this I earnestly apologize. But it has been years since I've been out on such a challenging course. Whereas, your Holiness seems to have achieved genuine mastery." Master Siger took the pipe from the Pope's hand and began to re-fill it. "My admiration is authentic."

"I happily offer the services of my golf pro, Sister Angelique of Tours," Pope Nicholas said. "Undoubtedly she will improve your stroke. And she is extremely good with a putter." When Master Siger finished refilling it, His Holiness took the pipe from his hands.

"But back to my instructive tale, and please pay close attention. Although Raymond had once again been excommunicated he was not entirely without allies. Into this political maelstrom stepped poor Peter II, the King of Aragon. No doubt with an eye toward a profitable marriage of one of his daughters to one of Raymond's sons, Peter foolishly volunteered to defend Raymond's lands and take up arms against Simon de Montfort. It surprised almost no one that his miserable little army was thoroughly over-matched by Simon at the battle of Muret, his army was decimated and Peter himself was killed. Count Raymond realized in an instant that his last best hope was gone. Once again he surrendered himself to the Pope. But Pope Innocent had grown tired of his wayward prince. The price of peace this time for Raymond was considerably higher; the Pope demanded he receive all of Raymond's lands. You see, forgiveness may be free, but it is never cheap." With a smile as smug as an accountants' at tax time, Pope Nicholas returned his attention to the cards in his hands. Master Siger took the pipe and lighted it.

"Now, on this next hole," the Pope said, "there's an acre of heavy woods about half way along a six hundred and thirty-seven yard dog-leg left. The green is bordered by a pond and there's a sand trap just to the left of the pin. You have my apologies, but this is a very tough hole for any golfer with a slice like yours."

Disguised within another cloud of billowing white smoke, Master Siger shrugged. Teeth clenched around the pipe's mouthpiece he said, "I am honored that your Holiness even tolerates my presence."

Pope Nicholas sighed with sympathy. "My son, you are no doubt severely discouraged by your progress. It is a deep disappointment to hone one's skill over many years, only to discover the goal of perfect mastery further away than ever. Instead, let me continue to divert you with this delicious imbroglio."

Master Siger no longer had any idea what His Holiness was talking about, and he was just high enough not to care. He endured a gust of relief from a direction he could not discover.

"Reluctant but without alternative," Pope Nicholas said, "Raymond agreed to the Pope's terms. Meanwhile, Simon finally responded to the Pope's decree and withdrew his army from the field. As a result, peace between Pope Innocent and Count Raymond reigned for several years. Yet, as so often happens in these situations, a few confused and hysterical half-thinkers renewed the Albigensian heresy which grew quickly into a confused and hysterical mob. And just as predictably, the local bishops again insisted to the Pope that Raymond was doing nothing to stamp out their heresy." His Holiness took the pipe from Master Siger's fingers, fingers that felt numb as bananas, a feeling Siger found almost pleasant after all.

Through his side window, Pope Nicholas watched a flock of birds rise and fly toward the rising sun in a wide graceful arc. He smoked. To Master Siger he seemed suddenly lost and alone. Then Pope Nicholas appeared to remember the pipe in his fist and passed it back to Master Siger. From under his seat, His

Holiness produced a small cooler. He opened it to reveal several golden bottles of chilled Mexican beer. He handed one to Master Siger. They each twisted a top and drank.

The clouds of his mind parted briefly for Master Siger and he said, "In truth and justice, the case against Raymond was circumstantial. His worst offence was the guilt of unwise association. He would not cooperate in the humiliation and abuse of his people by anyone, even forces loyal to the Pope. His crime was that he was unable to field an army strong enough to hold off attacks against his people, while he lacked the political strength to insist Pope Innocent call Simon de Montfort back. Raymond realized Pope Innocent was prepared to sanction the torture, rape and murder of thousands of honorable Christians merely in order to assert his own authority."

His Holiness grinned. He passed the smoking pipe to Master Siger. "Finally you're catching on, and for this I am relieved. But my tale gets even better, so pay close attention. The violence Simon and his thugs brought down on Languedoc paralyzed its populace with terror. Ultimately, this proved to be a very serious mistake. Pope Innocent had finally become nervous about the creature he had created. Simon's astonishing lack of scruples eventually forced even the Pope to reconsider. In an attempt to curb his creation's blood-lust, His Holiness turned once more to King Philip Augustus and renewed his invitation to lend aid. In response, King Philip sent his young son, Prince Louis, to Langudoc. The King felt no enthusiasm for combating heresy, but he was greedy for the Count's lands, and with Papal approval in his pocket he turned out to be even more unscrupulous than Simon de Montfort."

Siger shook his head and muttered, "I have the feeling this story does not end well."

His Holiness shrugged. "Every story ends happily for somebody."

As if recognizing Master Siger's discomfort, Pope Nicholas waved his hand to indicate the little world around them. "You need proof? Here we are, together on a lovely day. Birds are singing and crops are growing and the cold streams that pour from the mountains fill with fish. You and I sit having this delightful conversation as we enjoy the healthful benefit of a wonderful sport, all the result of the events I am attempting to describe. Now, through the participation of Prince Louis, King Philip's support of the Pope was demonstrated decisively in battle at Narbonne. As a result of that battle, Count Raymond finally was forced to abdicate in favor of his son. All that Raymond had left for his boy were a few small parcels of land in Provence that included some castles and some serfs. This inheritance, however, included our lovely Venaissin. You see, Count Raymond's loss was our gain. In this way, you and I are the ultimate beneficiaries of blood that was shed fifty years ago."

Master Siger shuddered. Suddenly he could see piles of mangled bodies, could smell the scent of burning and rotting flesh. He said, "But your story is not over. By your own philosophy, all that has happened so far is simply prologue, and the ultimate beneficiary has yet to be revealed."

Pope Nicholas studied Master Siger's face. The moment seemed suspended, yet Siger was no longer interested, the conversation had passed beyond the absurd. His hangover had reasserted itself, and now all he wanted was his bed and sleep.

But Pope Nicholas's smile seemed filled with admiration. "So, my philosopher has finally awakened. I told you I had invited you here with a purpose. Finally, words worthy of a mind. Now I see why it is that Paris is so warm for you. So I am certain you will be delighted by the conclusion of this tale. But before we continue, our other game must progress."

With the cards once again in one hand and the stump of yellow pencil in the other, Pope Nicholas began to write. "On the following hole, another water hazard of remarkable elegance and proportion will prove too alluring for your ball to resist. Unfortunately, the ball you have chosen is like Aristotle's fish, drawn to water because its flesh contains so much of that matter. Your chip-shot over a sand-trap that you will admire for its gracefully undulant outline will also fail. But I confess you have made great progress. This is a fifty-seven stroke hole, for which you have shot sixty-three. Be of good cheer, Master Siger, your score improves. Meanwhile, though a nine puts me forty-eight under, I confess I did not play that hole as well as I would wish."

"On the contrary," Master Siger said. "Your Holiness plays with remarkable style and imagination. Perhaps you have at one time considered turning pro."

"Sarcasm ill-fits your situation, scholar. Be careful or you'll make me forget where I was." Pope Nicholas tossed the empty beer-bottle into the back seat, reached down and opened another. "Our tale, meanwhile, moves ahead five years. The blood-thirsty but extremely useful Simon de Montfort has died. Taking his place is his son, Amaury de Montfort. Meanwhile, so egregious had been the behavior of de Montfort the Elder that an agreement was signed at the Fourth Lateran Council, taking the lands that had been bequeathed to Amaury, and returning them to Raymond's family, now represented by a son as well. But things just keep getting more interesting. Bereft of any hope of regaining Simon's conquests, young Amaury turned all his hereditary claims on Languedoc over to King Philip Augustus. You'll recall that King Philip had been thoroughly occupied with consolidating his conquests in the north, though he had sent his son Louis to battle in his stead. But through this gesture of submission, Amaury had given King Phillip a solid though unintended stake in this conflict. Rather neat, don't you think?"

"I suppose neat is one word that comes to mind. But there are others." His own words startled Master Siger even as he spoke them. But His Holiness simply chuckled.

"That's another thing wrong with you intellectuals; no sense of humor. Be that as it may, although you may not recognize what was about to happen, old Raymond saw all of it quite clearly. And he was determined not to let it happen. Having regained his palace at Toulouse, Raymond immediately made formal acknowledgment of King Philip's rights as ultimate ruler of his lands determined to forestall any charge that might justify an invasion. In Raymond's mind, his acknowledgment of fealty to King Phillip was simply a formality that would preserve his own power over his lands from any more predations by the Pope. Foolishly he did not anticipate his King. Because Raymond's act had legally given King Philip formal justification to assert what, in most other cases were purely ceremonial rights, and to confiscate Raymond's lands. And this King Philip did." He turned to face Master Siger and his face brightened with a smile. "You see? Contrary to the proverbial assertion, there are happy endings all over the place."

"But of course, this story still doesn't end there."

Pope Nicholas solemnly nodded. "Another five years pass, King Philip Augustus dies, and the now-King Louis VIII joins forces with the recently inaugurated Pope Honorius III, in another grand crusade against old Raymond, using one more Albigensian uprising as the excuse."

"Wait," Master Siger said, thoroughly confused. "Why go after Count Raymond when he has formally declared himself a vassal of the King?"

"Because, my friend, Raymond's declaration assumed that, in return, King Louis would follow his father by acknowledging Raymond as rightful ruler of his domain, merely standing locally as the King's surrogate. You must see the brilliance of it. A jumble of royal formalities had suddenly turned very literal. If Raymond expected to keep even a small portion of his lands, he now had no choice but to fight with whatever he could find. In a string of dazzling campaigns, King Louis made short work of Raymond's forces. Beziers, Narbonne, Carcassonne and finally Avignon. But then, just as Louis was about to conquer Toulouse itself, he fell ill and died."

"I begin to wonder," Master Siger said with a sigh.

"And well you should," Pope Nicholas responded. "Louis VIII's son, the heir to the Crown of France, was still in his minority. But Louis' wife, Blanche of Castile, managed a very diplomatic deal. She promised to withdraw the French army on two conditions. The first, that the Crown keep the territory it had so far conquered, and just as the Lord intends when a King conquers your land. But the second had Raymond's remaining lands pass, along with Raymond's daughter, into the hands of King Louis VIII's brother." His Holiness paused, smoked slowly and watched Master Siger.

"And that, my son," the Pope finally said, "is how it came to pass that an effort by the Papacy to deny territory to the French Crown, resulted in French kings living on the Papal doorstep." His Holiness paused, a look of melancholy passed over his face. "Paris has proved a very large and distressing neighbor." But then his expression brightened. "A tale of ambition gone wrong, do you think? One should certainly wonder."

Master Siger hesitated. "So, is that the lesson your curious story was intended to convey?"

Pope Nicholas suddenly looked over at Master Siger, but then he laughed uncomfortably. "Now that I think about it, that's something encouraging. Because now I realize I can't recall why I told you that story."

Master Siger waited, a thought growing in his head. And this new thought was so ghastly he trembled to say it. "Let me suggest that, though your Holiness recognizes the gambits of all of these players, their political intrigues and duplicities, yet you cannot remember the nature of the Albigensian heresy itself."

The Pope's smile became radiant. "And there you are! Now you've got it exactly, Master Siger! The whole story folded neatly into a single nut-shell." His expression became almost affectionate. "That is exactly the point of my elaborate little story." He went back to filling the bowl of the bong, a grin of supreme satisfaction wreathing his face. "Let me enlighten you about myself, Master Siger. I confess I have found in politics that it is more important to be feared by your enemies, than to be loved by your friends. What do you think of that? Pithy phrasing at least?"

"I'm confused," Master Siger confessed honestly.

"Look at it this way. Had Philip feared Raymond, or had Innocent been intimidated by him, neither would have made an attempt on his lands. And then, what would Raymond need of friends or allies? Now do you see?"

Master Siger shook his head. "I suppose I do. But to what end?"

His Holiness leaned back. "Well, I'll tell you. I was elevated to this office because I have studied the workings of power, all of its interlocking cogs and gears. And I have been taking notes. So I now believe the little guys of the world deserve a book written for them that lays out the rules of power. Something that finally explains to them how the big guys play the game, and what they expect for a result. And you, Master Siger, might be the very man to finish that project for me. I'm told you fellows from Paris are particularly good at this sort of thing. And as further inducement, don't forget that the thoughts and opinions of well-known personalities such as myself always do well at the book-stalls."

Pope Nicholas's suggestion came to Siger slowly, a cloud passing, thinning, to reveal a mountain. He was no longer certain of what he had been hearing. "With all respect, I must beg your Holiness's pardon. While I'm certainly flattered to be thought of in such a light, at this moment I have several projects at hand. Besides, such an exposure of the clock-works of power might prove unwise. Someone less conversant with those machinations might misguidedly conclude that Papal action always defeats Papal intention."

"And perhaps that is precisely the point. Perhaps, regardless of intention, the real purpose of this Crusade I've just described was its result; the French crown's conquest of Languedoc. Or perhaps the point is that there are times when the ideas of some men justify their torture and murder. Because the ultimate goal of torture and murder is the propagation of terror. And in politics, terror is always a precious weapon. A religious pretext for invasion and conquest is always sufficient since politics is simply religious control by other means."

"I'm certain I'm wrong," Master Siger said, "but your enthusiasm for politics seems to exceed your enthusiasm for heresy. Can you really not remember the nature of the Albigensian heresy?"

Pope Nicholas shrugged, a gesture subtly shaped by his shimmering robes. "And to what purpose? All heresies are equally actionable, regardless of their individual distinctions." He stretched then and yawned. "But look around us. The Lord has given us this beautiful day, let's not waste any more of it. We will finish our golf game and then enjoy a hearty lunch, or so I've been promised.

How's all that sound?"

Master Siger smiled, pretending his consciousness had not already gone disastrously astray. The glance from His Holiness told Master Siger he had not succeeded.

"But enough of our history lesson," Pope Nicholas continued. "We have a game of golf to finish. Now, the following hole takes us around that mountain you see about four miles from here. A par fifty-seven, I will shoot a twenty, which will leave me thirty-seven under par. You will shoot ninety-eight which will leave you forty-one over."

Master Siger re-filled the pipe. "I could not be more prescient, nor more embarrassed."

Pope Nicholas stared hard at Siger. "I dare say, embarrassment aside, prescience must fascinate you. We are aware that you have written extensively on causality and time." Master Siger looked up startled as much by the Pope's tone as the substance of his remark. "You should be flattered your articles always appear in the best journals." As if responding to Siger's surprise, Pope Nicholas added, "There, you see? We do try to keep up."

Perhaps it was the beer and dope talking, but finally Master Siger could no longer resist his own inclination to impertinence. "Since your Holiness admits an interest in current thinking, you must also be familiar with the Condemnations published just four months ago. With your cultured intellect, you must have observed that Bishop Tempier has mingled astrology with astronomy, physics with mysticism, and epistemology with taxonomy. Though I may be wrong, the Condemnations seem an intellectual disaster and their promulgation a fantastic injustice. Our saintly Brother Albertus has had to endure reprimand because of them, and even our late Brother Thomas has been condemned by them."

Pope Nicholas sighed with a weariness that surprised Siger. "Keep just one thing in mind. The issue is not the invincibility of the man over that of the office." The Pope leaned back and propped his knee against the steering wheel. "Back in Paris you probably don't think much of us, but out here in the wilderness we still manage to follow Parisian affairs closely. For example, I was very impressed by your article in *Playboy*. Of course I didn't understand half of it. All that stuff about contingency and all that just leaves me confused and annoyed. But even I, Pope of all Christendom, have a tough time getting published in *Playboy*." Pope Nicholas leaned forward and lowered his voice. "How would you like to meet the Playmate for that month? Miss March? I could set it up, we're very close. In confidence she's told me that yours was the only article she read in that issue. What do you think?"

When Master Siger said nothing, Pope Nicholas said, "I've watched you on the tv news shows. Always so cool and contained, arguments always charming yet cogent; nobody gets to you. Even the big name heretics from the University."

Pope Nicholas tossed his empty bottle to the back-seat, it crashed into the back windshield. Without turning to look, His Holiness brought out another. Master Siger discovered that he was thirsty and did the same. "Paris must be crawling with heretics this time of year," the Pope said. "Anyway, that's what my predecessor John XXI believed."

"And apparently so does Bishop Tempier." Despite the temptation, Siger could not resist the opportunity for sarcasm.

Pope Nicholas suddenly stared at Master Siger. "Nor is he the only one." But then he smiled, slapped Master Siger's knee hard and laughed. "Here you are sitting beside the Bishop of Rome prepared to argue for a God who is incapable of comforting the unfortunate, the sinful, or the poor. What do you expect us to do? People like you look down upon us simply for wanting to do our jobs. But these are our jobs, after all. What else would you expect us to do?"

"Humbly I remind your Holiness that Bishop Tempier formulated and issued the Condemnations at the suggestion of, but without formal approval from, the Holy See. That is, your predecessor. Since they did not originate from you, you have the power to suspend them for further study. Your Holiness has held this exalted position hardly more than a few months. Study and reflection in this matter is entirely understandable."

Pope Nicholas held the pipe toward Master Siger. When Master Siger took it, His Holiness said, "All right, speak your mind so that we can be finished with it and then finish our game."

Master Siger held the chill glass beer bottle against his forehead. Despite the air-conditioner he wanted to open a window, but he didn't. Encased in thick and hazy air by the murky windows, in the half-light of the front seat Master Siger feared he had become caught in a dream from which he would never wake. He said, "Bishop Tempier is an old friend of Cardinal Pontioni. Through the Cardinal's circle he has become friends with the Fantestri brothers and Elmira of Burgundy, all acknowledged supporters of the Ghibelline crowd. Of course, rumors are always to be ignored, but there was an openly expressed conviction that the Fantestri family had conspired with other Ghibelline supporters for another candidate for your job."

His Holiness slapped his own knee as he laughed in mild surprise. "And you believe this is news? Can you honestly believe I am unaware of all of this?" The Pope's surprise seemed genuine, and Siger decided to believe it. "Please, for both of us, understand just one thing. According to my belief in a Powerful and Immanent God, I occupy this position by His Divine Will and His Will alone. Any other so-called candidate was one only in his own mind, and perhaps the minds of a few delusional friends. Otherwise, you must realize you are suggesting that somehow, the will of a single human being could even slightly deflect the work of His Glorious Will. In effect, you suggest that a conspiracy among mortals could confound Divine Intention. This Sacred Office is a direct expression of the Lord's Will, and invulnerable to the actions as well as intentions of mere men."

Siger held his breath a moment and then muttered calmly, "Your Holiness claims the Lord chose you to occupy the Chair of St. Peter even at the moment He created the world. A subtle form of pre-destination and certainly harmonizes with my article. Perhaps your Holiness should tread lightly here."

The Pope glowered solemnly. "Humbly, I believe that in all ways I am simply a part of Christ's plan for this world and for the next. But take my advice, Master Siger, and recognize this. Individually, the Condemnations may not deserve the careful examination or lucid and convincing rebuttal of a mind as sophisticated as yours. But their creators, too, are a part of Our Lord's plan. And the Lord does have a plan. None of us should have any doubt about that. Perhaps the Lord inspired those Condemnations simply to test the faith of a certain arrogant master of arts who once lived in Paris. Perhaps this is the way the Lord displays His hand at work in the world. We cannot know the Lord's wishes except as those wishes become manifest in the long unfolding of time and history." Gradually a smile appeared on the Pope's face. The smile filled Master Siger with a sense of peace, a contentment despite the inscrutability of his future. For a moment Siger was almost grateful, and the sensation left him bemused.

"Now, what do you say, Master Siger? Let's finish this golf game."

Through a series of proofs based on the Pope's unerring estimates of Master Siger's skill at golf along with his luck, the remaining holes in the game of golf between his Holiness Pope Nicholas III and Master Siger of Brabant were played out in the front seat of a motionless car, from hole to hole, while the air-conditioner blasted and Bing Crosby sang "White Christmas. The car slowly became so filled with thick smoke that, by the time his Holiness reached the eighteenth hole, neither could see out through the windows.

But finally Pope Nicholas returned his score card to Master Siger. "Just sign this right there. It's one of those formalities that officious persons in the local golf league dearly love." When Master Siger had signed and handed it back, the Pope scrutinized each card. "So the final calculation indicates that I shot one hundred and thirty-three under par, while you shot three hundred and eighty-one over. Admittedly lop-sided, but I must congratulate you. Your game improved remarkably on the back nine."

"Your Holiness is too generous with his praise. And even more generous with his patient instruction. Without both, my score would have been infinitely worse."

"Holy Mother Church is nothing if not infinitely patient and infinitely generous. Now, what do you say we go see if our noon meal is ready."

When Master Siger stepped from the car he was amazed to discover how stoned he was. The ground seemed invitingly soft beneath his feet, as if he might sink into it and disappear from sight if he stopped moving. And the light unaccountably seemed to move five seconds ahead of his eyes. Pope Nicholas III stood stretching and then sighed. He said, "I love being out of doors. The beauty of Nature is a mirror of our Lord's love for His creation. The fragrance of the air and the warmth of the sunshine simply remind us of how well-loved we are by our Creator." He paused and looked about, and then he shivered. "Let's get going back to the palace before I begin to sweat."

Master Siger nearly had to run to keep up with the long Pontifical strides as they returned together to the golf cart. Struggling breathlessly he said, "I have meant to ask only one more question. Do you know what has happened to my colleague, Boetius of Dacia? He fled Paris when I did but by another route. I had expected to meet him here. Yet I've heard an unfortunate rumor going about that he has died."

The Pope stopped in his tracks so suddenly that Master Siger had to skip around him to avoid a collision. Master Siger said, "I hoped that with your contacts you could investigate."

The Pope turned to stare directly into Master Siger's eyes. "Really? Boetius dead? And he has not been heard from since you left Paris? Have you discussed this with anyone else?"

Master Siger gasped for breath. "Remember that in your chamber, Frère

Jacques said that Boetius had been delayed en route but that he would join us soon. That was three days ago. Meanwhile, at the Christmas Eve gala I was reliably informed by a mutual friend that he had drowned in the English Channel."

"Indeed." The Pope was obviously perplexed. "Perhaps your informant is not nearly as reliable as you believe. After all, it could have been another Boetius of Dacia who had this accident."

"I was informed Boetius met his end in an attempt to flee to England. Your Holiness is well aware that the Archbishop of Canterbury, Robert Kilwardby, is much in agreement with Bishop Tempier concerning the teachings of Aristotle. Though a potential antagonist, perhaps he might shed some light on what happened. You know so much about what transpires in your blessed kingdom, I had hoped you might make discreet inquiries."

His Holiness glanced into Master Siger's eyes with an empathy that surprised Siger. The Pope put an arm across Master Siger's shoulders. "You know, it is really too bad Frederick the Second is no longer with us as Emperor of the Kingdom of Sicily. A person of your abilities and inclinations undoubtedly would have added grace and brilliance to his court at Palermo." After a moment he asked, "Inquiries about whom?"

"Why, Boetius of Dacia. I was just telling you about him."

"Oh," the Pope said seeming suddenly confused "is that who we were discussing?" Pope Nicholas resumed walking with long, aggressive strides. "Bit confusing, all these Boetiuses of this hovel and that village. Tend to mix them up. Boetius of Dacia, you say? Sorry, never heard of him." They reached the golf cart, His Holiness returned to the driver's seat and started the engine. Over the motor's roar he added, "I'm afraid I've never heard of Dacia either. Nice place? Don't suppose it's anywhere near Brussels, is it? Wonderful chocolate in Brussels. Superb sprouts as well." When Master Siger took his seat, His Holiness put the cart in gear and stepped hard on the gas. Smiling broadly at Master Siger he slapped himself on the stomach. "But I have the Devil's own appetite. All of this exercise and fresh air has put a powerful thirst upon me as well. Let's get to the refectory before I begin eating these shrubs."

Let Us Cast a Last Long and Sympathetic Glance at Our Terrified Philosopher as He Disappears Over Another Rolling Hill of Provence, Careening In Horror In a Golf Cart Beside the Most Powerful Man in All Christendom. The Curtain of History Billows Once Before it Falls.

CHAPTER THE EIGHTH

LET HISTORY RECOUNT With Heavy Breathing Through Red, Half-Parted Lips That at Lunch the Day of the Great Papal Golf Victory, Master Siger and Pope Nicholas III Were Joined by Mistress Marguerite, Princess Alicia of Auvergne, Abbess Juliette of Padua, Marchioness Lady Gertrude of Copenhagen, and Princess Arcala of Seville.

Renowned for their intelligence and piety as much as their startling beauty, Master Siger was even more dazzled by the presence of these gorgeous women than by the sparkling wine, or the Pope's erudite disquisition. Yet, despite his pleasurable befuddlement, he still could remark to himself with relief that neither Dr. Simon de Brion nor Frère Jacques had joined them. For the moment, Master Siger enjoyed a temporary Papal dispensation from surveillance, or so he hoped.

Amidst a banquet-table spread with bloody flesh meats and burned fish, along with vegetables, fruits, cheeses and wines, Pope Nicholas III held forth on the current state of diplomacy in Europe. Gesturing emphatically with a thick brown chicken leg, he reviewed Ottakar's submission to King Rudolf of Bavaria, an event recently much discussed in the media. To the large, wet eyes and ruby, demure lips of his elegant company, Pope Nicholas explained that regardless of the permission Ottakar had received from the Holy See to retain the kingdoms of Bohemia and Moravia, considering Ottakar's enormous ambitions, he was bound to rise again in revolt. While Pope Nicholas denied any partisan feelings on the subject, His Holiness insisted that, recognizing the decline of the power of the House of Hapsburg under Rudolf, and taking into account the approaching demise of the Hohenstofen since Frederick's death, the Holy Roman Empire was in danger of being reduced to a quaint legend. Magyar domination had made the East uncertain, and with the Mongols already established inside Ottakar's fiefdom, the Papacy found itself with no choice but to look to Her west and south for advantageous alliances.

This collection of sparkling eyes and reddened cheeks, heaving pale bosoms and shivering strong haunches surrounding Master Siger reminded him that he had joined a world thoroughly unlike his own. In this world, the exercise of power reeked with its own seductive musk. Prognosticatory prescience, even in the world of grubby gangster potentates, was sufficiently akin to magic of the highest power. And power was that aphrodisiac Siger had merely tasted in his classroom, so his admiration for his Pontiff was without envy.

"It is said," Alicia of Auvergn said, interrupting the Pope's recitation with her warm, husky voice, "your Holiness has been enthusiastically wooed by Anjou." Her languorous smile exposed bright, even teeth. "It is even said the French cardinals have proven particularly seductive."

"Anjou has troubles all over the Mediterranean," the Pope said with casual disinterest. But as he spoke, Pope Nicholas's eyes took on an avuncular enthusiasm for the appearance of an apt pupil. "A spot of trouble east of the Alps is the least of her concerns." He then described the elaborate series of secret negotiations being carried on by Peter III, King of Spain, over the fate of Sicily. His Holiness spoke with a self-assurance and certainty that set the soft, pale shoulders surrounding him trembling.

Between bites of beef and draughts of wine, Master Siger indulged himself in scrutinizing his table companions. And he could not resist smiling. Though His Holiness might be reluctant to admit it, Power itself, undiluted and undisguised, set these gorgeous heads nodding, these shapely lips muttering and murmuring with coos of approval launched on the hot moist breath of desire. The last thing Master Siger wished was to interrupt his show, and it was most certainly the Pope's show. By what delirium could Siger convince himself that mere verses of Averroes might set this vivacious symposium, this brilliant bouquet, to begin to tremble? It was tales of rendered bodies and spilled blood that set these hearts beating, that held these tongues and quickened this breath. Master Siger shifted uncomfortably. Just as with the banquet of food and drink that burdened the table, this incomparable experience was Siger's only by the grace of His Holiness. His eyes moved admiringly over the faces around him and discovered suddenly that Mistress Marguerite was studying him. He reached for a roasted partridge from the serving tray and returned his attention to the Pope's monologue.

Without mentioning Papal claims to the island kingdom, Pope Nicholas described how he and Charles of Avignon would put the matter most urgently to the attention of the House of Anjou and its head, King Charles of Sicily. His Holiness then revealed with a knowing grin that parallel negotiations were going on with Rudolf of the House of Habsburg. Months earlier, his Holiness had negotiated the marriage between Rudolf's daughter, Clementia, and Charles of Sicily's son, Charles Martel. With this single stroke, the Anjou/Habsburg alliance had gained enormous weight. Clementia had received Burgundy as dowry, and his Holiness had sealed their contract.

This remarkably candid exposition of the hidden gears of power left his audience all but frozen with excitement. His Holiness breathed faster and perspiration glittered on his forehead. Sitting next to Siger, Princess Arcala of Seville began to rub her thighs together. With this gesture, Master Siger suffered a vicious stab of envy.

News that, despite their alliance with the Ghibeline party, the Habsburgs had thereby acquired a vital interest in the welfare of the Holy See left Siger unimpressed. His Holiness seemed certain that all of this put the Papacy in a much improved position as negotiator in the interminable dispute over Navarre between Alphonso X of Castile, and Philip III of France. Siger recalled the long recitation from the golf course, and inwardly shuddered. He remembered seeing the Pope's picture on a magazine cover at the time of his investiture accompanying an article that identified him as an individual about to effect major changes in European diplomacy. But Siger admitted to himself that this idea now left him oddly depressed.

When he looked again, he realized Mistress Marguerite had continued to watch him carefully. Sunlight poured through those wide windows high on the wall behind her, and rich bright light surrounded her thick dark hair, making her skin more luminous and her eyes glitter. The intensity of her scrutiny left Master Siger nervous.

The luncheon lasted nearly two hours. By its end, Master Siger's accumulating exhaustion led him to promise himself he would depart the moment it was over. Food had left him drowsy, and despite the glorious company gathered around him, the baffling talk of negotiations left him longing for a siesta. So he watched these beautiful women stand and gather to walk beside His Holiness, and then he chose a doorway in the opposite direction. He turned to leave when suddenly Mistress Marguerite stepped up beside him.

"Pardon me, Master Siger," she said with a warm smile, "but in my reading I have reached a problem Averroes raises concerning the unity of the intellect. Unfortunately, I am a bit confused by the writings of Brother Thomas on this subject. If you have a moment, I am eager to hear your thoughts on this."

Master Siger turned to see that the others had gone ahead, though he could still hear the Pope's heavy voice accompanied by delicate peals of feminine laughter. Master Siger's camouflage had moved on, and he and Marguerite now stood together alone. Cautiously he said, "Of course. If I can help, it will bring me great pleasure."

Mistress Marguerite said, "Perhaps we could discuss all this in the garden." Her eyes were bright with curiosity, and her dark hair swung provocatively beside her pale cheek. Though she was smiling, her interest seemed earnest.

Master Siger followed her out of the common-room, and they followed a corridor that brought them to the cloister. But they had hardly stepped into the sunlight of the cloister when Mistress Marguerite stopped and turned. "On second thought, it is rather too warm in the sunshine today. I have a much better idea. Please, if you will, follow me." Without further explanation she led Master Siger back along the cloister to a heavy, dark door he had not noticed before. He wondered if some enchantment compelled him to follow this beautiful woman. And then he decided that no enchantment would have been necessary.

Mistress Marguerite led him through the door and then along a corridor that had enough turns and stairs for Siger to become lost. Though he was tempted by this opportunity to ask her opinion of their Pontiff, he found himself simply too pleased by watching her. The corridor became narrow, forcing him to follow her, and he watched her back, watched her long thick hair as it moved, watched her heavy dark skirt sway seductively with her steps. Although several times she turned seeming to make certain he continued to follow, Siger surmised she was pleased that he was watching her in the way she hoped to be seen. Her smile was sweet and in their twilight her glance was bright. So he watched her body move and shift along the path, recalling her delightful shape subtly disguised beneath the folds of heavy cloth.

This narrow corridor opened into a small, high-ceilinged chamber. Grey light seeped through a band of small windows close to the ceiling. From the folds of her habit Mistress Marguerite produced a flashlight. "Arm yourself, Master Siger, because you are about to enter the Papal archives. Therein lay land titles that predate Julius Caesar, stacked beside compilations of laws and statutes dating to the reign of Emperor Julian. There are even manuscripts purported to be in the hand of Aristotle himself stored there."

From another hidden pocket Marguerite brought out a large black key. She led him to one corner of the room and an entrance barred by a heavy iron gate. Beyond the gate he could see only utter darkness. Mistress Marguerite turned the key in the lock and it yielded soundlessly. Flashlight in hand, she led the way through. When Master Siger had entered behind her, she closed and re-locked the gate. "I hate being interrupted when I'm reading. Don't you?" Her laugh echoed softly in the stairwell, the sound of cotton falling on cotton

With Mistress Marguerite leading the way they began their descent of a narrow spiral stairway that turned gradually to the right. The air was cool and dry. As the light from above faded, Mistress Marguerite allowed the light of the flashlight to dance along the walls bouncing with each of her steps.

At the bottom of the stairs another heavy wooden door blocked their path. Mistress Marguerite used the same large key and the door swung back. Inside the doorway, she reached to the wall and flicked on a switch. Lights at various places around the chamber came on. Master Siger was startled to see that they stood at the entrance to a wide, deep and low-ceilinged room. Sets of stout wooden bookshelves one after the next seemed to recede into obscurity. From where they stood, Siger could see the rows of shelves were interrupted occasionally with small tables surrounded by chairs and topped with reading lamps.

In a low tone of surprising urgency Mistress Marguerite said, "I must caution you, Master Siger. The complete contents of these archives are known only to His Holiness and the chief archivist, Peter of Swabia. As far as the rest of the world is concerned, this collection does not exist." She leaned even closer, offering him her cleavage as quietly she added, "There is enough controversial material here to threaten the foundations of the very Papacy itself."

"I have no desire to threaten the Papacy," Siger said dryly. "So tell me why have you brought me here?"

Beside the entrance was an alcove. Centered in it was a low, round table with a couch and several armchairs surrounding it. Floor lamps stood at either end of the couch. Mistress Marguerite said, "Though our visit is clandestine, I would expect that a brilliant scholar such as you would experience a bit more curiosity." Gesturing as if they were her personal possession she said, "These archives have been accumulated over a thousand years. The most obscure texts, treatises on the most arcane subjects, hidden revelations of a world-historical character are all catalogued here. Sex scandals of the Popes, secret letters of St. Paul, the lost lust-poems of Homer, love potions from ancient Egypt, revelations of extra-terrestrial visitations to the Earth. All of these and more are found on the shelves I have opened for your inspection." She paused as if waiting for his response. When Master Siger said nothing she said, "Perhaps I should give you a glimpse of the riches surrounding you."

"Wait!" Master Siger stood. "I have two questions I hope you'll answer first. How is it that you know about this archive, and why have you brought me here?"

"We don't have much time." Her whisper was again urgent, but the glint in her eyes was mischievous and excited. "Save your questions, and I promise all will become clear."

Leading Master Siger slowly along a wide center aisle between bookshelves, Marguerite stopped to point out an eighth-century manuscript from a monastery near Antioch. In it, she explained, its author announces the discovery of a passageway leading to that hollow beneath the surface of the earth. He reports that having made the descent, he has encountered an entire world of beings living upside down. He describes his adventures among these curious creatures and his discovery of their intention to invade the earth's surface. Using weapons unimaginable in their destructiveness, he insists they plan to wipe out the entire surface population. Why? For the simple reason that these beings are tired of living upside-down. The author then describes the only logical course that might save the human race; complete subjection of the planet to Papal authority. With the centralization of control of the productive force of the human race, the Pope would lead God's Chosen to victory.

Master Siger's look was dubious. As if in response, Mistress Marguerite named seven cardinals, an archbishop and two kings prepared to implement this plan, and added that there were more than a hundred bishops ready to join them.

Master Siger shook his head smiling. "Any true believer would feel great relief knowing that Holy Mother Church is prepared in every contingency to prevent chaos."

In response, Mistress Marguerite said, "Every true believer has the God-given sense to refrain from biting the hand that feeds it." With a disdainful grin she led Master Siger further along the shelves. She stopped again and pointed out a tenth-century history of the Roman Caesars written anonymously in Syracusa. The author explained that the legendary deification of these men and women was simply their return to their extra-terrestrial homeland. These so-called Caesars, the author insisted, were in fact sons and daughters of extra-terrestrial beings who, as a personal rite of passage, each took a turn serving as the leader or leader's consort in one or another earthly empire. The author insisted as well that every earthly empire had been created by these extra-terrestrial beings to provide a training ground for their young. Through a series of astrological observations and mathematical proofs, the author demonstrated that these beings must originate on the planet Jupiter, and thus they were superior to humans in every way since they live on the largest of the planets and that planet was closest to God. Though impressed by the subtlety of this conjecture, Siger remained unconvinced.

Mistress Marguerite then led Master Siger to an alcove in a gap between shelves. On a stand within the alcove stood a large wooden chest. Lovingly polished to a warm reddish brown, the chest was intricately carved with riotously cavorting naked figures of both sexes and all ages. Mistress Marguerite explained that it contained the entire collection of Papal golf score-cards beginning with those of Pope Linus of Tuscia. The intricate and salacious carving so captured Master Siger that he could not take his eyes from it. Mistress Marguerite paused before she said, "Perhaps you would rather examine a manuscript in the hand of Brother Thomas of Aquinas." Despite his disbelief, she succeeded in regaining his attention.

Mistress Marguerite led him further along to a set of shelves piled with notebooks and large bound sheets of manuscript. From the pile, she carefully removed one sheaf and handed it to Master Siger. The book itself was a commonplace school-child's exercise book. Master Siger carefully turned the first several pages. The handwriting he recognized as unmistakably Brother Thomas's.

Peering over his shoulder as she spoke, Mistress Marguerite said, "In this manuscript, Brother Thomas concludes that while it is in every way agreeable, and in many ways advantageous, that all of the power of Holy Mother Church rest in the hands of the Bishop of Rome, there is no historical or doctrinal basis for this centralization of power. And he adds that, however agreeable it may be for the moment, this concentration of power will lead inevitably to

profound abuses which will only end by dividing the Church against itself."
Master Siger sensed that she watched him with a bemused grin, a grin he was
beginning to enjoy. "Needless to say, you have in your hands the only copy of
this controversial work." She waited until he had read a few more pages before
she took the notebook impatiently from his hands and replaced it on the shelf.
"There's still more," she said and then led him to another alcove with its own
couch and tables and lamps.

Shelves along one wall of this alcove contained a jumble of oversized
manuscripts and large volumes in tattered leather bindings. Mistress Marguerite
leaned forward to scan one shelf, Master Siger stood back charmed to observe
her in that posture. Finally she pulled from the shelf a thick elephant folio. Its
spine was split and sections of the manuscript had become detached. The worn
covers and shabby binding showed that it had been referred to often. "Help
me," she sighed.

Master Siger lifted the volume startled by its weight. Mistress Marguerite
nodded toward a low table before the couch. As he placed it on the table, she sat
down on the couch and patted with her palm the seat beside her.

"This manuscript," she announced, "dates to the year 683 and comes from
a monastery near Paphos on the island of Crete." Master Siger opened the
cover, turned the first few large and dusty pages and found he was looking at
illuminations, painted in bold colors and explicit line, of thoroughly lascivious
scenes. Mistress Marguerite leaned over his shoulder when he stopped at one,
pressing her breast against his back. "These are the illustrated dialogues of
that notorious Roman, Lucian. I don't suppose there's anything like this at the
Sorbonne." Page after page, Master Siger found himself startled by a remarkable
feeling, as though his widening eyes could not fill quickly enough with the
sights before him. Scene after voluptuous scene of wanton gymnastics presented
themselves to his gaze. He discovered that his hand holding the page had begun
to tremble.

"One can only be astonished," Mistress Marguerite said softly, her lips nearly
brushing his ear, "by the verisimilitude this talented artist has achieved. Not
only do their faces gleam with ecstasy, but even the contact of flesh upon flesh
possesses remarkable anatomical accuracy. Look at the tints of flushed throats,
the sparkling black eyes and red-tipped appendages. They arise before the eye
as persuasively as a shimmering mirage in the sun-baked desert."

Master Siger realized that Mistress Marguerite's hand had begun to move among the folds of his robes until her cool fingertips touched his stomach. "A filthy pagan poet, no doubt corrupted by Satan himself," she said as her hand moved freely. "This artist is no less filthy or pagan because his craftsmanship is brilliant. His skill is diabolical and leads one almost to believe he has created his work from scenes immediately before his eyes."

Siger turned to the next page and then stopped. It took him a moment to realize he was looking at a drawing of a woman engaged in a most degrading behavior with two other women. But what startled him was that the central character looked exactly like Mistress Jacqueline, his Aristotelian love. Mistress Marguerite noticed his concentrated attention. "Do you like that one particularly?" Her voice betrayed a lascivious smile.

Master Siger studied this drawing a long time, and the longer he stared the more convinced he became that it was she. He reminded himself that a generous memory has many tricks which conceal even as they reveal. Without turning he asked, "You say this volume dates from the seventh-century?" When he looked more closely, he thought he could make out, through a window just above the right shoulder of the woman and beyond a cluster of trees, the twin towers of the cathedral of Notre Dame. "Look there," he said pressing his finger beside the incriminating element. "The construction of Notre Dame was completed only a few years ago. And it's construction wasn't even begun until after 1100."

Mistress Marguerite withdrew her hand suddenly from his robes and slid to the other end of the couch. There was sadness in her anger, as if Master Siger had spoiled a delightful game. "What's the difference? Looking at a picture like that, only a fool or a philosopher would challenge such a trivial detail. You philosophers are all so literal!" Then she stood, lifted the enormous volume with one hand and, as if with no effort, slid it easily back into its place on the shelf.

"Let's go," she announced impatiently. "There's something else I need to show you." Before Siger could stand she had already begun walking quickly along the long row of bookshelves.

To her retreating back he called out, "You mentioned some works by Aristotle down here." He began to trot to catch up. She seemed to glide along the aisles ahead as if her feet no longer needed the earth. She passed through the narrow openings between stacks, certain and economical in every movement. The images Master Siger had just seen in the volume continued to stir his mind in such a disturbing fashion that he found himself regarding her retreating figure in a new, hot light.

Mistress Marguerite stopped suddenly. Her hand darted to a shelf just above eye-level that included several octavo volumes fallen together. She brought one down, glanced at its cover, and then tossed it over her shoulder. Master Siger just managed to catch it as it spun through the air. The book appeared familiar. He flipped open the cover. The title was calligraphed in a dialect of Syrian Hebrew. Transcribed by Haiam of Aphrodisus, it bore the title, "On Comedy: Lecture Notes From The Words of Aristotle." His hands trembled as he turned to the fly-leaf. Master Siger discovered the inscription, "To King Leer, from Queen Sophia." He nearly staggered as he carefully turned its pages of elegant script. For a moment he intended to ask Mistress Marguerite how the book had come there, but looking up he discovered that she had continued walking ahead.

At the far-end of the bookshelves she stopped and turned to face him. "Really!" she said. Her voice was edged with impatience. Fists on her hips, she stood in the center of the aisle. "Bring it along with you, if it's so interesting. Perhaps you can refer to it in your oh-so-many hours of solitary boredom. There's a comfortable couch right over here." Then, through an opening between shelves on the left side, she disappeared. Master Siger snapped the book shut but clutched it carefully to his chest as he trotted to catch up to her.

When he reached the aisle where she had disappeared, he found that this one was wider than the others, and that a little further ahead it ended in a wide stairway down. Mistress Marguerite was not in sight, but he continued to hear her footsteps. He hurried to the top of the stairs and immediately started down. At the bottom, through a single wide door, he entered a small, dark and low-ceilinged room.

This room was decorated with dark blue brocade on the walls and richly colored pillows tossed everywhere on furniture and on the floor. Attached to the wall on the left was a large TV screen. Arranged in an arc before the TV were chairs and couches, with small tables scattered among them. On the right and occupying two walls were shelves filled with black cases of videotape. Mistress Marguerite stood beside one set of shelves, head tipped to one side and quietly muttered to herself. Master Siger asked, "Where are we now?"

Without turning, Mistress Marguerite said, "His Holiness likes to keep up, as I expect you've noticed. Speeches, interviews and documentary pieces fill these shelves, all filed and catalogued. But there are some things here I believe you should see." Gesturing blindly without turning she added, "The bar's behind you. Fix us something to drink." She continued to scan the titles and then over her shoulder she asked, "By the way, is that book any good?"

Master Siger carefully placed the book on the low table in front of the TV and then went to the bar. As he mixed and poured, he explained what he knew of the book and how crucial it was to an understanding of Aristotle's categories of representation. He did not mention Mistress Jacqueline, nor that he had surmised her image in the volume of illustrations. Mistress Marguerite chose several video tapes while he spoke, and then carried them to the couch. With a drink in either hand, Master Siger sat down at the end of the couch opposite her.

Mistress Marguerite nodded with polite indifference as Master Siger passed her drink while he explained that because critics have had only Aristotle's volume on epic poetry and tragic drama, they have consistently misjudged the profundity of any buffoonery that is not self-consciously satiric.

"Well," she said sipping from her drink as if finished with his disquisition, "you can put your book down now. I have a treat for you." She chose a tape from the small pile by her side and leaned toward the TV. "It is well-known you thought highly of Brother Thomas."

"He was the flower of his generation," Siger said with a hint of pride, "and an inspiration to everyone who knew him." Mistress Marguerite inserted the tape into the video tape machine. After a few moments of buzzing and whirring, Brother Thomas' face appeared on the tv screen smiling and shaking hands in a crowd of other Dominicans.

"This was shot in Naples," Mistress Marguerite said as she made herself comfortable at the other end of the couch, "a few days before Brother Thomas began his fateful journey to Lyon for the Council. The tape actually begins a little before this, but I picked it up where he's coming up the front steps of the Refectory at Santa Giacomo. About a hundred and fifty people including a dozen press and two TV crews waited inside the cathedral. A press conference was scheduled to preview the topics he planned to discuss at the Council. He expected as well to field questions about prospects for peace with the Islamic world." Mistress Marguerite pressed a button on the remote in her hand, the images advanced in trembling, rapid gestures, and just as suddenly froze. She asked, "Recognize anyone here?"

The color was smeared and the image blurred, but Master Siger could not mistake the face of Frère Jacques a few steps behind and to one side of the smiling Brother Thomas. "Better yet, wait." She pressed another button, and after a few seconds the scene changed, and Master Siger was watching ministers and high clergy wander smiling among tables as they held tall glasses or coffee cups. Eventually the camera found a table to one side. The image of the table that included two men sitting across from each other and talking grew large, and then with another press of the button the image froze.

"You recognize your companion," Mistress Marguerite said, "but do you know the other man?" She did not wait for his answer. "The Kingdom of Castile and Aragon has designs that reach far beyond the Pillars of Hercules. And the Papacy will accept nearly any support against the Crown of France." After a moment she asked, "See the man with the heavy mustaches to his right? Just remember his face."

"Wait," Master Siger said, "just what are you suggesting? That Frère Jacques sometimes acts as the Pope's emissary? That he works inconspicuously? Is this a reason for suspicion?" Master Siger felt his chest tremble even as he resisted his own suspicion. In his mind, he defied her to prove her suggestion.

Mistress Marguerite smiled as if already accepting his challenge. She turned at her end of the couch and positioned her knees in such a way that Master Siger could see well along both of her legs to their dark juncture. "I'll remind you that on the news of Brother Thomas's passing, remarks, albeit whispered, were frequent and pointed, to the effect that it was convenient though sorrowful for the College of Cardinals to be deprived of such an incisive mind."

The image remained frozen on the screen displaying faces Siger would never have linked together sitting with each other locked into a conspiratorial moment. Mistress Marguerite continued, "Though Brother Thomas always avoided speaking in public on the primacy of the Bishop of Rome, he had been less discreet in private, and once had been overheard to utter radical hypotheses concerning the Papacy's foundation in Rome. His Holiness may have wanted the Council to concern itself with Iberian politics and the coming Crusade against the armies of Allah, but Brother Thomas had been more interested in the fate of the refugees from the Inquisition. Particularly those in Castile, where measures against the victims of these interrogations were unspeakably harsh. And Brother Thomas might have complicated the issue by insisting that political support for the Pope from the House of Aragon and Castile had been exchanged for a free hand in dealing with political dissenters opposed to its expansion." As she leaned forward reaching again for her glass, a flap of her habit fell open revealing nearly all of her bosom. Without covering herself she added, "The Inquisition has enriched the Crown of Castile with the unimaginable wealth it has confiscated from those nobles it has declared heretics. And the Church has been pleased to share in that wealth."

"I'm sure I don't see any connection between the preservation of the Church and the death of Thomas," Master Siger insisted, despite his growing suspicion.

Without responding, Mistress Marguerite stood from the couch, removed the video tape and replaced it with another. "This next one reaches a couple of years further back, but you should find it even more intriguing."

In the new image on the screen, Master Siger recognized another old nemesis, Pope John XXI. Before his ascendance to the Papacy, this Pope had been known as Peter of Spain, Splitter of Hairs and Tyrant of Logic. He and Siger had battled on the faculty of the Sorbonne. Master Siger had managed to avoid his required classes in logic, classes taught exclusively by Peter of Spain, until he had been called to Rome. Now on the TV screen, Peter of Spain stood resplendent in his Papal robes dressed as Pope John XXI. From the decor of the room and the apparel of others in the scene, Master Siger assumed he was viewing an official function. Suddenly, from the left of the screen the camera captured a familiar, smiling face. Hand extended, Frère Jacques stepped forward to kneel and kiss the ring of Pope John XXI, then stood and was warmly embraced by the Pope. The camera swung around slowly, taking in other smiling faces around the Pope and Frère Jacques. Mistress Marguerite pressed a button, and this image became still. "He may not be so easy to recognize here. He was growing a beard at the time. I understand he has since shaved it off."

"The face is familiar, as is the beard," Master Siger said, both astonished and resigned. Standing several steps from the Pope, Master Siger recognized Bishop Etienne Tempier. It had initially been Pope John XXI's request that let loose Tempier and his scriptural weasels with their first set of Condemnations. Mistress Marguerite set the machine to advance images slowly so that he could watch Bishop Tempier muscle his way through the crowd until he stood at the left shoulder of His Holiness, and beside Frère Jacques. When Tempier turned to Frère Jacques and embraced him, Master Siger sat forward.

"You like that one?" Mistress Marguerite asked with barely suppressed humor. "This was a meeting at Viterbo eight years ago. What you just saw was a portion of the reception held in honor of the Pope's arrival. The conference had been organized to plan actions in defense of commercial shipping in the

Mediterranean from Moslem pirates. A multinational strike-force had been proposed. Aragon's insistence that this force must first rid Spain of Moslems was put aside in favor of commercial interests. The Pope arrived expecting to placate Charles of Anjou, just as he had done when he was negotiator under his own predecessor, Urban IV." Mistress Marguerite pressed a button that stopped the machine, and then ejected the tape. "There's one more I think you'll like."

This time, when Mistress Marguerite turned to remove the tape and then turned again to replace it, her habit rode so far up from below, and rolled so far down from above, that there was very little left of it to cover her pale, matchlessly formed body. Yet when the tape began to run, Master Siger found himself compelled to watch it.

"This is surveillance footage," she said, "very top secret. What you're about to see was shot just outside the lobby of the Excelsior Hotel on the arrival of Pope John XXI in Narbonne. The surveillance operative posed as a beat-camera for the local news affiliate. The picture is pretty grainy and jumps around, but you'll see what you need to see. The source is an anonymous organization with access to the highest circles of authority. The guests were almost all petty aristocracy who had made a bundle from the Albigensian crusade." She paused and watched the screen intently. "There!" she said as she pressed a button. "Recognize him?"

The image was fuzzy, as if the man had been caught in mid-stride. "Wait," she said, and advanced the image a few frames. Master Siger realized he was watching Frère Jacques pass through a hotel door with a spectacularly dressed red-haired woman on his arm.

"I'll slow this part down," Mistress Marguerite said and pressed a button. The images changed as slowly as a heart-beat. Inching forward from the left of the frame Siger recognized Dr. Simon de Brion. She said, "Watch carefully." She stretched herself out on the couch so that her feet lay in Master Siger's lap, and the rest of her uncovered body unfurled in a glorious arrangement.

Simon de Brion approached the couple, shook hands with Frère Jacques, then kissed and embraced the young woman with a wide smile. He leaned close and spoke into the woman's ear. The woman's head tipped back laughing. Then Frère Jacques spoke into her ear. As he spoke, Simon de Brion's arm slowly wrapped around her waist. Finally the woman laughed and turned. Accompanied by the two men, she returned through the door to the hotel.

"Had enough yet?" Mistress Marguerite asked with a teasing laugh and then poked her toe into his stomach.

"Is there more?" Master Siger asked, half hoping there wasn't.

Mistress Marguerite paused before she said, "Just one more. But then you have to come to bed."

Twisting and turning her exposed body shamelessly, she replaced the tape and pressed a button. "This will take a minute. I have to fast-forward to the right part." Unconsciously the fingers of her free hand raked the side of her thigh as she studied the numbers flashing past on the video tape machine. Finally she pressed a button on the remote and the machine stopped. "This should be the spot."

As the tape began she said, "This is that first tape again of Brother Thomas at Naples. Now, watch carefully this time." Again, Siger could plainly recognize Frère Jacques in the entourage of Brother Thomas. He watched again as Brother Thomas, with his prodigious girth, struggled slowly up the steps. When he stopped once for breath and to exchange pleasantries with his companions, Master Siger noticed Frère Jacques standing almost beside him. Then Master Siger thought he recognized Simon de Brion brush quickly past Frère Jacques and covertly pass something to the man. After Simon de Brion had passed, Frère Jacques stepped forward to embrace Brother Thomas. When Brother Thomas finished this warm greeting he continued up the steps. Frère Jacques paused to watch him before turning to walk away.

"Did you see it?" Mistress Marguerite asked.

Master Siger sat frozen, he could only nod, saying, "Play it again." Without waiting for her to respond he took the remote control from her hand, rewound the tape and started it again. When it finished he repeated it, this time moving the images as slowly as he could, staring at each, then advancing another frame, studying the next, an excruciating progress.

"How much longer will this take?" Mistress Marguerite asked petulantly. "Are we finished yet?" Master Siger could not take his eyes from the screen, even after the tape ended and the screen had gone white. Mistress Marguerite grew tired of waiting for him to notice her and resumed poking his stomach with her naked toe. Finally Master Siger asked, "What do you know about all this?"

She groaned and then turned onto her stomach, began slowly beating her feet, one and then the other, against the tops of his thighs. Her round glowing bottom displayed itself admirably. "The tapes are part of the Papal collection. Every Pope, no matter who he is, likes to stay on top of what's going on. But I know a few of the people who were there."

Suddenly she flipped onto her back again. She was smiling. The light in her eyes as she looked at Master Siger aroused his interest. "Suppose I told you I know a guy who was around Brother Thomas at the abbey. In fact, he was among the last people to see him alive." Master Siger waited. "Suppose," she added, "I told you I could introduce you to this guy." She rubbed her foot against his member through his robes. "Would you be interested?"

Slowly Master Siger leaned forward. With his eyes fixed on hers, he gently kissed her naked stomach. Eyes still on hers, he repeated his kisses, moving from one spot on her soft warm skin to another.

Mistress Marguerite giggled in a way that surprised Master Siger, a childlike delight he had not expected. As he burrowed his face further into her flesh and she laughed again she added, "You and I will meet first thing tomorrow morning at the garage. The weather will be perfect for a drive through the country. I promise to show you the most delicious scenery." Now her laughter, her warm damp smell, the excitement of her quivering flesh, all stimulated Siger's desire. On the couch and then on the floor, the ocean of their pleasure roared in storm-tossed waves.

Hours later, an exhausted Master Siger returned to his room, laid back on his bed and stared up at the roughly cut grey stone of the ceiling still obsessed with the images from the tapes. Mingled randomly in his mind's eye with visions of Mistress Marguerite, the scenes from the tapes dissolved every other thought. Still befuddled in the turbulence and agitation of his pleasure, he tried to distinguish his desire for her from his fears over what he had seen. So time passed before he realized he had left his Aristotle behind in the archive room. He wondered if there was any chance of getting it back. One more thing he would need to ask from Mistress Marguerite.

Let Fall the Gossamer Curtain of Memory, Let Gather the Silver Mists of Time. Master Siger's Via Dolorosa Has Only Just Begun, and It Stretches Before Him Piled with Sharp Rocks and Bedeviled By Blind Turns. Let the Light From That Past Dim and Fade, though Nothing Ever Ends.

CHAPTER THE NINTH

WITH A BRUSH OF PUREST LIGHT Let History Paint the Clear Azure Sky and Warm Sunshine that Poured Down upon Mistress Marguerite in her Bright Blue Habit, as She Led Master Siger of Brabant Into the Twilight of the Papal Garage.

Meandering between wooden shelves piled with black and greasy mechanical parts in a grey light perfumed with the aroma of gasoline and exhaust fumes, they approached a short, burly man dressed in grease-blackened grey overalls. His face was wide and thick, his hair and beard were wiry and rusty red, and his hands were black with grease. When he saw Mistress Marguerite he greeted her with a beaming hello. She left Master Siger's side and stepped up to him. They walked a few paces speaking quietly together. The burly mechanic suddenly laughed, patted her behind affectionately, and then handed her a set of keys. Without turning he continued to walk, and left the garage for the sunlight outside.

Mistress Marguerite rejoined Master Siger and took his arm to lead him further into the dim, cool garage. Master Siger asked, "Friend of yours?"

The weak light could not disguise Mistress Marguerite's grin. "Albert of Swabia. Nearly stoned to death in Lausanne for witchcraft. Accused by the Inquisition of putting curses on people's cars." With a warm, bright laugh she added, "Can you imagine?"

They entered a portion of the garage where a line of a half-dozen gleaming cars crouched. Each was a different model and color, but all bore the small gold Papal insignia on the hood. Mistress Marguerite walked to a black '67 Thunderbird with blood-red interior. "His Holiness offered Albert refuge," she said, "in exchange for his services. He's only the best mechanic south of Paris." When Master Siger closed his door she started the engine. "An exchange of favors, and Albert is accommodating. Within the walls of the Palace of the Pope, one cannot exchange too many favors, nor have too many friends." She backed the car out of the garage with confident skill.

"I have heard similar suggestions," Master Siger said, "so often I've been tempted to believe them. A favor to the powerful is never wasted. Or so I've been told."

"There's something new to be learned every day, Master Siger. It is up to each of us to put aside our pride and learn what we need to know."

They emerged through the Papal gates and into the narrow and winding streets of Avignon. Beyond the gates to the city they crossed over the Rhone River, passed Villeneuve and the fort of Saint Andrew, and then picked up the highway to Nimes. Mistress Marguerite drove fast, their speed surprised Master Siger. Soon they were passing farms and vineyards and sparsely grown winter hills, some topped by tumbled stone walls. He asked, "Where will we meet your friend?"

"Impatience is not among the virtues," she said. The cowl of her habit hid part of her face. "The Lord has given us a marvelous afternoon. Let's not waste it on the tedious."

The warmth of the winter sun, the acceleration of the car pressing against Master Siger's chest, and the company of this beautiful woman; everything at that moment delighted him. Mistress Marguerite drew back her cowl. Her long, dark hair tumbling thick to her shoulders and surrounding her face was caught by the breeze and swirled playfully behind her. With a glance she caught him studying her and she smiled. "Take a look in the back," she said. On the floor of the back seat Master Siger saw a large wicker picnic basket.

"A plot of some sort," he said.

"Of course! The Palace is a perfect nest of plots, and fabulously generous to clever plotters. Besides, a picnic in the country always cheers me up."

"It seems unlikely you need to kidnap companions for your excursions."

"And all the more reason for you to feel flattered."

"Do trips into the countryside improve your knowledge of biochemistry?"

"I expect my knowledge of Aristotle to improve."

They drove for a time in silence. Master Siger watched more farms and their low stone buildings pass as he wondered why he was suddenly certain things had gone wrong.

"This is delightful," Master Siger said earnestly. "And most generous of you. I confess that since our trip to the Archives I've been deeply troubled. And since then I've hoped you would add to what you have already showed me."

Mistress Marguerite tossed her head back when she laughed. Master Siger liked the gesture; it was generous and enthusiastic. "Don't you ever relax?"

"Do you think I should?" Master Siger asked, pleased with his own cleverness.

"I promise you we will spread our blanket where neither Thomas nor Aristotle nor the Pope himself will find us." Her expression was warm with delight, but the tone of her voice seemed almost a challenge.

"And what of our rendezvous?"

"All in good time, Master Siger. We should not enjoy the dessert before the main course."

When they reached the city of Nimes, Mistress Marguerite stopped their car in a parking lot beside the Roman amphitheater. A market had been set up in the shadow of the amphitheater's towering and weathered grey stone walls. Wide, brightly-colored awnings sheltered the noisy crowd of shoppers from the sun. Between the stalls, oxen harnessed to wooden carts shuffled and lowed in place. At openings between the awnings, religious fanatics standing on upturned wooden crates preached to whoever would listen. All the while, through the noisy and colorful crowd, groups of screaming, careening children played. Pasted to the grey stone walls above the crowd were huge wildly-colored posters of bulls and matadors that announced the weekend bull-fight card.

Mistress Marguerite led Master Siger slowly by the arm from stall to stall. Though she had pulled the cowl of her habit forward to cover her head and obscure her face, she attracted the eyes of everyone who saw her, and each vendor smiled at her approach. Master Siger had to confess to himself that all of this attention flattered him with a teenager's pride in his escort. Eventually they stopped at a fruit stand. As she scrutinized the display Mistress Marguerite said, "The most delicious fruit comes late in the season."

"The sweetness of enlightenment is the purest joy." In response to Siger's remark, she shook her head and again simply laughed. She reached forward for a single apple from a pile of dozens. As her hand approached it, Siger thought he saw that apple grow brighter, its red skin darker and richer. He blinked hard, determined not to believe his eyes. She put the apple and another beside it into her basket, and then stepped to the other end of the stall. As she scrutinized the fruit on display she described to Siger the variety of effects of soil, of nutrients, of rain and sunlight, and the cycles of the moon. Her hand then moved toward a peach, and again he watched this peach appear to grow more ripe, its color richer. Siger wondered if she was explaining the process of her selection, or attempting to disguise a phenomenon he could not mistake. When her hand moved toward a bunch of grapes that suddenly seemed each about to burst from its own sweetness, he decided to listen without reflection.

Mistress Marguerite expanded Siger's education further while she went about purchasing cheese and wine. And at a stall selling bread, the long, bright loaves she touched each took on a golden amber glow.

With a filled bag finally slung over one arm, she led Master Siger beyond the market and into a nearby park. When they reached an empty bench Mistress Marguerite sat down. She leaned her head back, turned her face up directly into the sunlight and closed her eyes.

"Do you ever wonder," she asked, "what they would think of us here, now?" She spoke without turning, as if addressing the sun itself. It took Siger a moment to realize she was speaking of the builders of the amphitheater whose walls towered over them.

"They would applaud our exuberant ignorance," he said while he took the opportunity to admire the elegance of her profile and the full roundness of her lips. "But they would also be appalled by our vicious fanaticism and fanatical individualism. And it would elude them that what they applauded and what they found appalling were halves of the same whole."

Mistress Marguerite seemed to consider his words. "And Aristotle? What would he think?"

Master Siger hesitated and then shrugged. "Probably the same as the Romans. That's one thing about the ancients. They found much more to agree about than we do. But let's not get sentimental." He nodded toward the amphitheater. "In there they threw Christian believers to the lions and cheered at their terror and misery."

Mistress Marguerite grinned coyly. "Now who's getting sentimental? They threw anyone to the lions they could get their hands on. The Romans needed spectacle. What better spectacle than to watch animals tearing human bodies apart?"

"Perhaps humans tearing humans apart?"

"When times get bad, spectacle gives people assurance that things are under control. Undesirable elements are being disposed of, malefactors and malcontents are disappearing. Such a spectacle offers the hope that it's only a matter of time until things get better. Things are being taken care of, and the rulers have the body-count to prove it. Christians were just another variety of malcontent insisting on their own repression. From the Christian point of view, all of this violence against them simply proved that they were right."

"A harsh estimate," Master Siger said. "Acceptance of God's will is the sacrifice that assures our salvation. To do otherwise is to risk losing the path."

A smile passed over Mistress Marguerite's lips. "So, do you believe they had something we have lost?"

"Who are you referring to? The Romans or the Christians?"

Mistress Marguerite turned to face Master Siger and, with her eyes now open wide, she leaned close to him. "In this case, is that a distinction without a difference?" The sharp blue of her eyes unnerved Siger, but he grinned as easily as he could.

"The progress of history," Siger said, "is a series of forgettings. We only progress by forgetting. But we risk forgetting what we most need to remember. We avoid the agony of choice by remembering what pleases us, and pleasing ourselves that our memories are complete."

Her look softened almost with sympathy. Her blue eyes became warm, while a sweet smile hovered over her lips. She slid across the bench toward him until their thighs touched. Suddenly Master Siger felt himself drifting within a dream where his actions were no longer the result of his will. He turned toward her, and then kissed her long on the mouth. In their caress his lips seemed to blend into hers, as if physical being and its world had utterly collapsed into a single point, and the two of them embraced at its center. A bright light appeared behind his closed eyes, and the bench beneath him seemed to move.

Breathing heavily Mistress Marguerite leaned suddenly away. The spell was broken, the other world returned. "So," she said panting for air, "what else do they teach at the Sorbonne?" Though she smiled, she did not wait for his answer. She stood and brushed her habit straight. "We'd better go. We still have some driving to do."

Master Siger staggered beside her as they made their way through the market. The sunlight seemed suddenly over-bright, while the air took on a crystalline precision. He stole glances at her profile in search of some sign in her expression, thought he was not sure what he was looking for. When finally they reached the car she turned to him asking, "And should Brother Thomas be left behind, too?"

Taken by surprise, Master Siger opened his door and leaned to get in. "The sights and aromas of this market have stimulated my appetite. Are we very far from our picnic?" The glint of light from the car door shifted, in a moment he realized his mind had cleared.

Mistress Marguerite shook her head, the curls of her dark hair obscuring all of her face except her eyes. "Some non-answers are as good as answers."

They followed the highway until it turned onto a smaller road. The road sign pointed toward Lodeve. They turned again, now the road was canopied by tall trees. Master Siger watched dappled sunlight splash golden onto Mistress Marguerite's face. She saw him watching her. "I asked about Brother Thomas and you evaded the question. He criticized you pretty strongly in his article in *Sports Illustrated. De Unitate Intellectus?* And he was even harder on you and your colleagues in his *Summa Contra Gentiles.*"

Master Siger shrugged with annoyance. She had said she wanted to leave shop-talk behind, and now she was talking deep-shop. "He only criticized my positions. What he said about my writing was penetrating and subtle. And I appreciated his scrutiny. His attention flattered anyone's efforts."

"Did you consider him your friend?"

Master Siger hesitated, struggling to sort through his thoughts. "Brother Thomas has been dead more than three years and still I miss him. He was generous to me in ways I cannot explain. But that generosity was simply his desire for reconciliation and consensus. His brilliant mind struggled to resolve every dichotomy, to harmonize Aristotle with Augustine, Bonaventure with Bacon, Plotinus with Avicenna, and Averroes with Peckham."

"A mind more engaged by synthesis than innovation." The tone of Marguerite's voice carried a hint of dismissal.

"For Brother Thomas there was no distinction. The act of thinking demanded first an engagement with what has already been thought. Only then could any claim to originality be justified. Otherwise, solipsism was inevitable."

"Your generosity to your departed colleague does you credit." Mistress Marguerite spoke without taking her eyes from the road. "And I find that very engaging." After a moment she said, "Brother Thomas was badly treated by Tempier and the others. But I hardly suppose you harbor hard feelings."

Master Siger growled, surprised by his own anger. "The Condemnations of 1270 were gratuitous and harsh. The Curia's treatment of Brother Thomas was irresponsible. None of the challenges against him would have withstood serious scrutiny. It was evident to anyone with a mind that all his efforts had been to reconcile those in error, and return them to the path of Divine Light. Brother Thomas never lacked zeal. But by his nature he would not condemn the error's creator, only the error itself. Instead of slaying the Church's enemies, he cultivated points of agreement with them. But such magnanimity earned him nothing from a Church too involved in the politics of State to protect its own honor or the purity of its message of salvation." When Siger looked he discovered no smile on Mistress Marguerite's face.

Master Siger continued, "What impressed the rest of us most was that, despite his treatment, he endured those horrendous proceedings honorably. He brought challenging positions into the light, and defended his own positions without needing to condemn others."

"What you describe is theology as a meat grinder," Mistress Marguerite said. "After all, he was never forced to defend a position he had not already acknowledged as his own. But his equivocations gave his enemies the stones with which to slay him. And curiously, he never denounced those men intent on silencing him."

Master Siger sighed. "You're right about one thing. The creation of religious dogma is like the manufacture of sausage. Observation of its process is in no way edifying or reassuring." He did not like the direction she had taken their conversation. The continuing turmoil of his own thoughts surprised him, and it gave his mind no rest.

"Well, speaking of sausage," Mistress Marguerite said, as though sensing the change in his mood, "perhaps my own appetite is beginning to cloud my mind." She laughed self-consciously, a gesture Siger suddenly found endearing. "But I promise you we will be stopping soon."

Their route took them high into the hills where the road climbed in a series of tight turns. Mistress Marguerite drove confidently through them, Master Siger was impressed by her easy maneuvering of their machine. Beyond a pass near the crest of the hills, the town of Lodeve spread below them as a cluster of low, grey stone buildings. Strung along either side of the road, the town followed the center of the valley. Behind the buildings on one side of the road, Siger spied a wide stream that tossed glittering cascades of water over grey boulders the size of small elephants. At the fork beyond the town she turned right onto a road that took them still higher into the mountains.

Mistress Marguerite slowed over this worn and rutted road saying, "Brother Thomas's detractors were Franciscans and followers of Brother Bonaventura. While most of the teachers being attacked were, like Brother Thomas, products of the Dominican schools."

Master Siger laughed uneasily. "Boys play rough, and the bigger the boys, the rougher the play. Brother Thomas was in their league and knew what he could look forward to. He just refused to play their game. He never searched for heretics, only errors."

Mistress Marguerite shook her head. "And as a commendation to Brother Thomas's compassion and as a memorial to his largeness of spirit, Bishop Tempier chose the third anniversary of Brother Thomas's death to promulgate the new Condemnations. How much will you wager the Franciscans were drinking more than spring water that night?"

Master Siger felt a moment of nausea pass over him. Whether it was the altitude and their rapid movement, or revulsion at the implication Mistress Marguerite seemed to suggest, he could not decide. "Brother Thomas was loved by everyone. Albertus Magnus called him the Angelic Brother. Students flocked to him. Three nights before his departure, the students of the University of Naples conducted an all-night carouse in his honor. And as he was leaving the city on that last journey, grown men with tears in their eyes lined his route and kissed the edge of his cloak as he passed."

"You astonish me," Mistress Marguerite said. She turned the car onto a still-narrower but now unpaved road, and followed it slowly along a steeply rising trail toward the top of a mountain. "Is it an act of will that allows you to remain blind to the envy that surrounded Brother Thomas?"

"Do you ask me to believe there were men in that gathering whose highest goal was other than the realization of Christ's Kingdom on Earth?"

Mistress Marguerite laughed sweetly. "Now I know you're teasing me. Brother Thomas simply failed to dispense enough favors."

"Or favors to the wrong people."

"Favors to the powerless are always wasted."

"Same thing."

"And worse than useless since the powerful expect their favors."

"And resent the donor when favors are awarded to the unworthy."

"You see," Mistress Marguerite said, "your education continues. So what I have heard is true. You are only willfully naïve, and this affliction is simply a pose. As if by not acknowledging disbelief, you will sustain your own belief. As if through a determined ignorance you will fail to see that what Aristotle has said is true. All men are political animals. Even your Brother Thomas had run afoul of Charles of Anjou. What could have been more political?"

Looking out the window Master Siger sighed, "Or merely that all men are animals."

The road ended, and Mistress Marguerite guided the car along a hidden dirt path into a small grove of trees.

"Tell me honestly," Master Siger said. "What exactly is the purpose of this inquisition?"

Mistress Marguerite's smile was impish, but a hint of the diabolic caught Siger by surprise. "Perhaps it is simply my curious nature. But as a member of the faculty of the Sorbonne and a product of her instruction, you must admit it is understandable that I probe your loyalty. As I am prepared to reveal secret knowledge, I must be certain you are worthy."

"If you suspect my intentions, why continue?"

"Because some of us only need to observe to know." Between a pair of tall thick trees she stopped the car and shut off the engine.

For Master Siger, the sudden silence and cessation of movement were unnerving. Mistress Marguerite leaned back, stared ahead through the windshield while her hands remained gripping the steering wheel. "Brother Thomas had been building a Dominican house of study at the University of Naples when Charles prompted Pope Gregory X's sudden announcement of a council in Lyon in the spring. Confident of defending himself and his ideals, Brother Thomas humbled himself and made ready for the long pilgrimage to attend the Council. His journey hardly begun, at the abbey of Fossanuova between Naples and Rome he suddenly fell gravely ill of some unknown ailment and died. He was just 49 years old. So sad, but also so convenient." She turned smiling. "You see, I do know the story."

Master Siger shrugged to disguise his surprise that she knew such details so well. He knew the official version, and he had guessed the secret political histories. "Then you also know as well that the Council was expected to reconcile the Greek and Latin churches, and to offer support to Alfonse X and his crusade to rescue the Iberian peninsula from the Moors. All of this in remarkable accord with the Mediterranean policy of Charles of Anjou." Siger recalled the sight of all those tonsured heads cracked and bleeding from the violent battles over the issue of the Iberian invasion.

"But what had been left off the official agenda," Marguerite continued, "was the suppression of certain radical mendicant orders, especially those whining about Church corruption and insisting that only absolute poverty could make those shepherds of their faith pure, since poverty is a form of chastity and, as one of the virtues, is just as absolute."

"You mean, as in the fact that one can neither be partly chaste nor partly poor?" Siger shook his head. "But as a gesture of conciliation, His Holiness confirmed both the Dominican and Franciscan charters, each of which asserted adherence to that most virtuous of virtues. His Holiness looked forward to a certain amount of purging of those men in love with poverty and hostile to Papal greed. But it was expected that all of this would be accomplished invisibly and in utter silence."

Siger added, "Meanwhile, errors involving Aristotle and the Islamic scholars would be denounced with great publicity. And the role of their defender would fall inevitably to Brother Thomas. In that conservative Augustinian enclave, he was as close as any of them would tolerate to an Averroist. So he would appear completely compromised over the issue of the another Crusade, and utterly ineffectual in his defense of the virtue of poverty. Had he survived his illness, Brother Thomas's views on Aristotle would have been sought after and discussed at Lyon, but perhaps it all would have come to nothing anyway."

"Travesty!" Mistress Marguerite muttered. "And Thomas knew it." She paused and her expression softened. "So tell me, why do you think he agreed to attend?"

Master Siger responded, "Positions he thought were all but holy were coming under attack. As an acknowledged genius, he was being offered the opportunity to discuss dangerous ideas in public and thus available for public scrutiny. How could he resist? Besides, his arguments against chance not to the contrary, Thomas was a bit of a gambler. Perhaps he just wanted to roll the dice and see what would happen."

Mistress Marguerite smiled. "So for the Holy Father's purpose, Brother Thomas's demise was as timely as he could have wished. The leading thinker of his age and an unapologetic Aristotelian and sympathizer to the Averroist camp, now at the very height of his mental powers and international acclaim, struck down by a mysterious illness within only a few miles of where he was born, and a few miles from Monte Cassino where he'd studied as a youth. One is almost reassured that the Hand of God is active in the affairs of men after all."

Master Siger shook himself as if from a disturbing dream. "Every good conspiracy theory lacks the same thing: evidence. If it weren't for the lack of evidence, every good conspiracy theory would be true." He felt himself tremble, whether from fear or anger he was not certain. "Others raised these same questions at the time of his death. In the end, nothing was proved, and Brother Thomas remains cold in his grave."

Mistress Marguerite sat quite still, and Siger wondered what she could be thinking now. With a quiet laugh Master Siger added, "Admit it. Those tapes you showed me mean nothing." He felt almost disappointed because he was certain this was true. "As evidence of a conspiracy, all they make clear is that these men knew each other and that they all knew Brother Thomas."

"The tapes put everyone in the same place at the time of the murder," Mistress Marguerite said quietly. "In most conspiracies, that amounts to quite a lot."

Master Siger trembled. "There was no murder. Everyone agreed he had been ill for some time, and his doctors had warned him of the precarious condition of his health more than once."

Mistress Marguerite remained motionless and silent. Master Siger said, "But you're right about one thing. I do not want to think this man was murdered. And I do not want to think these men could have done it. And happily, you've offered me no reason to believe otherwise."

When Mistress Marguerite finally turned to face him, she was smiling. "C'mon," she said. "You carry the blanket and the basket, and I'll bring the food and wine. And take that paper bag out of the glove compartment." Once again Master Siger found himself following that bright blue habit under a warm and generous sky along a steep and narrow path.

Let the Hand of History Pause in Reverence to this Scene of Light and Sun and Warmth, and to the Youth With Which This World Was Once So Rich.

CHAPTER THE TENTH

LET THE SHAPELY Yet Inscrutable Lips of History Report that with a Pounding Heart Master Siger Followed Mistress Marguerite Through a Narrow Path of Dry Golden Grass Accompanied Only By the Sound of Twittering Birds and Buzzing Insects.

The air was motionless and warm. Their path led past thick bushes and under low, wide trees. In moments Siger was bathed with sweat. They continued to climb, and when he looked back, he could no longer see the road.

Over her shoulder Mistress Marguerite called out, "I first came here with a Cistercian monk. Frère Ralph. He promised he would teach me a perfect meditation on the love of God and the mystery of Grace. I was sixteen."

Master Siger breathed hard attempting to devour the air around him. He watched mystified as Mistress Marguerite seemed to float without effort over the rough ground.

"He had beautifully thick and curly black hair," she said with a thrill in her voice that startled Master Siger. "It fell in ringlets across his forehead. He was so pale and drawn he could have been dead. But he wasn't as interesting as he should have been. We came here three times, and then he was sent to a monastery near Perugia. He wrote once inviting me to join him. I never answered his letter, but I thought about it a lot." She stopped and turned. "Do you think I should have gone?" Her look was suddenly so earnest all Master Siger could do was shrug.

Beyond the line of trees their path led them past large grey boulders ranged so close together he had to squeeze himself between them to keep up. Master Siger could only follow Marguerite's back, a sight appearing and disappearing in flashes of blue along these grey alleys. But when he reached the path's end he stopped.

Spread before them the ground was flat, as if the hand of God had cleared away the side of the mountain to leave a narrow shelf of thick dry grass, with a cliff that overhung the valley like a balcony. Master Siger paused with amazement.

Mistress Marguerite took his hand and squeezed it. "See? I wasn't kidding." Her face beamed with pride. Still holding his hand, she led him slowly to the edge.

The cliff fell away sharply down to the valley. They were so high that the road below them was a grey ribbon, and farmhouses and barns dotted the valley like charming bright boxes. "Feel privileged, Master Siger. You are the only person I've ever brought here."

Their isolation was so complete, Master Siger shuddered. The sky was clear and blue and seemed both overwhelming, and somehow closer to him than he had ever felt it. The cry of a single bird brightly calling startled him.

"Quite a drop," Mistress Marguerite said surveying the valley. Still holding his hand she stepped back. "Let's take our stuff over here." She led him to a spot well back from the edge but still in full sun. She took the blanket from Master Siger and spread it on the ground, then placed the basket and the food and wine in the center. Kneeling together they emptied the bags and brought out plates and cups. She held a bottle of wine toward him. "I understand the arts masters of Paris are particularly good at this job."

While Mistress Marguerite peeled and cored an apple, and then sliced its pale flesh into thin pieces, Siger uncorked the bottle and filled their cups then he held up his. "Thank you, Mistress Marguerite, for a marvelous inspiration. The Lord has provided in abundance."

Her hand darting quickly, she dipped a slice of her apple into the wine in his cup and then held it to his lips. "All praise to the Lord." He smiled and ate it. She said, "While I slice some cheese and bread, why don't you go to work on what's in that bag."

Mistress Marguerite sliced the cheese and quartered more fruit and then sliced large pieces of bread. She laid the plates near one edge of the blanket. When Master Siger finished rolling the joint he lit it and passed it to her. At that moment he realized that since first seeing this place he had not stopped smiling.

"I imagine," Mistress Marguerite said, "that being a major intellectual keeps you indoors a lot. So I'll bet you don't get many opportunities for this kind of research."

"And there's the pity." Master Siger shook his head. "All philosophy should reflect the beauty of Nature. A thing can only be true if it is as beautiful as Nature."

"And does Aristotle revere the beauty of Nature?"

"His fascination is indisputably a form of adoration."

"Adoration or acquisition?"

"The similarity is less significant than the difference."

They sat for a time eating. Master Siger listened as a small flock of crows called in the distance, and still more faintly, a dog barked.

In the bright still air Master Siger's heavy robes were making him miserable. As if reading his thoughts, Mistress Marguerite looked up at him. "Are you hot, too?" Without waiting for his reply she shifted onto her knees and in a moment lifted her habit over her head. Suddenly she was naked, her skin almost blindingly brilliant in the sunshine. She folded her habit into a pillow, then stretched out on the blanket on her back with her folded habit under her head.

Highlighted by the sunlight, her naked body was lustrous, each curve and hollow filling with blue shadow. For a time she stared straight up into the immense sky but then she closed her eyes. She smiled. "Tell me more about Avicenna's epistemology."

Master Siger laughed with surprise. Her closed eyes offered him a leisurely study of golden highlights, the pale blue net beneath her skin, the shape of the shadows of her breasts, the curve of her hip as it flowed to her waist. He said, "Tell me something about yourself that I need to know."

She hesitated and then her smile turned into a grin. "I don't really care about Avicenna's epistemology." Master Siger laughed again. She said, "Now tell me something about yourself that I should know." She still had not opened her eyes.

"I don't really know very much about Avicenna's epistemology." When she laughed he said, "Your turn."

Still without opening her eyes she shifted her hips as if to settle in for her recitation. "At the time de Monfort's crusaders reached Carcassone my grandfather was a lawyer there and a minor politician. My father described him as a cautious man in a dangerous age, and thus a fundamentally smart man. Under utterly fraudulent accusations of heresy, the most hideous tortures the human mind could imagine were being inflicted on honorable Christians. But it was Christians who kept themselves busy tormenting and killing other Christians. Impalement, castration, burning, white-hot iron pressed searing into human flesh, along with machines of surprising ingenuity; all came into use against my grandfather's friends and their families, most of them people he had known all his life. A shrewd and cautious man, he rightly decided not to wait to be robbed or to watch his wife and daughters raped, and then, along with his sons, slaughtered in their courtyard. So he led his family to safety behind the city walls of Montpellier. In this way, ours was among the few families fortunate enough to be spared. Some time later, his eldest son, my father, attended the university and became a doctor. His three brothers, my three uncles, meanwhile became prelates of high rank. So in an odd way, those wars blessed my family. The reason I hold an office in service to the Papacy is by the intercession of my uncles, his brothers."

"It is a rare war that does no one any good."

"You sound like our Pope. Give up his illusions; those wars were a disaster for my people. Their lives, their culture, even their language were all but destroyed."

"Yet here you are, in service to that institution responsible for their misery and destruction."

Mistress Marguerite paused as if considering something. She opened her eyes, turned and studied Master Siger a moment. "It seems our new Pontiff has concluded that success in wars which preserve political power and religious hegemony have in fact put the Papacy in greater danger. Ambition has put the Pope at the mercy of kingdoms larger and more powerful than his own. His Holiness can only gesture in broad stokes, because on the political stage he is increasingly a minor player."

"How can you say that, when you've described all the great and powerful men who pay court to him?"

With the slightest motion of her hand Mistress Marguerite waved his question aside. "For my people, the Pope's insecurity is our revenge. Besides, while he is distracted by Charles of Anjou we are left alone. Still, I think sometimes we would have fared better under the banner of Castile than of Paris."

Master Siger knew they were utterly alone, yet Mistress Marguerite's sentiments made him nervous. As if in a place where even Aristotle could not find them, the ears of Holy Mother Church still might.

Master Siger said, "I suppose I'm uncomfortable with politics because I really don't understand it. Like the Arabic language. Despite my admiration for the Islamic masters, I have never been able to make out more than a few words of their language. After months in Majorca working for Balthazar in his bookstore, and then those nights with Miriam, my Hebrew as well is still pretty awful." With her eyes now closed again, and with sunshine caressing each turn of her warm, motionless flesh, Mistress Marguerite smirked. Master Siger was relieved, and in that relief found encouragement.

Mistress Marguerite remained quite still, as if thinking something over. When she opened her eyes, she shielded them against the sun with the palm of her hand. She turned to look at Master Siger. "Now that you have seen him close up, what do you think of our Pontifex Maximus?"

Master Siger hesitated before he said, "In Our Lord's plan there is a use even for weak tools."

Mistress Marguerite laughed. "Very diplomatic for a philosopher. Though it will not benefit your knowledge of Aristotle, I am sure our New Year celebration will improve your knowledge of political affairs. Representatives of all the most important kingdoms will be there. Certainly you will see Charles Martell. The House of Anjou will not be left out. And of course, Charles of Sicily will also be there." Mistress Marguerite again closed her eyes, her arms remained by her sides with palms flat and fingers spread. "But I have no idea who will make the trip from the House of Habsburg this year." Master Siger noticed that her exposed flesh displayed no tan lines. "Last New Years, King Rudolf arrived so drunk from the flight from Zurich he was confined to his bed for the celebration."

"It is little comfort," Siger said, "to know that the hand on the throttle may be burdened with a hang-over."

"Take my word for it. If you haven't felt it already in His Holiness's presence, you will feel it that night. The thrill of limitless power will travel along the surface of your skin and bloom before your eyes, and you will know unmistakably that you are in its presence. At that moment that power will become tangible. It will arise before your eyes like an ectoplasmic presence. It will be there before you and you will know it."

Master Siger grinned. "Sort of a mist hanging in the air, like a fragrance."

"Mock me as you like," Mistress Marguerite said, "but I promise you will see it in the bright lights and the darting cameras. The women will be beautiful and young, while the men will be well-dressed and not. Power and notoriety will chatter piously over tall glasses of champagne around tables burdened with gold and crystal. Have you noticed that even the bathrooms have gold-lined bidets? Voices will rise and swell and crest with pauses of loud laughter. But no matter what is spoken or heard, every mind will be turned to the half dozen persons gathered around His Holiness."

She remained still and only her lips moved. "Each nod and gesture will be memorized and later retrieved for analysis or conjecture. Even the court of Paris is never so graced as this New Year party. Within the apostolic embrace of His Holiness, powerful conflicting dynasties will gather together fraternally under a single roof. Topics will seem simply to arise in conversation, and His Holiness will orchestrate grand agreements to which he will be both guarantor and beneficiary."

"And will you be there?"

Eyes still closed, Mistress Marguerite's smile became mischievous. "Depends. I will not attend without an escort."

"Too bad."

"You think I will not get a date?" Annoyance suddenly entered her voice. "You think no one will invite me?"

"No," Master Siger said hastily. "That is, I meant to ask if I might accompany you to the New Year's Eve celebration?"

"Perhaps you should reconsider this. Are you certain you wouldn't rather go with Mistress Celestina? Or perhaps you'd rather wait until the last minute to see if something better pops up?"

"What I meant to say was, I will not go if I cannot go with you."

"And what if I am suddenly taken very ill and cannot attend?"

"I promise I will sit by your bedside until you recover."

"And suppose I get a better offer and decide to attend with someone else?"

"I will remain in my room and bemoan my harsh but just fate."

When she opened her eyes again, their blue sparkle was hard and bright. "I am not fooled by your lies, Master of Obscure and Useless Arts, Siger of Brabant. But you may lie beside me and tell me more."

Master Siger removed his robes and did as she suggested. The air above them was motionless and blue as they made love, and very high up a dark speck circled. For a moment Master Siger imagined being up there and looking down on his and Mistress Marguerite's pale forms. Afterward, she shuddered, and then with a smile curled more tightly against him. He folded his arms around her. He followed the rhythm of her breathing as her thick dark hair rested against his cheek. He breathed the heavy smell of her hair. Master Siger began to doze on his back with Mistress Marguerite's head nestled in his shoulder.

In Siger's dream he saw Brother Thomas in Heaven. He watched as Thomas walked slowly beside Aristotle on his right. God walked on Aristotle's left, and side by side the three spoke together. Master Siger was too far behind, and he could not hear what they were saying. But then he saw God's head tip toward Aristotle, as if He was eager to hear what Aristotle thought.

Mistress Marguerite stirred in Siger's arms and he awoke. But remaining motionless and with his eyes closed Master Siger pretended to sleep. He felt her carefully turn and stand and then step away from their blanket. When he squinted she had already taken several steps toward the edge of the cliff. Her movements were slow and certain. Bathed by so much sunlight her skin seemed opalescent and shadowless. The light played evenly over every curve and rise as she stepped forward. When she reached the edge she stopped.

Standing very still, offering her back to Siger, she spread her feet, held her arms straight out from her sides, raised them slowly until her hands joined above her head. She stood this way for several heartbeats. Then she dropped her arms to her sides. She repeated these gestures twice more. After the last, as her arms descended the light around them both changed. It trembled as if Siger was looking at a reflection on the surface of a pond, so that it seemed as if the world itself trembled. Master Siger wanted to rub his eyes, but then he felt himself slowly begin to spin.

When he opened his eyes again, Mistress Marguerite had turned and was hurrying back to the blanket. As she drew near the world seemed to resume its appearance. Master Siger sat up. Mistress Marguerite saw him and smiled. When she sat down in the grass before him, panting and pearled glistening with sweat, she took his face between her hands and kissed him. "You should not drink if it only makes you sleepy." Suddenly she released a quiet laugh. "Imagine a philosopher who cannot drink."

Siger asked, "Did you see something, too?"

"Was there something to see?" Her look darkened, she seemed to study him carefully, as if she was considering the question behind his question. But then her smile returned. "Never mind. Get dressed, we've got to go." She stood and took up her habit.

"What's the hurry?" Master Siger asked. He reached for her already regretting the disappearance of her unadorned form, but she slipped easily from his grasp.

"It's getting late," Mistress Marguerite said while she slipped her habit over her head and then adjusted it around her hips. "And I still want you should meet a guy."

Master Siger surprised himself with his own sense of disappointment as they gathered up their things and quickly made their way back to the car. Suddenly he decided there were things more urgent than Brother Thomas' demise.

Once they reached the highway, Mistress Marguerite followed a sign pointing to Montpellier. Master Siger shifted uncomfortably. "Do you still have family there?"

Mistress Marguerite shook her head. "Dad is retired and he and mom moved to a little place near Juan Les Pines. Very nouveau riche if you know what I mean. My twin sisters are older than I am and married with families. But I have distant relatives there. And I still have a few useful friends." She grinned.

By the time they arrived at the edge of Montpellier, the sun was red behind the jagged mountains that ragged its edge. Mistress Marguerite stopped the car in front of what looked at first like a doorway into the side of a hill. After a moment Master Siger noticed a small square window. Through the door they entered a low dark tavern.

When they stepped inside, the gloom and cigarette smoke seemed impenetrable. Master Siger's eyes slowly adjusted and he saw several older men seated at the tables around the room, and they watched them enter with suspicious glances. Mistress Marguerite nodded to the tall, bearded man behind the bar. He returned her look and then reached under the bar-counter. Master Siger of Brabant followed Mistress Marguerite toward the back.

At the back wall, two men sat at a table. As she and Siger approached, one of the men stood, then lifted the curtain that hung across the back wall to reveal a hidden doorway. He held the curtain as Master Siger and Mistress Marguerite passed through the concealed door.

In the small room beyond, the flickering pale blue light of a small television cast silhouettes around the heads of three men who sat side by side on the couch that faced it, and with their backs to the entrance. One of them called out, "Close the damn door!" although none of them turned around.

The head on the far left was bald and emitted a quiet chuckle. The one in the center, black hair flat and shiny asked, "What're you laughing at?" and then slapped him. In the back-hand motion, his elbow hit the man sitting at his right in the face. This man's wildly tufted hair formed a pale blue halo above him. "Hey," he said, "watch where you put that thing?" The man in the center turned to him. "Another word out of you and I'll tie your tongue into a knot."

"Quit pushin' why don't ya?" the bald one on the end said.

"Now listen you two. I'm going to see the end of this golf tournament or I'll gouge your eyes out and box your ears in." But finally he turned to look around and discovered Mistress Marguerite. He nudged the one with tufted hair. "Look who's come to visit?"

The large, round face of the bald one turned and split wide with delight. "Hiya, toots!, nyka, nyka, nyka." All three stood together as they called out greetings. Just then, a door concealed in the far wall opened. In it stood a tall man with a thin, sharp face, dark skin, sharp black eyes and even darker hair. He wore a dark, precisely-tailored suit. In the weak light of the flickering TV his black eyes sparkled. Siger felt suddenly certain he had seen this man before, but he could not recall where.

"Mistress Marguerite," the man in the doorway said in a smooth deep voice, "I feel privileged to preside over this reunion with old playmates." When Master Siger turned he saw that she was grinning as well, and in a way that made him nervous.

Mistress Marguerite opened her arms and cried out, "Repollo! Pepino! Apio!" The three men from the couch gathered around and began to embrace her with much laughter and kissing and fondling. At first Master Siger was amused. But in a moment there were hands. So many hands. And each hand seemed to be in search of a portion of Mistress Marguerite to rest upon and caress.

The stranger stepped back from the doorway. "Why don't you young people go amuse yourselves? There's a quiet reception room just down the hall. Master Siger and I have many things to discuss." The quartet left the room with more laughter and fondling and kissing. When the tall man closed the door behind them Master Siger realized Mistress Marguerite had not turned to say good-bye.

"I have been most anxious to meet you, Master Siger." The man's voice was low and soft, and his speech seemed like a kind of purring. "Your reputation is known throughout al'Andalus. Please, sit with me and chat for a time. And I will return to my friends and tell them of my conversation with the great Siger of Brabant." He added, "Our scholars study your interpretations of Ibn Rushd and

Aristotle with admiration." In the flickering silver twilight from the television the man's teeth glowed white.

He sat down carefully in the chair beside the television while Master Siger seated himself on the couch. "First let me introduce myself. I am your humble servant, 'abd al-Malik. I have earned a small reputation in political theory at the University of Cordoba."

Master Siger smiled with surprise. "Your reputation precedes you, Doctor 'abd al-Malik. I have followed your series published in *Car and Driver* with fascination as well. And your volumes on the development of the State and its connection to the evolution of religious societies will be studied with profit for generations. I have read the works of the brilliant 'abd al-Malik since I was an undergraduate, but I never even hoped for an opportunity like this. I am at your service and offer my help for whatever is needed. But tell me this. Have you discovered any additional works of the indomitable Ibn Rushd?"

"Your enthusiasm for the glorious Ibn Rushd recommends your incisive mind. Unfortunately I can report no progress there. I am fearful that over-zealous believers have destroyed certain of his works under the misapprehension they contain heresies against the Koran. But I've been told there is an old ship's captain living near Korfu who may have helped smuggle a set of copies to a rug merchant in Constantinople. But please, pardon me that I must change the subject, for I have come with another purpose."

Though seated, the man held himself with such dignity and repose Master Siger felt embarrassed in his presence. And yet as he observed the man, slowly he became certain he recognized him. He just could not remember where.

"I have traveled here secretly, Master Siger, as the representative of a faction within our government that does not wish its presence known. Suffice it to say that, as far as either of our rulers is concerned, this meeting has never taken place." He grinned brilliantly. "I remain deeply grateful to Mistress Marguerite for generously facilitating our illicit rendezvous."

"Pardon my question, but just where has she gone?"

"Ah, we both know how it is with old friends," 'abd al-Malik said, his grin becoming sly. "There is always so much catching up to do and so little time. But speaking of old friends, the world continues to mourn the loss of Brother Thomas. Though it has been three years, each day reminds us all that we will never meet his like again. Deprived as we are, Allah has made our task of redemption more difficult, our struggle to recognize His intentions more arduous. In passing, may I ask how your own researches progress?" 'abd al-Malik brought from an inside pocket of his jacket a small pipe with a bright silver cap over the bowl. As he waited for Master Siger's response he tipped back the cap and lit the pipe, then drew pensively on it. The aroma of the smoke seemed to Master Siger sweetly familiar.

"My work," Master Siger began, "can never replace the brilliant research that Brother Thomas would have accomplished. As you have been in touch with Mistress Marguerite, you know that my humble accomplishments have been thrown into disrepute by colleagues hostile both to myself and to philosophy. The fate of my work is, of course, of little significance. What is important is that Brother Thomas's work and the work of philosophy continue."

"Spoken like a true philosopher." 'abd al-Malik's smile widened at the mention of Master Siger's conflict, and he drew thoughtfully for a moment on the pipe. "This conversation has brought to mind many memories of your magnificent colleague. I hope it does not upset you to know it was I who shot the video tapes Mistress Marguerite agreed she would allow you to view." This sidelight startled Master Siger. "And that I was with Thomas the evening he died."

Master Siger sat suddenly upright. Though the room's dim light and subtle vapors wreathed his mind in pale colors and soft fragrance, 'abd al-Malik's words sharpened his attention. Quietly he said, "I have a feeling you are about to tell me something I do not wish to know."

'abd al-Malik's face became impassive, as though the weight of his knowledge compelled a strenuous effort to resurrect it. "There is a profound distinction between knowledge and understanding. Unfortunately I possess mere knowledge. Perhaps if I convey this knowledge to you, you may infuse it with understanding. But I tell you bluntly, my colleagues wish you to have certain information. The threat to us all from an aggressive and hostile Papacy must be deflected."

'ab al-Malik's words stunned Master Siger. "Are you asking me to betray the Bishop of Rome? Forgive me, but how is it possible any knowledge you possess might threaten the Lord's Shepherd on Earth?"

'abd al-Malik leaned back in his chair, crossed his legs and then very carefully removed a piece of lint from his knee. "I will only tell you what I saw the night Brother Thomas died, and what I have been told in confidence since then. I will leave it to you to bring the personalities and their situations into focus. With your proximity to His Holiness, only you are in a position to reconcile any contradictions."

"Before you begin, let me offer this warning," Master Siger said. "Regardless of what you say, I will not act against the interests of His Holiness or of my faith. Tell me what you know, and with the help of God we may make sense of it. I promise only that this meeting is our secret alone."

'abd al-Malik hesitated. His hard dark eyes seemed to weigh options as they studied Master Siger. He sighed as if unsatisfied with his decision, and only reluctantly spoke.

"Very well, I begin at the beginning. I had already spent several days at the abbey of Fossanova when Brother Thomas and his party arrived. I had been invited to attend a conference in Naples, and my friend, a Dominican brother named Giovanni Villani, insisted I stay with his brothers and make use of the abbey's remarkable library."

"The arrival of Thomas and his entourage had been long anticipated, and preparations for it began days before. I confess the group that arrived with Brother Thomas was a surprising mix of men. But such was your Brother Thomas. The lives of men were the stones and mortar of his philosophy. Through the subtlety of his thought he reconciled their difficulties and returned their religion to them sturdy enough to withstand every unconventional suggestion."

"Though Fossanova is a poor monastery, on the evening of his arrival a great meal was prepared, as sumptuous as any I ever recall in Cordoba. The table was not cleared until well after midnight. Yet, the next day we learned that illness had discomforted Brother Thomas throughout the night. Since no other brothers were so affected, his illness was regarded as simply the result of the rigors of travel."

"The following evening a similar thing happened. Though again no one else was afflicted, Brother Thomas suffered mightily. No one was more stricken by the fact of his illness than Thomas's personal cook, an older man who had served him a long time and who now stood by with tears in his eyes. Even I felt considerable uneasiness and had difficulty sleeping."

Master Siger leaned forward. The smoke from 'abd al-Malik's pipe had somehow put Master Siger's head in a swirl, so that there were times when his voice seemed to be coming from within his own mind. But mention of the cook had startled him awake. "Can you tell me that man's name?"

'abd al-Malik shifted uncomfortably, the first time Master Siger had noticed him not completely in control. "Apparently my inquiries concerning the man were insufficiently discreet. He has disappeared. Though he has been reported lost in a raid by Moslem pirates, there are reasons which, though I am not free to discuss them, are adequate to conclude this explanation is impossible. But let me return to my tale. The Brothers of the abbey were frantic with concern that their sainted guest should suffer under their roof, and they made every effort to root out any rot or filth on the food. But while we slept, Brother Thomas spent the following night in a terrible fever. The rest of the night he was sweating and chilled by turns, while his stomach and bowels seemed to have no strength."

"The next morning Brother Thomas was unconscious and burning with fever. Our dear brother's torment lasted the entire day, until just before sunset when he was finally released from his torture and breathed his last. A quiet groan flew suddenly through the abbey, as if a cold wind had found its way to the heart of the congregation. By nightfall the ceremonies of the faithful took charge. The comforting movements of public mourning, I'm sure you understand. And though I was well-thought of by my table companions, as a non-believer my presence became incongruous. I gathered my things and moved on."

After a moment Master Siger said, "You confirm much of what I have heard, but I have never spoken to one who was there and witnessed the events surrounding his passing. To witness the passing of greatness is a burden. You have my respect and my sympathy. But why have you told me this? How does any of this relate to His Holiness?"

When 'abd al-Malik re-crossed his legs, Master Siger detected a look of confused anguish pass over his face. "I draw you attention to two points. First, peruse the back pages of the March 11th edition of the *Midi Libre* newspaper of that year, and you will find a notice concerning the death by poisoning of a miller's son. What the notice does not mention is that the boy had been at that time in the service of Brother Thomas, and that among his duties was kitchen service. The rumor persists that the boy died the same night Brother Thomas was struck down by his final illness. Of course, a coincidence is always possible. I can only leave it to you to find out. My second point is that there was among Brother Thomas's entourage a certain Franciscan brother by the name of Simon of Brion. I am sure you are aware he now serves as papal legate. Tell me this. Is it also true that he has proved especially burdensome to your efforts?"

Master Siger shrugged. "Brother Simon is among the most powerful men in the Curia, so any interest in me could only be mere curiosity." And then he shivered. "What you report of his presence has been revealed to me by an independent source. Thus, your report gains in credibility. Unfortunately."

Suddenly the door at the end of the room opened. The mop-haired man Mistress Marguerite had called Pepino entered. His straight black hair hung wildly around his eyes, his shirt was half buttoned and he held up his unbelted and open pants with one hand. He was smiling as he approached 'abd al-Malik. In the man's free hand Master Siger recognized a set of car-keys. "Here you are, boss," he said, "just like you asked."

'abd al-Malik took the keys and waved the man away without looking at him. As Pepino retreated, he turned to Master Siger. "Tough luck, sailor." He grinned as he passed through the door.

When the door closed, 'abd al-Malik shook his head. "Mistress Marguerite cultivates the oddest allegiances." He handed the keys to Master Siger. "In any case, it appears she will not be joining you for your return. You, however, must leave at once. I have told you all that I can. Her absence will not be noticed, but I expect an effort is being made to find you even as we speak." 'abd al-Malik stood. "I will remain here briefly after you've gone, and hope thereby that neither of us is compromised." He stepped to the door. "Please remember," he said with his hand on the door handle, "discretion is in both of our interests. The enemies of peace and harmony are everywhere, in every disguise."

Master Siger returned through the tavern. With a glance he realized that the same men were still there, but that none of them looked up to watch him leave.

A cold breeze caught Master Siger as he opened the door. Outside, twilight had nearly passed into darkness. He shivered and then hurried toward the car. Peering into the weak light he recognized the car, and then slowed when he saw a shadow leaning against its front fender. The figure wore clerical robes, and the cowl was drawn over its head. Mistress Marguerite. Now Master Siger began to trot. When he was a step away, the figure turned toward him, the cowl was pulled back. Master Siger stopped.

"What took you so long?" Frère Jacques whispered with impatience. "Give me those keys and get in." Master Siger handed the keys to him dumb-struck. Frère Jacques turned and unlocked the driver-side door. As he slipped behind the wheel he said, "You better like trouble, 'cause you've got lots of it."

The Hand of History Grows Weary as the Web of Life and Memory Grows Thick with Threads of Doubt and Regret That Are Heavy As Chains. Let the Curtain Fall.

CHAPTER THE ELEVENTH

LET THE SUPPLE AND ANGULAR Fingers of History Part the
Swirling Aromatic Mists of Centuries to Reveal the Dour Face of Frère Jacques
as He Stared Grimly Over the Steering Wheel While He Drove Very Fast.

The tires screamed in tight turns as Frère Jacques spoke through clenched
teeth. "Are you some kind of dope or what? Don't you know there's nothing
Popes hate worse than a broken promise?" Gripping the wheel he shook his
shoulders as if something crawled over them. "Popes always have reasons for
what they do and what they tell the rest of us to do. For a smart guy, you are
just one big dope. Not even the Pope begrudges you a good fuck, but outside
the Palace you've got no protection. And you're a guy who needs protection,
believe it." Frère Jacques rolled down his window, spat loudly and then rolled
the window up again. His sharp bright eyes never left the road. "Hanging out
with a drug-pushing murderer like 'abd al-Malik." His laugh was more a snarl.
"How can somebody so smart be so dumb?"

After the sunny day and the heavy warmth of the room, for Master Siger the
night fell hard and sharp. He shivered against the cold. Slumped down in his seat
he understood he was utterly caught. "What do you know about him?"

"Take my word, pal, there isn't anything worth knowing that we don't know."

"Such as?"

"You want to know what I know? I know he peddled that story about the dead kid. Am I right?"

"What dead kid?"

"And he fed you some crap about Brother Simon." Frère Jacques leaned forward and fiddled with the radio. Unsatisfied he shut it off. "Well, here's the big secret. We already looked into all of that. Talked to the cooking help, talked to the boy's parents. And that kid wasn't within a mile of the abbey that night. And Simon de Brion was there as Brother Thomas's personal guest. Hardly rock-solid, but it seems enough to sink your conspiracy. You get my point?" Finally he turned and looked at Master Siger. "You're hooking big fish you'll never land. Just looking at you makes me very sad." Frère Jacques did not smile.

"And who is we?"

"We is who knows, dumb guy."

Master Siger stared ahead watching the highway unroll in their headlights, their yellow glare burrowing through a night of dark blue and black. He recalled the smeared, luridly colored images of Frère Jacques's face on the video tapes. Now, Siger's stroll arm-in-arm with Mistress Marguerite at the market in Nimes seemed to have happened in another era. And where had she gone? And how had Frère Jacques found him? Some plan between Mistress Marguerite and Frère Jacques? The abyss appeared before Master Siger suddenly. He noted its sloping walls, the inevitability of accelerating descent, and the empty, endless beyond.

"Do you pray?" Frère Jacques asked. His voice had become soft with sympathy. The change in his tone startled Master Siger, and he remembered being asked the same question by Pope Nicholas. "I mean, if God is unaware of us down here, why would anybody pray?" Master Siger slipped further down in his seat. "Am I right?"

"I pray as every good Christian prays," Siger said smelling a trap, "as an act of worship to my Creator and Redeemer. I don't know if the Lord hears my requests, but I don't doubt He senses my worship."

Frère Jacques sucked a tooth and began to smile. He leaned back and tipped his head to one side. "Me, I pray daily. The ways of Our Lord are mysterious, His simplest creations confound me. So I respond to Him with an open-ended faith. A faith above all that He will not torment me with new threats. But that when He does, He will recognize my miserable confusion and so love me that much more. I pray against an arbitrary Universe." He laughed harshly. "It seems like a good idea."

When Master Siger said nothing, Frère Jacques continued. "I need to tell you about a friend of mine. Great guy. Honest, loyal, really smart and not yet thirty. Gets his doctorate with highest honors. A commercial publisher decides to publish his dissertation. So my buddy starts re-writing. One night there's a real bad fire. Next morning his apartment is still there, but his manuscript, hundreds of pages of notes, hundreds of note-cards and research files, all of it now just this wet, muddy, ash-black pile in the center of his bedroom floor. Years of work suddenly a barely differentiated mass of ink-stained pulp and pieces of burned wood."

Master Siger shuddered.

"My buddy moves in with his girl-friend dragging along his miserable pile of stuff. Eventually the stuff dries out, more months of work, and a year later he delivers the manuscript to the publisher. And the book gets good reviews."

Frère Jacques gradually drove faster. Master Siger stared nervously through the front window. It occurred to him the possibility he would never arrive at his destination had just increased.

"Meanwhile, all this time he'd been chasing a job about to open up as the archivist to one of the Papal collections housed in Toulouse. He'd worked there on his dissertation and he'd wanted that job ever since. Employment for life at excellent pay in a cozy library. With his book well-received and support from Count Robert, he got that job. But the world turns, Master Siger. Despite Ptolemy and Plato, it is the world that turns. And it doesn't stop just because you want it to."

The dark and sinuous road began a gradual climb into the mountains. As the car turned in the switch-backs, the headlights swung suddenly into absolute nothingness. A space so featureless that all motion was invisible. Master Siger could not ignore the lurch of his stomach and the glittering vertigo that swirled before his eyes.

"My pal's future looked so bright he decided it was time he and his girlfriend got married. So they pick a place and we all go and they get married and everybody has a great time on a beautiful spring day and everybody is so happy and they go away on their honeymoon. Meanwhile, ever since he was a little kid my buddy's had these awful sinuses. Infections and colds, and trouble breathing when the weather changed. Doctors tell him it's a pretty simple fix. Talks it over with his wife and decides okay. Twenty minutes into the operation they're cutting open his chest and pulling these blood clots, like red-black worms, out of his lungs as fast as they can, just trying to keep him from dying. It's a turning world, Master Siger, and you philosophers can't say a true thing about it."

At a turn in the road, the upward angle of the headlights lifted above the edge of gravel and low shrubs so that a complete void opened. Reflexively Master Siger's fingertips reached forward, poised against the dashboard.

"Allergic reaction to his anesthetic, they said. But after they sewed him back up the doctors said he'd be okay. He got to talk to his wife and a few friends. I made plans to see him. Didn't work out. He had some kind of relapse, they couldn't bring him back."

The car came to the top of the road, and for a moment Siger held his breath. At the end of the turn Master Siger noticed the change in their movement. They had begun their descent.

"We walked around for days like each of us had been hit between the eyes. As much dumb astonishment as pain. Makes you think. Or it ought to."

Master Siger waited knowing there was more. "I mean, look at you. Young, clever, good-looking, good table manners. All you have to do is stay in good with the Popes of this world is what I say. Because whatever you least expect to happen, that's what happens."

Master Siger said, "The Lord tests our faith because He loves us. The difficulties of the world simply offer us new and more profound ways to demonstrate our faith in Him."

Frère Jacques seemed to listen to another conversation. "See, I know that the Lord will test me in the future as He has tested me in the past. I only ask to be tested against what I know, and not what is unknowable."

The angle of their descent suddenly became steep. Bracing both feet against the floor, Master Siger pressed himself back into his seat. "Then surely," he said, "it is good that you pray."

Between braking and down-shifting, Frère Jacques stayed within the turns, but Master Siger noticed that gradually they were going faster. Dark hedgerows and black trees poised behind whitewashed stone walls flashed past. Speed pressed into his flesh. Master Siger glanced over. From the pale green dashboard light he could just make out Frère Jacques's smile.

"A person makes a lot of decisions in one life. And every one is a chance to be wrong. Take us, right now. Guys like us, we've been around the block and we've kept our eyes open. But cars wipe out on roads like this every night. It's just that kind of world. The thing to do is not make a mistake."

After a series of quick turns, the road suddenly disappeared into a black stand of trees. The world beyond the headlights went completely black. When they emerged, it was onto a flat highway. They had reached the valley. In the moonlight the road stretched ahead, silver and straight.

Frère Jacques leaned his left elbow on the window. "The rational mind disturbs reality simply by its presence. Lurking motionless like a spider poised at the center of a web, it snares bits of reality as they drift past, pasting them onto the grid of its web, co-ordinates in some vague approximation of symmetry."

The engine roared and Master Siger felt himself pressed further into his seat. "Put that rational consciousness into motion and the reality that forms increases the range of the web, but the spider is no bigger than before. He just thinks he is." Frère Jacques glared with a weird grin that shifted from moment to moment as he held his chin above the steering wheel. When Frère Jacques glanced up to the rear-view mirror, the grin left his face and he muttered, "What have we here?"

Master Siger looked back. An approaching spot of bright light gradually became two headlights. As he watched, another light at the apex of the other two began to flash red. Faintly over the engine's roar he heard a siren.

Frère Jacques muttered, "Wonder what the Franciscan Highway Patrol is driving this year?" Master Siger suddenly felt himself pressed even further into his seat, their car lurched ahead moving faster. He turned to watch the headlights slip back. But almost immediately they were growing larger again, advancing.

Frère Jacques quietly laughed. "Let's you and me see how fast a car full of shit-bags can go." Master Siger glanced once at the speedometer and resolved not to look again. Frère Jacques leaned forward.

Farmhouses, trees and stone walls flashed into their tunnel of light like images from a silent film. The car trembled, a continuous explosion of power screaming forward. Yet the car behind them drew closer. Siger could hear the siren clearly. Gradually the headlights flooded their car with white light.

For a moment the car behind seemed inches from theirs. It swung out suddenly and pulled up beside them. The Franciscan in the passenger seat motioned with his arm for them to pull over. Frère Jacques grimaced and their car leapt ahead. Siger turned to watch the Franciscan car slip back. But in a moment it had pulled alongside again. Then the Franciscans pulled ahead, began to move into Frère Jacques's lane. Master Siger could not hear what Frère Jacques muttered over the roar of the engine, but they began to slow. As Frère Jacques steered their car to the shoulder of the road he said, "Hide your hands inside your robes." Master Siger hesitated. Frère Jacques snarled, "Do like I tell you!" So he did.

When they came to a stop, the Franciscans' '69 midnight-blue Corvette with white interior pulled across their path. "Just don't say nothing," Frère Jacques said, "and look real sick." Master Siger did not need encouragement.

After a moment both doors to the Corvette opened. The driver walked to Frère Jacques's window, the other Franciscan stood beside Master Siger's window. Before the Franciscan could speak, Frère Jacques said, "What's the idea? This is a Papal car. I'm on urgent business for the Pope. Get that crate out my way if you don't want trouble."

"No trouble." The Franciscan driver smiled. "Had a report of a stolen Papal car. We're supposed to check stuff like that out. Why don't you two step out and show us some ID?"

"You're interfering with a Papal emissary," Frère Jacques said. "When the Pope hears about this, so will your boss. I bet you expect a pension when you retire. So instead of making like the big, dumb jerk you are, just get back in your car and go away. You can always tell your boss it was a mistake."

The Franciscan placed both hands on the window frame, leaned toward Frère Jacques still smiling. "Afraid I can't do that. We mean no disrespect, brother. Just do like we ask."

"Puss-licking friars, kiss my ass," Frère Jacques muttered. "Get out of my way!"

"Sorry, brother," the Franciscan said grinning. "Do like I say. Now!"

Frère Jacques nodded toward Master Siger. "See this guy? He's a leper. The Pope needs to talk to him real bad. No telling what might happen if he's delayed on the road. But maybe you want to shake what's left of his hands?" To Master Siger, Frère Jacques said, "Shake hands with the nice Franciscan. Franciscans like lepers. Especially they like the puss."

The Franciscan's smile disappeared. "They pay me to ask questions. I'm asking questions. I'm just doing my job." The officer lifted his hands from the side of the car, brushed them together and took a step back.

"What's the matter?" Frère Jacques asked pretending surprise. "The Lord protects the righteous. You got a job to do." The two Franciscan patrolmen traded glances.

"I guess you were right," the Franciscan said. "My mistake. No trouble, right brother?" He took another step back from the car. "On your way, and God's speed to you both." He nodded to the other Franciscan, and together they walked slowly back to their car. To their backs Frère Jacques said, "Just be sure to give my best to Simon de Brion."

When the Franciscans were back in their car Frère Jacques began to
laugh. He drove slowly around the front of the Corvette and onto the road.
As he drove past, Frère Jacques continued to grin. "Burdened by Plato and
Augustine, the visible is never real, so those guys couldn't wipe their own
assholes without instructions." He glanced into the rear-view mirror and his
grin disappeared. "You can take your hands out of your robes now," he said
as he continued to watch through the mirror.

Master Siger turned to see headlights far back, but continuing to follow.
"I could lose those pricks in a second," Frère Jacques whispered huskily. "I
know these roads like a farmer. But what the hell, we'll let them be our escort
and earn their pay." Frère Jacques leaned back into his seat, draped his hand
casually over the steering wheel. "By the way, just what did that guy tell you
back there?"

Master Siger pretended confusion.

" 'abd al-Malik," Frère Jacques said. "Did you guys just hold hands, or what?"
Master Siger studied his own hands.

Frère Jacques turned to face him grinning with contempt. "How many
journalists do you know dress like him? You think he makes that kind of
money writing about dim-wits and poor people?" Master Siger realized his
responses were unnecessary.

"Did he tell you he once paid a woman for a story about alien abduction that
got a bishop burned at the stake as an alien from outer space? And probably
he forgot to tell you why he was at the monastery in the first place. Running
from a tax-evasion charge. Castile demanded he turn himself in or they would
expropriate his lands. Pretended he was writing some behind-the-scenes crap
about the Council. He planned to follow the procession up the peninsula, make
himself useful to a bishop or two, so that when they reached Lyon he'd have
friends to support his plea to the Holy Father."

"So why invent this tale about murder?" Master Siger felt genuinely
confused. "And why tell me? Does he really expect me to do something?"

"We're all expected to do something. All the time. It's the nature of human
existence and a precondition of Salvation. Judgement by action. Don't just stand
there, do something. As for the question, why you? Are you being intentionally
naive? In his eyes at least, who else would be likely to believe his bullshit and
dig around on Brother Thomas's behalf? The man's been dead three years, most
everybody don't even remember his name. Except for you. You're the only one

to care one way or the other. You have remained faithful to your most vigorous opponent. You have maintained his memory as Brother Thomas would have wished. No wonder you keep getting into trouble. "

Street lights appeared, and Siger recognized they had reached the edge of Avignon. Master Siger looked back. Their escort was gone.

"So, tell me what you two love-birds talked about."

Master Siger knew that within a few minutes they would be driving through the center of town and into the Palace grounds.

"Seems like you already know most of it. Just about the food-poisoning of the boy from the village. He seemed to know something more, but he was very nervous."

Frère Jacques smiled. "That's how he hooks you. Pretends that what he knows is so important he can't tell it to you. He's slick. And he's smart. His on-the-scene news stories around Brother Thomas's death and then his funeral got him exposure everywhere. By the time the gravy-train got to Lyon, His Holiness was ready to grant him anything. Even Castile had to back down. 'abd Al-Malik turned over a miserable little farm in the hills north of Madrid and the Crown forgave all outstanding tax obligations. He's one slick bastard, I tell you."

They drove rapidly along narrow, winding streets. The heart of the city was deeply asleep. "By the way, not to change the subject," Frère Jacques spoke without looking at him, "but it seems there's been a change of plans. The debauched citizens of Rome have been listening to the worst demagogues, and now they're holding His Holiness responsible for every little thing that goes wrong. As if the Bishop of Rome could cure every ill. So we're going to hold over at Orvieto for a while."

Master Siger said nothing, still confused and depressed, and now wondering when he might see Mistress Marguerite again. "Terrific town," Frère Jacques said. "And there's Etruscan graves there. Ever heard of those guys? The Etruscans are deep people. They were these druids who spoke some Celtic language and they were the first magicians, and they could fly. Very profound people. Just by using their minds they could make a car driving by blow up. And nobody can read their language. They were actually space aliens related to the aliens who lived on Atlantis and flew in rocket ships. I hope you're impressed."

"None of that is true," Master Siger said flatly.

"So what?" Frère Jacques said. They drove up the ramp and through the gates of the palace. The palace was utterly dark and seemed abandoned as Frère

Jacques brought the car to a stop. "The question is not truth. The question is, do I believe it."

"And Mistress Marguerite? What about her?"

Frère Jacques turned off the engine, Master Siger listened to it tick quietly as it cooled down. Frère Jacques sat still for a moment, then turned slowly to face Master Siger. "Forget her. She's in a whole other world. Just forget her. She's so completely different from you and me it isn't even worth the thinking." Master Siger thought about this as he got out of the car.

Frère Jacques accompanied him through the palace to the floor of his room. "Try to get some sleep," he told Master Siger. "Every day in the company of the Pope is a busy day."

As Siger followed the corridor hung with thick, dark tapestries, he considered its utter silence. Each firmly closed door he passed could be a barrier that simply disguised another conspiracy. Though he could not be certain why, his sense of loss and regret over Mistress Marguerite suddenly overwhelmed him and left him depressed. But when finally he reached his room, he saw a slender band of yellow light glowing under his door. Thrilled he would find Mistress Marguerite inside waiting for him, he swung the door open wide.

In a chair reading his breviary by candlelight sat His Holiness, Pope Nicholas III. He looked up as Master Siger opened the door. "Ah," he said with pleasure, "you've returned at last." He smiled brightly. In the candle light, the creases in the Pope's face gave his grin a look of avuncular affection. The glint of his wire-rim glasses reminded Master Siger of Santa Claus.

"Please," His Holiness said, "close the door. Come and sit down." He pointed to the chair across from his. He marked the page and closed his breviary, then placed it on the table between the two chairs. "I've waited quite a while for your return. I'm told you've had a busy day. No doubt you want very badly to sleep. And believe me, I do not wish to deprive you." The Pope poured wine from a bottle into two glasses on the table. While he took a glass for himself, he slid the second toward the other chair. "There are just two or three things I must ask about your undoubtedly exciting adventure. And I'd like to hear about it while your memory is fresh. But please, drink up."

Master Siger knelt and kissed the Pope's ring, then he sat down in the chair, took up the glass and emptied half the wine at once. He returned the glass to the table, folded his hands and sat back. "What has become of Mistress Marguerite?"

The Pope's smile broadened. "Of course, I should have expected that question. A charming and remarkable woman. I've known her since she was a child. Her uncles supported my nomination for the Keys of Saint Peter. Remarkable people, her family. But I expect she's moved on. She accomplished the task I set her, and now she is on her own, free to do what she wants. I have heard she is considering an invitation to join a convent in Ireland. Apparently there are monasteries there eager to acquire her services. In any case, please don't bother yourself about her. Believe me, she is as remarkably resilient as she is utterly fearless."

Master Siger remained silent. After a moment His Holiness nodded slightly as if he had come to a decision. "Perhaps I can find a way to get word to her, if you'd like to send her a message." When Master Siger said nothing, the Pope continued. "Allow me to change the subject and ask you to recall that you met with a certain 'abd al-Malik." Master Siger struggled to keep surprise from his expression. "I expect Frère Jacques asked one or two questions about your discussion. What exactly did he want to know?"

Master Siger decided to tell the Pope as little as he had told Frère Jacques. "His interest was vague and general. He only asked if 'abd Al-Malik told me anything new about Brother Thomas's death."

It was the Pope's turn to appear surprised. "And what exactly did you tell him?"

Master Siger paused, debating how far to co-operate. "It seemed I only confirmed what he already knew. That 'abd al-Malik had been present for the dinner and that later he had heard a rumor about a young servant dying of a mysterious ailment."

The Pope studied Master Siger's face. Master Siger decided he had said too much to someone, and couldn't decide to whom. Suddenly, as if relieved, the Pope smiled. "Our Frère Jacques is a remarkable character, don't you think?" He took up his glass and drank. Master Siger drank with him. When he returned his glass to the table, His Holiness refilled it.

Smiling, His Holiness said, "You appeared utterly distracted at our lunch the other day when the discussion moved to international politics. I take it you do not concern yourself with that sort of thing."

"Was it so obvious?" Master Siger asked.

"But let me ask you one more question. I've been told that you and Frère Jacques were detained by our esteemed brothers, the Franciscan Highway Patrol. Tell me, was their meeting harmonious and fraternal?" The Pope continued to smile, while his eyes seemed to study Master Siger's face even more intensely.

"Put simply," Siger said, "Frère Jacques had a few choice words for the officers and then adopted a ruse to avoid their scrutiny." His Holiness's eyebrows rose with interest. Master Siger described what happened and what part he played. When he finished, His Holiness laughed.

"A rare character. No doubt about it. Products of the Cistercian brotherhood always seem to have a bit more resourcefulness about them. They conduct themselves as independent agents, yet all share the same ideals and objectives." His Holiness paused as if preoccupied. "Getting back to your deplorable disinterest in politics, suppose I told you our Frère Jacques is deeply embedded in a curious alignment of interests."

Master Siger took a deep breath. "Your Holiness occupies the very center of the attention of every Christian in the world. It is not difficult to recognize that such a powerful center would attract the attention of other circles. And Your Holiness does not seem above the expedient of granting a service in exchange for a service."

The Pope shrugged and looked away. "It is not mere expediency. Where the Holy See derives a benefit, that benefit must first and always be granted to Holy Mother Church Herself. If an alliance does not benefit the Church and Our Flock, then there is no true or lasting benefit."

"Do you suggest that some among our fraternity are in league against His Holiness?"

The Pope sighed as if Siger's question possessed weight and bulk. "The Papacy is under attack from many sides. You and your philosopher friends are the least of our troubles. Heresy is merely bad public relations. But when fights break out between ordinary clergy and mendicants, the money stops flowing. Rich merchants start leaving all their earthly possessions to cock-eyed religious fanatics instead of that Church which baptized them and nurtured them and promised eternal salvation for their souls in the presence of Jesus Christ. This is more than a public relations difficulty. So, yes, there is dissension within our congregation. The conflicts between the religious orders have proven a terrible burden. Factions compete for Church leadership supported and directed by earthly rulers for their own benefit. Our beloved predecessors have left the Church a heavy burden of factionalism and political meddling."

The Holy Father drank down his wine and refilled his glass. "These are difficult times. The Holy See can ill-afford to lose the opportunity to use every talent available. Frère Jacques has proved invaluable in several delicate situations.

Still, we must remember that not all of his objectives are necessarily in the best interest of Holy Mother Church." He leaned forward, lifted the bottle and slowly refilled Master Siger's glass. "So I have a request to make."

"Will it be possible for me to refuse?" Master Siger asked.

His Holiness looked deeply into Master Siger's eyes, the lines of his face seemed to shift. "It is always possible to refuse. Our Christian brothers and sisters devoured by lions under the eyes of the Roman tyrants could have renounced their faith and refused their martyrdom. The real question is, refusal to what end? And if I told you your refusal could bring down the entire Church, would you even consider it?"

Master Siger smiled. "Martyrdom does not fit my profile. Suppose we begin by your telling me the plan."

His Holiness paused as if in a moment of debate. "The kingdoms of Europe sleep with their swords drawn. Crowned heads conspire to divide up Papal lands and Papal alliances. But most dangerously, the Papal prerogatives to negotiate and arbitrate disputes between Christian nations have begun to lose their grip. The Christian world sways on the brink of an anarchy that only the all-embracing arms of Holy Mother Church can prevent. Only the Christian Church can ameliorate those conflicts that threaten to set Christian against Christian in a race to spill the most Christian blood."

"These are issues far beyond my skill or knowledge," Master Siger pleaded. "I am utterly ignorant of these diplomatic forces at work. I am further ignorant of the powers supporting these threats. There must be others more suited to your need."

The Pope hesitated and then shook his head. "I call for help from every man of rare knowledge, whenever that knowledge will advance our cause. And not knowledgeable merely of economics, or military strategy, or political history. My need is for counsel that is innocent of political ambition. Holy Mother Church must disentangle herself from this web of conflicting interests She has been sewn into. And to accomplish this I need clear and methodical thought. I need exceptional analytical skills. Because you are comfortable thinking outside the opinions of others, you offer guidance few others could provide."

Master Siger leaned forward and took up the wine bottle, refilled both of their glasses. Then he picked up his own glass and drank. "While I would joyously live in a world ennobled by that Peace of His Universal Church, suppose you tell me how I will directly benefit."

His Holiness smiled with relief. "Had you not asked, I would need to question the wisdom of my choice. Of course you will have no official title or official position. Your controversial views are too well-known and would merely complicate matters. However, you will remain in the comfort and security of my residence so that our counsels will be conducted privately. Meanwhile, the resources of the Holy See will be at your disposal. In addition to your help in counsel, I expect you wish to continue your questionable philosophic speculations. We will provide time and accommodations to pursue those studies. And if you so wish, everything you write will be clandestinely published by a disreputable printer in Amsterdam under a pseudonym and false imprint."

Master Siger could not ignore his own mistrust. "Suppose I agree to all this, but a year from now I decide to quit. What happens then?"

His Holiness's look became suddenly grim. "Should you accept this offer, and it seems impossible that you will not, I will inform you when your services are no longer needed. Let me remind you, my wish to keep you here is only for the benefit of Our Holy Mother Church. Brother Thomas, whose broad shoulders would have carried all of us out of this darkness, is no longer with us." The Pope sighed, and for a moment closed his eyes. When he opened them again he smiled. "So I suppose that leaves us stuck with the likes of you."

"How much time do I have to consider this request?"

The Pope rubbed his eyes and then yawned. "Pardon me, Master Siger. It is late and I am tired, as I expect you are as well." He stood slowly, picked up his breviary and slipped it into the folds of his robes. "You have until I reach that door to agree. Good night, Master Siger, and sleep well." Pope Nicholas III turned lifting his shoulders as if shifting a great weight. For a moment, it was as if Master Siger could see the burden of his years piled onto his back. And as if he recognized Master Siger's thoughts, His Holiness smiled. "A fellow learns a lot being pope."

Before His Holiness had taken a second step, Master Siger stood. "I am grateful for this opportunity to serve that Church which has nurtured and sustained and supported me in this life, and which assures my salvation in the next."

His Holiness nodded saying, "You will find this is not a bad place to spend your time. And intangible rewards can turn suddenly tangible right before your eyes." Master Siger knelt and kissed his ring. His Holiness closed the door as he left.

Master Siger trembled with confusion. What His Holiness had explained seemed unlikely, not the least being the Pope's insistence on his respect and concern. Yet, Master Siger decided the man had been earnest in his request. Master Siger tossed all of the conflicting possibilities together in his mind. If there were truly a choice to be made, he was willing to try it.

His accumulated exhaustion attacked Master Siger so suddenly he could hardly keep his eyes open as he undressed. He brought the candle to his bedside and crawled under the blankets. Suddenly the door to his room opened.

A black-robed figure whose cowl was drawn completely over its face, and its hands hidden within sleeves, moved slowly through the shadows of his room until it reached the side of the bed and it stopped beside the table and candle. The figure loomed over Master Siger, though the face remained completely hidden. Then the figure shivered. In a moment the robes opened and fell to the floor. Mistress Celestina, in her fairest, most naked and unadorned splendor, stood before him. She said, "I hear you'll be staying around for a while."

"Seems that way."

"Then we must both consider ourselves lucky." Thick, golden curls danced beside her face as she laughed. "On a whim I decided to drop by. I didn't think you'd mind." She leaned down then and blew out the candle.

A Perfect Decision Which Neither History Nor Master Siger Could Dispute, Let the Curtain Fall.

CHAPTER THE TWELFTH

LET THE SALACIOUS HAND of History Conjure the Dreaming, Opaque Eyes of Master Siger of Brabant Opening Gradually, Hesitantly, Reluctantly From a Warm and Sheltering Bed onto a Grey and Hostile World.

In a moment he realized he was looking out through his chamber's window. The sky resembled the rippled underbelly of an angry grey beast, threatening cold and rain and more darkness. And then he discovered the undraped figure of Celestina, Mistress of Computerology and Conjurer of the Database. She stood with her back to Siger, her chin in her hand and her elbows propped on the window sill, looking up to the sky. Thick golden hair cascaded in undulating waves down her sinuous, brightly pale back to her glorious opalescent globosity. As if speaking to the world beyond the window, with a sigh she said, "You don't need a weatherman to know it's going to be a lousy day." When she turned, her green eyes were bright with pleasure.

"Lousy days come and lousy days go."

"On the other hand," she said suppressing a smile, "we could turn this dismal and dolorous day into a learning experience." Master Siger studied her undulant and vivacious unclothed form in the pearl grey light with dumb amazement, and his member stirred.

She stepped away from the window and moved toward the bed with easy grace. Her bright blond hair billowed beside her smiling cheeks, and her high, firm breasts seemed to float before her chest. With a charming smirk she said, "His Holiness thinks you're a pretty clever guy. So, tell me what you know about algorithms."

Master Siger watched, unsure of what he heard, but mesmerized by the pleasure of observing each of her approaching steps. He said, "That mathematical stuff I always left to Boetius. But he talked to me about them."

When Mistress Celestina reached the edge of the bed she crawled slowly across it cat-like on her hands and knees toward Master Siger while staring into his eyes. "Suppose," she said teasingly, "you and I spend the rest of the day in bed watching movies and smoking dope so that I can teach you all that someone in your exalted philosophical station ought to know about algorithms. How does that sound?"

"I don't know what station you're referring to, but this is a remarkable coincidence," Master Siger said. "For days I've been thinking that it was long past time I learned everything I could about algorithms." Celestina leaned past him and pulled the bell-rope. As she reached up, her breast drew close to Master Siger's lips, and he did not resist its temptation.

Mistress Celestina laughed. "Breakfast first," she said. Then from the night-stand beside the bed she took a small cigarette box, sat cross-legged in the center of the bed and balanced it on her ankles. Out of the box she took rolling papers and a bag. There was a quiet knock at the door. Without looking up, Mistress Celestina called out, "Angelique?"

"Yes, mistress," she answered in a voice hardly above a whisper. When the door opened, Siger discovered that the small, soft voice belonged to an even smaller woman. She entered and then stopped to stand just beside the door. Oval-faced with large dark eyes, her hair was long and nearly black, and by the smoothness of her pale skin she appeared to be very young. Without looking up and with her fingers continuing to work, Celestina said, "Please bring us some breakfast, and include fruit and wine." With an intimidated glance toward Master Siger, Angelique bowed and closed the door.

"The basis of the algorithmic function," Celestina began as if addressing the white cigarette paper held in her slim, pale fingers, "was first introduced by 'al-Khwarazmi in his book *Algoritmi de Numero Indorium*, written in Persian around 850 AD, and then translated into Latin about fifty years ago. In this truly marvelous book he introduced many fundamental advances in mathematics, including a numeral system that uses zero, and the first extensive discussion of algebra. This single work revolutionized Western mathematical science." Then she looked up. "But of course, you already knew all that."

Master Siger nodded. Though he was familiar with the book he was loath to interrupt his gorgeous lecturer. "No offense, but do you plan on lighting that thing sometime today?" With a surly grin Celestina continued as if he had not spoken.

"After that one book everything mathematical, from double-entry bookkeeping and accounting to computers and space-travel, became possible. The entire world around us is a direct result of the mathematical universe conjured by that single book." As she spoke, Celestina's shoulders trembled with excitement. "Of course, bits of the mathematics were older than the Greeks, but no one had ever thought to assemble all of it in one source." The movements and contours of her unadorned flesh made Master Siger breathe slowly. "All of it gathered and organized by a single mind's brilliant insight." With the white joint completed and held aloft in one hand Mistress Celestina laughed with delight. The way her body moved caused Siger to gasp.

After another knock at the door, Angelique entered without waiting as she pushed a loaded breakfast cart. Mistress Celestina asked, "Angelique, have you been introduced to Master Siger of Brabant?"

Angelique curtseyed with a coy smile. "No," she said. Nodding toward Master Siger she muttered, "It is my pleasure to serve."

"Master Siger," Celestina announced with a darkly serious tone, "is the only person in this palace unlikely to pinch your bottom." Angelique laughed, one hand covering her mouth, as she backed out of the room and then closed the door behind her.

Before the door had completely closed Master Siger called out with a tone of injured feelings, "Not necessarily." He turned then, reached toward the cart and poured coffee into two cups. To Celestina he said, "Before we continue, at least tell me what has led you to decide to educate me in the ways of the algorithm? What do you expect me to find interesting about this mystery of mathematical logic?"

Mistress Celestina lit the joint and passed it to Master Siger. "First and foremost, I know yours is the appropriate sort of inquisitive mind. So I know you will be intrigued because this is an intrinsically interesting form of expression, possessing a beauty that becomes obvious with even casual contemplation." Master Siger smoked from the joint and then passed it back to Celestina.

As she took it she said, "But I have another reason, and this reason will appeal to you as a philosopher. The method of solution to algorithmic functions is easily recognized as a higher form of algebraic logic." She took the cup of coffee offered by Master Siger in one hand, and passed back the joint with the other. "As just one example, consider the function of nesting. The setting of a piece of instruction within a larger and more elaborate piece of instruction resembles the placement of an algebraic operation within parentheses in an algebraic equation." Her large eyes looked into Master Siger's with an expectant gaze, curious and excited, as if waiting for him to be as aroused and delighted by this notion as she was, and join in her excitement.

Master Siger sipped his coffee and thoughtfully chewed his croissant. Finally he asked, "So tell me before this gets any deeper, what movie do you want to watch?"

Mistress Celestina pouted as she sipped from her cup. "First I get to tell you about algorithms for a while. Then we'll watch a movie."

Master Siger leaned back smiling, and with his free hand stroked her thigh. "Fair enough. Begin, then, at the beginning."

With the hyperbolic enthusiasm of a used-car salesman, Mistress Celestina began by describing control structures. While Master Siger alternated stokes along one of her thighs and then the other, Mistress Celestina described the operations of sequencing and branching. Then she moved on to the operation of iteration. She took a pillow from the head of the bed and leaned back. "Iterations are of two types: bounded, and unbounded, or conditional, if you prefer." She closed her eyes and with a dreamy smile explained that through iteration, an operation could be repeated either a specified number of times, or until some unspecified number of times yields a specified resultant. Only an infinite iteration is excluded.

The grey light from the window created silver highlights around the hollows of her throat and along the fine bones of her shoulders. Her skin beneath Siger's hand was warm. She continued, "We have now reviewed the basic control structures. They all can be combined in nested loops, where a loop is defined as a cycled internal activity, iterated some non-infinite number of times, and whose resultant is inserted into a sequence of further activity until commanded to stop."

Mistress Celestina slowly opened her eyes and then sat up. She leaned forward, took Master Siger's hands into hers and drew him toward her. "I am confident you are now prepared to penetrate that most transcendent of mysteries, the bubblesort." Master Siger smiled, leaned down and then with a growl pushed his face between her thighs. Mistress Celestina laughed and fell back onto her pillow.

Later they watched a movie chosen by Siger where the hero searched for the murderer of his partner, a man he did not like very much but felt obligated to revenge. Master Siger asked if they could watch the movie with the sound turned off.

"What good is that?" Mistress Celestina asked as she dipped thin slices of the peach Master Siger had cut for her into her glass of wine, and then ate them, red wine and golden peach syrup sparkling around her soft mouth. "How can you tell what's going on if you don't know what the characters are saying?"

Without answering, Master Siger stood and turned the sound of the video off, then returned to the bed. He sat down behind her running his hands along her sides up to her arms and then down again. "You promised me the mysteries of bubblesort." When he reached her arms again he slid his hands over her breasts. Slowly he moved his hands in circles, trailing his fingertips lightly. Mistress Celestina reached her arms back above her head, locking her hands across the back of Master Siger's neck.

"Bubblesort: a fundamental sorting algorithm that involves an un-ordered but finite set of elements. It is based on the fact that any list, traversed in sequence a single element at a time, such that each element is compared, and where possible, reordered sequentially with an adjacent element, can be repeated until a total reordering of the list into a certain predetermined order is established."

Mistress Celestina rolled onto her side as her back nestled against Master Siger's chest, then described the intricacies of goto. While he stroked her back, she explained the schematic conventions of a flowchart. At the conclusion of goto, Master Siger embraced her from behind while she moved onto her knees.

They finished making love and then watched another movie. In this one, the hero's best friend turned out to be a criminal, and it became the hero's mission to bring him to justice.

When this movie ended, Mistress Celestina said, "Our discussion of the enumeration categories and operations has merely prepared us for the heart of the algorithm: the subroutine. By definition, a subroutine must have a specific parameter by which it will stop its operation. Each subroutine is invoked, and once completed, fades back into sequence while the next is called. And the heart of these subroutines is recursion, a sort of formal iteration taken to another level of domain."

"You really want to keep telling me this?" Master Siger suddenly asked. He turned, sliced a piece of cheese and then placed it on a small piece of bread.

Mistress Celestina's sparkling blue eyes widened with a look of surprise. "I thought you were the sort of person who would appreciate all of this formal elegance. It's a beautiful thing. Take a step back, and you'll recognize the power of its beauty. It's also the way some AI theorists expect to reproduce human thinking. That's pretty interesting all by itself. I simply assumed you would be fascinated." Mistress Celestina hesitated, as if expecting Siger's response. When he remained silent she lifted her nose slightly into the air. "Anyway, I love it. The way it elaborates itself into arabesques of information thrills me."

Finally Master Siger laughed. "Forget I asked and let's move on to whatever's next."

Mistress Celestina grinned. "Just tell me when you've had enough. I never have a problem finding a man curious about algorithms." She reached across the bed until her back arched, glistening in the ashen twilight, and she lifted the wine bottle and refilled his glass. "Now that we have arrived at flowchart, we can resolve the mysteries of data-types and structures, and variables as well. And then we can enumerate the various arrays: vectors or lists, as one-dimensional arrays, and tables as two-dimensional arrays. And there are two additional variations of the list-type, or one-dimensional, array: the queue, and the stack."

Master Siger studied her eyes, waiting to discover if this was all some odd joke, or if she was actually serious. Finally he asked, "What movie should we watch next?"

"Will we only watch this one, or will we hear it as well?"

"If you need a change of pace, I could watch you and listen to the movie."

Accompanied by extensive fondling, they watched a film in which the hero discovered his wife cheating on him. But instead of leaving her, he decides to get revenge. It was a comedy but Mistress Celestina laughed at the most unlikely moments. Master Siger could not decide if she laughed because of what she saw on the screen, or the enthusiasm of his caresses. When the film was over he embraced her again with romantic intent. She continued to laugh, but her interest quickened as he pressed hard against her body. His passion seemed to surprise her, and her response was enthusiastic. Afterward, they slept.

When he opened his eyes again, the quality of the light had changed. Despite its overcast and depressing unevenness, he knew they were well into afternoon. And evening would fall soon and quickly. Mistress Celestina lay asleep breathing heavily beside him. At rest in their watery light, her face seemed luminous. The curled rim of her upper lip gave a tender and pouting contour to her profile. Soft, wavy locks of her golden hair caressed her face. With one finger he lightly stroked the side of her face beside her ear. Quietly he asked, "What do you know about Brother Thomas?"

Mistress Celestina's eyes fluttered open and then she squinted sleepily against the light. "Did you fall asleep, too? I'm hungry. Did you just ask me something?"

"I asked what you know about Brother Thomas. I want to know what you know about how he died." Master Siger continued to smile.

Confused, Mistress Celestina seemed even lovelier. She laughed uncomfortably. "I have no idea what you're talking about."

"You do," Master Siger insisted. "That's why I'm here. And that's why you're here. I know something, and you have come here to keep me from realizing it. I already know the answer, I just haven't thought of the question yet. And you are here to keep me from recognizing it."

"That's a pretty crazy idea." There was mild surprise blended with concern around her eyes. "Besides, why would I get myself involved in something like that?"

"Maybe I'm supposed to believe you're not intended to realize you're involved. Maybe you're supposed to believe I really care about this algorithm stuff."

Celestina's eyes took on an injured look. "You mean you're not really interested in anything I've told you?"

Master Siger smiled. "I want to know what you won't tell me."

Mistress Celestina studied his eyes and after a brief smile, covered her body with the bed-sheet to her throat. "That's a lot of questions that have nothing to do with algorithmic functions. Are you always this grumpy when you wake up hungry?"

Master Siger studied her face. It was a beautiful face that refused to tell him anything. "Suppose I suggest that all of this, including the charade of instruction in symbolic logic, has been executed simply to keep me in this room. And further, that you have been convinced by someone that keeping me here is for my own good, to protect me from some danger."

Mistress Celestina's sudden burst of laughter surprised Master Siger, and it continued for a while. "You must be as hungry as I am. I'll ring for Angelique. These delusions of yours will make perfect topics for dinner conversation." She let the bed-sheet fall away as she reached for the bell-rope just above her head. Her movements struck Master Siger as so artlessly unself-conscious he could not resist smiling, or doubting himself.

"While we're waiting," she said, "we'll choose a movie to watch. And this time with the sound turned up."

"We'll watch with the sound turned down so that we can continue our discussion of the death of Brother Thomas."

"I'll meet you half-way," Mistress Celestina said smiling coyly. "We'll leave the sound turned down. But since I know nothing about the death of Brother Thomas, I'll tell you all about trees."

Master Siger sighed with frustration. There was a knock at the door and Mistress Celestina called out, "Angelique?" Without answering, the dark-haired woman opened the door and entered the room.

"There you are," Mistress Celestina said to Master Siger. To Angelique she said, "He hasn't stopped talking about you since this morning. It has been all I could do to keep him distracted from lascivious thoughts about you. The things he has said make even me blush. I don't know whether you should feel flattered or frightened."

Angelique's face became red, and again she covered her smiling lips with her hand. Startled, Master Siger said, "That is absolutely not true."

Mistress Celestina's eyes widened with disbelief. "Spoken like a true and gallant gentleman. You like to make a girl feel appreciated." She turned to Angelique. "He has even suggested that both of us come to bed with him together. Have you ever heard anything so outrageous? It appears to be an obsession with him. Of course, I assured him you are not that kind of girl. But will he listen to me?" She turned to face Master Siger with a look of innocent surprise.

Confused, Master Siger said, "Could we decide on dinner first, and continue this discussion later?"

Mistress Celestina smiled with triumph. When she asked Angelique to bring their dinner she added, "And I expect that it will be you who brings our meal." Then she winked at Angelique. Still blushing, Angelique curtseyed and left, closing the door behind her.

When she had gone, Master Siger asked, "What was that all about?"

Mistress Celestina smiled. "Not what you think." Then turning she asked, "Shall we watch a movie and talk about trees, or will we turn up the sound of the movie we watch? Or perhaps you have something else in mind?" She reached her hand under the bed-sheets and grasped a part of Master Siger. Invigorated by the fantasy of these two women in bed with him together,

Master Siger responded with enthusiasm. When finally they lay side by side, breathless and glistening with sweat, they heard a quiet knock at the door. The timing of the interruption left Siger wondering if whoever it was had waited listening to them. The door opened and Master Siger was surprised to see their meal cart pushed by an older, dour-looking woman. Mistress Celestina smiled at his surprise.

Master Siger could only laugh. "I suppose I will now hear about trees."

The woman departed with a bow. Mistress Celestina asked, "Did you think the evening would end without my telling you all you could wish to know about them?" She took the flagon of wine from the cart and filled two cups.

Without waiting for his response Celestina continued, "Trees are also referred to as hierarchies. A tree is simply a hierarchy of data. Data-trees have a root and offspring, and can be most easily visualized as inverted compared with the trees of nature. But just as with the Lord's trees, our data tree has leaves, or nodes, and branches, or alternate paths. But trees are not limited to data. Any sequence in an algorithmic series can be represented as tree-like. In fact, they represent the special kinds of structure found in most of the useful algorithms."

"How fascinating," Master Siger said, glancing from Mistress Celestina's breasts to the silent video image of two men shooting guns at each other. "So what you're saying is that trees are our friends."

"Be frivolous if you must. Having broached the subject of trees, we must move on to tree-sort. As with all sort-routines, it is actually a sequence of recursive subroutines. Thus, if vectors and arrays represent data structures, and loops and nested loops are control structures, then all tress fall into the group of recursive routines. One of the beauties of recursive routines is that they can be structured to affect self-adjustment in response to demands on the performance of the algorithm. Are you as excited as I am yet?"

Master Siger realized he was more concerned with Mistress Celestina's breasts than either trees or those men shooting their guns on the video. He asked, "Didn't you say something about rolling another joint?"

She reached for the bag and the rolling papers. "All of the effort expended to create structures and routines that is at the heart of the algorithm has a single purpose, which is to give us the ability to query a database. Databases are themselves structures. Some use relational models for arrangements of data into larger blocks or tables, others work hierarchically in networks or multi-layered tree-like organizations. But the purpose is the same: to be able to take fragments and create reliable and useful wholes. This is the way simple data becomes knowledge. All structuring is intended to process information into knowledge. Kind of like making sausage."

"Bravo!" Master Siger said with his mouth full of chicken. "Masterful summary of an obscure and sophisticated science. I am awestruck at your precision of mind and eloquence of tongue. Let me be only one among the undoubted many to praise your grasp of subtle distinctions in logic and epistemology."

Mistress Celestina blushed and lowered her eyes in acknowledgment of Master Siger's praise. "With all respect due the most subtle mind since Brother Thomas, you and I have hardly scratched the surface. After all, I have yet to address the issue of syntax."

Master Siger wiped his lips with a cloth with one hand, while the other caressed Mistress Celestina's thigh. "No doubt we will plunge into even darker waters momentarily. But let me pause and survey the marvelous landscape you have revealed to me." He took the joint from Mistress Celestina's fingers and lit it.

They watched the end of the film where, as a finale, everyone in the film shot everyone else. When the credits began to appear it was impossible to see if anyone was still alive.

"That wasn't very good," Mistress Celestina said, though Siger could only hope she referred to the movie.

"How could you tell, with the sound turned down?" Master Siger's hand became adventurous.

"It's hard to imagine a stretch of dialogue that would have justified all that shooting."

"Hard, but not impossible," Master Siger said. His free hand became engaged.

"Impossibility is sometimes impossible to prove." After a moment Mistress Celestina asked, "Tell me seriously, would you really like to be in bed with two women?"

Master Siger laughed. "How serious should one be in bed? Besides, isn't it true that to be in bed with one woman is to be in bed with all women?"

Mistress Celestina's eyes widened with shock. She moved her legs away from Master Siger's caresses. "You are most generous with your compliments tonight. Perhaps hurting someone's feelings is as far as your technique for seduction goes."

"Wrong answer, right?" Master Siger asked thoroughly baffled.

Mistress Celestina studied his eyes. "What you don't know will kill you." Then she took his hand and placed it on her breast. "The naive are the most dangerous, so they break the most hearts." She sighed, leaned forward into his hand and closed her eyes. "I was certainly right to keep Angelique out of your cruel clutches."

"But not yours."

"Forewarned is forearmed. My experience suggests that time and indulgence have already rendered you incorrigible."

"But, on the other hand?" Master Siger prompted optimistically.

"On the other hand, if you demonstrated unusual remorse for your cavalier attitude, I might discover a reason to reconsider. After all, you are not entirely without charm."

Master Siger hovered over her with his lips close to her ear. Mistress Celestina opened her eyes and looked back into his. Outside the window, the darkness was thick, sculpted with broad strokes. He said, "Have we finished with algorithms for the day?" Her embrace was sudden and passionate. The smell of her skin warmed him like wine and his head seemed to float as he returned her embrace. Later, while Mistress Celestina slept, he drew the blanket over them both and blew out the candle. He fell into a deep sleep almost immediately.

Suddenly he realized he was being shaken by the shoulder. A voice whispered, "Hurry and get dressed." When he opened his eyes, a black-robed shape hovered in the darkness beside his bed. "You've got three minutes to get your clothes on. Let's go." The whispering voice belonged to Mistress Celestina.

"What's going on?"

Mistress Celestina hissed, "Be quiet and get dressed. If you value your life, get dressed right now and follow me."

His legs felt soft beneath him. The darkness was complete and maneuvering within it made him dizzy. With Mistress Celestina's urging, he managed to dress quickly.

From somewhere in her habit Mistress Celestina brought out a small flashlight and turned it on. She shielded the light with one hand and began walking toward the door.

The door opened suddenly. Filling the small disc of light Angelique stood just inside the door, and in her hand she held a large knife. "Stay where you are, please," she said quietly. She was not smiling.

Mistress Celestina stepped forward. With a slashing blow from her hand she knocked the knife to the floor. On the backhand she struck Angelique hard across the mouth. "Fool!" she snarled. Cringing from an expected second blow, Angelique cowered in a corner beside the door. "Stay there and don't make a sound." Then she ushered Master Siger out.

In the dark hallway, Mistress Celestina locked the bedroom door behind them. "She'll be screaming in another minute. We should hurry." With their robes whispering in the still darkness, she led Master Siger down the stairs. At the bottom she led him through passageways and down more stairs in a dizzying sequence. Suddenly he realized they stood outside the Palace and in the open air.

Mistress Celestina whispered, "Hurry, please, we aren't there yet."

Breathless, he walked quickly to keep up with her. "Where are we going?"

"My esteemed Aristotelian," she spoke quietly as she walked, "lest Rome repeat the crime of Athens, we are getting you out of here. Now, no more questions."

Mistress Celestina led him through alleys and past storage barns, until they reached the Palace walls. "It's along here," she whispered. Moving slowly along the wall, they approached a stack of wooden shipping crates. "Help me move these," she said. Master Siger put his shoulder to the stack. It moved easily, as if all the crates were empty. Suddenly Mistress Celestina was on her knees. "Right here," she whispered, "we have to crawl. Pull the crates back as you come through." Then Mistress Celestina disappeared through the opening.

Master Siger had nearly to lie on his chest in the muddy, foul-smelling mess as he grasped the edges of the crates and dragged them back to cover the passage.

He emerged to find himself on a side-street in the lower city. Mistress Celestina stood beside him. The sky was starless and almost as black as the hills in the distance. "We have to get outside the city," she said, "and we've got a long way to go." With quick silent steps she began to walk. Master Siger hesitated. Some steps away, already invisible in the darkness, Mistress Celestina stopped. "Make up your mind. Follow me and save your life, or die." She did not wait for his answer, the hush of her footsteps faded into the darkness. Master Siger broke into a run, relieved to catch up to her.

"But where are we going?" he asked.

"You have friends," she said panting. "I am taking you to them. We cannot run and speak at the same time."

Down narrow streets and even smaller alleys, she led him quickly through the town, until they arrived at a small, unguarded gate. Beyond it, they hurried across fields that seemed familiar to Master Siger. Beside a small stream she turned, followed it through a stand of trees and along a path that took them toward hills glowering ahead. Suddenly she began to walk faster. "We must not be late. Please hurry yourself." Though Master Siger was now nearly running, he could not quite catch up with Mistress Celestina.

At a crest between two higher hills they began to descend. Master Siger could see nothing from their vantage point, except that the city laid dark and brooding behind them. Their descent brought them into deep woods. Approaching the bottom Mistress Celestina led him into even more dense trees, and he could hardly hold to the path.

Suddenly Master Siger found himself standing on the edge of a large, open field. Without pause, Mistress Celestina was already walking quickly. Emerging from the darkness, Master Siger made out a cluster of tress near the center of the field and Mistress Celestina seemed to be heading toward them. He broke into a full run until he caught up to her just beneath the trees. He leaned against the coarse bark of one, panting and dizzy. Mistress Celestina seemed completely calm and rested. She looked at the sky and then glanced at her wristwatch. "Not three minutes to spare."

Master Siger struggled to catch his breath. His blood roared in his ears and his breathing was loud with exhaustion. But suddenly he heard something: a sound like the wind rushing through far-off trees. Mistress Celestina looked up. The sound grew louder. Even in the darkness he could watch her smile. "You are a man of remarkable luck, Master Siger. Lucky to be alive, and lucky to have friends who want to keep you that way."

The sound quickly became a roar. Soon it seemed to be overhead, but Siger still could see nothing. Then a beam of light suddenly pierced the darkness to shine down on them. A moment later, a helicopter settled gently in the field beside the trees.

"Let's go," Mistress Celestina yelled over the noise. The rotors of the helicopter continued to turn slowly. She took his hand and led him toward the machine.

The front of the helicopter was a round glass bubble. Mistress Celestina opened the door and got in, turned and held the door open for Master Siger. "Hurry!"

"Where are we going?" he asked. Suddenly the pilot of the helicopter turned. Sitting at the controls was 'abd al-Malik. "Do not delay," he cried out over the roar of the motor. "Your friends are waiting for you."

"Ask no more questions," Mistress Celestina added. "Delay means death."

"We fly to Marseille," 'abd al-Malik said. "Then a freighter to Amsterdam."

Master Siger hesitated. "But I must not leave now. I am too close."

"Are you insane?" Mistress Celestina screamed. Even in the darkness he saw concern distort her face.

"The truth is in my grasp," he insisted. "I am near the solution of the mystery of Brother Thomas' death. I cannot turn away." To 'abd al-Malik he said, "Why are you doing this?"

"The only good reason there is," he answered. "Money."

"And who is paying you?"

"Boetius of Dacia!"

"But he is dead!" Master Siger said.

"Alive enough to pay to get you out," 'abd al-Malik answered. "Now, let's go!" Master Siger hesitated. 'abd al-Malik said, "You have five seconds."

But Master Siger stood frozen, his desires torn and shredded and flapping in the wind, his confusion a roaring inside his head louder than that of the helicopter.

'abd al-Malik slammed the door shut and then the motor suddenly howled. Master Siger glanced through the glass bubble and into the eyes of Mistress Celestina. For a moment he thought he saw something glitter. The helicopter rose quickly, blowing dust into his eyes. Siger could not watch the helicopter but could only follow its sound. Gradually that sound faded.

When finally he cleared his eyes, he saw that a dozen black shapes surrounded him moving quickly across the field toward him. Master Siger decided he had once again made the wrong decision.

When the first dark shape reached him, Master Siger recognized his robes as Franciscan. The faceless voice asked, "Did you believe you had a choice?"

"Do you believe that you have a choice?" Master Siger asked.

"Questions are not answered by questions." When the others joined them, the group escorted Master Siger back to the gates of the Palace.

Once inside the Palace, two Franciscans continued as his escort. But instead of leading him back to his room, they took him through a section of the Palace he had not seen before. Along halls and through doors and up stairs and through additional halls, he followed them by the faintest of pale light. At the very top of the tower, his escorts led him into a small room, then left, closing the door behind him.

There was a couch and table and side chair near the center of this room, and bookshelves all around. The only light was from a single candle on the table. In the furthest shadow Master Siger made out a large writing desk. Suddenly a shadow-shrouded figure behind the desk stood up within the darkness, and took two steps toward the candle.

"Sorry to keep you from your sleep." The voice was smiling. "I needed to see you immediately. And now I must congratulate you on the wisdom of your decision." Even before Siger had made out the features of his face, he recognized Dr. Simon de Brion's voice.

Let the Talons of History Release Its Curtain and Spare Us the Witness to the Misery of Master Siger, A Fury of Regret and Despair Which Has Yet to Reach its Limit, Adrift in the Churning, Acid Perfidy of Sanctimonious Ambition.

CHAPTER THE THIRTEENTH

LET THE SILVER STYLUS of History Write in Sinewy Cursive Script on Panels of Brightly Polished Titanium that Master Siger Remained Still as Dr. Simon de Brion Emerged From the Sable Shadows That Surrounded Them.

De Brion took a seat on a chair across from Master Siger at the table that bore the single flaming candle. Simon de Brion's thick dark hair he wore short and fringed across his brow. Beneath his thick eyebrows his hard dark eyes seemed as empty as glass. Simon's dark face cast into shadows by the flickering candlelight revealed nothing. He spoke quietly.

"Too well do I recall the heady excitement a young man experiences when confronted with the terrible temptation to flee the confusion and contention surrounding him. Your decision to remain here with us demanded an extraordinary resistance. Your act was morally courageous, admirable and pleasing to God in every way. I offer my warmest congratulations."

Master Siger waited. De Brion continued. "Though this occasion of our meeting is less than ideal, your decision has provided us an opportunity to renew an old acquaintance." The faintest aroma of fatigue blew over Master Siger, and in a moment the pleasures of the day passed through his memory.

"Wish as we may for reconciliation," Siger finally said, "such is not always possible. Except through the Lord's total and eternal love for us." Master Siger turned his attention to Simon de Brion's hands, as if they might reveal what the man's expression withheld.

"Reconciliation is eternally available to all true believers," Simon said firmly. "Stray as far as we dare, the arms of the Church remain open and inviting. So please believe that my desire for accord is genuine."

"Though my deepest wish is that this be so," Siger said evenly, "my thoughts recall me to my present circumstance. I have been rejected by my superiors and sent here in exile. My work has been repudiated, burdened by accusations of heresy, and my friends and allies have been either imprisoned or have been forced to flee. Reconciliation demands reciprocity."

Simon de Brion laced his narrow, dry fingers together and placed them on the edge of the table. He leaned forward. The candlelight deepened the shadows and brightened the edges of his face. And then very slightly, he smiled. "For a washed-up professor possessing neither savings, nor wife nor friends, with just a single look around here I'd say you've done rather well for yourself."

Stung, Siger said nothing. After a moment Simon de Brion leaned back. "For reasons known only to himself, His Holiness has decided to place his faith in you."

Master Siger stifled a yawn. "But not completely."

Simon barely nodded and then continued. "Regardless of our shared past, it is only natural I should wish to renew an intimacy with someone held in such honor, and burdened with such responsibility. And to do this I am prepared to ignore all of those controversies that brought us into conflict in Paris. Let them fade into the mists of history, I say." De Brion's lips parted to reveal uneven grey teeth. Slowly he rubbed his hands together and his pale waxen fingers appeared almost alive. "If only that gesture affords me the opportunity to probe your fascinating mind. Without doubt all the Christian faithful will profit thereby."

"I am flattered by His Holiness' attention and confidence. And I assure you I will dedicate my best efforts to his service."

Simon de Brion's hands stopped moving and then folded upon each other like sleepy kittens. He sat back into his chair. "I confess I was greatly relieved that His Holiness decided to add you to his entourage of advisors."

Master Siger smirked. "How recent it was that some urged His Holiness to throw me into prison, and then execute me for heresy."

Simon de Brion grimaced. In the candlelight his expression made Siger shiver. "I never subscribed to that view. Nor, thankfully, did His Holiness. A few of us always knew we merely needed to speak with you in private and earnestly. So much would be resolved. And you bring such intelligence and experience to our struggle. We never abandoned the faith that eventually you would embrace your destiny and join in the Church's work."

Master Siger shifted certain he was being played a fool and annoyed he could not figure out how. "And once I had been separated from every colleague and supporter, my enlistment in those efforts became inevitable."

A look that could have been mistaken for sympathy played over Simon de Brion's eyes. "Many among us were confident of your value. Your decision tonight has been your recommendation. Respect for your mind is already universal. Admiration for your courage will spread just as widely. His Holiness has offered you a grave mission. He has asked you to take up that burden abandoned by Brother Thomas. Happily, yours is that powerful mind capable of illuminating areas of thought that continue to assault us from outside Christian dogma. But that mind must be determined to protect the health of its soul. And this, by your decision, you have shown."

Perplexed by the suggestion Siger said, "I can only be flattered by this display of your faith, since I can offer no obvious demonstration of my abilities."

"The Church has only survived because She instantly recognizes Her most valuable allies. Generals may plan great campaigns, but it is the soldier in the front-line who wins battles."

Master Siger forced a quiet laugh. "I am an even worse soldier than I am a general. Always turned to look in the wrong direction, at the wrong time, and at the wrong thing."

With a glint in his eyes that could have been generosity Simon de Brion tipped his head to one side. "There is so much about you that reminds me of a head-strong and impetuous young Brother Thomas. Without doubt you will hurl yourself recklessly against every bastion of heresy, never acknowledging the danger, or the cost, determined to defend your faith. I tell you now, Master Siger, the Church has terrible need for such zeal. We need your help, Master Siger, and I am not embarrassed to admit it. The fate of our mission on earth is in your hands."

Siger struggled to appear concerned. The fact that Simon de Brion had humbled himself, hiding and disguising his contempt for Master Siger, suggested how secure Siger was in the Pope's good opinion. It would not improve his security, however, to antagonize him or the Curia behind him.

"Our need is profound," Simon continued with dry despair. "You must not abandon us. You must not leave Holy Mother Church defenseless against marauding intellectual terrorists bent on the obliteration of Christ's work."

Now Master Siger could not resist laughing. "Surely you over-state the danger. No reasonable man could justify insisting Averroes or Avicenna or Maimonides or Brother Boetius or even Brother Thomas himself was any sort of intellectual terrorist. But that is what your unfortunate Condemnations have done. By insisting that, in order to continue their honorable researches, the schoolmen of Paris first needed the permission of the bishop of Paris, you robbed them of a gift given specifically to each by God Himself; his conscience. Guided by that supreme gift, each mind must investigate itself and that world it finds itself in, even at the risk of death. And this work, I insist, is holy to God."

Simon de Brion's smile reminded Master Siger how unlikely anything he was being told was true. "Youth is the only time appropriate for facing death without illusion. Upon finding oneself at the center of a great controversy, one might come to believe that certain acts are not merely desirable, but obligatory. Self-sacrifice occupies a high place in that arsenal of Christian weapons deployed against Evil." Simon de Brion paused suddenly. "But here we have been speaking and I have forgotten my manners. Let me offer you something to drink." He stood and stepped into the shadows to a small cabinet beside the desk, then returned carrying a crystal decanter of wine and two stemmed crystal glasses.

As Simon de Brion poured, Master Siger said, "I no longer believe Boetius of Dacia is dead." Though he watched Simon's face, the man betrayed no reaction. "Since your security surveillance is exceptional, I am certain you can tell me exactly what has happened to him." ·

Simon's expression darkened, he leaned forward and brought his face close to Master Siger's. "You have never lost your talent for the blunt question." Moving carefully, Simon de Brion returned to his chair and sat. "You remember that cafe near the Pantheon? Something with a rooster in its name. You and Boetius and a few of the others all hung out there together. When other students arrived they went directly to your table. I watched you and them, and I admit I was envious. But not even daring to admit this to myself, I was satisfied merely to be envious of those others, the ones with whom you shared your attention." Simon turned the slim bright glass between his fingers by its frail stem, as a look of bemused nostalgia surrounded his eyes.

"You and Boetius and your little inner circle," he continued, "all sitting together surrounded by so much interest, such animated faces excited just to be there with you. And always with all those charming young women surrounding you as well. All of you sitting together, such enthusiasm and such pleasure, and all looking down on me." Simon de Brion paused, then lowered his eyes and spoke quietly. "But perhaps I digress. To answer your question, there is no doubt in my mind, and there should be no doubt in yours, that our poor brother, Boetius of Dacia, is dead." Simon de Brion passed the full glass across the table to Siger.

"Is that all you will tell me?"

Simon de Brion stared at his own full glass. "It is all any of us ever really needs to know."

"So says you." Siger felt his impatience rise for what he no longer believed to be true. "But for the moment we'll let that pass. And Mistress Marguerite? What can you tell me about her?"

Simon de Brion sighed. In a consoling voice that seemed to have softened he said, "My sources agree she has gone to Tunisia. To do hospital work among the heathens. One story has it she was attacked and beaten outside Cyrene, and then during her convalescence had a profound religious awakening. I hear that since then she has dedicated her life to the service of the poor." Master Siger was startled to the point of pain on hearing these words. But it only took a moment to conclude he had just been told another lie. He waited in blank-faced silence.

De Brion paused and then offered his uneven grey smile. He tipped his glass toward Master Siger. "I offer a prayer and a toast. A prayer for the redemption of your immortal soul, and a toast to the uncommon good sense you have displayed by remaining in the consoling and protective arms of His Holiness, and those faithful who support him." Master Siger watched him sip from the glass.

After Master Siger sipped from his own, with a sigh he said, "I remember hanging out at the Strangled Rooster very well. And I remember that I never cared to talk to you. So here's your chance to finally tell me something interesting; something I don't already know. Tell me how Brother Thomas died."

Simon de Brion's expression betrayed his annoyance. He leaned back into his chair so that his eyes disappeared into shadow. "It is widely remembered that you took his loss most personally. All of us who recognized your affection for dear Brother Thomas regarded your grief with special sympathy. Yet, the death of our dear brother continues to haunt us all."

"I am deeply moved to hear that," Siger said in a tone that dripped sarcasm.

"And even were the world as we wish it, his eventual passing would have saddened us beyond heartbreak. But the timing and sudden nature of his death was uncanny, you must admit."

Dr. de Brion shrugged. "The Lord called our good brother to His side long before his time, of this I will certainly agree. And just as certainly, had he remained among us he would have shattered the very heart of the world with his penetrating support for Christ's mission of universal redemption. All of Christendom agrees that more was lost in that one day than we will ever understand. As to how he came to his fate, this is a path known only to God Himself. Brother Thomas had his weakness just like every man. And his health had been troubled. His sudden passing still came as a shock, though his health, already so unpredictable, had been at least suspected by those who knew him intimately." De Brion paused and then sipped from his glass. He glanced once at Master Siger over its rim.

Master Siger sipped and returned his glass to the table, grateful to be reminded he was being observed. "Some suggest Brother Thomas died from the administration of poison."

Simon de Brion glared suddenly. The planes of his face sharpened, angled to catch the candle's muddy orange light. "There is no limit to the deviltry to which some will descend, even as far as to make money from such a death. I am told there is a vile little Moslem reporter who has profited very well by spreading that false rumor. Twice false because it was never even a rumor. No one else has ever attempted to allege a conspiracy to harm Brother Thomas. Of course, I have met with this man and interviewed him on his experience, as was my responsibility. Just a miserable and worthless little liar. But every liar needs a fool for a partner."

Master Siger watched Simon compose himself. His back straightened and his shoulders squared, as if unfolding himself. "There is not a corner of this Palace that does not grieve over his loss to our mission on earth. By calling Brother Thomas to His side, the Lord added another test of our determination and love for Him."

The sudden ringing of the telephone startled Siger. Simon de Brion stood, stepped into the shadows of his desk to answer. He spoke quietly, the conversation was brief, and then he hung up. He returned to the table and refilled his glass before he sat down. "That was the Franciscan Highway Patrol. Very efficient fellows. The helicopter went down near Tolon. Engine trouble, apparently.

Mistress Celestina and that lying Moslem 'abd Al-Malik were captured hiding in a rain sewer along the road to Mende. They're being taken to Montpellier. That's in the jurisdiction of the Inquisition now sitting at Lyon."

"I will advise His Holiness to claim them," Master Siger said, "and put them under Papal protection. His Holiness will save their bodies from the rack, and in this way save his own soul from mortal sin." Master Siger's thoughts turned suddenly to those last moments in the field, the helicopter's rotors turning slowly above him in the darkness. And then the helicopter rising with friends determined to help him and yet without him.

Simon de Brion smiled. "If His Holiness did as you suggest, he would risk being seen sheltering heresy. On the other hand, a display of such compassion and generosity might reflect well on His Holiness' concern for all sinners. Perhaps he can be convinced."

"No true believer could ask for more."

"I am certain His Holiness will make his wishes on this matter known." Simon de Brion smiled as if suddenly recognizing something that pleased him. "I am relieved that you are not as naive as you appear. But answer me this. Do you have even a glimmer of an idea of the role you are about to play?"

Master Siger paused to sip thoughtfully from his wine. "I have a decisive role in the salvation of my soul. Whatever other work Our Lord finds for me, I will take it up with all my heart."

Simon de Brion chuckled and finished his wine. "No doubt, we will get past all this pious humbuggery eventually. To state it all in your own terms, you are about to become a key figure in a profound conflict. And we—you and I—are here tonight because His Holiness is certain you will play your part well." Simon de Brion refilled Master Siger's glass.

Master Siger studied the hand encircling the bottle's neck with round, slim fingers the color of cheese-rind. "Faithful," he said, "to my Church and Her teaching, I remain fascinated by the Universe the Lord has placed to surround us. Its beauty is uncontestable testimony to the love our Creator holds for us. Aristotle, and Islamic mathematics, and chemistry, and astrology; all of these are keys to His world and certain to reveal His grace in the commonplace."

Simon de Brion stood slowly, his eyes wide and staring at Master Siger. And then he burst into loud laughter. "How could I have been so wrong?" He began to pace, stepping into the deep shadows as he spoke, emerging unexpectedly and then retreating into invisibility. "For a moment I convinced myself you were at least not naive. So much for that. Let us follow your example and look squarely at this question. You ask why you are here, and what role you are expected to play. In fact, what you really want to know is why you have not been sent to the Inquisition. And that by itself is a very good question."

Master Siger remained silent, certain now that Brother Thomas had been murdered, though he still could not say why.

"You have acted as the ring-leader for a heretical mob of over-educated and impious hot-heads. And let me remind you, those condemnations were not the direst suggestions made against you and your horde. When impatience with your heresy spread, certain influential individuals considered rounding up the lot of you and shipping you off to slavery in Syria. There are people who practice that sort of thing, as you must already know. Still, a question might arise. Some misguided Benedictine monk from Baghdad might take it into his head to help you. Besides, I ask you, would your arrest and exile really have ended the thing?"

Master Siger smiled. "Exploration of this world given to us by God will continue," he said, surprised by his own passion, "regardless of kings or priests or other despots. And part of that world includes those institutions of political and social control, a panoply of resources from which despots derive their power. Can you believe I am surprised the firmest resistance to investigation of this world comes from princes and bishops?" Siger paused to watch de Brion.

Simon remained standing halfway between his desk and the table, his hands hidden in the sleeves of his dark robes, his eyes flat with scorn. Master Siger continued. "The fact that His Holiness combines the roles of Earthly Prince and Heavenly Shepherd has had the unfortunate result of leaving the Papacy twice suspect. Yet, rather than recognize an opportunity to create a domain anchored by incontrovertible reason and positive knowledge, the Curia regards every question, no matter how innocuous, as a dagger at the very heart of the Church on Earth."

Dr. Brion's laughter was edged with scorn. "Sophomoric ranting, convincing only to a crowd of drunken and lecherous undergraduates. I remind you we are no longer on the street corner nor in the lecture hall." From his position away from the table, Simon leaned forward as if to share a secret. "Now we will speak about what is real. At this moment the Papacy is in the greatest danger it has endured since the time of St. Paul himself. The Holy Office has always faced challenges to its power, but now conflicts arise over its authority. The people of Rome, subjects of His Holiness on earth as in Heaven, have risen up to the cry that his political authority is an illusion in which they will no longer participate. Meanwhile, earthly princes no longer seek his approval or counsel, and some even dare to ignore his direct commands. They take upon themselves their mantles of authority without seeking His Holiness's blessing. Treaties, agreements between princes, even arrangements of marriage; all are being accepted and formalized without regard to the Pope's disapproval. And as horrible as it all is, this is not yet the worst."

Simon de Brion shook himself as if disposing of a burden. He stepped back to his chair and with his hands still hidden sat down. "At this very moment, the material support for his Holiness and His Church—money from Papal lands and farms, taxes from its villages and towns, tithes and income from the administration of sacraments—is being diverted by these princes for their own use. Control of Church appointments to positions of authority, and the wealth that these appointments provide, are being taken out of the hands of His Holiness by earthly powers for unsanctified use. These princes even dare to take issues of dogma into their own ignorant and bloodied hands. Times are dark, Master Siger. His Holiness has come to you for aid, not contention or contradiction."

Master Siger hesitated at the urgent tone of Simon's recital. "Your passion only increases your eloquence, Dr. de Brion, and I must congratulate you for that. But only remember that the Church refuses to confront Her own failures. His Holiness struggles mightily against his bondage, yet he appears content to sleep with lions. Those who contest for earthly rewards with the likes of Charles of Anjou or Rudolph of Habsburg or Peter III of Aragon know they risk more than merely a family's wealth. His Holiness has all of Christendom and Christ Himself to answer to."

Simon de Brion's lips curled as if he'd just smelled something vile. "His Holiness has agreed to protect you, and you offer only derision and scorn in return."

Siger ignored the assertion. "Let us return to your original hypothesis. Do you truly believe Brother Thomas was so enamored of the princes of Earth that he would have exerted himself to save even one of them from the consequences of their own unholy ambitions? Their souls he held precious, but their earthly fortunes appeared to him as less than brass."

De Brion leaned forward in his chair startled. "Had he lived, there would be no doubt which side Brother Thomas would have supported. He understood what you prefer to ignore; that the power to do good must include possession of that power itself. This fact alone should make any suspicion of our complicity in his death preposterous. His ability, his loyalty, and his determination would all have provided His Holiness with great strength."

Though he was loath to admit it, Siger knew his beloved teacher's weakness for conciliation, and his willingness to collaborate even with those who despised him.

Simon continued, "And since you insist on your higher responsibility to the acquisition of knowledge of this most imperfect and inconstant world, let me remind you what Brother Thomas most surely would have told you. That education and that training which you insist you value so highly, even this muddle-headed thing you call a philosophy, all of it has been provided to you by the Church which you are now being asked to defend. And please remember, by this request we ask no more from you than we would have received from Brother Thomas himself."

Master Siger flinched at the nettle that had been planted in his soul so long ago, and which only awaited precisely this moment to awaken and turn and sting. But he tried his best to smile defiantly. "You believe I will help the Church despite Her rejection of all I hold most dear in my philosophy, simply because She taught me to read."

"On the contrary; precisely because of it." Simon de Brion's eyes grew bright, his pale hand reappeared, thin fingers clutched his wine glass. "But let me clarify something that remarkably appears to have eluded your recognition. Through Her determined resistance to every new idea, the Church has forced each challenger to sharpen arguments and gather evidence of absolutely unquestionable integrity. In short, the Church has recognized that its highest obligation is to put forward assertions only vulnerable to the most vigorous and scrupulous challenge. By this I hope you will recognize that we provide assistance to those intellectual adventurers like yourself by resisting you, by contradicting you, by condemning you and by condemning any and all who purport to agree with you."

Master Siger could not resist a smile. "Shall I express my gratitude now, or should I wait until the kindling beneath my feet has been set ablaze?"

Simon de Brion laughed quietly, but his smile did not reach his eyes. "Just as the music performer becomes profound by learning to play for those passionate about music, so, too, will you conjecture most brilliantly under the hot bright light of our absolute incredulity."

Siger realized his head had grown heavy. Wine and exhaustion and the lack of sleep gathered over him like a deepening fog, and he struggled to maintain his attention and he was not consistently successful. He said, "Whatever danger the Papacy faces, it is the result of handing supreme power to a certain coterie of dim-witted, devious and greedy men who in their hearts hold the Chair of Peter in contempt. For generations and with hardly a murmur from the Curia, these men have abused their power and privilege, and so have abandoned those souls dependent on the true source of that power and privilege. You have such audacity. Your request that I support this crumbling edifice suggests you no longer believe His Holiness or the Curia capable of that responsibility. But even worse for you, you find yourself dependent on the likes of me."

Simon de Brion shrugged and looked away. "Our Lord demands honesty of all of us. There is no good purpose for me to contradict you or defend the indefensible. Decisions have been made and positions taken that accomplished little except to endanger the very structure of the Church. But understand a single, simple fact. The gravest danger the Church faces is that of being rendered suddenly headless and left to stumble and lurch, blind and uncertain as to who will lead and who must follow, incapable of perception or action, yet still and no less responsible for salvation. The controversy over these purported philosophies you flog to the media is merely a symptom and not even the worst. With its prestige in decline and its ability to enunciate dogma challenged, the Papacy is in danger of losing its power to guide souls to the loving embrace of Jesus Christ."

Simon de Brion paused to refill his glass, and his small smile grew as his glass filled. "Believe me; if you wonder how it is I manage to put aside animosity and make this request for your help, realize I have disciplined myself as all of must to submit my will to the ultimate goal. It has always been clear to me that every attempt by the Church to stifle these trivial philosophical conflicts would end in mutual suspicion and humiliating failure. So over time I have pondered whether there was some other way these controversies could be made harmless. For some time I have given this question deep thought, and offered many prayers."

"Did you ever consider," Siger asked as his impatience returned, "that these voices would refuse to be silenced because they were certain they had recognized the truth?"

With a dismissive wave of his hand Simon continued, "But one morning as I read my breviary, an intriguing solution occurred to me. His Holiness would go about his affairs making a great show of struggling against these errors, and even categorically insist his words on the subject are final and can never be contradicted. But otherwise he would do nothing. In fact, through you he would invisibly sustain and even encourage this perverse notion of a philosophy elaborated without reference to the will of God."

"I must protest!" Master Siger cried as panic constricted his throat. De Brion's suggestion so startled him that he stood up. "My faith in Christ and His Gift of Eternal Life has never wavered, even for a single moment. And nothing within my mind or within my heart contradicts that."

But de Brion continued to speak as thought he had not heard Siger. "Though you are the master of the salvation of your own soul, in the world outside the Church you and your so-called philosophy are but a dust mote at the bottom of the Universe. Yet we realize that individuals like you and schools of thought like yours will unfortunately arise in each new generation. And as each of these pernicious philosophies emerges, those who are weak and misguided among our faithful will fall into their heretical embrace. Those who remain confused, uncertain or simply weak will succumb and leave our loving guidance without so much as a tremor. And thus it is by this awful, this hideous, process the Holy Body will gradually rid itself of skepticism and indecision. The chaff will over time drop away. And thus purged, the Holy Body will become more powerful and resilient."

"By the strategy you describe," Master Siger said with unconcealed mockery, "the Church will find itself left voiceless and inarticulate, only able to speak of God, and yet unable to speak to souls."

But Simon's eyes hardly flickered, as if the strand of his thought strung out before him bright and straight, and he would not be deflected. "Meanwhile, exhausted and injured by their flirtation with dismal reason, those wavering faithful seduced by these pathetic philosophies will eventually, inevitably, recognize that their experimentation with rancorous individual thought has simply left them more frightened, more vulnerable, and ultimately more miserable. Miserable in their rational isolation and helpless to resolve it, when reminded of the Church's constancy and inexhaustible strength these souls will return avidly to that faith we have preserved, purged finally of their hubris and thereafter even more dedicated to the needs of our universal mission."

Master Siger nodded, and he did not try to hide his indulgent grin. "By your description then, my presence can only prove exceptionally useful. In brief, you believe it is inevitable that minds will become disenchanted with reason, dissatisfied with understanding the world around them, and ultimately bored with Aristotle. Reasoned exploration of the world around them will only result in their insecurity and ennui. At the end of this grand exploration will come the question; was all of that doubt and fear and insecurity finally worth their misery?"

"You misunderstand my intention completely, philosopher. To the contrary." Simon de Brion leaned back again into the shadows. Master Siger moved the candle to one side of the table, but he could not dispel the darkness. "As much as any other human, I have succumbed to the seductive caresses these questions stimulate in weak minds. The desire for them, I confess, is unshakable. No threat of ultimate punishment could ever deter such perverse yet delicious obsessions. And as you also must acknowledge from personal experience, those so burdened with this obsession will blithely pursue it even at the cost of ill-health, impotence and incontinence, madness, poverty, and humiliation. Nothing, in fact, will deter those fallen souls from wallowing in their shit-bath of beguiling but inconsequential rationalism."

"My good brother can't be serious." Master Siger recognized that his patience for this lecture was nearly gone. "I cannot believe you regard the exercise of human reason as a form of disease."

"Let me remind you of something, philosopher." Simon de Brion straightened himself as if confident he was about to deal the winning blow. "Logically, all progress in the intellectual project of Aristotle and his system of natural science will, simply by its own terms eventually and inevitably demand the examination of the very smallest parts of the Universe. In the same stoke, it will also demand examination as well of the largest, the most complex and the most distant. This rationalist, empiricist and materialist project will be forced by the very logic upon which it is constructed to describe and explain phenomena that eventually can no longer be directly observed by the human inquirer, but must henceforth merely be assumed. And because it is no longer possible for these phenomena to be observed directly, belief in their processes will be forced to rely on mathematical, and not empirical, proof. At that moment, with the need for empirical evidence discarded and the very existence of the material world thrown into doubt, in a blaze of glorious white light, Plato and Augustine will return."

Despite de Brion's grin of satisfaction, Master Siger remained impassive. Fatigue and wine helped sustain his dispassionate expression but de Brion's suggestion touched something deep within him, leaving him suddenly frightened. As absurd as the man's suggestion appeared, something about it stirred Siger's mind in a way that left him chilled to the bone. So he watched Simon in silence, and he waited already vaguely recognizing the shape emerging from de Brion's fog of words.

Simon continued, "Left to investigate armed only with mathematical models, your conjectures eventually will fly about no longer anchored in anything even remotely resembling perceivable reality. Your instruments will only be capable of examination by indirection, and even your language concerning the results of those measurements will itself become honeycombed with imaginative reconstructions. And worse, their only proof will be found in their relationship to that system of coordinates derived by mathematical conjectures, themselves decisively distant from immediate experience. The rationalists at that moment will have nowhere else to go with their methodical disassembly of the cosmos. In their attempt to grip Reality ever tighter, they will find suddenly that in the final analysis, all is vapor and smoke, and nothing is real."

Struck suddenly by a wave of terror, Master Siger's laughter was closer to a scream. "I salute you, Dr. de Brion, and your very clever conjecture, as elegant and ingenious as it is suggestive. But suggestive is not compelling. In brief, you suggest a most unhistorical process. You offer a notion of history in which cause and effect proceed or follow each other randomly and without predictable consistency. Your assertion assumes that a blockhead's notion of linear progress is not only possible but necessary. This alone makes your argument suspect. Your model precludes even the possibility that reason and nature will embrace as lovers in a dance. And just as in a dance, positions change, perspectives shift, observations are revised and must be revised again. Your ludicrous theory of progress forces you to assert the absurd; that a time will come when the limit is reached of what can be directly observed and pondered and thereby recognized as a new source of hypothesis. If Aristotle said only one true thing, it was that wherever the natural mind turns, it will find a facet of nature that it will recognize as part of itself, and therefore appropriate for contemplation."

The expression on Simon de Brion's face became still darker, and Siger wondered how deeply he had stepped into the whirlpool, and whether it was too late to retreat. "Always the undergraduate and never the master; you remain incapable of acknowledging error." He folded his arms and tipped his head back. "Do not mistake the nature of my appeal," de Brion said. "It is assumed that a simple request for assistance is more palatable to someone as arrogant and deluded as you." Simon laced his fingers together tightly. "Philosopher, heal thyself!" He leaned further back and his face disappeared in brown twilight. "You underestimate us, Master Siger, and more the worse for you. You have an enviable reputation as an exciting yet erratic personality. But please, at least try to stretch your imagination." When he leaned forward and refilled both glasses, around his lips appeared a shadow of excitement.

"Suppose as you insist," Simon continued, "that your brand of so-called scientific observation continues another thousand years. Let us further suppose that at the end of those thousand years there are still many earnest people interested in continuing its project. And assume that project continues on still another thousand years. In fact, without prejudice to my hypothesis, assume the project continues another ten thousand years. The actual length, you'll agree, is of no significance so long as we recognize that the project itself can only be logically finite. It is inevitable that the day will dawn when the last Aristotelian philosopher will join his Maker. With that death, I insist, the project itself will die, becoming as inconsequential as it was before the birth of Aristotle."

Though he was startled by this proposition, Master Siger could hardly force his eyes to remain open. His mind was alert, yet his tongue lay large in his mouth, and his head wobbled on his neck. "Your argument teeters on three rotten legs. That progress exists, that progress is linear, and that the goal is finite." But finally, Master Siger realized he had lost his ability to sustain speech, or even to sustain a thought. So he sat back.

"When the day of final Aristotelian destruction arrives," de Brion continued but now with a smile that grew, "Holy Mother Church will be found still standing, sturdy and bright. The One and Only Church of Christ will have endured. If, by some Aristotelian miracle, humans sail off and discover new worlds and new souls for Christ, the Church will be there and will save those worlds, too. Let the heathen wander misguided, let the atheist mock, let the Anti-Christ challenge, our Church will remain. This has been promised to us by Christ. Every other philosophy will be abandoned. Let every doctrine rise up and strut its day in the sun, let it march the gullible over the precipice, let each label every other as heresy, let this round continue from generation to generation, let doctrines proliferate and multiply until a different one can be assembled for every misguided soul in creation. All, I tell you, all inevitably, must return to the

Church. Within Time and before the extinction of the species. All will be drawn together into One, Holy, Apostolic Congregation. No soul will be excluded, no soul will become lost. The Shepherd will for all eternity gather His sheep into its single Heavenly Pasture. By the promise of Christ, all that I have described, as I have described it, must come to pass. The number of years is literally without meaning. How many grains of sand on the beach; how many stars in the firmament? The Church will wait and the Church will endure. Until the Kingdom of Christ is on Earth as it is in Heaven."

Master Siger studied Simon, and waited, but for no reason he could understand. Finally, half in astonishment, he said, "So that's what you think?" His eyesight blurred and doubled, and he struggled to make out Simon de Brion's face, nearly featureless in the shadow. "I could envy such certitude. That much assurance must be wonderfully comforting."

"Saved is the soul that is at peace with itself."

"Or a soul that must dream its reality rather than bear the burden of consciousness in a material world." Master Siger finally found himself annoyed at Simon de Brion's own arrogance, as if content with the hubris to lecture him as though he were a schoolboy. "But tell me this. In the assured future you describe, how can my support of the Pope bring such events to pass even a moment earlier? If this victory is as you insist inevitable, why drag me into it? I am unworthy of such power and clearly incapable of its exercise. I am overwhelmed by the mere shadow of such towering responsibility. The ability to affect the course of human salvation has always seemed far beyond my reach."

Simon de Brion leaned forward again into the light and revealed an uncomfortable smile. "Each of us is merely a tool in the Hands of the Lord. We cannot decide of what material we are made, but only that the material be put to its best use."

"But as a convinced adherent to Aristotelian science," Master Siger said, "I am thoroughly tainted and therefore more easily corrupted. So do I not, therefore, threaten His Holiness and his power over dogma? Though I am an exceptionally weak instrument, do I not pose a danger? Can His Holiness wish to give me such power, with the assistance of the Holy Office, to corrupt Christian philosophers and scientists, enlisting them in a heretical crusade, the result of which would unmask their heresy to the Curia and the Inquisition, and lead inevitably to imprisonments and executions? My certitude concerning Aristotle must indicate my completely corrupted soul."

"All that is mortal is flawed," Simon said quietly, patiently, as if this admonition was both obvious and explanatory. "Only the Church is immortal and therefore without flaw. Still, I believe I have been misunderstood. No one wishes to discourage your thinking or writing. Nor should you concern yourself over your co-religionists. We already know who they are and where they are and who they are sleeping with. I ask only that you consider what is being offered. Burdened with irresolvable doubt though we may be, the Church offers guidance to light our way back to the True Path." Simon's smile deepened, as though he suddenly recognized something. Master Siger struggled with his own confusion. Simon de Brion continued, "While we are on the topic of flawed mortals, I need to ask what you think of our dear friar, Frère Jacques?"

Master Siger was startled.

Recognizing his confusion, Simon de Brion said, "He does strike one as a sort of amiable rogue. I cannot decide whether it is his coarse language or his loud laughter or his bluntness of thought and speech that is most immediately appealing. As a tool of Our Lord's work, Frère Jacques seems perfectly imperfect. Yet, I am told he is resourceful, loyal, tenacious, and energetic. These are characteristics rarely found together in one person. And he seems to have taken a great liking to you. You should be flattered. As imperfect as he may be, value his counsel and take comfort in his support."

"How well do you know him?" Master Siger asked.

Simon of Brion shrugged. "Not well, which is why I ask my question. He has taken an interest in you and has been anxious to share your attention exclusively."

"And His Holiness sees Frère Jacques as an able assistant to my researches?"

"His will provide indispensable companionship. Dedicated scholars like yourself must occasionally stand from their desks and partake of more substantial human company. Frère Jacques will refresh your mind to renewed philosophic investigation as his companionship will augment your repertoire of human foibles and profundities. Fear not, this companion will sustain your heroic struggle to unlock the mysteries of Creation."

"You must allow, however, that a bold and roguish bearing can hide merely a petty felon."

"Petty felons, whether made or born, occupy a particular place in the plan for salvation. As I said, we all remain mere tools in the hands of the Lord." Simon de Brion glanced at his wristwatch and then leaned back, folding his hands across his stomach in a way that made Master Siger angry. With a smile Simon added, "The hour is late, and you have much to do. I suggest you take this opportunity to retire. In a few hours we will leave for Orvieto and you'll need a solid night's sleep for the journey."

Master Siger hesitated and then stood slowly. He was nearly upright when he realized how drunk he had become. He struggled a moment to focus on Simon de Brion who remained sitting beside the table. "No doubt," Siger slurred, "Frère Jacques will know everyone who is anyone in Orvieto." He turned and took shaky steps toward the door when Simon de Brion spoke to his back.

"Before you go, let me assure you our security is a bit better organized than your recent experience might suggest. An attempt to escape will undoubtedly end in another embarrassing recapture. Sleep well."

Master Siger bowed dizzily and then managed to leave the room without knocking anything over.

He moved along the corridors slowly, distracted by statuary lining the hallway and the sparkling crests mounted to the walls. Words and images moved through his mind as slowly as his feet moved over the carpet of the hallway, a montage so utterly confused he was no longer certain what had happened and what he imagined. Somehow he had been both praised and warned, he had been rewarded and punished, he had been delighted with hope and depressed with suspicion. Despite the fog swirling behind his eyes Siger decided he would find the key, the source, and that he must do this, if only to vindicate the memory of Boetius. Perhaps it was as near as this own head, or as far as Orvieto. But at the thought of being confined to another hovel so far from Paris and populated by self-righteous parasites, Master Siger trembled. A vacuum bloomed in his chest, the Tuscan sun would be useless against the gloom that seized Siger's thoughts.

Somewhere in the series of long corridors between the rooms of Simon de Brion and his own, Master Siger came upon a door partly open. Through it he could see a street that seemed to lead beyond the Palace and the walls of the city and directly into the mountains. It took a sleepy and dazed Siger to recognize it and understand its invitation to freedom. He stood beside the door swaying for several moments hazily determined to consider the possibilities inherent in this opportunity. In the effort to gather his thoughts, Siger suddenly discovered he no longer had any. Somehow his mind had emptied itself, and not refilled. According to the laws of quantum physics as Master Siger understood them, one of Simon de Brion's guards was both out there just beyond the open door, and also not out there. Only at the moment that Master Siger took action and passed through the door would one or the other reality come into being. Either he would be captured, or he would successfully flee. Had he had the inclination or the right inducement and had he been sober, he might have attempted a probability distribution that would describe his situation. Suddenly, he needed to sit down. He looked along both sides of the corridor for a chair, but found none. So he stood looking through the door for a long time.

But Master Siger had to ask himself if abject and head-long flight was, as de Brion suggested, merely a prelude to certain recapture. Would it be a matter of days or only hours until he was recaptured? A humiliation repeated, multiplied and amplified, so that now suddenly he was an even greater danger to others. Or worse, would His Holiness finally conclude that Master Siger was no longer worth the effort to protect him? Siger leaned his shoulder against the wall, tipped his head forward until his chin was pressed to his chest. Could his position be any more threatening? Everyone who had tried to help him apparently had come to regret their generosity. Would another failed attempt at cowardly escape exonerate even a single one of his many failed obligations?

Master Siger straightened from the wall and turned toward the corridor leading to his rooms. The honor of closing the door to this invitation to freedom Siger would leave to someone else.

Let Fall the Gossamer Curtain of History as the Past Slips Back Into Its Ordained and Reassuring Place; All That Was Both Is and Is No More.

CHAPTER THE FOURTEENTH

LET HISTORY'S GOLDEN, Slim-Fingered Hand Part The Opaque Curtain of Time Woven of the Gray Strands of Months and the Red Threads of Years, To Reveal Bright Sunday Morning Over Sleepy Orvieto, and Over Master Siger Lying Within a Heap of White Sheets and Fat Pillows at the Center of His Bed.

Eyes shut tight against his thudding hang-over and against that searing sunlight flooding his room, Siger weakly reached out his hand and searched the bed beside him. His smile of misery grew slowly. He was, after all, alone again. He was also hungry and thirsty, and the pain in his head was blinding. Yet his smile affirmed that at least he was alive. One could go somewhere from there; one could count that a starting point.

With a burst of dazed determination, Siger pulled on his clothes and stepped out onto the balcony outside his window.

Parched sunlight painted the grey stone buildings before him with honey, and set their red-tiled roofs aflame. Beyond those ruby rooftops shimmering under the bright, hot sun, the certain and solid blue of the sky mocked his confinement, and its apparent benevolence insulted his insecurity. The palace was as silent as a mausoleum, and from his perch he saw no one moving in nearby windows or in the piazza below. He would not allow his chance to slip away, a whiff of a freedom he had not tasted since Montpellier stirred something. Siger's legs began to move before he did, as if knowing more than he did, and better.

The irony was not lost on Master Siger that he now resided in the town where Brother Thomas had lived for more than seven years back in the early Sixties, and where he had produced some of his most sophisticated and challenging theology. And after all, was not his *Summa Contra Gentiles*, composed while at San Dominico during his residence at Orvieto, essentially a diatribe against Latin Averroist thought, and specifically against Master Siger? At Urban IV's request, Brother Thomas had also written a liturgy for the newly-established Feast of Corpus Christi, the most subtle and beautiful of service oratories. It included the glorious hymn "Pange Lingua, Gloriosi Corporius Mysterium," asserting the miraculous presence of the Holy Flesh of Christ under the aspects of bread and wine. Brother Thomas had been residing in Orvieto at the time of the Miracle of Bolsena.

A certain Friar Peter of Prague, tormented by doubt over the presence in the sacramental host of the Holy Body, was celebrating Mass at a nearby church when he realized that the host he held aloft for the blessing had suddenly begun to bleed, and the droplets of its blood fell to stain the caporal beneath. When word of this miracle spread, that piece of cloth was ordered delivered to the cathedral at Orvieto where it was now displayed for the congregation's veneration. In the midst of all these events, Brother Thomas had somehow convinced himself despite all logic to embrace the Church's explanation of this mystery, and his decision had left Master Siger depressed and deeply confused.

Blinded by the sunlight and hobbled by the throbbing pain in his head, Siger stepped out of his room in the Papal Palace of Orvieto, and into the soothing darkness of the hallway. He passed along the palace's maze of silent halls and closed doors until finally he stepped out onto the patio at the top of the grand staircase. Once again, sunlight struck him like a physical blow.

Spread below and around him, the Piazza del Popolo lay deserted. Even the chairs and tables ranged before Sargenti's café had been taken in. Siger remembered this was the Feast Day of Saint Alphonso the Obsessive. Every citizen of Orvieto was at the Santa Maria Cathedral, known as the Duomo Cathedral, attending the High Mass offered in celebration of that controversial saint. Master Siger guessed that the congregation had reached the high-point of its celebration, the communal washing and re-washing of hands. Siger could no longer doubt the wisdom of his inclination. This holiday was important, and his absence from his seat in the Papal pew would be noted. So this, he decided, was a particularly good time to flee the party.

The stairway descending before Siger was wide and fearfully steep, and his vision remained uncertain as a vertigo threatened. Master Siger's legs trembled beneath him with each step, so he held carefully onto the stone banister, step after quavering step, until he reached the piazza. He followed the piazza's edge keeping to the shade of its buildings and reached the Street of Dogs. Its passage was narrow, and the height of the buildings on either side put the street into blessed grey shadow. Siger moved slowly, waiting for his sense of balance to return. Cool in this watery light, he followed the street until it ended at the Piazza della Repubblica.

Several weeks had passed after Siger's arrival in Orvieto before finally he made his visit to San Dominico. It was to its congregation that, in 1261, Brother Thomas had been sent as conventual lector to instruct the friars in theology, since they would be unable to attend a stadium generale. Master Siger wondered, considering the exhausting round of parties and social occasions he struggled to survive, how Brother Thomas with his enthusiastic notoriety had managed to get anything at all accomplished while he was there. He continued to marvel at the remarkable pile of manuscript pages Thomas had filled while in Orvieto. Because by comparison, even after more than three months, Siger's own pile was embarrassingly puny.

Master Siger stepped out of the shade of the street and onto this piazza to be struck so hard and suddenly by the sun and heat that it startled him, and he hesitated. He looked over to the tables outside Giorgio's Cafe and Gelato Bar, the only café in town that remained open despite the holy celebration. At a table under Giorgio's dark green awning and well-back from the street he recognized two Templars, Bernard of Lyon and Robert of Anglia, sitting together, tall half-empty glasses of red wine before each. Robert of Anglia recognized Master Siger and half-stood and waved for him to join them. Misery loves company, and both of them had attended the same party Master Siger still seemed unable to recover from. Siger hesitated. Each man was well-connected to the Curia, and cultivating their acquaintance offered Siger tangible benefits. He remained in the hot and breathless light confused. Should he join their table, as if he was just another refugee from a burdensome celebration? But after a moment Siger shrugged his shoulders, a gesture of helplessness. He had to leave, his gesture seemed to say, and he was on an errand of some importance. Before either could detain him,

Siger turned and crossed the piazza as quickly as his condition would allow, only hoping that neither attempted to follow.

Master Siger was unsure why it had taken him so long to make his pilgrimage to San Dominico. Certainly Frère Jacques had kept him amused and entertained to the point of exhaustion, but Siger could have made his visit at any time. So he had to wonder if it might have been simply the result of petty cowardice. What, after all, could he have feared to confront there? It was widely known that while Thomas was in Orvieto he had experienced a shattering crisis of faith. Was Siger wary that the resolution of Brother Thomas' crisis would tempt him as well? Or worse, did he wish simply to avoid confronting the depth of Thomas's abject betrayal?

When finally Siger crossed the piazza and reached the Street of the Club-Foot, the sudden cool breath of its shade calmed him. Beyond the first turn and finally invisible to the cafe, he stopped and leaned one hand against the damp stone wall. His body trembled and sweat from his forehead bit at his eyes. Yet it seemed he had surpassed a hurdle, and he resumed his shaky path. Pausing to rest every few steps, he made his way slowly along that curving, narrow street. In those pauses he recalled scenes from the previous night's carouse, and hugged himself to quiet his shudders of despair. His hangovers, both physical and spiritual, were his burdens alone, and sweating and trembling he dragged them to the Porta Maggiorie.

Reaching this street, Siger stopped and turned back to survey the piazza, and he was relieved to find he was still alone. Then he crossed to the Porta Romana. Its long steep path down from the fortified town only ended at the floor of the valley. At his side, the rocky drop along the edge of the path was abrupt and sheer, the cliff-sides towered nearly vertical. Clustered on a plateau surrounded entirely by steep, straight walls, the town of Orvieto was a natural citadel for His Holiness in his time of trouble. For Master Siger, on the other hand, the town proved a disheartening prison, made even more dispiriting by the debauchery of its inmates.

Perhaps because of the numbing sunlight, or perhaps only because Master Siger was already inclined to move, he took the first downward steps. A moment's indecision, and the steep slope captured his uncertain legs and insistently carried him forward. After that, it became simply easier to continue. He smirked at the way he had colluded in the completion of his own fate. The brilliant, shimmering sunlight left his head throbbing, and he could hardly

open his eyes to steer himself away from the precipice at his side. The slope
and his weak legs conspired so that he staggered downward along its stony path.
But the times had been wild in Orvieto. He smirked in his dazed stumble at
memories of his elegant incarceration.

As a well-known member of the Pope's retinue, Master Siger had arrived in
Orvieto in an explosion of color, sparkling polished brass, silver and gold, a
shrill cacophony of trumpets and booming thud of drums. Siger recalled the
crowd's deafening cheer when His Holiness entered the Piazza del Duomo, and
then climbed the low steps into Santa Maria. Titular leader of the Guelphs, His
Holiness was a natural ally of the Monaldeschi family, the single most powerful
clan in the valley. But His Holiness took every opportunity to express his warm
wishes of Christian fraternity toward the Filippeschi family, a powerful clan of
Ghibellines, allies of the Hohenstaufen emperors of Germany, and enemies of
the Monaldeschi and the Papacy.

From the moment of their arrival, Master Siger's personal popularity startled
him. Hardly an evening passed when he was not answering an invitation to a
party or dinner. His presence was entreated by the wealthy and powerful families
allied to the Mondaleschi. But to his greater surprise, Master Siger soon found
himself circulating among like-minded thinkers, an odd coven of eggheads cast
upon this gorgeous and isolated haven. Men very much like himself, engaged
in philosophical speculations and the translations of obscure writings. And
at Orvieto, Siger discovered a trove of volumes that had been smuggled from
the archives of Constantinople. He had arrived at the perfect environment to
advance his studies, quietly sheltered within the protective shadow of the Pope,
and as good as invisible to the Inquisition.

So despite Siger's best efforts to remain above and apart, this sleepy village
on a plateau dominated by its magnificent and very holy cathedral had begun
to feel like home. The only irritation to this idyll in the backwaters had been
the constant presence of Frère Jacques.

But about what could Master Siger complain? Frère Jacques had proved to be
the very best companion. Seemingly a friend to every bartender and baron in
town, Frère Jacques had introduced him to people high and low. He always knew
where the best parties were, always counted among his friends the most powerful
men and the best-looking women. To Siger, it seemed there wasn't a door in
this village Frère Jacques could not put his head into without being greeted as a
friend. He introduced Master Siger to some very amiable card players to whom

he lost a large amount of money, money which Frère Jacques then graciously replaced. He took Siger to a cinema where films made at the local film school were shown. Frère Jacques even introduced him to a night-club where naked people did startling things on a stage and in front of everybody. Master Siger could not imagine a more gracious or enthusiastic host. As if Frère Jacques was prepared to pull rabbits out of his hat to entertain and divert Master Siger. So it seemed only Siger's miserable constitution left him at the end of every party, festival or soiree with embarrassing regret and a hearty hangover.

But Spring had finally returned, and with it Master Siger's thoughts returned to Paris. He could only account for this desire as the result of a jading disillusionment. The public parties, the card games, and the film festivals, like the rounds among his philosopher-friends, all eventually seemed to come full circle. Party hostesses and drug dealers began to recur like rhetorical strategies in philosophical discussions, so that no matter how circuitous the route, they seemed always to return to the point where their party had begun, debaucheries that invariably degenerated into a new source of scandalous gossip. This realization had cost Master Siger several hangovers. He wondered how many more such evenings he could endure.

When at last Siger paid his visit to San Dominico, it had been just past mid-day and he found himself alone within the chapel's cool twilight. Some thoughtful cleric had placed the chair Brother Thomas had used when delivering his lectures to the left of the altar, and looking at it Siger could almost conjure the image of Brother Thomas's rotundity overflowing the chair's stout wooden arms. After a brief wander around the chapel Master Siger took a seat simply to rest and perhaps reflect.

Brother Thomas had arrived at Orvieto burdened by a crisis, and here Siger sat bedeviled and confused by a crisis of his own. So perhaps Siger finally made his pilgrimage with the hope that he would find the reassurance that Brother Thomas had found.

Yet Master Siger remained skeptical. Because what Thomas had discovered in this chapel was something that Siger still found unacceptable. So perhaps his visit had been doomed to disappoint him. Through prayer and contemplation while residing in Orvieto, Brother Thomas had managed to embrace one of the deepest and most frightening of the Church's mysteries; the transubstantiation.

Master Siger studied the crucifix above the altar, the same one that had spoken to Thomas assuring him of the truth of that terrible mystery, and promising him that the very salvation of his soul depended upon his acceptance of its truth. What bothered Master Siger was that, despite Thomas' close study of Aristotle, and having lectured so brilliantly on his philosophy, he had finally come to accept this most un-Aristotelian account. Siger remained astonished that Thomas had confronted a crisis of reason, and resolved his crisis with mere faith. Siger's disillusionment had arisen because, despite all that Thomas had studied of Aristotle's writing on Substance and Essence, Brother Thomas had finally accepted the confusing notion of God's exceptionalism; the idea that God had created the material world and all the laws that govern it, and yet had permitted Himself the luxury of exempting His Own activities from those laws. So at least for Master Siger, it seemed as if Thomas had abandoned Aristotle. Unfortunately, by this decision Thomas had also betrayed Master Siger and all those who had studied Aristotle's words seriously, through the expedient of trimming his conviction to fit this need.

At the time, Siger had almost managed to stifle his disappointment over Thomas's decision, but he had known even then that his decision would result in their decisive break. The debate over this mystery had offered Thomas the perfect opportunity to openly embrace, and thereby validate, the double-truth theory; that what was true in faith could simultaneously be false in reason. The absurdity of the doctrine of transubstantiation had all but demanded such a compromise, and the double-truth theory would have permitted believers to continue to believe without feeling like idiots. Had Brother Thomas done this, he might have saved numerous Parisian masters from the thoughtful attention of du Val and the Inquisition, including Boetius of Dacia.

Master Siger had lingered in the chapel a long time with his heart burdened by his struggle. Brother Thomas had held in his hands the means to resolve a crisis that troubled more than merely some Parisian masters. Men in all walks of life, exposed to new learning that was emerging from the most unlikely sources, had begun to find themselves caught up in identical crises. It had remained in Thomas' power to give the minds of men a status equal to that of their souls. Thomas had the opportunity to bring peace to hearts divided against minds, but in the end he had walked away. He had abandoned Aristotle and every man who had approached the Philosopher's writing with an open mind. So Master Siger had remained in the chapel with his eyes upon that crucifix waiting for something, he did not know what. Had he expected Thomas to suddenly materialize seated in his chair, offer to hold Siger's hand and tell him that everything would be all right? Or had he expected the Lord God Himself to suddenly begin dictating for Siger's benefit? Though Siger had remained in the chapel struggling with his doubt, in the end he had simply dozed off in the cool silence, and no revelation had appeared to him in dream. But when he awoke he realized he must return to Paris. If he held out any hope of resuming the battle that Brother Thomas had abandoned, he would need to begin in Paris, and among the Parisian masters. And he would need to trust that the Lord would understand the honesty of his intention. Master Siger's wobbly legs came to a stop so suddenly that he nearly fell forward.

Finally he reached the valley floor, to stand at the gate of the Etruscan village of the dead. Just beside its entrance towerd a broad, old chestnut tree, its wide and thickly-leafed branches forming a canopy of seductive shade. Master Siger sat down beneath the tree, grateful for its shelter from the terrible sunlight, and he sighed.

Beyond the rasp of his own breathing, Siger heard only the chatter of birds and buzzing of insects. Then from the plateau far above him, he listened to the tolling of the cathedral bells. Master Siger enjoyed a comforting solitude. Gradually regaining his breath, he turned his attention to the gate.

The lane that opened before him was paved with wide grey stones. On either side as if guarding the path stood the remains of two winged lions of gray stone mounted on tall grey stone pedestals. Every detail of their features had been worn away or broken off, but their outlines remained alert sentinels frozen at the moment of flight. Master Siger glanced back along the long, steep climb upward to the town intimidated and discouraged. He rested until his head finally cleared, and then he stood. With a nod to each of the sentinels he walked between the beasts and entered the necropolis.

Shaped like small houses, the tombs were ranged along either side of the main path evenly spaced in rows, with smaller alleys opening at right angles. The cemetery had been laid-out like a village, with doorways of the tombs directly facing each other across the lane. Lacking exterior decoration, their surfaces in many places had acquired a thin layer of moss. Though the sunlight seemed brutal enough to wither wherever it fell, it was still Spring, and even these grey stones appeared sheathed in bright green. He looked down to discover parallel grooves worn into the stones beneath his feet that could only have been made by the wheels of ancient chariots. He conjured the image of an Etruscan chariot passing along this way on another bright afternoon in early spring, but two thousand years before. This image pleased Master Siger. It seemed to assure him of something he could not clearly grasp. Something about the permanence of the past, but also something about the universal individuation underscored by these particular tombs. Even in Death, we are only merely ourselves.

The line of tombs that straddled the lane led into a deeper shade of clustered trees. When he reached that shade Master Siger again paused, and he sat down on a pile of stones to rest. He looked up to see that above the sealed door of every tomb was a lintel inscribed with something that could have been lettering. Siger guessed he was reading the name of a family or a clan. Though these symbols were indecipherable, he understood that these marks were intended to particularize the spot. These symbols said to Master Siger that, of all the people who have ever lived, or who will ever live, only these particular people inhabit this particular plot of this earth. With an uncontrollable sigh of melancholy, Master Siger recognized the inhabitants of these tombs as men and women like the men and women he knew, had known, and would know. And he saw with aching clarity that these had come here to rest, earthly endeavors, failures and successes, all ultimately blended into an obscurity that would never quite disappear, finally shrouded and disguised by the returning verdure of the earth. Though the human world had struggled to remain, the natural world had claimed its own.

Sitting among the remains of these humans and their artifacts, Master Siger felt even more strongly the power of the surrounding forest, its exuberance and its shadows. And sheltered within these woods, that natural world so beloved by Aristotle, Master Siger felt welcomed. He sat quite still under the shifting and dappled twilight, surrounded by the play of sounds and the aromas and textures of the air. The sighs of the forest drifted around him, a breathing world, the in-flow and out-rush of air, a cooling tide, whispering and muttering with an unjustifiable contentment. Siger could only sense this contentment as outside and beyond him, forever distant though always present, yet as palpable as his own heart-beat, or the rush of air into his own throat, or the taste of the air on his tongue, or that insistent murmur within his ear. The Nature that encircled him flaunted a fruitfulness that belied Master Siger's own weakness and sterility, a power of creation beyond his own fragility. And this frailty, his recognition of deficiency, reminded him that he remained incomplete, and that his mission, this adventure, had collapsed into the rubble of its effort. The murmur and mutter of the forest resembled the quiet laughter of women. Siger was tempted to laugh along, to acknowledge the joke and surrender to his own absurdity. Instead, he stood and resumed his walk.

Siger discovered further ahead that some of the tombs had collapsed into mounds of rough stone half-buried in the earth. In their overgrown desolation, Master Siger almost expected to see a centaur step into his path. Under the uneven light that filtered through the trees, these tombs seemed hardly imagined, as if they could have been created simply to confound him. He wondered if Nature was also making fun of him, placing these objects here simply to confuse and discourage and frighten him.

As he walked, Master Siger remembered drunken rambles through the Luxembourg Gardens in the company of Boetius. Shrouded in fading twilight walking and arguing, drinking and walking, sitting and arguing, it had been a kind of life that now seemed so remote it might have happened to someone else and in another century. And so he found himself again missing Boetius, a sense of loss that brought tears to his eyes. He longed to believe that all he had been told about Boetius was wrong, and that the man remained alive, somewhere. Would de Brion have told him honestly if he was still alive? Did it make any sense even to wonder what had really happened? So what began as thoughts turned to anguish and nagging doubt. He wondered again about the helicopter. Would Boetius have risked a nighttime landing against Franciscan security? Could that apparent rescue-attempt have been merely a temptation calculated to fail and created by an enemy who used Boetius's name as his cover? With a shudder Master Siger reminded himself again that Mistress Jacqueline may have told him the truth: Boetius was dead, lost at sea unburied and unmourned except by Master Siger himself. If that was so, Master Siger hoped Boetius had found the chance to recant his infamous assertion that the life of the philosopher is the most perfect on earth.

And in thinking this, Master Siger had to acknowledge that his own situation provided an embarrassing contrast. His life at the Papal Court was pleasurable to the point of decadence. Having chosen a life among scoundrels, Siger was relieved he had chosen to pass his time in the company of wealthy and educated scoundrels. But Master Siger could see clearly the mark of death that was upon them all. They were as dead as the inhabitants of these tombs. A thousand years dead? Two thousand? These before him had once been as alive as Master Siger, and now they were just as dead as they ever would be. A thousand years forward? Two thousand? In that world, a world just as real as the one Master Siger shared with the others, he and those around him were already dead. The day Siger died he would be just as dead as those he stood among now. The fact that somewhere in the future his death had already taken place disturbed him. Unhappily, once conceded there was only to pick a number, any number found on any calendar, and that could just as likely be the date as any other. Such a number had found its way to Boetius. Except for a delicacy of feeling, did it make sense for Master Siger to exclude himself, or anyone else, from their position in that fatal lottery? Only the Lord Himself could know.

Master Siger followed the avenue of shade cast by more tall, overhanging chestnut trees. As the shade became deeper, Master Siger felt his strength returning. Oddly, the further he walked, the better he felt. He followed this path partly out of curiosity and partly because its gentle slope continued to coax his legs forward. He was simply glad to be shielded from the sun.

As he passed these monuments, ancient even during Aristotle's life, the words of Simon de Brion returned to Master Siger. Snatches of their Avignon conversation seemed to echo from the remains of these tombs. Just as they were built before the time of Aristotle's powerful thought, so might there also be an end to natural philosophy, beyond which all would be forgotten. Simon de Brion had insisted on this so bluntly and with such effortless certainty that Master Siger still could not dispel its possibility. Like those drops of the Blood of Our Lord that stained the caporal now hanging encased above the main altar of Santa Maria cathedral, as the centuries passed those blood-stains would grow dim, but they would never completely disappear. No matter how far into the future, in every future world it will always be the case that those stains had miraculously appeared on that caporal. Just so, it will always be the case that Aristotle thought.

The twilight from the trees arching over the lane became still deeper. Master Siger walked recognizing fewer of these piles of rough stone as tombs. More and more lay opened, blocks of stone pushed over or missing completely, goats and bats now their only inhabitants.

Would the future regard systems of thought like Aristotle's the way Master Siger looked upon the tombs of these illustrious Etruscans whose very names were lost forever? Would it all finally amount to just so much corrupted theory, mixed and blended without consideration of method, result or consequence? Would it ever be possible to discuss knowledge of the material world without mention of Aristotle? Would the time come when systems and their systematizers were simply piled together and shoved into a corner abandoned to collect dust? Or worse, to stand as warnings of what should not be speculated? Master Siger shuddered. Thus would Aristotle be reduced to an example of failure. He wanted to know that at least his own thoughts and writings had had some value for his contemporaries, and perhaps even would grant him some small portion of that future. Despite the endurance of the objects around him, Siger decided this was unlikely.

The trees crowded closer overhead. Tombs he passed now hardly amounted to more than piles of different-sized stones. Within the fragrant green twilight, a gentle chaos of moss, plants and flowers shrouded the rubble adding to its silent grace. Master Siger walked as the path continued to narrow and the darkness thickened. The path finally disappeared into tall grass and scattered bushes. Distracted by his thoughts, Master Siger continued on. Gradually he realized that the end of the lane was cloaked in profound darkness. Yet he felt as if he had no choice except to continue. He was less eager to pursue a quality of the light than he was anxious to overcome the dread he had discovered enveloping his thoughts. As though, if he walked far enough and long enough, the darkness within him would finally relent. He reminded himself that such dark thoughts were not the same as prophecy, yet he was determined to wrestle with his possible place in the intellectual chorus.

Finally the lane ended in impenetrable shadow. He stopped at a barrier of interlaced tree branches and tall, heavy bushes, already intending to turn and retrace his steps. But suddenly he was certain he heard beyond that vegetal barrier the sound of water splashing, blended with a sound that could have been voices.

At first he could not hear those voices clearly. He took another hesitant step forward, and then another, until the voices separated from the sound of flowing water. He was startled to realize that at any moment he might recognize a word. The path had disappeared in the darkness, so he chose his steps cautiously, enticed by a hardly-discernable sound of voices gradually becoming clear. The voices were soft and high-pitched and young, and female.

Master Siger took another careful step between the bushes and those tree branches woven and entangled before him as if placed there to block his path. As he pushed ahead, the foliage seemed to whisper his name.

The voices became clearer and Siger decided they spoke in a language he could not decipher. High-spirited cries punctuated with splashes of water were followed by glittering laughter that inexplicably thrilled him. Master Siger tried to move only when the laughter was loudest, yet the sound itself paralyzed him.

Confronted finally by a wall of heavy branches and wide, thick leaves that seemed determined to keep him back, with two fingers he parted this living wall gently. He discovered that he had reached the bank of a wide and quick-flowing stream. But what he saw in the water so startled him that he trembled and half-turned to run away.

The Curtain Must Fall, Yet The Eloquent Hand of History Hesitates. Bemused By an Unaccountable Fear, Master Siger Must Move Forward, He Cannot Do Otherwise, Even While Reluctance Hobbles Him. But There Is No Return For Master Siger, Though He Still Does Not Know This. That Path Of Retreat Has Disappeared, the Past is Another Country. He Belongs to History, and History Must Remain His Home.

CHAPTER THE LAST

Let the thin yet perfect Ear of History Recall the Laughter
of Female Voices as Its Sound Enticed Master Siger's Attention to a Shallow
Portion of a Sparkling Blue Stream Shaded Beneath the Broad, Thick Boughs
of an Old Chestnut Tree Whose Darkly Gnarled Roots Reached Out into the
Stream To Form a Glittering Pool, Surrounded by Golden Air Bright Under
That Noonday Sun.

Through the screen of green leaves that concealed him, the startled Siger
of Brabant, professor at the prestigious Sorbonne and Master of Natural
Philosophy, discovered three women standing in the stream playfully bathing
each other. Amid caresses and handfuls of water, they laughed in the bright
voices of schoolgirls. Thigh-deep in the glittering water, their naked figures
seemed almost too elegantly proportioned, their forms too splendidly well-
shaped, rounded swells and curving hollows blue in their bright twilight
world, and droplets of water on their skin sparkled with fire. Master Siger
gasped and then held his breath.

Though sheltered by the shade of tress and standing in cunning disguise
within foliage so dense he had to force an opening, the light emanating from
these gorgeous beings assaulted his eyes. Tricks perhaps of the eye itself, eyes
which Master Siger wondered if he should trust. What his eyes presented
as real, Master Siger could not believe. If reason had been Siger's anvil,

observation had been his hammer. But this vision beside this stream and under this light left his anvil shattered, his hammer pliant. His disbelief was formally complete, yet he could not look away. He discovered himself forced to accept the impossible.

Treacherous light, traitorous eyes, he observed the color of each woman's hair which, by some fragmentation of the light, appeared alternately fair or red or brown and then nearly black. This shifting of tones and shades of color with each movement of the light left Siger lightheaded and enchanted.

As amazed as he was by the effect of the light upon their hair, its effect on their skin astonished him. Even dappled and shadowed beneath that huge tree, their flesh shimmered with iridescence. Light fell upon it exploding like the shower of golden sparks from a shattered wood-fire. But what most astonished Master Siger was an illusion so powerful and compelling, it left him rooted in his hiding place and unable to move, his legs merely numb sticks, his hands bags of cement, and he could not even turn his head. This effect, Master Siger observed stiffly, was uncanny, but its chimera left him powerless.

One of these remarkable creatures, Siger was compelled to accept, bore an impossible resemblance to Mistress Jacqueline. The second, he was convinced, appeared to be the twin of Mistress Marguerite. And the third could be none other than Mistress Celestina herself, in her opulent and apparent flesh. Master Siger discovered he was barely breathing. And then he began to panic. Because the more closely he observed these beings, the stronger these resemblances grew.

Breathless and trembling, Siger watched as the woman who could only be Mistress Celestina turned tipping her head toward the other two, and then spoke in a voice Siger could not hear. The others laughed and began to splash each other, while the one who appeared to be Mistress Celestina turned away striding gorgeously toward the shore. Her wet and sparkling body shimmered in the half-light, her movements were lustrous with the grace of breathing as she approached a cluster of bushes and then stepped behind them and out of his sight.

Master Siger returned to watching the two remaining women continue their play. Gradually their play became rougher, and soon they began to wrestle. And as Master Siger watched with increasing excitement, the women began to take turns pushing each other under water and laughing louder still. Enjoying the simple pleasure of watching these frolics, Master Siger fell into a pleasant lethargy, as if he could have remained hidden there forever simply observing this display of terrifying delight. For a moment he surrendered, his power of thought abandoned him and flew utterly from his grip. Moments floated beneath him on a series of rolling swells of rapture. His motionless breathing seemed to harmonize with the laughing voices of these two women, naked and brilliant, at play before him. The behavior he observed, along with his muddled thoughts about everything occurring before him, even the sound of the rushing stream and singing of birds, seemed to happen outside the drift of time. And he questioned nothing, as certain of all he saw as he was of the breeze that caressed his face.

The bushes behind him rustled. Before he could turn, Master Siger was embraced from behind so fiercely his breath was forced from his chest and circles of colored light appeared before his eyes. A voice from behind him cried out, "I've got him!" Master Siger recognized this voice as belonging to Mistress Celestina.

The two women in the stream stopped their play and turned in his direction, and then resumed their laughter. Still confined from behind, Siger was lifted until his feet waved in the air, then was pushed forward through those bushes that had hidden him, and out into a clearing at the edge the pond beneath the tree. Whenever his feet stumbled, the arms encircling him lifted him with startling ease. From the stream, the two women cried out in unison, "Bring him here!"

Master Siger was pushed along the bank to the place shadowed beneath the tree. Its thick, black and gnarled roots reached out forming a wide, deep pool of perfectly clear and motionless water sheltered within the deep shadow of its broad and leafy boughs. Along the pool's edge the bank fell off sharply. Carried with seemingly no effort by the arms around him, Master Siger was made to sit at the edge of the pond with his feet trailing into the water. Without releasing him, his captor sat down behind him. His awkward position squeezed his head between his captor's substantial breasts.

The other women approached to within an arm's length, and then sat and reclined in the clear, shallow water, its motionless and glistening surface reflecting and so doubling the allure of their perfect forms.

"So!" said the one who resembled Mistress Marguerite. "Finally you've brought us a philosopher."

"Finally," the one who looked like Mistress Jacqueline said, "you've brought us a live one to play with."

"A live one indeed," the one who looked like Mistress Marguerite added, laughing and clapping her hands.

"He has seen us!" Master Siger's captor announced darkly from over his shoulder. "And he must be punished!" Though her voice was clear and bright, its tone insisted his situation was serious.

"Yes!" the two women before him cried together. Their eyes glittered with unnatural intensity. "He must be punished!" They clapped their hands with delight and splashed each other with water that sparkled in their twilight. "We must punish him!"

"Wait!" Master Siger cried. To the one, he said, "Don't you recognize me, Jacqueline?" The woman he addressed shook herself, her skin shimmered like a pearl. "And you," he said turning to the other, "I have known you, Mistress Marguerite." The sound of her sigh came to him like a breeze. Half-turning to his captor, Master Siger added, "And tell me that you are not Mistress Celestina."

Suddenly all three women burst into loud laughter; their voices so harmonized that its sound resembled church-bells. They laughed together so long and loud that for a moment Master Siger's captor's grasp loosened. Believing this was his chance, he shrugged to break her embrace. But the arms around him closed immediately and with remarkable strength.

"Philosopher!" the voice behind him warned. "Be still if you hope to be enlightened."

The woman who resembled Mistress Marguerite stood. Glittering in her pale and perfect form, she folded her hands. "Whoever it is we most resemble among your mortal friends, Master Siger, know that you are in the presence of immortal goddesses. Hear and acknowledge that throughout all possible Universes I am known as Goddess Kim. Beside me in her perfect splendor, your mortal gaze falls upon Goddess Tina. And know yourself as among the most fortunate of men, for you are held in the gentle but certain embrace of none other than Goddess Stacey."

Master Siger realized the two women before him were staring at his waist. Looking down he saw that his member had stiffened so thoroughly it formed a tent beneath his robes.

"Bring him here to me," said Goddess Tina, the one who resembled Jacqueline. His captor, whom he had known as Mistress Celestina but who he now must acknowledge as Goddess Stacey, pushed him further toward the edge of the pool. Goddess Tina reached up and tossed back the fold of his robes exposing his excited state. She grasped its base with the grip of an iron clamp. To Master Siger she smiled. "Now you must remain, prepared as you obviously are to entertain goddesses who have condescended to reveal themselves to you." Goddess Stacey laughed as she released him and stood.

Master Siger moved to stand, but in an instant Goddess Tina's grip moved lower and she squeezed sharply. The pain sent Master Siger flat onto his back. Quietly, Goddess Tina said, "We will agree that you will not do that again." When she released her grasp, her hand moved immediately back to the base of his member where she resumed her grip.

Majestic in her splendid resemblance to Mistress Celestina, Goddess Stacey stepped back into the water, approached Goddess Kim, embraced her and caressed her face with water. Though she continued to smile, Goddess Kim said, "Of course, he must be punished!"

"He must be punished!" Goddess Stacey agreed, and then kissed Goddess Kim lightly on the throat. Goddess Kim giggled and splashed her in response.

Goddess Tina nodded. "There can be no equivocation. For his impertinence he must be punished."

Finally Master Siger raised his head. "But Jacqueline," he began. Before he could continue, she gripped his member sharply.

"That's Goddess Tina to you, mortal dimwit philosopher, if all that is not a simultaneously redundant oxymoron. You are in the presence of goddesses. Where is your humility? Where is your decency? Where is your respect?"

Goddess Stacy asked, "And where is your fear?"

Goddess Kim said, "He has seen us naked and at play." Her smile disappeared.

"He has seen us together," Goddess Stacey said.

"He has seen how we are together," the three chanted in unison.

After a moment Goddess Tina grinned sheepishly. "I know how this one would be punished best." Suddenly she pulled hard on his member. The pain was so great Master Siger could not even cry out. "I shall relieve him of this!"

Goddess Stacey shook her head and sighed. "Don't bother. He's a philosopher. He'll just grow another one."

Nodding in agreement, Goddess Kim said, "We must think of a punishment from which he will never recover."

"The punishment must be as severe and as painful as the offense," Goddess

Kim said.

"A terrible, fierce punishment!" Goddess Tina and Goddess Stacey declared together.

Suddenly Goddess Kim smiled. She stood, her eyes suddenly bright in the shadows. "I know what his punishment must be!"

"Tell us!" Goddess Tina and Goddess Stacey said in unison as they laughed. Then they began to splash water at Goddess Kim until all were laughing. All except Master Siger. "Tell us! Tell us now! Tell us, please!"

As she wiped water from her eyes, Goddess Kim said, "We will tell him his future!"

"Yes!" the other goddesses cried together. "Yes! A sublime punishment! We must reveal his future! Knowledge will be his punishment. Reveal his future so that we may watch him writhe in the exquisite misery of incontrovertible knowledge."

With a burst of laughter and splashing water, Goddess Kim asked, "Which of us will begin?"

"You have discovered a most excellent punishment!" Goddess Tina said as she caressed Goddess Stacey's back. "You have earned this privilege. Please begin." Goddess Stacey turned on Goddess Tina splashing her with water.

"All right," Goddess Kim said. "But you both must pay close attention that I make no mistake." She came toward Master Siger, half-swimming and half-crawling in the clear, shallow water, so that her lithe and sinuous form was perfectly displayed to his fearful and disbelieving eyes. In the water beneath his feet, she reclined opposite Goddess Tina, whose grip remained firm. Her expression suddenly darkened. "But where should I begin?"

"I suppose," Goddess Stacey said, "eventually we will have to tell him about his death."

"That is true," Goddess Kim said sadly. "But that we should leave for later."

Goddess Stacey said, "We should begin, then, by assuring him that all that he writes will be published."

Goddess Tina said, "Yes. Since he thinks what he thinks is so important that he must write it all down, this certainly concerns our scholar. Undoubtedly he tells himself that all that matters is that inquisitive minds have the opportunity to read his oh-so profound thoughts." Goddess Kim and Goddess Tina burst suddenly into loud laughter together.

"So be it," Goddess Kim said. Turning with a look of great affection she said,

"Let me assure you, Master Siger, that everything you write while under the protection of His Holiness, he will agree to publish." She paused as if observing his reaction. "I expect this pleases you." His look of relief provoked her. "But understand that none of it will ever actually be printed."

As if enjoying the stunned confusion on Siger's face, Goddess Stacey added without prompting, "And you want to know what else? When you die, everything you have written will be burned. Like in fire. Consumed in the highest and brightest flame."

"And their ashes," Goddess Tina added, "will be turned into compost."

All three goddesses became quiet as they watched Siger struggle to accept what he could not understand.

Finally Goddess Tina said, "Though this may be difficult for you to comprehend because you are mortal, understand that all that you have written will disappear." Smiling lewdly she added, "It will be as if you had never thought."

Choked with horror, Master Siger attempted to speak, but Goddess Tina simply increased her pressure. Master Siger groaned. "Do not mistake this for a dialogue, philosopher. Accept your fate as your punishment!"

Goddess Stacey said, "Now let's tell him about the Pope."

"Perfect!" Goddess Kim said splashing water at Goddess Stacey. "But it's your turn. You should tell him about the Pope!"

"Tell him about the Pope!" Goddess Tina and Goddess Kim repeated together. "Tell him about the Pope!"

"Should I tell him everything about the Pope?" Goddess Stacey asked coyly.

"Just tell him the good parts," Goddess Tina said.

Goddess Stacey nodded and then turned to Master Siger. "I have unfortunate news, Master Siger. Giovanni Gaetano Orsini, whom you have known as His Holiness, Pope Nicholas III, will leave this earthly realm. He will shrug off his mortal shell and take on the mantle of the Blessed Elect. In short, sadly, His Holiness will die. As for philosophers, so also for popes. As Aristotle is, so Pope Nicholas III will be. And it won't be long."

"Really!" Goddess Kim added with bright charm. "When you think about it, for a mortal it might seem very long. I mean, to a mortal, a few years might seem nearly an eternity."

"Wait!" Goddess Stacey said sharply. "We should not tell him how far in the future these events will take place."

"But I said nothing about that!" Goddess Kim said.

"She didn't!" Goddess Tina agreed.

"You told him this would happen in a few years," Goddess Stacey said.

"That's true," Goddess Kim agreed. "But it could be any few years. To an immortal goddess, a year is hardly more than a moment."

"Fair enough," Goddess Stacy said. "We will permit this confusion, and encourage him to speculate pointlessly."

"You haven't told him the best part yet," Goddess Tina said. "Tell him the best part!"

"Can there be," Goddess Stacy asked, "something better than foreknowledge of the death of another?"

Goddess Tine and Goddess Kim squealed with delight. Goddess Kim said, "There's always the knowledge of what will come after."

Composing herself Goddess Stacey said, "Master Siger, as you well know, when in the fullness of time His Holiness, Pope Nicholas III joins his Creator, a new pope will be sought."

"The Pope is dead, long live the Pope!" Goddess Tina said, and all three laughed.

"The search for the new pope," Goddess Stacey continued, "will be extensive and meticulous. The final candidate must be a man of great wisdom." Goddess Stacey's laughter burst from her throat.

Goddess Kim added. "The new pope must be a man of unassailable virtue." Then she, too, was overcome with laughter.

Goddess Tina barely controlled her own laughter as she said, "And the new pope must be a man of sterling self-control, perfectly submissive to the will of his Creator and Redeemer." But with these words she was overcome as well. The other goddesses joined in her hilarity, so that the two rolled in the water embracing and laughing.

Weak from her gaiety and rubbing water from her eyes, Goddess Stacey finally resumed. "Deliberations in Viterbo will continue for months. Names will be put forward only to be passed over. Powerful men will gather behind locked doors to advance one candidate and then another, yet consensus will elude the proceedings for many weeks. But finally, springtime will come to Holy Mother Church. A candidate will emerge who embodies the achievements and aspirations of the Church. A Knight steadfast in his defense of His Church, but also a Shepherd vigilant for the safety of His Flock will be put forward."

"Tell him who it will be!" Goddess Kim and Goddess Tina said in unison. "Tell him who the new pope will be!"

Goddess Stacey smiled cunningly. "His Holiness will take the name Martin IV, and his reign will last a number of years. He will wield power firmly, and under his leadership the security of the Chair of Peter will increase. He will be respected and feared by the earthly powers, and when his time has come, his passing will be deeply mourned."

Goddess Stacey stood and approached Master Siger. She leaned forward and brought her lips close to his ear. Her full, pale breast was hot as it brushed against his shoulder. She whispered, "And now, I will tell you that the man who will become His Holiness, Martin IV, is no one other than your dear old friend, Dr. Simon de Brion." And into his ear she began to laugh. Goddess Kim and Goddess Tina joined her, and the laughter of these three gorgeous goddesses set the leaves of the tree over their heads shivering, rippled the water around them out to the middle of the stream, and shook the reeds ranked behind them. Their thrilling laughter traveled through the earth and through the water and through the air, so that there was nothing, living or dead, anywhere on the earth that was not laughing at the venerable Master Siger of Brabant.

As Goddess Tina laughed she pulled harder and harder on his member. Yet this pain was nothing compared to the agony of Goddess Tina's laughter. But the true source of his misery was not obscured. The thought that Simon de Brion would achieve absolute control of that Congregation created by Jesus Christ to bring salvation to every soul living and dead, caused his heart to quake and then shrivel with despair. He realized that it was all much worse than he had ever imagined. And Aristotle had given him no help.

"That's right!" Goddess Kim said. "Your friend Aristotle was totally useless to you. Nothing you ever read could prepare you for Simon de Brion securely ensconced as Prince of Princes and Christ's Shepherd on earth. But why should we care what concerns your Aristotle? He was indifferent to us. It is only common courtesy that we return his favor."

"Besides," Goddess Stacey announced haughtily, "someone like Simon de Brion is precisely the man to preside over your faith. He is more representative of the type your religion demands than anyone we can imagine."

"He is perfect!" Goddess Tina and Goddess Kim chanted, "He is perfect! He is perfect! He is perfect!" Goddess Stacey joined them. "He is perfect! He is perfect! He is perfect!" Then to the accompaniment of more glittering laughter they began to splash each other with girlish awkwardness, indifferent to Master Siger's devastation.

A wave of dizziness overwhelmed Master Siger. He tried to imagine the world of Simon de Brion's Papacy, and that image was not comforting. But he also realized that with Simon de Brion in possession of the Keys of Peter, Master Siger would become thoroughly expendable.

Yet, even when Goddess Stacey announced the man's name, Master Siger recognized how appropriate his choice would be, and how shrewdly the game would be played to secure it. A new structure of alliances, a new community of interests would gather. Despite protests from those locked out of that community, Goddess Stacey had just assured him that all competitors would fail, and every delay or diversionary tactic would prove useless. Master Siger's vision dimmed. He could foresee only terrible consequences for his Church and the Chair of Peter.

Goddess Tina suddenly asked, "And just what concern might all of that be to you? What could you possibly care?"

Master Siger realized she had somehow heard his thoughts and now addressed him directly. She studied his face with an intensity that startled him. She said, "You have always been indifferent to the ways of the powerful. You have always held yourself above their inelegant struggles. For you, the Papacy and the Curia and the Inquisition have always been a hardly bearable embarrassment of self-promotion and self-aggrandizement. Why should you feel concern now?"

Master Siger opened his mouth to speak, but Goddess Tina pulled harder than before. Glancing over her shoulder to the other goddesses she said, "It's time we told him."

Though they continued to smile, Goddess Kim and Goddess Stacey nodded, and then became very still. Finally Goddess Kim said, "It is the only thing these mortals really want to know, anyway."

"For all mortals," Goddess Stacey said, "it is the only knowledge that is of any value, yet it is impossible to find."

"But Master Siger will be the exception," Goddess Tina said bright with confidence. She watched his eyes as she spoke. "Of all men, Master Siger will know the occasion and circumstances of his own death."

"And there will be nothing he can do about it," Goddess Tina said sighing with regret.

"He will have knowledge," Goddess Kim said, "that is without power. His knowledge will offer him no alternative action. His knowledge will not permit him to change even one single moment. Not the slightest gesture, nor even the smallest instant of light."

Solemnly Goddess Stacey said, "Just as for Aristotle, so also for Pope Nicholas III."

Goddess Kim added, "And just so for Pope Nicholas III, so also for Master Siger of Brabant."

Where she had fiercely gripped, Goddess Tina now caressed, her hand moving smoothly along the length of his member. Goddess Stacey said, "Though it takes an infinity of forms, Master Siger, understand that Death knows no strangers."

"Well put!" Goddess Kim said. "But what concerning his death would our philosopher most desire to know? The time of this event, or its method?"

Goddess Stacey said, "Remember that this is his punishment. Remember that his crime is severe, and so Master Siger must be punished severely."

Smiling brilliantly, together Goddess Stacey and Goddess Kim said, "So we must tell him all!"

"Our philosopher," Goddess Tina said, "will acquire the Ultimate Knowledge. He will learn the moment and circumstances of his own death."

"Be reassured, Master Siger," said Goddess Tina calmly. "Know that your death will not be by your own participation. No blame for it will be held against you."

Goddess Kim said, "You must be aware that Pope Nicholas III has taken it upon himself to be your protector."

"Whatever he may think of you," Goddess Stacey said, "he has decided he must not allow you to fall into the hands of the Inquisition. And he will succeed, as he must. Otherwise he risks alienating a powerful opposition within the College of Paris."

"And also because he knows," Goddess Tina added, "that any recantation from you must expose numerous clergy, particularly in the mendicant orders, to insupportable scrutiny. And if he removes his support from you now, it would be the same as admitting that the scurrilous methods of the Inquisition are proper and justified. It would vindicate the misery caused by their intrigues and paranoias."

"So be of good cheer," said Goddess Kim, "for he will protect you."

"He will defend you until the end of his life," Goddess Stacey said.

"But at his death," Goddess Tina added, "you will lose your defender. And the man who takes his place will have no reason to protect you, and every reason to make an example of you." Goddess Tina's caresses continued insistently.

"You should entertain no doubt," Goddess Stacey said, "that he will be persistently encouraged to turn you over to the Inquisition."

"Do not think too badly of him for this," Goddess Kim said. "By doing so, he only gains in prestige among those supporters waiting for him to strike the first blow against heresy. His abandonment of you will expose an infestation of heterodox thinking, and he will be expected to exterminate it as certainly as he has done in the past. And his zeal will be appreciated by the appropriate interests."

"Of course," Goddess Stacey said, "the new Pope's opponents will not be powerless. And they will be happy to use your cause to their advantage. But they will fail to rally sufficient support, and so will be forced to withdraw. At that moment you will be as welcome to them as a fish dead three days."

"But believe us, Master Siger," Goddess Kim said, "though the outcome is already decided, that is no reason to allow Simon and his allies an easy victory. The battle must still be fought."

"It will all happen very quietly," said Goddess Tina, her caresses growing more artistic with each stroke.

"Months will pass after the investiture of the new pope," said Goddess Stacey, "as your fate is argued. Powerful alliances will clash, and your skin will be their trophy."

"But finally all the deals will be made," Goddess Kim added. "The compromises will have been conceded, all of the oaths sworn."

"And then," Goddess Stacey said, "all that is left will be to deal with you. But fear not. The Inquisition will never reach you. You will continue far beyond their grasp, and beyond the reach of any mortal being. Save one."

"Your end will be sudden," Goddess Kim said stroking her own arms and chest with water. "Despite all that we are telling you, your death will come as a surprise."

"And it will be over quickly," Goddess Stacey said. "What struggle you offer will be useless."

"Was Brother Thomas murdered?" Master Siger blurted out this question without pause and before Goddess Tina could react. The goddesses looked to each other in vague confusion.

Finally Goddess Stacey said, "It doesn't matter."

"What?" Master Siger asked. This time Goddess Tina was prepared for him.

Master Siger's groan echoed across the stream.

"Really," Goddess Kim insisted. "Believe us. It doesn't matter."

Turning to Goddess Kim, Goddess Stacey said, "On the other hand, if it really doesn't matter, then it really doesn't matter." In response, Goddess Kim shrugged and then returned to splashing water over her chest.

"The fact is," Goddess Tina said, "he died of natural causes."

"Right," Goddess Stacey said. "Or at least that's the best information we have."

"That is, as best as we can guess," Goddess Kim said.

"What?" Master Siger said. Goddess Tina was even quicker in her reactions. Master Siger braced himself, and he was not disappointed

"Well, what did you expect?" Goddess Stacey said with exasperation. "Just because we are goddesses doesn't mean we can be everywhere all the time. We're only goddesses. Some things you learn yourself, but some you believe because of your source. It wasn't like any of us was around him every second."

Laughing with embarrassment Goddess Kim said, "We only became interested in you after he died."

Goddess Stacey said, "We expected you to be next."

Goddess Tina said, "But we would have gotten around to you eventually. We were on a schedule to make the rounds among all the Latin Averroists. And then the Thomas-thing came up and all the priorities got changed."

"Our best guess is that Brother Thomas died naturally," Goddess Tina said. Turning to the others she asked, "Now, can we get on with the rest of his punishment?"

"Yes!" said Goddess Kim and Goddess Stacey together.

"So we must tell him first about the pope," Goddess Kim said.

Goddess Stacey said, "I will begin with the passing of Pope Nicholas III."

"Which also will be very natural," Goddess Tina interjected. "We will be with him the entire time, thus our certainty."

Goddess Stacey said, "Unfortunately, with the completely natural death of His Holiness, Pope Nicholas III, once Simon de Brion is installed as the new Pontifus Maximus, the clock on your demise will begin to tick."

"And that time will not be very long," Goddess Kim said.

"But what can mortals know about time?" said Goddess Tina. "Mortals can know only the sequence, but true duration is beyond their sensibilities. Their parcels of uniform time cannot be adapted to real time. So we will simply limit ourselves to the sequence of events. References to real time will only confuse him."

Goddess Stacey smiled as if satisfied, splashed water on Goddess Tina, who used her free hand to splash water at Goddess Stacey, who had already turned to splash water on Goddess Kim, who was ready and waiting for her to turn so that she could splash water on Goddess Stacey. For a time, water flew so thickly that the goddesses disappeared in the billows of its snow-white froth. With a final cascade of laughter, the goddesses became quiet. Goddess Stacey stood again wiping water from her eyes. She stepped to a rock jutting out of the water near Goddess Kim, and then sat in the water with her back leaning against it and her delicious bosom heaving as she paused to catch her breath.

"Much to the new Pope's surprised relief," Goddess Stacy began, "he will discover himself surrounded by a legion of men determined to demonstrate their loyalty to him, and their utility to his schemes. There will be one among them who, though he has been a member of Pope Nicholas' inner circle of confidants, and has pretended indifference to Simon de Brion as the Papal Legate, will offer to Pope Martin IV fanatical, passionate support."

"One day," Goddess Stacey said, "the newly installed Prince of the Church will denounce you and deplore your continued annoyance. And one among those who hear his words will conclude that he, personally, has been challenged to demonstrate his utility and loyalty to this new Prince of the Church by bringing his annoyance to an end."

Goddess Kim added, "This man is of that tribe who discover themselves loyal to whoever holds power. He will make certain his demonstration of loyalty is visible only to those who need to see and to be reassured by his efforts. Because he understands that only this will grant him a generous reward."

"So this man," Goddess Stacey continued, "will look around for the most valuable service he can render. And he will recognize that the ultimate reward is only offered for the ultimate service." She seemed suddenly to become tired of talking or perhaps merely bored with the progress of her narrative. She slipped her entire body and face under the water and remained there.

Goddess Kim smiled at Master Siger and then resumed. "What greater service can there be than to accept a responsibility, even at the risk of physical danger, in order to eliminate a threat that cannot be confronted directly. Such a demonstration of loyalty would prove thoroughly convincing. Especially since the new pope knows he will need many dedicated hearts for those battles in his future."

Goddess Tina broke in suddenly as if anticipating Master Siger's thought.

"How, in his heart of hearts, does any man come to this conclusion? How would a man prepare himself to perform the ultimate act? Do not assume, Master Siger, that you can know his thoughts. But more, do not believe he has any more choice over his own actions than you have over yours. And worse for him, unlike you he is not gifted with foreknowledge of these events. In fact, at this very moment even the possibility of such an action has yet to occur to him."

Goddess Stacey emerged suddenly from underwater and splashed Goddess Kim. Then turning to Master Siger she said, "Remember that as you hear these words, all of this has already come to pass. Otherwise, how could we know it?"

Goddess Kim's smile was full of sympathy. "But take some heart, Master Siger, for you will be revenged. Upon your demise, your murderer will be confined by the Inquisition under the accusation of possession by Satan himself. After many uncomfortable months providing his torturers with despicable amusement, your murderer will be sent to a particularly impoverished and primitive monastery near Bucharest. Though it will seem a long time to him, not very long after these events, as he is returning one night from the house of a notorious woman, he will be attacked by bandits. Horribly wounded, he will spend the little time remaining to him in agony. But in the end his wounds will prove fatal. So much for the exquisite rewards for service to His Holiness."

Master Siger wanted to confirm that he knew the identity of the man in question, but instead he asked, "And what of Boetius of Dacia?" He waited for pain. Instead, Master Siger heard a sigh of frustration, as if the gust had come from all three goddesses at the same moment.

"He is alive and well," Goddess Kim volunteered with exasperated bluntness. "He is living in Amsterdam, married to a thirty-five year old virgin with a pile of money and a printing press. How much curiosity do you expect to have satisfied? After all, we are administering your punishment."

Goddess Stacey added, "He has set himself up to print pornography to earn enough money to publish books of philosophy. Given the precariousness of your situation, none of this should matter to you. Yet for sentimental reasons you no doubt wish him the best. Your loyalty to a friend you half-believe is dead does you credit."

To Goddess Tina, Goddess Kim said, "Perhaps we should not have told him this. Satisfying his curiosity concerning his dearest friend who he believed was dead seems more an exceptionally generous reward than a painful punishment."

"His punishment comes precisely," Goddess Tina said, "in that he is invited to imagine a future in which he cannot participate. His future is lost, while his past can be of no matter."

Master Siger hesitated, his thoughts gone astray for a moment in a vision of the past that seemed to be happening again before his eyes, yet also seemed to encompass the goddesses as well, all in a blanket of violet night.

Goddess Stacey said, "Believe us, philosopher, there was no possibility that you could have gotten onto that helicopter. What was apparent was never real."

"I could have gotten on," Master Siger protested. Goddess Kim pulled firmly, the sudden shock caught Master Siger by surprise.

Goddess Kim smiled. "An unavailable choice is no choice at all."

Languidly stretching her body immersed entirely in the water Goddess Stacey said, "Just as an event can seem to be merely one of several possibilities, in retrospect, that same event will be recognized as the inevitable result of an unrecognized choice. What appears the result of a conscious decision can be recognized only later as unavoidable and inevitable. Like all mortals, you mistake reality for its model."

Goddess Tina said, "Recognize yourself, Master Siger, as merely one sub-routine in the algorithm that is weaving the cloth of life itself. An algorithm in which no sub-routine is disposable, no sub-routine is more or less critical to the operation of the algorithm than any other. An algorithmic function in which every choice is fixed and every inevitability disguised by a forest of illusory options. Laws are the imperfect representations of paradox. Every paradox is true because every resolution is imprecise and therefore false. Paradox rules, the type is the exception." Goddess Tina's hand continued its caress. Under her attention, Master Siger's member became utterly rigid, and Goddess Tina's smile grew with it.

Goddess Kim slithered through the clear, cool water and approached Master Siger, who lay flat on his back across the stream's bank, with his legs in the water to his knees, and all of his lower body exposed to the cool, dappled sunlight. Watching Goddess Tina's hand, Goddess Kim said, "We have punished him severely. His pain will be excruciating. It will torment his sleep and leave him exhausted at sunrise. Our punishment has been severe."

"Perhaps too severe," Goddess Stacey said standing. She strode toward Siger, her skin glittered with diamonds of water. "As his crime has been serious, his just punishment must also be serious." She sat down in the water beside Master Siger's legs and opposite Goddess Tina and Goddess Kim. "The world has now been set aright. What would happen has come to pass."

Watching Goddess Tina's hand she began to stroke Master Siger's right thigh. "And yet, can justice be too well-served?"

"It is possible," Goddess Kim said, "that the demands of justice can be exceeded." She began to stroke his left thigh. While watching Goddess Tina's hand she said, "Perhaps, in the case of Master Siger, the harshness of our punishment has exceeded the severity of the crime."

Goddess Tina asked, "And are we not goddesses? Gifted as we are with unerring judgment, are we not also gifted with incomparable compassion and unjustifiable generosity?"

"We are not goddesses," said Goddess Stacey, "if we are not also generous." Her hand on Master Siger's thigh moved closer to his hips.

"If our justice should be unearthly, so also should be our generosity," Goddess Kim said. Her hand moved along Master Siger's hip while she watched Goddess Tina's hand. And I have observed that, on occasion, one generous act can overcome a multitude of injustices. But the act must be large, even perhaps enormous. And the act must also be utterly generous. The recipient can only be entirely unworthy as the act is without the slightest hint of self-interest or benefit. An example of the purest altruism."

Raising her eyes, Goddess Tina's gaze locked suddenly onto the eyes of Master Siger. Her eyes seemed to grow large, and as he watched, appeared to grow absolutely black. Gradually, a hint of the very darkest blue appeared. Goddess Tina half-stood. While her hand continued to confine his member she slid her body along his chest, until her face was just above his and her knees were each beside his hips. "The generous act must be unmistakable," she said bringing her lips close to his as she lowered her hips onto him. With a turn of her hips she invited him inside.

"To be unmistakable, the act must be grand," Goddess Kim said. She brought her face to rest beside Goddess Tina's and above Master Siger's.

"It must not only be large, it must also be powerful," Goddess Stacey said. She brought her face to rest beside Goddess Tina's other cheek.

Goddess Tina shifted above him. On her first downward stroke Master Siger felt something that brought to his mind a bolt of brilliant crystal energy that coursed suddenly through him and set his body trembling.

When he opened his eyes again, the faces of the three goddesses together hovered side by side just above his. Goddess Tina's dark eyes grew larger, so that he thought he saw within them a midnight sky. She lifted and descended again, and again his body shuddered. For a moment Master Siger held his breath. When he looked again he realized the faces to either side of Goddess Tina's had begun to merge with hers. Their individual features began to blend and then disappear within each other. And the features of Goddess Tina's face blurred so that Master Siger seemed to see the separate faces of each goddess superimposed one over the other. All of their aspects hovered together just above his mind.

Goddess Tina lifted and then descended again, and then again. Master Siger was overwhelmed with fits of an exquisite pleasure that sent him trembling and shuddering as if he floated on a wild and cresting sea. Goddess Tina/Kim/Stacey's face hovered as it grew even larger over his, until it blocked out the entire sky, and all he saw was the faces of those superb goddesses smiling down at him. Eyes became large enough so that he seemed to look through them into a night sky splattered with stars. And among the stars he could just make out a sliver of yellow moon, a slim and yellow flower-petal laid against a black velvet sky.

As his body trembled and shook, this slice of moon grew larger. As if moving toward him now, this sliver continued to grow. Master Siger still heard their sparkling laughter of pleasure, a sound that made him smile. The moon became larger as if approaching, then still larger, and then looming.

Suddenly, as if in a unified concession, the voices announced, "Oh, all right! Not all of your books will be burned! Satisfied?" Master Siger closed his eyes tightly as a cascade of blissful fire poured through his veins so powerfully he heard himself cry out.

After several breathless moments Master Siger opened his eyes. The face above his disappeared as slowly as a slip of fog, and suddenly he recognized above him a broad, leaf-covered tree bough. Then he heard footsteps. Glancing around he realized there was no water, there was no stream, there were no goddesses. Suddenly, staring down over him appeared the grinning face of Frère Jacques.

"So this," he said with a broad smile, "is what philosophical contemplation is all about. Accept my deepest apology if I have disturbed your study. It appears as if your philosophical speculation, though successful, is unlikely to bear fruit."

Master Siger glanced down to find that the lower half of his body was completely exposed, and that his hand was in an area and situation that startled him completely. With a single gesture he drew his robes to cover himself and wiped the pearly liquid from his hand onto the dry grass at his side. Then, to Frère Jacques's continued and obvious amusement, he sat up.

"No wonder," Frère Jacques said with a smile, "Boetius of Dacia claimed the life of the philosopher is more pleasing than any other."

Master Siger discovered himself sitting under the broad chestnut tree that sheltered the crossroad before the gate to the Etruscan necropolis. Though he sat beside the tree, he realized he must have been completely visible from the road.

"I can see why," Frère Jacques continued, "the Church wants to be rid of you philosophers. Your insatiable appetites are not limited only to truth." Still smiling, Frère Jacques sat down beside Master Siger.

Looking around further, Master Siger could see no sign of a grove of trees or of a stream. Instead, beyond the distant edge of the necropolis laid a field of pale and sun-brightened straw grass and weeds that continued flat and even and golden across the valley and up into the hills in the far distance.

Frère Jacques said, "So you skipped the High Mass. I wondered where you'd gone. I asked one of the Papal guards and he told me I'd find you down here."

"I must have fallen asleep," Master Siger said, though his mind seemed still fog-bound. The sound of crystalline laughter chimed in his ears even as it slowly faded.

"You and I," Frère Jacques said, "are expected at His Holiness' table for dinner. I thought I was coming to rescue you from some horrible intellectual struggle." From behind his ear Frère Jacques produced a thin, brightly white joint. "Little could I imagine how fearsome a struggle I would discover." He placed the joint between his lips and lit it. After he had smoked at it a moment, he passed it to Master Siger.

"I would have thought," Frère Jacques continued as for an instant he held back the smoke before he exhaled loudly, "that our circle of female acquaintances would have been sufficient for even your most complex and demanding philosophical speculation."

Master Siger took the joint and smoked, still unable to form a coherent thought. He looked out again across the broad yellow valley stretching before him, open and unobstructed to the foot of the far hills. He could have kept walking. This thought came to him suddenly and painfully. Beyond the Etruscan graves and the line of bushes, and then further on. On and on he could have walked, into those hills and lost. Lost to His Holiness, to Simon de Brion and Frère Jacques, lost even to the Inquisition. Lost and gone for good and all. He could have simply kept walking. Or so he wished to think.

Watching Master Siger carefully, Frère Jacques took the joint from his hand in silence. The sun was setting; its light bathed the hills behind them and the fields all around with a warm amber glow. They passed the joint back and forth as Master Siger's mind continued to swirl. The colors of yellow and red and green and brown gradually sharpened, the music of the birds and insects sweetened, more harmonious than a moment before. Gradually, bits of his memories formed chains, but he could not link sequences of words and images. His thoughts seemed suspended beyond his ability to gather.

As Frère Jacques stubbed out the remains of the joint he asked, "So tell me, as late in the day as it is, and as hard as you've been working, are you ready to get drunk with the Pope one more time?"

Master Siger looked at Frère Jacques's face, searching for a certain glimmer, a cast of eye that would reveal that he possessed foreknowledge similar to his own. But then he realized it didn't really matter. Such knowledge would make no ultimate difference. He realized he would probably never really see Frère Jacques. Frère Jacques would maintain his mask until the very last moment.

"After dinner," Frère Jacques continued, "I'm taking you to a party a friend of mine is throwing. She's been asking me to introduce you for days. I'd planned to do it anyway. You're going to love her. And this seems the right time."

Master Siger studied his face but found no guile or self-consciousness.

Frère Jacques placed his hand on Master Siger's shoulder. "Are you feeling all right?"

To his own surprise, Master Siger was convinced Frère Jacques's concern was sincere. He nodded and then stood. "Let's go," Siger said. "My stomach is so hungry it's about to bite me in the ass." With a loud, bright laugh Frère Jacques stood beside him.

Together the two men stepped out from beneath the tree and onto the brown and dusty path. The setting sun was large and cast a golden glow onto the road before them. Master Siger squinted, overcome with inexplicable relief, and then hesitated. With a glance he measured the path's long steep ascent back to town. Something in his chest softened. Suddenly he felt all the doubt concerning his past rise up off of his shoulders, up away from him like a fever passing.

Still smiling, Frère Jacques threw his arm across Master Siger's shoulder. "You know, I think this is the beginning of a beautiful friendship." With a nudge he urged Master Siger forward. Bathed in that light drifting to the color of brass, the men began their dusty climb up the long, steep road, and home.

The Hand of History Grows Weary. The Hand of History is Pearl-Grey, Its

Narrow, Pale Fingers Grasp Loosely the Gossamer Folds of Time's Curtain. All that Was Predicted Came to Pass. Though the Planet Turns Unceasing, No Gesture, No Syllable, No Moment, But Those The Goddesses Had Assured Master Siger Came to Pass. The Goddesses had Opened that Book and Allowed Master Siger the Sight of This Particular Page. And Upon That Page Had Been Written All He Had Needed to Know, All That Could Be Known, a Knowledge Profound yet Vain in Its Uselessness. The Hand of History Has Inscribed the Names of Popes and Kings and Philosophers and Knaves, Those Lines Inscribed Even at the Birth of the Universe. Let the Hand of History, in Broad, Finely-Etched Letters, Inscribe All That the Goddesses Had Predicted Onto the Bright and Crisp Page of that Cosmic Tome. Let the Opus Universalis Reverberate With These Deeds, Brave and Cowardly, Exactly As Here Described. Let Their Passions Resound, Let Every Gesture and Sigh Leave its Mark Unalterable and Unaltered for Every Eye of Every Future to Behold. All Thought Has Been Thought, and Yet Must Be Thought Again. All Hope Has Been Cherished and Denied and Retrieved. All Hearts Have Desired and Then Withered and Disappeared, Empty and Without Reprieve. History Has Inscribed All of This and Moved On. There Is Only History, Its Recognition and Loss and Revelation. That Which Once Was Will Always Have Been, and Thus Must Always and Forever Be.

A. W. DEANNUNTIS lives in Philadelphia and has published fiction in the following journals: *Silent Voices, The Armchair Aesthete, Timber Creek Review, Lynx Eye, Los Angeles Review, Yemassee, First Class, Pacific Coast Journal, Short Stories Bimonthly, Luna Negra, CrossConnect, Spout, The Iconoclast, North Atlantic Review, Nite-Writer's International, Onionhead, Nuthouse, Mind in Motion* (Pushcart Prize nomination), *Kiosk, Cimarron Review, California Quarterly, Dog River Review* and *Coe Review.*